PERDICION

Perdicion

The Other Blue Planet

Alec J. Ott

OPEN ROAD
INTEGRATED MEDIA

Copyright © 2024 by Alec J. Ott

ISBN: 978-1-5040-9808-3

This edition published in 2024 by God of the Desert Books/Open Road Integrated Media, Inc.
180 Maiden Lane
New York, NY 10038
www.openroadmedia.com

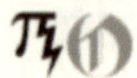

To my lovely wife Marygrace. Although she's not much of a sci-fi fan, she loves me and I love her right back.

PERDICION

INTRODUCTION

THE SISTER PLANETS

Nestled in one of the vast spiral arms of the Milky Way galaxy, about twenty-four thousand light-years from the galaxy's center, a rather ordinary yellow star was the nurturing mother sun to a system of orbiting planets. Average in most respects and among a hundred billion stars that made up the galaxy, the yellow star was middle-aged, solitary, and relatively set apart from her neighbors. The distance from her nearest neighbor, the Alpha Centauri star system, was fairly substantial, even in galactic scale. Even the light from this neighbor took more than four light-years to reach her. She did not mind her seclusion, for this common little star had her duties as a mother to keep her busy. Her most distant children spun in vast orbits as giant balls of swirling gas, yellow, orange, and blue. Her closest offspring were four small inner planets whose orbits were close enough to really benefit from her warming light. The closest of these inner planets was essentially a large rock in space, a stillborn. The outer planet in this group was the angry sister, who had once had oceans and a brief, abortive attempt at life billions of years ago. This Red Planet stalked in the distance as if resentful of her two middle sisters.

3

The two middle sisters were the sun's dearest daughters—the two sister planets. They basked in the sun's light as exquisite blue spheres in the blackness of space. Like twins, they had formed at the same time about 4.5 billion years ago and evolved along identical paths. One was the second planet from the sun and the other was the third. One had a moon, the other did not, yet they were more alike than they were different. As twin worlds, they traveled as the largest planet in each other's night skies for billions of years. The beauty of their blue globes with a white, wispy cloud cover could be seen for millions of light-years. Yet, this was not the source of their distinctiveness—their true character came from within their atmospheres. Unlike the now-barren womb of the Red Planet, the fertility of the twin worlds was unprecedented. Both were pools of life, with vast oceans and green forests that teemed with plants and animals—life of countless varieties. As the billions of years passed on, species after species of animals and countless varieties of plant life came into being, lived, and died in a constantly renewing cycle. The newest generations continually took their place while their ancestors merged back into the depths of the planets' crusts—their remains building and collecting beneath the surface, as if to stock up on unlimited resources for their inheritors to come.

Then, about twenty thousand years ago, *they* arrived. A new and radically different form of animal began to appear on the sister worlds that was far above all the other creatures who had ever lived before. Unlike all the other animals that had come before them, who lived their lives driven by instinct alone, these new creatures walked upright with intelligence and self-awareness. And they quickly took their place as masters of their respective worlds. For thousands of years, the inheritors were completely unaware of each other's existence. Their own worlds were quite enough to occupy them as they made homes for themselves, hunted for their food, defended themselves from enemies, and played under the stars at night. When time permitted, they sought meaning in their existence and something higher, larger than themselves. In primitive times, they found divinity in the sun, planets, and stars. The sister planets thus became known as goddesses of beauty in each other's nights.

Considering the billions of years the sisters existed together, it was amazing how closely the planets' peoples resembled each other. But there came to be a difference in the two peoples' development. Perhaps it was chance. Perhaps it was due to the inner sister's harder environment. It might have had something to do with the inner planet's smaller orbit and thus its shorter year. Perhaps the Creator had granted the inner planet favor. No one knew for sure. Whatever the reason, after hundreds of millions of years of life, and after twenty thousand years and untold generations of people, the inner planet made faster technological progress than its outer sister. While virtually meaningless in the vast time scale of the solar system, the inner planet, which her people called Perdicion, was about two thousand years more advanced than her sister, which came to be known as Parthénos, or simply the Blue Planet, to the people of Perdicion. While the most advanced peoples of Parthénos were just learning how to make sea voyages in small wooden sailing vessels, the inner planet was already flying advanced aircraft in her skies and orbiting satellites in space.

While Perdicion was already advanced, the discovery of life on Parthénos helped to speed along Perdicion's technological advancement. To see why, just imagine for a moment the incentive it brought to know there was a nearby world that supported life! The desire for space travel became more than simply a quest for knowledge and some vague achievement of conquering space. Perdicians had a concrete goal of voyaging to another planet just like their own, where they could land, visit, and meet their fellow inhabitants and travelers in their own solar system. Proof of intelligent life on Parthénos spawned a space race among Perdicion's leading nation-states. This economic and political incentive sparked incredible technological advances in space travel and, unfortunately, weapons and warfare. It did not take long before world wars began to break out. Mighty battles raged on the land and seas, in the skies, and eventually in space. Fleets of ships patrolled and battled for control of space above Perdicion's continents.

Then after years of misery and death, the people of Perdicion grew weary of warfare and the largest allied nations agreed to merge to form a one-world government, which became known as the Supremacy. But the wars were not over. A rebellion took place on Ishtaria, a large northern continent. As the violence and terrorism increased, the Supremacy offered Ishtarians passage to Parthénos to make a new beginning in a new world. Millions, including many of the leaders of the rebellion, took up the Supremacy's offer. Sleeper transport ships were booked and left the planet on regular schedules.

While their passengers slept, each transport ship passed Parthénos' orbit and continued further and further out into the solar system, out to the Red Planet (or Soror Furioso, as it was less commonly known on Perdicion) to an environmental domed city named the Red Colonies. Originally constructed for mining operations, the Red Colonies had been expanded and enhanced in secret for several years for the eventual housing and controlling of the Ishtarians. The betrayed Ishtarians awoke to find themselves in a bleak, unnatural existence, having to breathe filtered air and walk only on metal floors. Their outside world now required pressure suits and helmets.

Thinking that they had benevolently solved the Ishtarian problem once and for all, the Supremacy left a fleet of ships in the Red Planet's sector on permanent assignment to keep the peace. However, within a few years, the Ishtarians embarked upon a massive revolt in the colonies and not only took control of the domed city but managed to capture the orbiting space station and many space vessels (including Supremacy military ships) in the Red Planet's sector. Mining operations and production facilities all fell into the hands of the Ishtarians. Soror Furioso thus became a hostile enemy to Perdicion. Emboldened by their victory, the Ishtarians pledged the destruction of the Supremacy, the force behind their misery and the continued denial of their greatest desire—populating Parthénos. While at a numerical and technological disadvantage, the Ishtarians made effective use of their captured weapons of war. Over the years since the revolt, they intermittently attacked the Perdicion home world and its space fleet using hit-and-run attack tactics. The Supremacy fleet had not yet countered with a major attack against the Red Planet, but as the planets were nearing a rare conjunction that made the travel time between them shorter, it was rumored that a new front would be starting soon.

CHAPTER 1

PROTECTING THE BLUE PLANET

Commander Solus had been on continuous patrol in the Blue Planet sector for nearly half of the planet's orbit year, guarding the planet in his attack ship against intruders from the Red Colonies. Just coming off a thirty-minute watch, he let his attention wander towards the planet, which dominated his view screen. It was his favorite sight.

Knowing that his Prolix would alert him in case of trouble, he gazed out over the black emptiness into the bluish glow of the planet's outer atmosphere, gently taking in the nurturing sun's light and warmth. Using his command viewing screen, he focused on the wisps of clouds floating serenely over the vast expanses of ocean, and on to the dark tan and gray formations making up the landmasses. It was beautiful even from this dark distance, but this was nothing compared to the dizzying splendor of the planet's surface. Truly, Parthénos—the Blue Planet's formal name—remained the totally pure, untapped natural wonder of the solar system.

While Solus' home planet, Perdicion, had its lovely spots, it had become so very crowded, commercialized, and polluted.

There were no frontiers there, no challenges anymore. Everything about it had already been discovered and conquered. Yet a whole new world sat below him, just aching to be explored.

Perhaps the environmental laws were a good thing, Solus thought. The laws forbade any interference with the natural processes of the planet, to keep modern Perdicians from polluting the place with their mere presence. Solus had never liked that aspect of the laws, but he realized that once Perdicians started living down there, the people of Parthénos would be forever changed.

This reflection shifted Solus' thoughts toward the intelligent life of the Blue Planet. Genetically, these simple races of people were identical to Solus' own people. Amazingly, there were Parthénos counterparts for almost every race of people living on Perdicion. When this was discovered, it confounded Perdicion biological sciences for years, and science had never to this day been able to explain the phenomenon. There was the twin evolutionary theory, which suggested that each of the races had independently developed features that best suited its environmental conditions. Others proposed the common ancestry theory, which suggested that the various counterparts on each planet were indeed related and that an outside intelligence had taken a sampling of each race on the originating planet and planted them on the other. It was a matter of debate among proponents of this theory as to which planet was the originating planet.

Yet, looking down on this beautiful world, Solus was reminded of the old legend of the Creator. The Supreme Being, the god who supposedly created all this. That old faith and other superstitions had been wiped out by the Supremacy long ago. But looking at that blue globe, Solus felt like something was written in his very heart, like a longing for more, for something bigger than himself and his home, the space fleet. Something bigger than that planet down there, or the solar system, the galaxy, the entire universe for that matter.

He was tired of the emptiness of space, tired of the war . . . the cause. His heart did not burn as it once did, as it did when he had entered the Perdicion space fleet. He was beginning to wonder if there was something else, something more; about what was right and what was wrong . . .

"Okay, stop your daydreaming. We've got company!" said Solus' Prolix, awakening him from his dream.

"Commander." The voice of Ensign Fleek, the ship's scansman, joined in the abrupt interruption of Solus' thoughts. "That incoming asteroid I've been watching is coming within range of the planet. There's some suspicious-looking space debris along with it."

Solus reviewed the readings. Their enemy, the Ishtarians, practiced the art of concealment. Hiding a ship near asteroids that passed close to the Blue Planet was a common tactic. A ship not wanting to be detected needed to camouflage herself with whatever background that presented itself. Asteroids, comets (when one happened to fly through), and space junk offered opportune hiding places. In this relatively crowded section of the solar system, there was always something to be found to hide behind. "I concur, Fleek, it is suspicious," Solus remarked. "Bas, initiate stealth mode and intercept."

"Yes, sir," responded Warrant Officer Bas, the helmsman, as he complied with Solus' order.

The dull black hull of Solus' attack ship, *Shadow*, slipped silently from view as navigation lights winked out and the ship made an automated maneuver that kept its low-profile nose pointed towards the intended target.

"Bring us about to intercept course, 1-3-6," Solus ordered.

Stealth mode hid their ship in the blackness of space, but if they positioned themselves with the very bright Blue Planet to their rear, the enemy would very likely notice a rather large and sinister black spot moving towards them.

"It's definitely a ship, sir," Fleek reported. "My low-energy scan indicates a crew aboard."

"Time to make our presence known," Solus said as he prepared to hail the ship via broadcast frequencies. "Ishtarian vessel approaching the Blue Planet," Solus announced in broadcast mode, "this is the Supremacy attack ship *Shadow*. Your presence has been detected. You are in violation of the Blue Planet planetary quarantine law. Stop your engines and respond to my signal."

The unidentified ship appeared to have one action plan if detected—make a run for it. Making no further pretense of subtlety, the now fully visual transport vessel fired its launching thrusters, and darted ahead on a direct course for the Blue Planet. Her engine's orange fire brightly lit the ship and its surroundings, chunks of gray rocks floating in the black nothingness.

"Full thrusters," Solus commanded, "and initiate attack mode."

"Yes, sir!" Bas responded with a touch of restrained excitement. This was to be their first action of the patrol. As one of the most advanced ships in the fleet, *Shadow* was designed for combat in both space and atmospheric environments. The low warning sirens sounded.

Attack mode involved a silent transformation of the vessel, which spread apart the ship's aft-pointing wings and separated the nose of the ship into two sections. Silently and invisibly, the ship's wings began moving apart and spreading wing-mounted thrusters and weapons to either side of the ship's main hull, allowing for maximum maneuverability and forward firepower.

In turn, after the separation walls had risen and divided the bridge crew into two cockpits, the pointed nose of the ship split in two—each side sliding gracefully away from the other. The now separate nose sections each contained fully redundant functional command modules, a specialization in case of heavy damage to one or the other side. The primary helmsman and navigator were in the starboard cockpit; the scansman and weapons officer were in the port-side one.

Solus, as captain, remained in his own self-contained command center in the middle—just above and behind the two nose sections.

"They're using up all their fuel," commented Fleek. "I guess they don't want to turn back now."

Solus smiled and met Fleek's quick upwards glance. He could just dimly see Fleek and Warrant Officer Chamers, the weapons officer, encased in the port nose section. Solus was tall with brown hair and a pale complexion, the typical build and coloring for a native of Ouda Regio, the homeland of the Supremacy. Fleek was also from Ouda Regio, and tall and brown-haired, but very lean compared to his commander. Solus glanced over at the starboard side and could just make out Bas and Rowling, who was the navigator. Rowling was another Ouda Regio native; tall and blonde. Unlike the rest of his crewmates, Bas was dark and stocky, a trait of his people who were native to Southern Ishtaria, Perdicion's largest northern continent. However, Bas' family had moved to Ouda Regio when he was a boy. They had a proud tradition of service to the Supremacy.

The attack ship shot forward, visually indicated only by a slight decrease in the rate that the transport moved away from them. Solus broadcasted another command: "Ignite your breaking thrusters or we will fire on you."

The unheeding transport continued on its course straight towards the planet.

"They're making no evasive maneuvers, sir." The long yellow tube streaked towards the planet.

"I don't see any landing apparatus," added Bas. "How are they expecting to land?"

"I presume that they are planning a controlled crash," Solus replied. Someone this desperate was simply glad to have a ship at all for the journey, even if it was unsuitable for landing. "But they're not going to get that close," Solus added. "Prep the cannon." The splitting of the ship's nose had also exposed *Shadow*'s primary weapon platform, a large burst cannon.

"Yes, sir," responded Chamers, another native of Ouda Regio, who was pale and thin, often ignoring his Prolix's warnings about his diet.

If the transport ship had any defensive weaponry, then *Shadow*'s glowing weapon would provide the enemy a target to shoot at, but this could not be helped. An ominous circular orange glow appeared between the two nose sections.

"Target their engines. Weapon intensity to disabling strength." The crew could feel and hear the weapon's build-up surge. "Fire."

Shadow's burst cannon fired a hellish blob of orange radiation, which streaked out through space towards the transport. Solus watched as the energy burst rapidly decreased in size, moving across the distance between the ships with staggering speed. Ensign Fleek monitored the weapon's progress from his controls. "Impact in 46 seconds," he reported.

Solus noted that they still weren't making any evasive maneuvers. The yellow tube shot ahead as if ignorant of its impending doom.

"Thirty seconds," Fleek continued, "direct hit inevitable, unless they've enhanced their maneuvering capabilities."

"Something is odd about this," Solus remarked.

"Fifteen seconds; they're still on course."

Solus turned to his monitor to watch. The energy burst closed the distance rapidly, and still the ship made no course changes. The two signals on his screen then became one.

"Impact!" Fleek called out. Solus zoomed in on his display on the impact zone. An explosion had engulfed the transport.

"She's breaking up!" Fleek reported.

"That's odd," Solus said, perplexed. "Our burst should only have disabled them. Keep watching—something's not right."

Solus scanned the impact area. The escaping oxygen from the ship created energy flames from the explosion. Already he could see pieces of debris flying out from the waves at every angle.

"Destruction confirmed, sir."

The crew watched in silence at the expanding explosion. Solus then noticed something else. "Scan that piece of wreckage that's heading towards the planet. It seems to be conveniently on the same course as the ship was on."

This piece was not spinning and flopping at random like the rest of the transport as it flew apart. Solus zoomed in on the object and saw at once what it was. Fleek confirmed Solus' judgment: "It's the transport's command module, and it's intact."

So that's their little trick, thought Solus. They exploded their ship around them just as the burst hit to keep our attention while they kept going. Ships' command modules, as a standard, had heavy shielding and could remain intact if the ship around it was damaged. It was certainly a gamble, however. There wouldn't be much room for the passengers and cargo— most of which would have been sacrificed with the rest of the ship. They'd be able to maneuver, but could go no faster than their current speed. "Engines to full speed!" Solus commanded. "We've got to knock them off course. Prep the weapon again. Set for disabling."

"Yes, sir," responded Chamers.

"Burst the weapon off their port bow."

The attack ship was closing in on the remains of the transport, and again Solus felt a tingling of disquiet. "Bas, give that wreckage a wide berth." And just as they altered course, something within the wreckage erupted. A second and third explosion immediately followed. The force of the explosion violently shook the ship, and impact sirens blared in the cockpits. Solus quickly regained his senses and checked his status monitor. They were intact; his and the other command modules remained online. "Bas, Rowling—how you doing over there?" Solus queried. "How about you, Chamers?"

"We're still functioning," Bas replied.

"A mine detonated off the port bow," stated Rowling.

"We're okay in here," Chamers reported.

It appeared that their opponents had strewn some mines about just after the explosion. They had to have timed it exactly to avoid detonating the mines along with the rest of the transport. "Another little surprise," replied Solus sardonically. "Apparently these people mean business. Keep the weapon locked on the target. Target just off their left bow . . . fire!"

Again the burst cannon emitted an inferno of orange radiation. "Burst in ten seconds . . . five seconds."

This time, the opponent did move. At nearly the last second, the tiny capsule veered to starboard. But it was not enough to escape *Shadow*'s weapon. The orange ball burst just close enough to send the command module tumbling away in a crazy spin. At first it looked like pieces were coming off the capsule as if it were about to break up, but it remained intact.

A moment later Fleek reported: "I'm detecting small-arms fire inside the capsule."

"I don't think they want to be caught," Solus replied.

* * *

A short time later, *Shadow* had closed the distance and drew close to the now flopping capsule. Bas positioned the ship above it, and with gentle positioning thrusts managed to steady it enough to grab it.

"Extend the umbilical tube, attach and enclose their escape hatch," Solus ordered. "Secure from attack mode."

Shadow's nose united again, covering the now-dark weapon platform, and her wings slipped silently backwards. As the ship transformed, and the cockpits' separation walls retracted, Solus reported his action to the other ships in his attack squadron, designated in the Supremacy fleet as the "Blue" Squadron.

Positioned all around the planet, Solus' command included five attack ships of the same class as *Shadow*, and one support vessel. The Blue Squadron was part of a much larger battle group controlled by the command ship, *Singularity-SBS*, a vast space battleship that served as the base for the sector and the flagship of the theater commander. *Singularity*'s battle group was composed of six heavy cruisers, a hundred attack and assault ships, organized into twenty squadrons, as well as various other support ships.

This battle group had deployed months ago, leaving only Solus' undermanned Blue Squadron behind to guard the Blue Planet. Solus' ships normally had a larger crew of seven each, but not an extra man could be spared in the battle group's mission, which was classified. Solus was one of the few officers in the fleet who knew where they were headed. He also knew that several more battle groups normally stationed for home defense had deployed from Perdicion as well. To Solus this meant only one thing—the beginning of the end for the Red Colonies. The Supremacy was finally making its decisive move against the Ishtarians.

And he looked forward to that, even if it meant the end of his career in the fleet. After all, once the system was rid of the Ishtarian rebels, there would never again be a need for a large battle fleet. There would be no need for wars ever again. The very existence of the battle fleet was due to the wars between Perdicion's nations, as each fought for control of the planet and the solar system. But that had all ended when the Supremacy had won the day and taken control. Each absorbed nation's forces had been taken into the Supremacy, and if it weren't for the Ishtarian rebellion, the fleet would have been reduced years ago.

Of course there would always be some form of planetary defense apparatus, Solus reminded himself. Perdicion science had not completely ruled out the possibility of life outside the solar system. But even if there were other worlds similar to their own in far-off solar systems, the incredibly vast distances between Perdicion and the rest of the galaxy made visits, or even contact, extremely difficult to imagine.

Yet, unlike the inhabitants of the Blue Planet, the people of Perdicion had proof that they were not alone in the universe. This made the idea of life in other worlds seem all the more possible. Perhaps when this was all over, thought Solus, they could get on with exploring the rest of their own system. They hadn't really even ruled out the possibility of other undiscovered life in the outer solar system. The largest of the gas planets, for example, had a huge moon that could, in theory, support life of a sort. Maybe Solus himself would lead an expedition to that moon and find out.

But then again, perhaps not. He knew where he wanted to go next. Settlement of the Blue Planet would surely begin once the Ishtarian threat had ended. That was the world he wanted to explore.

After completing communications and sending his long-range reports to Supremacy Command, Solus ordered Fleek to continue monitoring the area for any incoming space objects. As they saw nothing on the long-range scan in the sector, Solus decided to get on with the unpleasant business of boarding the captured capsule. "Bas, join me in the main deck for a moment."

The thick, curved cockpit doors slid open and Bas emerged from the forward cockpit into the brightly-lit inner hull of the ship. Solus climbed down the stairs in back of his command module and joined Bas a moment later. Attached to the main deck by artificial gravity, the two men eyed one another. Solus noticed that Bas' combat suit, colored with many combat decorations, now sported dark singe marks on the arms. "Bas, are you injured?"

"Just a flare-up from the controls, sir," Bas responded with a smile. "It didn't hurt."

"Well, thank goodness," Solus said, but continued reproachfully, "but why didn't you report it?"

This omission was due, Solus realized, to Bas' ever-present desire to demonstrate his self-sufficiency and that he did not require constant hand-holding from his commander. And this was true; for an upgrade, Bas was amazingly capable, including having independent thought that was well above average for his class.

Bas looked crestfallen. "I'm sorry, sir, I didn't think about that. I didn't want to bother you about it in the middle of the action."

"That's okay," Solus said reassuringly. "I know you can think for yourself, but you've got to keep me informed. My indicators didn't show any damage to the command modules, yet you had a flare-up. That's important to know."

"Yes, sir," Bas said. "I'm sorry, sir!"

"Just keep that in mind in the future. Now I'm going to get suited up and secure that capsule." Bas nodded respectfully, although he knew his commander was not following regulations. Upgrades were far more expendable than their officers. They were supposed to do tasks such as securing a captured ship. "Return to your post and monitor my progress from your position. I don't want to be surprised while securing the capsule."

"Yes, sir."

Bas returned to his cockpit, while Solus, after suiting up and arming himself in zero-atmosphere gear, made for the conveyer tube at the center of the ship, which he used to get down to the ship's bottom hatch. With a shoulder weapon locked in place on his combat suit (which freed both of his hands for navigating in zero gravity), Solus cautiously made his way down *Shadow*'s extended umbilical tube.

"Bas is the designated upgrade for this duty, you know," Solus' Prolix pointed out.

"Yes, I know, Xoxon, but I want him to remain at the pilot's post to keep watch." (Solus had named his Prolix Captain Xoxon in his childhood after a legendary space hero. The name had stuck with him throughout the years.)

"You know it's not that. Bas has been designated as the shipboarder. He's supposed to do that. This is, well, risky."

"What—are you telling me you're scared?" Solus replied sardonically.

"Nothing of the kind. I'm simply reminding you of regulations—"

"I know you have my best interests at heart at all times—"

"You are the commanding officer—"

"And I am commanding," Solus interrupted. "Look, I appreciate your kind thoughts, but I know what I'm doing. This is basic leadership stuff, something that's been forgotten by many in the officer corps these days. In my opinion, we've relied too much on Prolix technology for discipline. Upgrades are people too, after all."

"Yes, with less-enhanced Prolixes, shall we say?"

"Of course," Solus replied wryly. "Regardless, the upgrade non-coms still need to be led. It doesn't hurt to show them every once in a while that we are willing to do some dirty work too, or risk our precious skins for them."

"Radical thoughts. You're lucky the command node's not around to hear this."

"Yes, yes, but what are you going to do about it, rat me out?"

"Don't tempt me," Xoxon replied wryly.

Solus was a highly decorated combat veteran of the Perdicion Space Fleet. He had proven his abilities to his commanders over and over again in countless campaigns in space. Because of this, his judgment and loyalties were beyond question. Thus, with the great respect he had justly earned from the chain of command, great latitude was granted in allowing him to speak his thoughts. His Prolix logs, when monitored, seldom caused him any sort of trouble.

"Besides," said Solus, turning back to the subject at hand, "Bas is special. He's not your ordinary upgrade. He's quite gifted, and I would hate to lose him as my helmsman. But enough of this now; I am reaching the end of the tube." As Solus approached the opening at the tube's end, he could see the captured command module's escape hatch enclosed at the bottom. The ship's robot arms had just completed opening the circular hatch. The opened entrance was as black as space within. All had been silent in there since they had registered the small-arms fire several minutes before. "Bas, I'm at the hatch opening, and I'm going in."

Bas acknowledged.

Solus released his gravity boots and pushed his head through the hatch opening below him, looking into the tiny chamber. He peered upside down into the darkness, his helmet lamp illuminating two rows of benches facing away from him towards the front of the capsule. He felt a strong surge of adrenaline.

As he pushed himself in, his first priority was to secure his feet to the floor. After flipping, he planted himself immediately across from the opening. Firmly in position on the floor, he looked around. There was no place for concealment other than behind the benches. He moved between the back two benches and peered left and right. One was occupied by a woman, dead with a wound to her chest; the other chair was empty but burned and torn from a weapon's burst.

He moved forward to the pilot's seats and saw another woman in the co-pilot position. This woman had a shot wound to her shoulder and neck. As Solus turned to the pilot's seat, his helmet light illuminated a man staring fixedly at him, a red bubble slowly expanding from his gaping mouth, with a red mass floating out from behind his head. The dead man's arms floated crazily in the air among many small driblets of red. A pulse gun bounced in the air beside him. "Bas, they're all dead. The pilot shot them all before eating his own gun."

"Understood," Bas replied.

Looking away from the horror, Solus checked for the ship's data logs in the main console. With reflections of red and orange lights swimming around his face, he began to transfer the ship's log to *Shadow*'s memory drive.

The memory transfer was seconds in length. "I'm done here, Bas. We'll close her back up and leave her for *Guru* to pick up. Once we've detached, give the coordinates for retrieval." *Guru* was Solus' support ship. Her crew would need to put the bodies out to space and clean up this mess.

"Understood, sir."

Solus glanced again at the dead, and then looked around through the main screen. The Blue Planet loomed before him. He could almost feel the planet's gravity pulling at them, as if she were beckoning them in. These people had made it so close, but died within its sight. Solus had done his duty, but he did not enjoy having contributed to their deaths. So desperate they were to avoid capture that they chose death, the only escape route left to them.

Solus looked out at the world below him. It was a wild place, everything constantly on the move. And because the planet's axis of rotation was slightly tilted off from true north, her inhabitants experienced varying seasons of weather as the planet orbited the sun. The planet had its nights and days, but its nights were not always quite so dark as Perdicion's nights, because the Blue Planet had a large white moon to light the night skies. Its presence caused the oceans to ripple and the tides to hit and splash against the landmasses. Yet, everything seemed just right there, as if the Creator after using Perdicion as a model had gotten it just right the second time.

He heard a low moan beside him. Startled but with trained precision, Solus' eye movement targeted his shoulder weapon towards the sound.

"I'm detecting faint life signs from the woman in the co-pilot's chair," Xoxon reported. "It's harder to tell with these people without a Prolix."

The woman's eyes were closed, but her lips moved. Her mouth opened slightly.

"Bas, one of them is alive after all," Solus called out. "I need a medical transport mat!"

Later, back onboard *Shadow*, Solus looked at the unconscious woman, now lying prone in the ship's tiny medical chamber. He had alerted the squadron's medical officer, Dr. Nevek, and the doctor was now monitoring her readings remotely from *Guru*. The support ship carried the medical officer and contained a fully-equipped sick bay.

With Nevek's guidance, Solus had already removed the patient's environmental suit, treated her neck injury, and administered medication to heal the wound on her neck. "Sol, her injury was not severe—burns and a concussion from a close-proximity pulse-gun shot. With the stimulant you just administered, she should be coming around soon."

"Understood, Nev. Then I can question her?"

"Well, yes, but I'd prefer to have an in-person look at her first," Nevek responded. His youthful appearance due to his round, freckled face and reddish hair often disguised his years of experience.

"You're going to have to trust the medical monitoring systems."

"You know very well how I feel about that . . ."

"I do. Your senses—your fingers—tell you more than some blighted piece of equipment," said Solus, in order to head off that oft repeated quote.

"Well then, give me a chance to examine my patient!"

"We simply can't rendezvous right now. You know we're spread out too thinly for that—"

"Additionally," the doctor interrupted, "she does not have a Prolix within her; therefore, the monitoring equipment is not as accurate—"

"Accurate enough."

"My recommendation, then, is to let her rest. Not that you will listen to that."

"I listen to and highly prize all of your recommendations."

"Then why didn't you marry my sister?"

"I didn't want to be related to you."

"At last the truth comes out . . . Nevek out."

With his old friend dispatched for the moment, Solus looked again at the patient. Now that she was more than simply a corpse or an enemy combatant in a space suit to him, Solus began to notice her very attractive female features. The sheets of the bed luxuriously exhibited the feminine curves of her long and lean body. She was unusually tall for an Ishtarian. He had heard somewhere that some Ishtarians from the northern regions were taller, and that even though they shared an olive skin tone with those from the south, they were not really ethnically related to them.

In spite of himself, he had always been secretly attracted to Ishtarian women, tall or short. It must have been that sense of the exotic in them that intrigued him. This woman's hair was wavy, long, and black. Her skin was smooth and olive-colored. There were no signs of prolonged space travel there—none of the unhealthy paleness that showed in Solus' own face.

She slowly showed more signs of life, and after another few moments opened her eyes and looked around at her surroundings.

Solus stayed in the room but kept silent and in the corner away from her.

All at once, she noticed that her clothing had been removed and instinctively pulled the sheets closer to her neck. As a note of alarm flickered across her brow, Solus chose this point to speak. "You are safe," he said. "You are aboard my ship. I have treated your wounds."

At first she was startled by his voice. Filled with dismay, her eyes quickly scanned her surroundings. Yet, focusing her gaze on the Supremacy officer standing nearby, her alarm slipped away, and her eyes flashed at him. "Safe in a Supremacy ship?"

she replied with a strained voice that did not capture the fire in her heart.

"Quite safe. At least compared to your colleagues who, I'm sorry to report, are dead," Solus answered. "May I ask why the pilot shot you?"

"He was not my colleague," she answered.

"You know that travel to the Blue Planet is forbidden."

"I do not recognize that law—it is against the Natural law, as is the Prolix."

This response aroused a flicker of an old anger within Solus. "Your people had the choice to reject our technology—" he began.

"Yes, as long as we lived by your rules and stayed where you forced us to live!"

"Our government was patient and tolerant with your people for many years, but we would not put up with terrorism."

"A couple of extremists blow up some buildings, and that's all the excuse you need, isn't it? Did that justify the mass deportation of my people, who had every right to live on the planet where we were born?"

"The situation was intolerable. Your people ruined our world, and the government was certainly not going to allow your people to come here and corrupt the people of this planet. The Supremacy acted for the best," Solus stated.

"That's right. In the cold logic of the Supremacy—the answer was so easy! Marooning millions of inhabitants from your own planet in an over-crowded domed environment on a cold, lifeless, red ball of dust," she answered.

"I prefer cold logic to irrational hatred."

"Either way, it always ends in death and destruction."

Solus could not help but feel a sense of disquiet within as he pondered her last statement.

"It's pointless arguing with her," Xoxon interrupted.

"Xoxon, please!" Solus called out in frustration, eyeing the ceiling. He looked over at the woman, embarrassment quickly replacing his anger.

"You're talking to your Prolix, aren't you?"

"I was," he replied, with evidence of his embarrassment coloring his cheeks.

"I can't imagine why anyone would take that inside themselves voluntarily," she commented.

"I didn't," said Solus. "I was born with it. Nevertheless, I accept it as a wonderful tool—"

"Then you have no choice but to accept it."

"Possibly, but I can't deny its usefulness."

"But then again, you've got the command version, haven't you?" she continued. "Not as mind-numbing, is it?"

Solus did not respond.

"Still, it does control you, doesn't it?" she added. "Maybe not directly, but you do have to be careful what you say and what you do, don't you? It sees everything, doesn't it? It reports everything to your superiors, doesn't it?"

"I'm sorry, but I must break in here," Xoxon interrupted again. "I don't report anything! It's the command node that takes the logs—I can't help that!"

"I know," Solus whispered. "Please be quiet!"

"Getting some more negative feedback?"

"Yes, in fact," he said coolly.

She smirked.

In his annoyance, he was about to counter with a vicious salvo, but he stopped himself. The news he was about to give her would be hard enough to take without him adding to it. He then decided he had better not delay in telling her. "Listen, I know you Ishtarians hate the Prolix, but I am under standing orders to—"

"What are you saying?"

"I am ordered to administer the Prolix to all captured prisoners."

At this her expression immediately changed from defiance to anguish. She began to cry pitifully, and he immediately regretted telling her. After all, he realized, her former companions had chosen suicide to avoid being captured.

"What's your name?" he asked, trying desperately to change the subject.

She did not reply, but continued to cry.

"Please, it's nothing official," Solus continued. "I just want to know."

"Her name is Myra, born on Ishtaria in Supremacy Year 2050," Xoxon reported.

"Myra. What a lovely name. It fits you."

She looked at him with swollen, red eyes. "You're trying to make friends with me now? You just destroyed my ship and stopped me from getting to my new home. Next, you'll be taking my mind from me. Please, just leave me!"

"Very well," Solus said softly. "I will leave you alone." Seeing that she was safely secured to her bed, he made his way out of the medical bay. Her renewed sobs haunted him as he climbed back up into his command module. As he regained his seat, he was struck with how beautiful she was—and indeed, how lonely he was.

CHAPTER 2

INTERPLANETARY JOURNEYS

The action just experienced by Commander Solus' Blue Squadron was just the beginning. The interplanetary journeys had begun months prior when three cargo ships left the Red Colonies, unbeknownst to the authorities there. One had just been intercepted by Solus as it reached the Blue Planet. While that engagement took place, the doomed transport ship's sister vessels lurked in the darkness, watching the outcome of this uneven battle and waiting for their chance.

The solar system had not seen such traveling between planets in her entire history. It had all begun months prior, as three of the solar system's inner planets began to come together in close conjunction. This meant that the planets were all as close as they ever came to one another on the same side of the sun. Soon they would be in a straight line with each other, stretching out from the sun.

Perdicion orbited the sun at an extremely fast pace, every 224.7 days, as reckoned on the Blue Planet. As such, it came in conjunction quite often with both the Blue Planet and the Red Planet. There were essentially two interplanetary routes taken by ships from Perdicion. One was a direct, non-stop route to the Red Planet. The other route was a comparatively short journey to the Blue Planet, with the option of a second, much longer leg to the Red Planet. A large part of the Supremacy fleet had just made the latter journey. This immense battle group had been in proximity of the Blue Planet for several months, awaiting the right time to continue to the Red Planet.

But the outward journey to the Red Planet was not the only route being taken in this busy section of the solar system. Also taking full advantage of the planetary convergence, the Red Planet had several pilgrims leaving its vicinity. Months before, a group of ships well known by the Ishtarian Ruling Council, the leaders of the Red Colonies, had begun a journey from the Red Planet on course for the Blue Planet. Consisting of a transport ship and two attack ships in escort, these travelers did not wish to be seen, and they moved in complete radio silence, in an arching course that considerably lengthened their journey.

On a mission that began some eighteen months ago from the Red Planet, another ship was now on a direct course for Perdicion. While on her journey, the ship had crossed the Blue Planet's orbital path while it was on the other side of the sun, and continued directly to Perdicion's orbital path. The ship was now in Perdicion's path, traveling towards the planet to rendezvous with it as it came in the opposite direction.

Captured during the Red Colonies revolt and re-christened *Vengeance*, the vessel was an old fifth-generation stealth ship. Although acting under orders of the Ishtarian Council, the ship's crew of two each had their own personal reasons for completing the mission. The commander was named Gapp, a former freighter pilot who had joined the Ishtarian cause after the revolt. As a young man seeking his fortune, he had moved to the Red Colonies to become an apprentice freighter pilot as such, he had been one of the few who had voluntarily re-located to the colonies. He had hoped to remain there for only a short time before building up his accounts and then moving back home. With this plan to keep him going, Gapp had accepted his paltry sleeping chamber and squalid living conditions as a temporary sacrifice that would someday reap greater rewards.

But it was never meant to be. He had achieved his goal of learning to pilot spacecraft, but his work had remained confined to ferrying loads of raw materials to the space station, where it was then transferred to deep-space freighters. But after nearly ten years at the same job, he still had not been able to make the leap to the larger vessels, and resentment flooded within him.

The real reason Gapp had never been promoted to deep-space piloting duties was his refusal to have a Prolix integrated within him. While from Ouda Regio, his family had fostered within him a dreadful fear of the technology, fearing possible health consequences of having his body modified with the technology. He had certainly seen the effect it had on the lower classes, noting the alarmingly common glassy-eyed stares and mechanical manner of their speech.

His resentment toward the government overflowed, when he was left behind to his fate on the colonies. Incoming freighters, which would have been his only escape route, had been warned off from approaching the Red Planet due to the Ishtarian revolt. Gapp's short stay had become permanent. While his choice to remain Prolix-free had always kept him down, it had now saved him from death at the hands of the Ishtarian authorities.

Left to his own devices, he knew his survival depended heavily upon a well-developed pragmatism: his sympathies for the cause were quickly rearranged within himself. With a new Ishtarian-centric worldview and an inescapable usefulness as a pilot, Gapp was spared from the initial bloodletting of the revolt.

And as the mind can fool itself so well, he soon came to believe that he had always been sympathetic to the Ishtarian cause. Good things followed him now. He had finally achieved his goal of commanding a space vessel, but even better: he was the captain of a military ship. Moreover, as this was the most important mission ever undertaken by the Ishtarians, his selection as captain was a high honor.

Placing the ship on autopilot, Gapp got up from his cockpit seat and went out into the interior main deck to get something to eat. He was bearded, slovenly, and a hulking man. His environmental suit needed cleaning, marked with the stains of many past meals. "Blog!" he bawled out as he entered the ship's center deck, where the mission's most critical member, after himself, was stationed. "I've just plotted a new course towards an asteroid that will be passing Perdicion's orbit within days. If we intercept it and move in unison with it towards Perdicion, this will be our best chance of getting close to the planet without being spotted. Is your cyber-attack program ready for action?"

"My program is and has been ready," replied Blog, who was sitting at his computer station, playing a video game. "As I've indicated several times, you just need to get me in range of the planetary node." This conversation was annoying to Blog, since he had explained this necessity to Gapp on what seemed like countless occasions. Blog was a smallish man; his face was clean-shaven but surrounded by a large head of long blonde hair.

"I'm aware of that," Gapp replied. "It can't be delivered any other way, because it would be picked up by the security scans if transmitted from outside the planetary node. I got that. But I want to know if your program will work."

"As I've already said countless times, I believe so. It has worked in all tests, but I can't guarantee it, and you know that.

I never said it was certain. I can't know certain variables—they may have made changes to the systems since my departure, things I cannot anticipate."

"I don't want to hear that. We're past all that—it's got to work! If it does not, we will lose this war, and this ship will be destroyed. Do you understand that?"

"I know that."

Gapp looked intently at Blog. "This is too critical for any hedging—it has to work. I will personally kill you if it does not."

Blog's annoyance converted to a pang of anxiety. "I don't need this, Gapp!" he said sharply. "I don't need this kind of pressure from you."

Gapp stepped closer to Blog and leaned over him. "I think you do."

Blog, who had been looking at his screen and not at Gapp, now looked up at his fellow human crewmate.

"I want you to understand something," Gapp continued. "It's my job to get you to that node, and once we are there, you must do your part."

"I am aware—" Blog started to interrupt.

"No, let me be rightly understood—there will be no excuses, no shirking of the responsibility. You are responsible. This is not just another little hacking job. You *must* get it done, or we are toast. All of us. Do you understand?"

"Yes," Blog said, after a short pause, saying it simply to end the conversation. His face showed what he felt about his counterpart—that he could not possibly understand the complexities of launching a cyber-attack against the most heavily secured system on the planet.

"I hope for all our sakes, but especially yours, that you do."

Gapp, for his part, was sick of hearing this little man's "excuses for failure in advance," as Gapp called them. Blog needed to take ownership of his role in this mission. He had a great gift with technology, and as such had been pampered for most of his life by those seeking to benefit from his gifts. He'd had no hard knocks and could easily buckle at any moment under the pressure. As it was, Gapp was serious about his threat.

Gapp grabbed a drink container and a ration from the pantry and left the inner deck to return to the darkness of his cockpit to eat by himself. This was typical—the two men did not associate with each other much, especially at meals. Blog was not sorry to see him go, and looked at the closing cockpit door with flashing anger. He also had been nurturing his anger for a very long time as yet another stepchild of the Ishtarian problem.

Blog had been at one time, an elite programmer in the Supremacy Science Bureau. He had reached the heights of his profession at an early age, but had soon grown restless in his job, which involved the tracking of bugs in the cognitive interface components of the network. He considered this to be far beneath his skill set, and took to finding satisfaction in hacking access to more critical systems and then deploying his own little creations of code. This provided him with an outlet for making his mark on the world. The mysterious improvements and enhancements kept appearing, many times to the bewilderment of his superiors. He took silent gratification when his anonymous work was noticed, and reveled silently in his secret power.

Then one day, one of his little gems, a visual imaging improvement that added rounded corners to a visual display, created some interface problems with related visual systems. The effect of his little goof was that a few Prolix beta testers lost their sight temporarily—until the release was removed from them. The extracurricular code was analyzed and traced back to Blog, who had gotten careless by reusing some of his previous work code. Having been caught, Blog was taken off the Prolix team and quickly shipped out to the Red Colonies to maintain the mining operations' output tracking systems.

With deep resentment as a bridge, Blog was recruited by the rebel Ishtarians just prior to the revolt. His services in covertly accessing Supremacy military systems provided the rebels access to boundless intelligence information from the network, while his hacking of the upgrade network provided the rebels an easy victory. For his part, Blog saw the revolt as a wonderful opportunity to sow his revenge on the Science Bureau and the Supremacy. His little master plan, which he was now about to deploy, had been something he had been nurturing as an illicit progeny for more than a decade. It was only now that the Ishtarian Command had decided to put it into operation. It would, after all, mean the end of their secret inside look at the intelligence network. But it was also their last alternative.

Blog thought about Gapp's threat, and despite his annoyance, he began to understand Gapp's meaning. If he did not get this right, they would indeed die.

Their ship slunk through space waiting for Perdicion to meet her.

JOURNEYING IN SPACE BETWEEN THE RED AND BLUE PLANETS' ORBITS

Vestige was aptly named. A remnant of the Red Planet's revolutionary government was secretly aboard. The group of officials and their hangers-on occupied the large sleeper ship, one of the many ships used by the Supremacy to move the Ishtarians to the Red Colonies. It was designed to haul large numbers of people long distances in the relative comfort of sleeper compartments. It had been docked in the Red Planet's space station on the day of the revolt and became a prize of the new government.

Two years prior to the present orbital conjunction of the inner planets, the Ishtarian-led Red Colonies council, normally fraught with disharmony on any decision, grew more and more convinced that the Supremacy would be acting against them soon. Moreover, they knew that they could not withstand an attack from the Supremacy fleet.

The only thing that had postponed a Supremacy counter-attack until the present was the distance involved in traveling between the planets. It was coming, and it was only a matter of time. While no enemy ships had been spotted entering the vicinity of the Red Planet in the years following the rebellion, unmanned scout probes had been picked up and tracked. Clearly the enemy was patiently biding their time, gathering intelligence and plotting and planning their final attack. The Red Colonies would be re-taken, the Ishtarian government there would be destroyed, and the leaders would all be killed. If they were found there.

They rested their hopes on the Blue Planet, and many missions had already been undertaken in attempts to establish foothold settlements on the planet. The Supremacy forces stationed there had intercepted or destroyed every single ship the Ishtarians had sent. But things would be different this time. The Ishtarians realized that, if an attack was imminent, it would involve a vast majority of the Supremacy fleet.

This was the way of the Supremacy—attack in overwhelming numbers to guarantee victory. This tactic would, in turn, greatly reduce the number of ships protecting the inner solar system to dangerously thin levels.

What was dangerous for the Supremacy was an opportunity for the Ishtarians. While the majority of the Supremacy fleet was kept busy out at the Red Planet, the remaining Supremacy forces left behind would have to be dealt with, but that's where

Blog and Gapp's mission came into play. If that was successful, they would simply land on their new home and spread the revolution to the Blue Planet.

They just needed to get there. For that, there had been much debate about which ships to take on this mission. There were several to choose from, including three large cruisers at their disposal, all captured during the Red Colonies' rebellion. These could accommodate a large complement of passengers, but as military ships, they were not designed for the comfort of the passengers. Even more, their large size would make them harder to conceal upon approach to the planet.

Far better, it was decided, to leave the cruisers to the defense of the colonies, and take the *Vestige*. While she had limited defensive capabilities, the *Vestige* would have two stealth attack ships as escorts if trouble appeared.

Leaving a skeleton governmental body behind, the Ishtarian Council abandoned the Red Colonies to start the new world order on the Blue Planet. The transport ship and its two escort vessels crept along on a long, arching course. The commander of the ship was Captain Jimbal. As an Ishtarian combat veteran at the time of the armistice treaty that ended the global Perdicion wars years ago, Jimbal was then given the opportunity to join the Supremacy armed forces. He turned it down, not wanting the price tag for joining, the Prolix. Instead, he took a job as a passenger ship pilot, and was the *Vestige's* pilot at the start of the rebellion.

During this present journey, he and the ship's engineer were the only crew awake. It had been an uneventful trip thus far, although at times infused with steadfast, mind-dulling monotony. The scenery never changed, even though they were traveling at an incredible velocity. Jimbal often sat on the darkened bridge of the vessel (dark to avoid casting too much light out into space) and stared out at the stars all around them. He managed to remain alert by keeping a constant lookout for the Supremacy fleet, which he understood from intelligence reports would be passing their position going in the other direction.

They finally appeared in his sensor scope one day. He was on the bridge as usual, several months into the journey, when the ship's long-range scanners picked up the presence of a huge fleet of ships headed towards the orbital path of the Red Planet. Jimbal quickly switched off the ship's surveillance and radar equipment to avoid being picked up by the fleet.

Knowing from experience that advance scout ships from the fleet would soon be passing below his current position, Jimbal positioned *Vestige* and her escorts dangerously close to a near asteroid and then matched its course and speed. With their ships' power reduced to the bare minimum to lower their scan signature, the hidden ships' pilots watched from the darkness in awe as hundreds of vessels passed under them.

One of the great Supremacy battleships, several cruisers, and countless support, stealth and attack ships all passed below them. It was practically Perdicion's entire space fleet. The three ships lingered by the slow asteroid in dread, waiting for the alarms to sound, announcing a missile lock on their hulls.

After what seemed like hours, the last of the enemy ships passed out of the vicinity of the asteroid that was their cover. In reality, the battle groups had coursed past the Ishtarian ships' position in tight formations and were gone very quickly. But the hiding ships had to wait where they were until the enemy was far away before they could fire their engines to get back on course for the Blue Planet. After a time, Jimbal decided they had waited long enough so that, even if they were spotted, it would not be worthwhile for the Supremacy to give chase.

Jimbal got his little convoy back on course for the next leg of their journey without further incident. He had opted not to wake the council. He reasoned that they were better off in their blissful ignorance of what was going on around them. What a collection they were, thought Jimbal. Most of them would drop their own grandmothers out of the nearest portal for a better cabin. The rebel cause was just a way for them to jockey for power. Yet, Jimbal reasoned, they were still better than what the Supremacy offered, which was technology that controlled your life. He would wake them up at the proper time, when they were very close to the Blue Planet. It would then get a lot noisier on this ship, and he would miss the silence. But then again, he hoped to be out of space in the very near future. He fully intended to land on the Blue Planet and live as one of the natives. He would slip away at his first chance.

He didn't have much concern over this bunch taking over the Blue Planet. They were much too inept for that. Of course, if this so-called "cyber-attack" that they were always talking about worked, he just might be able to return to the home world and live there. That would be nice too.

THE SUPREMACY BATTLESHIP ARMEGO IN ORBIT OVER PERDICION

In a high orbit above the planet Perdicion, the battleship *Armego* was one of three battleships left behind to protect the home world. The three enormous ships orbited the planet in a continuous line, each going into full alert as it reached the orbital sector on the side of the planet facing the outer part of the solar system, code-named the Red Zone. This was the area where incursions from the Ishtarians were most likely to occur. This defense pattern had been in place since the orbital conjunction of the three planets had begun, and it had been going on for many weeks. The crew was getting weary.

There seemed to be no end in sight either. Captain Fame certainly felt the strain. A middle-aged man with gray hair covering only the sides and back of his head, the aging space veteran was headed to the bridge to oversee the full alert as *Armego* entered the Red Zone for what must have been the thousandth time.

"Battle stations!" he called out as the bridge doors opened at his arrival. Proceeding to his commander's station, Fame watched the activity of his bridge crew. All around the ship, the crew manned their battle stations and would remain in those positions for the next three hours until their slow orbit took them out of the zone, then giving the *Nebula*, *Armego*'s sister ship, sole responsibility for guarding the zone. *Blanco* followed her, now on the far side of the planet.

"Broadband scanners to full power," he ordered.

It was all routine—his crew knew exactly what to do. But he could see the strain on their faces. It had been a long and tedious duty station. Fame took his command chair and reviewed the shift reports. The upgrades were not giving any troubles. But then again, they rarely did. The Prolix network hardly ever had glitches, and the only source of problems occurred when an update was sent through the network. Nothing of this nature had been forthcoming for several months, but he was aware of a major upgrade scheduled to be delivered in the very near future. The Science Bureau was calling it a "conversion," which indicated an overhaul of the network not seen since the upgrade version of the Prolix came out over twenty years ago.

This worried him in his status as a battleship commander. Such an upgrade was likely to cause all kinds of disruptions aboard his ship. According to the latest bulletins, the upgrade personnel could be out of service for anywhere from an hour to a day, depending on the individual. It would wreak havoc with the duty roster, and all of his officers would have to remain on continuous duty throughout the process. And who knew for sure what would be the result? There were all kinds of rumors floating about as to the extent of the changes and the control the Prolix would have over the individual. The new upgrade supposedly offered improvements in maintaining readiness, both from physical and mental standpoints. The new Prolix would keep the bodily aches away, and the blues as well, by stimulating the body's own natural chemicals to manage pain and mental states.

For a commander of upgrades, this was certainly a good thing. They could be on a seemingly endless planetary defense mission, and the crew's alertness and morale could remain unchanged indefinitely. But what did this all mean to Fame as a Supremacy citizen? The changes of course meant much more government control over a vast portion of the population. He didn't like to think about this.

"Subcommander Robards!" he called out to an upgrade at the scanning station.

"Yes, sir!"

"Pay close attention to the asteroid objects scheduled to come into our sector during the alert. There're several large ones that are due to pass Perdicion fairly closely."

"Yes, sir. We are closely monitoring two large objects, both within proximity of the planet. Neither will pass close enough to pose a danger to the planet, but ships may be hiding near or on their surfaces."

"Exactly—stay on top of it," the captain said. He thought about the enemy they were protecting the planet from. This upgrade conversion would be yet another confirmation of the righteousness of their cause. More government control meant less freedom. And, facing it frankly, Fame could not suppress his own disquiet over the issue. "Are we in contact with our friendlies?" he added, meaning the small attack and support ships that had also been left in the sector.

"Yes, sir, they are both currently maintaining synchronous orbits in the Red Zone. The skimmer is stationed above the northern continent. The guppy's above the southern hemisphere." "Skimmer" was the nickname for Supremacy attack ships, a nickname the class had acquired for the ease in which they could enter the planet's atmosphere. Guppies were the support ships. Someone must have found the name amusing, and it stuck.

"Good, keep their signals and positions locked in the sensors. Lock in on the space station above Ouda Regio too. I don't want another friendly-fire incident."

CHAPTER 3

THE ISHTARIANS BREAK THROUGH

Faith in technology. That was the real point of contention. And it was not just about using technology, but about actually immersing yourself in it. But not just yourself. Your choice was made for your descendants as well. That was the truth of the Prolix, and it was the real source of the Supremacy's power. As Perdicion computing technology evolved, those wonderful assistants and connections to all sources of data became ever smaller, more complex and indispensable. In earlier times, these tiny devices were the requisite assistants and toys of the rich. They were networked for instant communication and access to data and entertainment. But far better, they brought a certain incalculable sense of security. With these devices, you always knew where you were and that help was but a call away. Even more, these devices constantly monitored their host's medical condition, a life-saving service that brought widespread demand.

The rich man's luxuries quickly became the common man's

necessities. These life-saving devices then evolved from hand-held devices to tiny implants inside the scalp. Then the first true Prolix came about through a significant breakthrough in the combined fields of bio-engineering and computer technology. With this new development, the Prolix technology code could be merged with a person's DNA, making it a permanent fixture in the person's genetic makeup. When inserted into a body, the Prolix code enabled a computing technology that allowed the person to receive and send digital communications with his or her body using the brain. The technology stored collected information in the brain and was powered by the central nervous system, using the same electrical impulses that powered the body itself. Accepting the Prolix became the ultimate act that symbolized the planet's love affair with technology—a perfect blending of biology and technology.

The net effect of the Prolix was that people were connected in a bio-technical network. The devices connected the individual with the collective culture and information of the planet. Books, telephones, and all other forms of entertainment and communication media became obsolete. Each Prolix could locate and communicate with all other Prolixes within a certain range. And Prolix nodes strategically placed around the world and onboard command ships in space connected the Supremacy's entire dominion.

The Prolix became your constant partner. It was the little voice in your head that you could use as you saw fit. It would speak up as often or as little as you chose. It reflected your own personality and had the potential to take on many roles in your life—your guardian angel, your mentor, your advisor, your valet, your best friend, even your parent. It presented information to you by spoken word, music, and sounds, and by text and images before your very eyes, superimposed on the real world.

While the Prolix could not read your innermost thoughts, it could interpret a vast number of the electrical impulses of your brain as commands. Thus, you could interact with external technology by merely thinking about it. For example, you merely had to think about switching on the lights for it to happen. This had especially effective applications in the use of weapons technology. For example, a pilot could fly his ship and manipulate its controls and parts as quickly and efficiently as if they were extensions of his own body.

Once the Supremacy gained control, this wonderful technology was made freely available to all. However, a budding rebellion against the technology began to question the government's generosity. There was of course a tradeoff. With the communicative power of this technology, the government had the absolute power to track all Prolix users' actions and movements. While this created a virtually crime-free environment, since it was so easy to catch the guilty, notions of privacy also had to be revisited. For most Prolix users, the benefits far outweighed any misgivings about the government watching them. And as time wore on, for the sake of safety, the Supremacy took greater control of its citizens' day-to-day lives.

Not all people accepted the gift of the Prolix. Some found the very idea abhorrent. The rebellious viewed the technology as a grave threat to the very heart of what it meant to be free.

ABOARD THE SUPREMACY ATTACK SHIP SHADOW *STATIONED ABOVE THE BLUE PLANET*

Myra stared out at the glowing blue planet via the viewport in *Shadow*'s medical bay. She had longed to migrate to the Blue Planet since she was a little girl. This was as close as she had ever been to it. She had made it to the outer atmosphere only to be snatched away from its grasp. Where she sat now, imprisoned in the enemy's ship, it was like peering at an open, gleaming treasure chest that sat in all its glory just on the other side of an unbridgeable chasm. Tears of sorrow and frustration welled in her eyes as she gazed upon the planet's shining beauty.

The planet was so beautiful to look at—so much better than that dead world she had been marooned on for the past ten years. From this distance, the planet below looked mostly the same as Perdicion, even if the continents were larger and arranged so differently. Perdicion's largest southern continent, Ouda Regio, was tiny in comparison to any landmass below. Even so, Ouda Regio was the population center of the planet and the home of the Supremacy. It was not so much a continent, but really the largest island in a gigantic chain of islands along Perdicion's equator. Many of these islands were also the bases of enormous volcanoes, and the tips of submerged highlands that extended for almost ten thousand kilometers across Perdicion's largest ocean, the Ishtaratic. The other largest continent was in Perdicion's northern hemisphere. This was Ishtaria, which was essentially a gigantic basin with dry land in its center.

Myra had been born in Northern Ishtaria. Her parents were farmers, as their family had been for generations. During the day, when the sun was at its hottest, her family stayed indoors in their home, which, as was the way of their people, was crafted to look like the environment around them. Their snug little farmhouse resembled an outcropping of rocks on the side of a hill. Myra remembered sitting on the cool floor on hot afternoons with Darod, her brother, in front of the chairs of their father and mother. They were given their lessons, learning the ancient crafts and studying the family and cultural history.

They also got lessons about their religion. They were

descendants of a small community that followed the Old World Religion. They were taught about the legend of the Fall of Man and their banishment from the garden of paradise, which had been planted by the Creator on Parthénos. Myra and Darod were taught that their Perdician ancestors had been exiled from Parthénos to live on Perdicion. As such, Parthénos was the paradise to be attained by those chosen by the Creator to make the journey back. "We will return there one day," Myra's father would say. "It is God's will that we do. Parthénos is a precious world, filled with many beautiful things."

Myra's father often taught them about the many peoples found on the planet. "The more primitive natives dress in skins of animals and often make war on their neighbors," he said once. "Yes, they, like us, never quite learned to co-exist peacefully with their neighbors. Unfortunately, we face a more pernicious enemy in the government . . ."

"Darling, let's not go on about the government," Myra's mother broke in gently. "The children don't need to hear about that now."

"Yes, of course," her father replied.

That was the juxtaposition set in Myra's mind from an early age. Freedom and natural splendor went together, as did government and servitude. To the farmers of Ishtaria, the serpent in Perdicion's garden was the Supremacy. Its poison was its all-controlling Prolix technology and the environmental laws, which would not allow the Ishtarians to farm profitably. Their home planet had been thus spoiled, but the contagion had not yet spread to the Blue Planet. It had become a shining example of the purity of nature.

One day, however, an announcement that they all hoped for came through the media. "The travel ban has been lifted. Ships are leaving now for the Blue Planet. Book your passage now!" Myra's father read to them with incredulous hope. "They are offering free passage to the Red Colonies," he told the family after reading the lengthy advertisement. "And guaranteed work. But for those that want to migrate to the Blue Planet, it will cost."

The terms of the passage were extremely specific. Each person had to agree to follow all environmental laws to the letter. They were to be placed only in specific colony locations, previously uninhabited. It had an air of truth about it.

Myra's family was among the first to take up roots and book passage. The preparation for the space journey was a most amazing time for Myra. Her family excitedly readied for the biggest adventure of their life. They sold their farm and used most of the proceeds to pay for the journey. They packed only their handheld belongings, and then the day came when the family entered their transport ship ready to spend the next few months sleeping and dreaming about their new life.

"Here are your sleeping chambers," the attendant said, leading the family down a small corridor with seemingly endless rows of tube-like compartments. "You are in Corridor 12-C, 345 through 348." There were four open chambers with storage for luggage below each opening. The family all looked anxiously at the small openings. "Don't worry, once you're all settled in, you'll be able to see and talk to one another through the intercom."

Myra could see the tops of people's heads in several of the other closed chambers.

"You'll note that you have company already. We've got another family across the way from you, already tucked in and asleep," said the attendant, noting her scan of the corridor. "You'll be asleep too in less than an hour. And then the next thing you'll know, you'll be awake and at your destination."

"Pardon my asking, but will the ship be leaving soon?" Myra's father asked.

"Oh, we'll be leaving shortly," the attendant said evasively. "We are still in the process of boarding, and it may take another few days. Then I'll be getting tucked in as well. They only keep a small skeleton crew awake for the journey." The family looked at each other. "But don't you worry about that," the attendant added hastily. "You'll be well looked after. And you won't be aware of time passing. Like I just said— the next thing you'll know is when we wake you up at the destination."

"So, the ship will be stopping at the Blue Planet, then going on to the Red Planet?"

"Yes," said the attendant. "There are two legs to the journey."

"Will you get us all up at the Blue Planet stop?" Myra's father asked. "What if there's some mistake?"

"Now don't you worry about that," the attendant responded. "It's on your travel manifest. These tubes are programmed to open at the destination." He pointed vaguely to the controls on each tube. "There will be no mistakes. Now let me assist you in climbing in," he said. "We'll first lock up your baggage."

Once the baggage was stowed and locked up, the attendant opened the first chamber and slid out the sleeping platform. Myra's parents wanted the children in place before them, so Myra was to be the first, being the oldest. She lay down on the bed. The attendant put monitoring bracelets on her wrists, and then pushed on the end of the bed to slide her into the chamber.

Myra had to fight off a wave of claustrophobia as she was

inserted inside the wall. It was well-lit inside, with a monitor screen directly in front of her, but it was very close. She could not stretch out her arm before touching the top of the chamber. She had plenty of air, she had to remind herself.

"You'll be asleep in no time," the attendant said reassuringly. "She's very brave," he said to her parents. "We often have to put the children out before placing them in the tubes. We'll keep the hatches open until you're all safely stowed."

Myra heard the associated noises of placing Darod, her mother, and then her father into their chambers. Once they were all in place, their monitors showed each of them on split screens. The attendant, seeing that they were all comfortable, closed their hatches. They were alone with one another, and before long, they began to feel sleepy. The automatic stasis process had begun. "Dream about the Blue Planet," her father said, "and then we will be there."

They drifted off.

Returning from her memories, now aboard *Shadow*, Myra gazed out at the blue-and-white globe in her window. The pain and frustration of it all got the better of her, and she began to struggle in vain against the restraints holding her to the bed. After a moment, the medical systems fed her a sedative. She was forced off into a fitful sleep . . . a dream began . . .

She was in space standing on an invisible plane. A solitary man, clothed in red, stood before a dragon. It stood on its hind legs stories above him, inhaling deeply in order to spew out a column of fire at him. The man readied himself to take the onslaught for the others. The lava poured from the dragon's mouth and flowed all around the man and then beyond him to the planet that she had not seen before this. It encircled and enveloped the planet, making it glow orange and black. The man, blackened with soot but otherwise unhurt, stood there still—seemingly protected by his clothing. The dragon roared in anger and frustration . . .

Even under sedation, Myra struggled in her bonds as the images flowed in her head.

At his command station, Solus was trying to picture Myra's face. As often happens when you meet someone new, especially a woman to whom you are attracted, he could not quite picture her features in his mind. He wanted very much to see her face again. Of course, he could simply turn on the monitor to the medical bay and look at her, but that seemed wrong, a violation. He resisted the urge.

"Alert, sir," piped in Bas, interrupting his contemplation. "It's a ship-to-ship transmission."

"Acknowledged," Solus replied. He noted from the communication's encrypted identifier that it came from *Traverse*, one of his squadron's attack ships. She was commanded by First Lieutenant Grand, another of Solus' old friends who had served with him for nearly half of his career in space. Grand was a hulking man, with black hair and a dark complexion. Grand's dark, handsome face now appeared before Solus.

"Commander, looks like we've got some company in my sector today as well. We're picking up a small transport ship coming in. It's making an approach using the moon as a cover, but we detected it via the sensor on the dark side."

"Understood. Intercept and board the ship."

"Yes, sir."

"You'll have to be on your own on this one. I'd be leaving my own sector wide open."

With only the five ships, Solus' small squadron was strategically deployed in zones around the globe. Any teaming up of ships would leave an entire zone of space around the planet unprotected.

"It's a comfort just to know you're there, sir," Grand responded. "We'll be fine."

Solus forgave the sardonic tone. He'd known Grand too long for anything else. "I'm alerting the other ships."

To Xoxon, Solus ordered: "Bring up my other ship commanders and Lieutenant Foglet, please."

In response, four faces of those who made up his command were projected in front of his eyes.

"Commander! Good to see you—all quiet here," said Lieutenant Thump, commander of *Orion-SAS*. Short and stocky, with blonde hair, Thump was the most junior officer in the squadron. Even so, as a veteran of the Red Colonies rebellion, he had seen enough action to rate his own ship command.

"Hello, Commander," spoke red-haired Lieutenant Quash, commander of *Radiate-SAS*, another old friend of Solus. "Something's up, I expect."

"Commander," Lieutenant Prop, commander of *Corona-SAS*, said in greeting, as did Lieutenant Rodd, who commanded *Guru*.

"Foglet, here, sir," piped in Lieutenant Foglet, another dark-haired Supremacy officer and the Blue Squadron's overworked engineering officer. Presently aboard *Radiate*, Foglet was typically stationed on *Guru* and performed maintenance on the attack ships when they docked with her. As the squadron was spread so thin, the ships could not dock with the *Guru* for any length of time, so Foglet was transferring to any ship requiring maintenance. *Radiate* was having some non-urgent difficulties with her environmental systems.

"Gentlemen," Solus began, "we're seeing more activity today. What with the planetary convergence, this is undoubtedly the beginning of a new wave of incursions. We need to keep on the alert."

"Yes, sir," they said together.

"Grand is about to intercept another transport," Solus continued. "Since I am the closest, I will be his cover in case of difficulties."

His officers acknowledged again.

"Commander, do you think word has gotten out about our weakened presence here?" queried Prop.

"Good question, Prop," Solus replied. "It's quite possible. Regardless, we know there will be increased incursions with the planets in such close proximity in their orbits."

Solus realized at times like these how ironic it was that space-fleet movements and tactics resembled those from the days of wooden sailing ships, when it took weeks and months to move fleets to different parts of the oceans. How similar that was in space! Given the nature of the orbits of the planets and how the distances between them differed as the planets neared one another and then grew apart, the timing for travel was vital. "Thank you, gentlemen. Rodd and Foglet, stay on please." The other heads disappeared. "Rodd, what's your ETA on picking up that enemy command module that I left for you?"

"Sir, we're on our way there. We're approximately forty minutes away," replied Rodd, whose tall, lean form was not seen in the link—only his long, serious face.

"Understood. Keep on the alert for new orders. We may need you in Grand's zone."

"Acknowledged, sir."

"And Foglet, how're the repairs on *Radiate*'s environmental gear?"

"I think I got it worked out, sir," Foglet said. "I replaced a faulty system junction. I'm just testing it to make sure that was the only issue. The diagnostics are checking out." Foglet's face was bearded and handsome, but had the aspect of a nearly constant wiriness.

"Good work," Solus responded. "I want you back on *Guru* as soon as a rendezvous can be arranged. Then I will be picking you up. I want you to inspect *Shadow* for damage after our little action."

"Yes, sir."

"In the meantime, stand down. *Radiate* can't meet with *Guru* at present. Take it easy while it lasts."

"Thanks, sir. My thoughts exactly. Foglet out."

A few moments later, Solus watched Grand's engagement from his monitor. *Traverse* closed in on the unidentified spacecraft in stealth mode, and her prey gave no outward sign that she had been spotted. Then, just as Solus had done, Grand announced his presence. Solus could hear Grand's transmission: "Ishtarian vessel—this is the Supremacy attack vessel *Traverse*. You are in violation of Supremacy space laws governing planetary quarantine. Stop your engines and respond to my signal."

The ship, appearing to obey, fired its stopping thrusters. *Traverse* moved closer to the vessel. Then, as Solus watched, a large explosion flashed out near Grand's ship. Grand's voice rang out in Solus' cockpit. "Commander, we've been hit. We stopped the other ship, but then it deployed some kind of mine and detonated it."

"What's your status?" Solus asked, with practiced outward calm.

"I have no power, and I can't get my crew to respond."

"I'm scanning your vicinity," Solus stated as he focused his sensors on the area about the two ships. *Traverse* was quite dead, and the enemy ship was flopping in an uncontrolled fashion.

"I'm going out into the main deck and see if I can restore the ship's power," Grand reported.

"Very well," Solus responded. "I'm calling in the *Guru* to assist you."

Accordingly, Solus communicated with the support ship. Rodd responded immediately and altered course, but it would take them at least a half hour to get to Grand.

Grand reported after a time. "I've restored partial power. Our port cockpit was damaged and we had one casualty, Nocab. Ham was also in the cockpit. He was injured, but he's going to be okay."

"Understood." Solus scanned the enemy vessel for signs of power. He could detect nothing, but the situation made him feel uncomfortable. "Grand, can you maneuver the ship at all?"

"I've got thrusters, sir."

"Good. Move away from that ship; you're in no condition to board her." He could see the protest register in Grand's eyes. "It's not going anywhere. I want some distance between you and that ship."

"Very well, sir."

Solus monitored as *Traverse*'s positioning thrusters began moving her away. The pace was deadly slow. Displayed on his instruments, the two ships seemed hardly to be separating at all.

Grand reported again. "Commander, I've got partial sensors up. I'm detecting some strange energy readings emanating from that ship."

Solus' thoughts raced—what could he do? Then it happened before he could do or say anything. The enemy ship exploded. As usual, time itself seemed to slow down. He watched in stunned silence as the blast's shock wave expanded out and caught *Traverse*, which before his eyes quickly broke up into countless pieces. Only Solus' experience and training helped him remain in control. "Fleek, monitor the explosion . . . check for the command modules."

"Searching, Commander." After a brief pause, Fleek reported back. "Commander, I am picking up two cockpit modules, both from *Traverse*. They appear to be intact. I see none from the enemy ship."

Hope flooded Solus. "Rowling, plot a course to get us there as fast as possible. Bas, take us there, maximum speed."

They both acknowledged, and an instant later *Shadow* was racing towards Solus' old friend.

"You're leaving this sector unprotected," Xoxon said.

"I know, but it can't be helped."

The action had taken place on the far side of the moon, and the support ship was out in space on the other side of the planet. *Shadow* was closer, and every minute would count if Grand and his crew were still alive.

"Sol, Nevek here," piped in Dr. Nevek from the *Guru*. "I just wanted to let you know that we've got our emergency medical equipment up and ready here."

"Thank you, doctor."

"I'm sure Grand is okay. He's always led a charmed life."

Years ago, Grand and Solus had served a tour together in the Red Colonies sector, just before the revolt that had driven out the Supremacy presence on the planet. The conditions were about as miserable as any in the entire solar system. With the significant infrastructure required for expansion of the facility, slow construction, and a swollen population from the forced migrations, the Red Colonies expanded in size at glacial speed. That was the challenge of working and living on a planet without a breathable atmosphere.

Originally the Supremacy had planned the colonies as an

operation for exploiting the untapped natural resources of the Red Planet. Only after the forced migration of the Ishtarians had the authorities worked towards making the colonies self-supportive. As such, there were plenty of jobs to go around. But no matter what, the population was unhappy with the terrible living conditions, and without the Prolix to control them, they had proved difficult to manage. Underneath it all was a simmering rage at the Supremacy—the entity responsible for their exile.

The Red Colonies always reminded Solus of a vast, endless, and over-crowded civilian airport terminal; some hurrying, some waiting, but no one really going anywhere in particular. The most habitable place was the great dome at the center of the colonies. The transparent ceiling rose into the air to a hundred-meter height. Hanging plants grew all over the place, giving it an almost tropical feel. Around the dome, large entertainment districts had popped up at every entrance, and there were several. This area, needless to say, was a favorite for the Supremacy forces when on leave.

Grand loved the crowds. He dragged Solus to every imaginable kind of nightclub in the district. While Solus grew anxious and dispirited by the atmosphere of the place, Grand would walk along cheerfully, patting children on the head as he passed, making casual observations about people that they saw as they made their way around the crowded hallways. "That one there looks as if he's made up entirely of cartilage, the way he's waving about," Grand said once, indicating a man selling packaged snacks in one of the countless vendor booths that lined the hallways. "What an odd little guy," he noted about another passing figure. "He creeps along in sort of a slither, rather than walking. Graceful, I suppose, but odd."

There was one character in particular who Grand liked to visit who was a regular in the dome. He was a crazy sort of fellow who stood on a box and preached to the passing crowds. His name was Zealrot, and he practically foamed at the mouth in his vehemence. He stood there many an evening sermonizing to all who would listen. His belief system somehow involved turning the Blue Planet's inhabitants into slaves and forcing them to worship him as their new god. Solus believed him to be nuts, but Grand was convinced he was a complete fraud. "I know a con man when I see one," Grand said, watching the man's convulsive arm gestures.

"I don't know; he seems pretty sincere to me," Solus replied.

"Oh, I can tell. A fraud can see right through a fellow fraud." Grand's manner could have been taken as being uncaring and aloof, but it really wasn't that. He just refused to be brought down by his surroundings. If anything, he tended to brighten the places he visited. He simply would not reflect back someone else's bad feelings towards him, even those who hated him. He could visit any drinking establishment, no matter how tough the crowd, without any discomfort. Grand could take over a place, accepting equally good humor and every ill-willed utterance made towards them. He sometimes even succeeded in turning bad feelings into passing toleration of their presence. Suffering agonies himself, Solus was always amazed at these performances.

As *Shadow* hastened to the scene of the explosion, Solus repeatedly tried to reach Grand, but got no response. Between transmissions, Solus had time to analyze *Traverse*'s and his own recent action. It was obvious now that the Ishtarians were using new tactics, deploying mines around them when engaged. Solus' first disabling-strength shot in his action must have detonated the mines around that ship, which had caused its destruction.

There also must have been some unexploded mines in his path, which he had thankfully avoided.

He would need to warn his squadron and then update Supremacy Fleet Command. To complete his report, he would need to interrogate Myra. And to his growing annoyance with himself, he could not fight off a budding attraction towards her, in spite of her being a rebel Ishtarian. More to the point, she clearly loathed him. It was impossible.

Was he that lonely that he could have feelings for an Ishtarian woman? Truly, women were few and far between in the deep-space fleet. A small number served in medical and support roles on the command ships, including some officers, but here Solus was outnumbered by other competing men. And unlike Grand, who accepted this challenge delightedly, Solus had neither the desire nor the time to do any wooing in that kind of environment.

Forgetting his resolve not to look, he checked in on her using his command monitor and read her life-sign readings. As expected, she was still there, head to her side, unconscious; the log showed that she had been sedated. Solus gazed at her parted lips and imagined their softness.

"Solus, you must not get emotionally involved with this woman," said Xoxon.

"She is lovely, though," Solus responded.

"Myra has many classically beautiful female traits." To illustrate the point, an image of Myra's face appeared before Solus. "For instance, her facial features are all in good proportion to the size of her skull; they are neither too big nor too small and are symmetrical. Her eyes are large and her lips are full. Her hair is long, shiny, and healthy-looking. Her figure—"

"My, aren't we the romantic one?" Solus said sarcastically. "You'd make quite the poet!"

While Xoxon objected to Solus' characterization of his analysis, Solus thought of several examples of females he had known who wouldn't have fit with this "classic" criteria. Somehow, they had pulled it off anyway, and they fit his estimation of beauty. Subjective, maybe, but there were some things that a computer mind, even an extremely advanced one, could not comprehend. Yet, Xoxon was right about one thing. Myra was classically and extraordinarily beautiful.

The Blue Planet's moon loomed large and white in the distance as they approached the scene of destruction. Upon arriving, *Shadow* immediately proceeded into the ships' wreckage to locate the two cockpit modules. The flames had long since burnt out as escaping oxygen had dispersed into space, but electrical sparks ignited and winked out in reds and blues all around them as the wreckage twisted and spun off in all directions and angles. Bas set an erratic course to navigate through the spinning wreckage towards the flopping capsules.

While Bas made positioning maneuvers and extended the ship's grappling arms and umbilical tube, Solus again went down to the ship's bottom to retrieve the survivors. As he passed into the center of the ship, he glanced into the medical bay and saw that Myra was still asleep. There were extra fold-down beds in there, but he hoped they would not be needed.

Bas managed to grab first one capsule and then the other in the ship's grappling arms. The first one was attached at the end of the umbilical tube. As before, when Solus reached the end of the tube, the captured capsule's hatch was already open. This time, however, Solus saw a head poking out. It was Grand. "Commander, good to see you!" he said with a smile. "Had to come in person to help out your old friend?"

Solus smiled back. "Glad to see you're all right. What's Ham's condition?" He noted that the other two crewmembers were apparently no worse for wear and would be freed from their capsule next.

"He doesn't appear to be in pain, but I think he's in shock."

"How's that?"

"Well, he's acting funny. Come on in and see. We'll need both of us to coax him out of there." Grand ducked back down, and Solus followed him into the tiny compartment.

"I sat him down in the command chair to make him more comfortable," Grand explained. "Most of the controls are junk."

Solus went forward into the remains of the port-side command module of the late *Traverse* and advanced to the chair where Ham was sitting. He looked far worse than Grand. His environmental suit was completely burned away in places. His skin was burned on his arms and chest. Mumbling to himself, he twitched and moved his head from side to side, looking at the damaged controls. "Ham, how are you doing?"

"I-I can't get anything to move. I'm numb all over. I can't feel anything," he stammered, seemingly on the edge of losing control.

"Stay calm, Ham," Solus tried to reassure him. "You've been through a lot today."

Solus tried to make eye contact with him, but Ham would not meet his eyes. "Ham, look at me."

"I can't get anything to move. I tell the control to move, but it won't . . ."

This was disorientation from losing his Prolix mental control powers over the instrumentation.

"Ham, the ship's damaged. The systems are not working."

"I'm disconnected. I can't work anything!" Ham's voice was starting to rise, on the verge of hysteria.

"Ham, I'm going to speak to your Prolix now, and see what's happening, okay?"

Ham continued his writhing, not seeming to have heard.

"Xoxon, patch me in to Ham's Prolix, please."

"Connecting . . ."

"What's happening in there?"

"Greetings," responded Ham's Prolix. "Ham is in shock. He has sustained second- and third-degree burns over ten percent of his body. I'm managing his pain by disconnecting his nerve impulses. I've also disconnected him from external technology to avoid any accidents. This appears to be causing further disorientation. I'm attempting to calm him now."

"Can we move him?"

"He can move, but with difficulty."

"Disconnect," Solus ordered.

"Disconnecting . . ." Xoxon responded.

Grand returned with a transport mat. As soon as they strapped Ham on the mat, he was sedated. Solus watched as Ham's twitching ceased and his head drooped into unconsciousness.

"That's for the best," Grand said. "He looked mighty uncomfortable. It's disconcerting to have your mental control ripped away like that."

"Yes," agreed Solus. It was like having your extended limbs suddenly ripped from you and removed.

A few minutes later, as Solus and Grand pulled Ham's body up into the ship's conveyor tube, Fleek's voice rang out. "Commander! I'm detecting another ship coming into range of the planet!"

With the umbilical tube extended, the ship was vulnerable. "What's their position?" Solus responded.

"They're coming into sector A—the zone we left unprotected."

The ship was not in imminent danger, but Solus' relief was short-lived. An enemy ship was getting through his blockade. He was failing in his mission.

"They're coming in at a high rate of speed on an angle to enter the planet's atmosphere. At this distance we will not be able to intercept them in time," Fleek reported.

Solus, however, was not left without an option. "Bas, reposition the ship. Chamers, target that ship. Prepare to fire two spears." Housed in its wings, *Shadow* was equipped with eight missiles designed to hit long-range targets.

"Yes, sir. Repositioning the ship."

Solus heard the thrusters firing and could feel the ship moving around. *Shadow*'s wings swept forward, positioning themselves at the ship's sides with two missiles now deployed below them.

"Ship targeted," Chamers reported.

"Fire," Solus ordered.

Instantaneously, the spears roared away from the ship and towards the planet. Solus and Grand felt the tremors from the thrusts of their engines. Then, like a bird of prey retracting its talons, the missiles' deployment pods merged back within *Shadow*'s wings, while the wings themselves swept gracefully backward again. In the meantime, Solus and Grand completed the rescue of Grand's two other crewmen. Once the cockpit modules were empty of survivors, *Shadow* abandoned them for later retrieval by the *Guru*.

"Rowling, plot and execute a course to follow those spears. Fleek, monitor their progress," Solus commanded. (Dr. Nevek would be mad at Solus for leaving with his patients, but it couldn't be helped.)

"Yes, sir," they responded simultaneously.

As they made their way up the conveyor tube, Fleek kept them informed as to the Ishtarian ship's movements and the missiles' progress towards them. The interception point would be dangerously close to the planet's outer atmosphere and could possibly be seen from the surface. Minus the explosion, it would probably look like ordinary shooting stars to the people below.

Meanwhile, they got Ham into the medical bay and placed him onto one of the fold-down medical beds. After pulling off his suit, they enclosed him in the automated caring unit to tend to his wounds. The unit began at once to clean and minister to his burned skin. Just as Solus had predicted, Dr. Nevek called in to complain bitterly about Solus' leaving before *Guru* could get there. "Solus, I need to get him under my care as soon as possible," Nevek said, after reviewing what they were doing to care for Ham. "He's suffering from Prolix technology disconnection."

"I understand, Nev, but I can't wait for you. We've got a breach of the blockade in progress."

"You get him to me as soon as possible."

Myra watched them as they cared for Ham, but she was having trouble distinguishing reality from the surreal world of sedation. Her mind became garbled with memories of her past life on the Red Colonies.

A repeating alarm sounded in the distance. Growing ever insistent, it roused her from her sleep. She was back in the past—back in the sleeping tube of the vast transport ship that took them from Perdicion. "Attention! Attention, passengers—the ship is being evacuated," a voice spoke through her monitor. "There is no need for alarm," the voice continued. "Please follow the attendants in an orderly fashion."

"Mom? Dad?" she called out. But before they could reply, her chamber door opened and her bed slid out into the corridor. Myra looked around and saw that her family members were all being ejected from their chambers. Their belongings were spread out on the deck floor.

"Come along," called out their attendant, who appeared from

the shadows of the corridor. "We need to get you moving. The ship is being evacuated."

"What is going on?" called out Myra's father, gathering their bags.

"I'm not quite sure," replied the attendant. "I've been told to get the passengers off as soon as possible. Please hurry!" The attendant hurried the family down corridor after corridor until they reached an exit. When they opened the door into a larger chamber near the bottom of the vessel, they could hear the roar of crowds of people being herded out the exits, all being moved out into the darkness outside the ship.

"Where have we landed?" Myra's father asked. "Why's it so dark out there?"

"Please keep moving; you will be safe in a few moments," the attendant replied. "It's night out. There is a processing center right outside, then you will be free to go." The attendant, after pushing them into the moving crowds, disappeared back into the recesses of the ship. They held each other to avoid getting separated as the crowds pushed out of the vessel. They had arrived in the cold reality of the Red Colonies' refugee processing center. There was no return passage.

Now Myra's mental streaming morphed into a dream.

She was in space and saw a blue planet large before her. She could not tell if it was Perdicion or Parthénos. Regardless, she was filled with delight. She tried to go towards it, but could not move. Then, a creamy brown cloud seemed to envelop the planet. It quickly covered the planet's surface, snuffing out the wonderful blue air and oceans. In spite of her being in space, she could smell sulfur and burning. Lava spewed forth into space, within inches of splashing her arms. She wailed in agony at the sight.

Then it was gone. The Blue Planet was before her. It was blue but mistier, like clouds were escaping the atmosphere and drifting into space. She looked at it, transfixed. A voice spoke.

"Find hope in me." The voice penetrated her very being. "Come and know me better."

Aroused from her dreams, Myra came back to the present. She saw Grand and Solus working on Ham's burns. "Another casualty of this awful war," she uttered.

Hearing her, Grand looked around, and Solus could see his instant appreciation of her beauty. "Your Ishtarian comrades did this," Grand replied, but not in a hostile tone.

"They were not my comrades. I was merely a passenger."

"You're not an Ishtarian?" Grand asked.

"I am, but I am not a rebel. I am a Harmonian."

"Harmonian?" Grand said, then remembered. "That's right, I know, the peace- and nature-loving group."

"We always sought peaceful solutions to end the system's strife," Myra replied. "We did not approve of the Ishtarian Council's violent course of action."

Solus had heard a little about this group. He knew that their association with the rebel Ishtarians came solely through their mutual dislike of the Prolix and their desire to colonize the Blue Planet.

"Commander, perhaps I should debrief her while you attend to that Ishtarian ship," Grand suggested.

"No, I need to do that personally. Take my command position and monitor the spears, please."

Grand nodded and said quietly, "Okay, I get the point; you saw her first." Smiling at Solus' obvious discomfort at this, Grand went out of the bay, crossed the center deck, and climbed up into the command module.

When he heard the door sliding shut after Grand, Solus looked at Myra. "I need to ask you a few questions."

"Is this going to be a two- or three-way conversation this time?"

"My Prolix will not interrupt me unless there's something urgent," Solus replied for both her and Xoxon to hear.

Myra smiled in spite of herself. "What do you want to know?"

"I want to know, among other things, how you got here, how many ships came with you, and the nature of your mission."

"If I answer freely, will you still force the Prolix on me?"

"Well, frankly, I should have administered it to you already."

"Please don't!" she implored.

Her pained expression hit him unexpectedly like a jolt. "I will not—for now—if you will answer my questions truthfully," he replied.

"What choice do I have? Please let me out of this bed!"

At Solus' thought command, the bed released its hold on Myra, and she sat up immediately, holding the sheets to her body. "May I have some clothes to wear?"

"Yes, of course," Solus replied. "Let me get you something." He reached into a compartment and pulled out a yellow jumpsuit, some black socks, and the smallest undergarments that he could find and laid them out on the end of Myra's bed. "I'll wait outside while you get dressed. Please come out here when you are ready." As he stepped into the center deck, he closed the bay's door. "I'll get you something to eat and drink." He went over to the galley and began to prepare a food tray. Not waiting for a report, he contacted Grand. "What's happening out there?"

Grand's face appeared before him. "The spears have locked onto the target. Impact in ten minutes."

"Thank you. Keep me informed. And keep sending updates to the squadron."

Grand looked back at him. "Having a little tea party back there, are we?"

"Keep your eyes out of the medical bay and on those spears, please!" Solus said testily. Grand acknowledged, very pleased at seeing his commander's discomfort.

Myra opened the medical bay door and came through. As her body had graced the sheets of her bed, so it did, as well, with the jumpsuit, in spite of its somewhat shapeless cut. Solus could easily distinguish her shapely curves beneath them. Her long black hair cascaded about her shoulders.

"Please sit down." Solus gestured towards the round table and chairs near the center of the deck. To this he brought over a tray. She seated herself. He set the tray with sandwiches, cookies, and a cup of tea in front of her and sat down himself. "Let's begin. I need to know how many ships were with you."

Myra answered between gulps of tea. "Since telling you this will not jeopardize anyone else, I can answer. There were three ships. You stopped the one I was on, and, from the wreckage I saw outside a little while ago, you intercepted the second one, and now you are after the last one."

"We engaged two ships, that is true, but both were destroyed by the ships' own crews," Solus responded, wanting to correct any lingering notion that he had simply destroyed two unarmed transport ships. "Was this part of an organized Ishtarian operation to break our blockade?"

"No, the Ishtarian government would not allow us to leave. Our ships were hidden from them."

"I see," Solus responded, then continued. "You said that you were a passenger, that your fellow travelers were not your compatriots. Please explain."

"As I told you, I am a Harmonian. Our only motivation in all of this is to live harmoniously with nature. We seek to live on the garden planet below. We do not seek to change it, for it is perfection itself. To live there in harmony, we must change ourselves and blend into the environment we live in."

"You mean you wish to live on the Blue Planet as the natives do? Go back to nature, as it were?"

"That is precisely what we wish."

Solus looked at her incredulously, but in a way he understood. He had often thought about this very idea. He knew from secret intelligence that Perdicians had been on the planet before. There had been several expeditions and scientific explorations made, but only a handful of the inhabitants had actually come in contact with them. Yet, once the Supremacy started colonization in earnest, the Blue Planet's ignorant people would be changed in a profound way, and the planet's untouched mystique would vanish forever.

But perhaps change wasn't so bad, either. The Supremacy would bring them technological advances that would help them feed themselves more efficiently, extend their lives, and improve their living conditions in countless ways. With a mental effort, Solus dropped this line of thought and continued his questioning. "So, there were others with you in your journey here who were not Harmonians?"

"We were betrayed. We had grown impatient with the new government that was set up after the revolt. They had proved no better than the Supremacy in leading us. For their own reasons, they would not permit us to leave the colonies. We had three small ships and left on our own, and we got away. But the leader of the mission betrayed us, and our ships were taken over."

"And who was this?"

"Zealrot."

The name was instantly familiar to Solus. "Zealrot? You mean the crazy man who used to preach in the dome?"

"Yes, that was him. You saw him there?"

"Many times. I was stationed in the colonies for a time," Solus replied. "But back to Zealrot—how did he get involved with your movement?"

"He found out somehow that we had hidden ships, and devised a scheme to publicly renounce his old beliefs and join our movement. He captured the trust of our leadership and even convinced them that only he could break through the Supremacy blockade. With his extensive background in smuggling, it was hard not to agree. No one in our movement had that kind of experience."

Myra stopped speaking for a moment to collect her thoughts. She was becoming dangerously close to revealing too much about the Harmonians back at the Red Colonies. She could not reveal the secret of their hidden base on Phobos, one of the Red Planet's dark moons. This base, an abandoned secret Supremacy facility that remained unknown to the Ishtarian authority, was concealed inside one of the many crevices on the surface of the small satellite. They traveled between there and the orbiting space station in secret, using space station shuttles—and often emergency escape pods.

After considering, Myra decided that she could tell Solus about the journey, and she did so with some detail. She told him that Zealrot's compatriots were stationed on each ship and killed the Harmonian men by sabotaging their sleeper chambers. Once he had control of the ships, Zealrot threw off any pretense of being a Harmonian. His old, crazy goal still lived— he planned to come down to the surface of the Blue Planet in glory and be hailed as a god.

"What ship was Zealrot in?" Solus asked. "It wasn't your ship, or I would have recognized him."

"His second was in command of our ship. It was he who shot

me and Melva, my sister Harmonian. He was in one of the other ships; I'm not sure which."

Thinking it through, Solus strategized that Zealrot was likely commanding the ship they were now chasing, and had very likely ordered the last transport to destroy itself. He was still thinking it though when Grand appeared before him. "Commander, the spears are coming within range of the ship."

"I want a direct hit," Solus ordered. "Destroy that ship.

Myra, although she could not hear Grand instantly understood the situation. "Two of my sisters are probably on that ship!" she broke in. "Please do not hurt them!"

"Myra, I will not let that ship get past me," Solus replied. "I can't allow Zealrot to land on the planet."

"But they are entirely innocent!" She looked into his dark eyes, pleading with her gaze. He looked back into her brown eyes.

"I will do what I can," he said after a moment. Still looking intently back at her, he made a command decision. "Grand, prepare to detonate the spears within one hundred meters of the ship. We're going to disable it."

Meanwhile, the spears rocketed towards their target. Rather than using a ship's monitor screen, Xoxon placed the spears' transmissions before Solus' eyes, assuming that Solus didn't want Myra to see what was about to happen. The ship, another yellow tube-like vessel, was centered in the missiles' targeting grids. "They've altered course. Evasive, away from the spears," Grand reported.

"Acknowledged."

"They're sowing mines behind them," Grand added. "They were easy to spot once I knew what to look for."

"Alter the spears' course to avoid the mines," Solus responded. Explosions began to dot the path behind the running ship.

Indeed, mines were going off. The spears avoided this area and continued on towards their target.

"Our missiles are in range," he said to Myra. "I'll let you know when it happens."

"Sir!" Fleek called out via Prolix link. "The target ship. The scanners are picking up explosions at the ship's bow. Pieces of the hull are exploding off of it."

Xoxon displayed the scan for Solus. Explosions had exposed the ship's command module. Solus watched as another explosion marked the ejection of the module, which was visibly shoved out from the front of the ship. "Chamers, do you see that?" Solus asked. "Reposition the spears. We need to delay the detonation. They're too far away to stop that module."

But it was too late. The spears exploded at precisely one hundred meters from the ship. The explosion took out the ship's engines and sent the yellow tube flying off at an angle away from the planet. The unaffected command module continued insolently on its way towards the atmosphere.

Solus transferred the image of the escaping capsule to a monitor on the wall. "Zealrot has made good on his blockade-running boast," he said to Myra. "After sacrificing two of his ships, he managed to escape our spears in his command module, and is now headed for the planet's surface."

Myra looked intently at the screen. "They made it," she said, happy for her friends.

As they watched, the capsule began its orbital descent.

"I'm going after them," Solus stated.

Myra looked at him and saw that his eyes seemed to show regret, not anger. "I will help you to catch Zealrot, if you promise not to hurt my Harmonian friends."

"I'm afraid that is not—"

"And you must promise not to infect me with the Prolix."

That was a promise he could not make, but one he badly wished he could.

ABOARD THE ESCAPING ISHTARIAN COMMAND MODULE

With the explosions from the enemy's missiles still flashing in their rear, Zealrot was feeling exuberant at getting away. He piloted the clumsy thrusters of the command module towards the planet's atmosphere. It would be a rough entry and landing, but he welcomed the ending of this journey. "We have done it!" he exclaimed to his crew and passengers, who sat strapped in their chairs to the side and back of him.

"You were as good as your word, master," said the man in the co-pilot seat. This was Waltron, Zealrot's large and loyal bodyguard. The other passengers were two of Myra's Harmonian sisters, Mondra and Zeeni.

"Well, my dears, we're almost there," said Zealrot, half turning towards them. "You will be my queens in my new kingdom, starting tomorrow!" he gloated.

"We want nothing to do with you," Mondra replied wearily, very much tired of repeating this line.

"Have you forgotten what I did to your friends? Are you so foolish as to risk my wrath?"

The two women did remember, and the memory of it sent pangs of horror down their spines. Zealrot sensed their emotions and snickered at his power over them.

Zealrot's life's journey had taken him to many places prior to this grand adventure. He had sprung from an Ishtarian family with an extended history of criminal activity. He was olive-skinned and black-haired, with a pointed beard. His short stature was more than made up for by a commanding voice and an imposing personality. In addition to giving him his physical looks, Zealrot's family had heavily ingrained in him their warped worldview. Zealrot had joined the rebellion against the Prolix for less than the noble and idealistic reasons that drove most of his compatriots. His driving motivation was the fact that the Prolix made it extremely difficult to conduct larceny, fraud, robbery, and all the other countless anti-social behaviors that seemed to come as second nature to him.

Smuggling was his family's chief source of income, and Zealrot himself had learned to pilot many types of craft and ships in his quest for more profitable smuggling opportunities. He met up with Ishtarian leaders when the underground Prolix rebellion movement came into association with the underworld that Zealrot frequented. With extremely profitable exchanges, he assisted the Ishtarians in obtaining explosives and other items needed for terrorist activities. As more and more weapon orders came in, his fate became more and more linked with the Ishtarian movement, both for its profitability for him and the false air of legitimacy of a worthy cause that enveloped him.

When the first Supremacy crackdowns began in the southern hemisphere, after several terrorist bombings in which he had been a principal supplier of materials, Zealrot had himself smuggled out of the south back to Ishtaria in the north, where he re-emerged in a stronger and higher position within the rebel movement. Later, when the Supremacy began allowing mass migrations off the planet, Zealrot joined one of the space transports under an assumed name. He left the planet, never to return, and entered his sleep chamber quite pleased with himself for having put yet another one over on the authorities. It had been almost too easy to slip away. His new home would be primitive, yet eminently corruptible! Upon arrival at the Red

Colonies, he realized,of course, that he himself had been snook-
ered, and quite grandly at that. The boarding authorities at the
space port had cared very little about identities and security—
the ship on which he had been booked had simply been taking
the trash off the planet.

In the days after awakening from his journey, Zealrot went
into a rage that seemed to destroy his sanity. In this state, he
experienced what was, to him, a religious epiphany. He discovered something that gave him a new purpose in life. It became
his driving force.

Some men in his condition have gone on to take over entire
countries, while others have founded new religious movements. Zealrot, himself, was consumed with only one goal—
descending into the primitive world of the Blue Planet and
assuming his ordained role as the people's new god and master.
His old associates wondered whether Zealrot had gone crazy.
They did not recognize the new person that he had become.
Gone was the quiet, shadowy manner that had been so essential
in his previous employment. Unchecked in the unruly environment of the Red Colonies, Zealrot spent his days proselytizing
his new vision and recruiting members. His force of personality
alone won over many to his movement, and his fame rose in the
community.

His growing movement had started to become a threat to
the occupying Supremacy forces, but before he could be dealt
with by them, the revolt took place. And while Zealrot's forces
had aided in the takeover of the colonies, allies soon became
enemies again. He quickly gained the admonition of the new
Ishtarian government as a disruptive force in the small community. And this government was no more willing to allow him to
leave than the Supremacy had been.

Not deterred, Zealrot began to seek new allies to his cause.

He began to realize that his new persona as a religious leader had become a detriment to his goal of getting to the Blue Planet. Moreover, he began to hear rumors of hidden ships being harbored by other groups in the colonies. That was when he decided to infiltrate the Harmonians. With a lifetime of experience in deception, it was quite easy to assume a new persona as a Harmonian. It was not hard to convince the Harmonian leadership that he was absolutely vital to a successful mission in establishing a Harmonian outpost on the Blue Planet. As to his former ideology of enslaving the inhabitants of the Blue Planet, that was merely misguided bitterness, he told them, over his confinement in the Red Colonies. While not everyone believed in his sincerity, the Harmonian leadership was convinced that he should take part in the first mission to the planet.

With the command module's limited power, the only atmosphere entry point available to Zealrot would take them over a large but somewhat secluded continent on the planet's northern hemisphere. This continent contained no advanced civilizations, and was populated only by primitive migratory and agrarian people. They lived in tribal communities in what was essentially a gigantic contiguous forest that comprised the entire eastern coast and middle section of the continent. This was not exactly what Zealrot had planned for, but it would do for a start. Once he had established himself properly in this hemisphere, his armies of primitives would then conquer the more advanced civilizations.

The destruction of the rest of Zealrot's ship had taken from him most of the equipment that would have made his path to power so much easier. Much of it had been Supremacy gear that had been acquired after the revolt in the Red Colonies. But, just prior to their run for the planet, Zealrot had ordered Waltron to pull into the command module whatever weapons and equipment that he could fit. It was not much, but it would be the small seed from which his new kingdom would sprout. Just a tiny demonstration of their power would spread awe and fear far and wide. Surely much larger things had grown from smaller starting points.

Waltron broke Zealrot's train of thought. "Master, will I get a woman?" he asked imploringly.

"You may have your pick of the native women below—but only after I have personally rejected them," he replied condescendingly.

"And will you divide up your cattle in a similar fashion?" asked the other of the two Ishtarian women in unrestrained disgust. The two were bound to their chairs. The one who spoke was Zeeni, an attractive dark-haired Harmonian sister.

"Silence! I will not tolerate impertinence!" Zealrot shouted. "The only reason you're alive is because you are both experts on the natives below! Besides, a god must have his goddesses, and I will be their new god! I will be worshipped and glorified! My kingdom will last—"

"Until the Supremacy comes and takes you away," Zeeni broke in.

"Oh, I don't think they will be giving us any problems," Zealrot smiled. "The Supremacy's time is about to come to an end."

"What do you mean?" asked Mondra, a formidable Harmonian sister in both mind and body.

"This is something that I know," Zealrot responded mysteriously. "Their ultimate power is about to become their ultimate undoing."

The nose of the capsule was beginning to glow orange as Zealrot began his descent. The new king was coming down in a giant ball of glorious flames.

CHAPTER 4

THE BATTLE OF THE RED COLONIES

According to official Supremacy history, the Red Colonies' migration was the Supremacy's benevolent solution to the Ishtarian problem. Myra remembered it much differently, as did most other Ishtarians who were transplanted without their consent to the colonies. Her first weeks there remained vivid in her memory. After the humiliation of the processing center, her family was provided quarters in one of the countless tenement sections of the colonies. Their passage money had actually paid for a private apartment—a two-bedroom suite, with a small kitchen. Myra's family began their new life there in a sort of stunned denial.

It was always dark in the colonies. Even when the tiny sun was up in the sky, the sunlight barely illuminated the uninhabitable world outside, much less the family's apartment from the single window it contained. Myra's father would spend hours staring out through the thick glass of this window at the dead world outside, watching the dust swirling red and coating everything in sight. He loathed it all, yet at the same time envied the men he saw from time to time working outside in environmental suits. It was far better out there even without air than living in their enclosed metal world.

In addition to their living quarters, their new hosts gave the family a living by providing them with jobs in the colonies. Myra's parents got horticulture work raising vegetables in the colonies' vast greenhouses. Myra got work in a lunch counter operation that did business in the colonies' main dome, while Darod bused tables. Their paychecks primarily paid for the utilities, rent, and their food.

Children can be quite adept at dealing with negative changes in their lives. In spite of conditions quite the opposite to her rural way of life back on Perdicion, Myra learned to tolerate their new restricted, indoor-only existence. She coped by living internally, always staying in the natural world in her heart and mind. She often lay awake at nights, reminiscing about the life she had in her old home, and in turn, dreaming of a future life on the Blue Planet.

While Myra worked hard to keep her memories and dreams alive inside her, her parents fared more poorly in their new life. Her father turned to drink as his descending avenue of escape. Her mother, so deeply connected with her husband, could not help being pulled down with him. When off work, Myra's mother moved about their rooms at all hours like a ghost, absentmindedly straightening up, cleaning, and cooking.

Watching her parents' slow, heart-rending decline made it too painful for Myra and Darod to remain in their quarters for any length of time. As a result, they both stayed away as much as possible. Darod soon joined one of the many gangs of boys that roamed the dark and dirty corridors of the old mining operation. With his new friends supplanting his unhappy family, Darod seldom returned, and his appearances were barely noted.

Yet, in spite of their present hopeless condition, Myra's parents' previous labors to instill their beliefs and traditions in Myra and Darod throughout their childhood had taken solid root within Myra. With their old religion as a foundation, her dreams of living on the Blue Planet were not just a dream but a belief system. Following this framework, she joined the supplanted Harmonian movement, whose ideals of living harmoniously with nature on the Blue Planet could not be quelled by the enclosure of metal walls. Rather, the movement had gained new strength in its new claustrophobic environment. While its adherents were physically further away from their goal, their cause and determination were never more intense.

The Harmonians had been studying the Blue Planet for as many years as they had existed, from both Perdicion and the Red Colonies. They had done so by tapping into the Supremacy monitoring satellites in place all over the globe. They spent their time memorizing every bit of territory and studying the habits and customs of the natives. Even in the Red Colonies, Myra became well-versed in surviving in the natural environment of the Blue Planet. While she had no practical experience, from her studies she knew as much as the people living there did about how to survive in their environment, from finding food in the forest to keeping warm and dry.

ABOARD THE SUPREMACY ATTACK SHIP SHADOW *ABOUT TO ENTER THE BLUE PLANET'S ATMOSPHERE*

Just prior to *Shadow*'s descent into the atmosphere, the attack and support ship met up and linked briefly to permit the transfer of personnel and equipment. As such, Ham was moved to *Guru* to be placed under Dr. Nevek's care. While this transfer took place, *Guru*'s automated systems replenished the complement of spears within *Shadow*'s wings. During the transfers, Solus transmitted his log to fleet headquarters on Perdicion.

As *Shadow* sped towards the Blue Planet's atmosphere, Solus gave orders for his squadron to reposition more broadly around the planet to make up for the loss of Grand's ship. *Guru* would have to cover temporarily for *Shadow* in her zone while she was within the planet's atmosphere. The support ship had limited offensive weaponry, but was still more than a match for any non-military craft that might approach the planet.

Shadow then entered the atmosphere and converted into atmospheric mode, sweeping her wings forward to create lift and a stable airfoil to fly in the air of the planet. This design made her just as effective a fighting machine here as she was in space. Her dull black hull flew across the darkening skies towards her destination, the zone where Zealrot had made a soft crash landing. Solus noted that the crash site was on a large northern continent populated by primitive migratory peoples. The Supremacy had named this land New Ouda Regio after the Supremacy's own home continent on Perdicion.

As they closed in on the landing zone, Solus ordered a "hover hop" to deploy the landing party as quickly as possible. This meant that the ship would float within inches of the ground, drop the landing party, and immediately take back off again and regain space. The squadron was dangerously over-extended as it was, and *Shadow* could do little to assist while sitting on the ground waiting for the landing party to return.

Solus made a command decision to lead the ground mission personally, and ordered Grand to take command of *Shadow* while he was on the surface. Solus also decided to keep the party small by taking only Bas and—controversially, if it were discovered by Fleet Command—Myra. Bas was an easy choice; he was one of the fiercest hand-to-hand fighters that Solus had ever known. And from the intelligence he had gained from Myra, he knew Bas would be needed in taking on Zealrot and his huge bodyguard.

As to Myra, Solus had outwardly accepted her arguments for taking her with him. For one, Myra argued that she knew Zealrot well and could thus help Solus find him more quickly. Perhaps more important, she gave him ample proof of her knowledge of the planet and the natives living there. She would be extremely helpful if they ran across natives in their pursuit. But ultimately, Solus knew that she wanted more than life itself to be on the ground of the planet, and he secretly wanted to give her this gift, even if it was only for a short time.

Even more problematic than taking Myra with him, Solus had delayed administering the Prolix to her. If he injected her with the upgrade, he reasoned, the software would begin to assert control over her mind and body, make her unable to function, and would likely reduce her to a sobbing heap. Because this would not help the tactical situation at all, Solus felt justified in delaying its administration. But this was also a dodge. The truth was that he could not bring himself to do it. He did not want her to hate him for it.

So, there they were. Solus, Myra, and Bas sat together in the circular deployment compartment at the bottom of the ship as *Shadow* made her descent. (Down the compartment's middle was the tube used to extend the compartment below the ship's belly and connect to other ships.) Solus and Bas had donned full combat gear, designed with variable camouflage to match the forest environment below. Myra wore the same protective camouflage and gear, minus its weaponry.

As the ship reached a lower altitude, Grand deployed their

compartment, extending it down outside the hull, which exposed the compartment's windows and hatch. The trio watched as the windows revealed the world passing below. Solus felt a lump in his throat at the sight. The gigantic green forest beneath them extended out in all directions. Numerous blue lakes shimmered and rippled as they raced by. It was the beginning of spring here, and the entire world below was blossoming and renewing itself.

"Commander, we're getting close to the landing site," Grand reported via Prolix link. "I've detected a clearing up ahead that's a relatively short distance away from it."

"Understood," Solus replied. "Come in low over the treetops, so we're not seen."

"Executing," Grand replied. He had already switched the engines to silent mode to muffle the roar of the ship's maneuvering thrusters. Surely the fugitives would be expecting their visit, but it would not be wise to announce their arrival.

The ship's thrusters slowed them down rapidly as the landing site came into view. Grand then floated the ship down into position close to the ground, close enough that barely a small step was needed to climb out of the deployment compartment. In an instant, the landing party was out and running for cover under the trees, and the ship was already climbing up and away with only the sounds of a brisk wind blowing through the area.

Bas immediately swept the area with his rifle-mounted scanner to ascertain the tactical situation. As he did so, Solus gave some last-minute commands to Grand. "Keep on the alert for fleet transmissions," he said through his Prolix communication link. "I want to confirm that they have received my last report."

Grand acknowledged.

"And keep me informed if any other ships are detected. If you lose contact with me for more than a few moments, assume command of the squadron."

"Yes, sir," Grand responded. "I've got the situation well in hand. You take care of yourself down there, and get that jackass for me. I've got a score to settle with him."

"You got it. Out."

"Sir, I'm not detecting any hostiles," Bas reported. "The crash site is that way," he continued, pointing into the forest in a direction to the northwest.

"Is there a path near us that we can use to get through to it?" Solus queried.

"Yes, it's right over here this way," Myra said as she made her way directly towards a gap in the trees and brush. Solus looked at Bas, who, after checking his scanner, nodded in confirmation. The men smiled at each other, noting her assertiveness, and followed her. After months of walking on a ship's metal deck, the ground felt wonderfully soft and uneven under their feet. As they made their way into the forest on the single-file path, Myra explained that it had been shaped by the migrations of deer and was used by the local people to get through the woods.

For the first time since they arrived, Solus began to sense things around him. The scented breezes carried in smells of spring blossoms and the sounds of animals echoing in the forest. It was now getting dark under the trees, but their night-vision equipment was not quite necessary yet. It was all very wonderful to him, and he could see that Myra was in heaven.

"There's a large animal crossing the path far up ahead," Bass said, looking at his scanner. This halted the party. Myra turned and looked at Bas' scanner screen, showing an image of the animal.

"That's a black bear," she said. "They're only dangerous if confronted or surprised. We'd better wait a minute or two to give it a chance to move on."

This was exciting, Solus thought. This truly was the

wilderness, complete with large and dangerous animals. Most of these animals had long since vanished from vast parts of his own world. "Very well," Solus answered. "We don't want to make a lot of noise fighting off an animal."

"And you might kill or hurt it in the process," Myra added.

"Yes, that too," Solus replied, not having considered that before.

As they waited, Myra looked closely at Bas for what seemed the first time. "You're from South Ishtaria, aren't you?"

"Yes, my family is from there, but they live on Ouda now," Bas replied. "My family have always been farmers and soldiers," he added, smiling.

"My family were farmers too."

"Were?" Bas asked. "What do they do now?"

"They live in the Red Colonies now."

"Oh, yes, of course," Bas said. "I'm sorry."

"It's not your fault," Myra said with conviction.

Solus broke in. "I think we've given that bear ample time to get out of our way." They began moving down the path again deeper into the woods. The light continued to fade. He wanted to view this world as much as possible through his own eyes, and only after it had gotten very dark did he order the group to pull down their night-vision shields.

Their vision equipment augmented their eyes to see further and into the X-ray spectrum. He looked up a passing tree and saw three little mammals with striped tails coming out of a hole in the tree. They looked down questioningly at the passing strangers.

Myra noted them too. "Nocturnal animals are starting to awaken," she explained. They began to hear hoots and screeches echoing in the night air. "Those are night birds calling back and forth. They're hunting for rabbits and mice." Myra was the perfect guide—she seemed to know everything about the trees, the plants, and the animals.

"Commander, we're getting close," Bas reported.

"Okay, let's halt."

Following Solus' lead, they crouched down into the brush beside the path.

Solus then consulted with Xoxon. "Tie in to the scanner's readings, please. What's your assessment?"

"The capsule is resting on the ground near a small clearing," Xoxon reported. "The landing parachute is not visible, and there's no apparent landing damage to the vehicle; therefore, it must have been retrieved. I can detect footprints of four individuals around the capsule that go about in various places, but ultimately lead away from the capsule in a direction heading west."

"Can you detect any human readings?"

"Not within the range of the scanner."

"Do you have any idea where they might be going?" Solus asked Myra.

"I believe . . ." She paused. "I think they are looking for a native encampment. The people here are both farmers and migratory. There is a small village near a lake about a 30 minute hike from here in that direction."

Solus noticed her hesitation. "You seem troubled. Are you concerned about something?"

Myra eyed Solus' sidearm intently, one of many weapons on his combat gear. "Yes, of course—I'm concerned about the fight that will start when we catch up to Zealrot. I am very worried about my Harmonian sisters. And if a firefight starts near a native village, many could get killed. I do not want anyone killed."

"Listen," he said firmly. "I am here to stop Zealrot from

harming these people. I will do what I can to avoid a confrontation, especially when there're people about."

"So, you do regard them as people?" she asked, surprised.

"Well, yes," he answered. It had not occurred to him to think of them in any other way.

"Not many from the Supremacy would agree with you, you know," she said. "In fact, many think of Ishtarians as being less than human. Bas here would be considered by most to be a non-person, correct?"

"The Supremacy has always been good to me and my family," Bas responded.

"Bas, go and make a further tactical assessment of the capsule," Solus ordered. "Do not get too close, because it might be booby-trapped."

"Yes, sir," Bas said, and got up at once and moved off into the darkness.

"Listen," Solus said to Myra, "I know that you are used to speaking your mind, but you cannot criticize the Supremacy in any way around Bas."

"You don't want him to hear it?" she replied.

"You are not doing him any good at all. Understand that his Prolix records everything he does and says—everything about him and around him. You will only make him anxious and uncomfortable talking in that way, or worse, he could get into trouble with the authorities."

"Oh, I did not think of that."

"I thought as much."

"You really do care for him, don't you?"

"He's one of my men," Solus said stiffly.

An explosion interrupted them, which rocked the ground and knocked Myra and Solus together and over onto their backs. Immediately regaining his feet, Solus reached out for

Myra and helped her up. He looked her over carefully to ensure she was uninjured.

"I'm fine," she said.

Armed with this knowledge, he grabbed Myra's arm and they ran in the direction of the explosion. As they drew nearer, they found Bas sitting in the midst of a bed of ferns, rubbing his un-helmeted head. The burning remains of the capsule lay smoldering in the distance. "Are you hurt?" Solus asked as he and Myra both helped Bas to his feet.

"I'm fine, but I did a stupid thing," Bas replied. "The hatch was left wide open, and I just had to see what would happen, so I picked up a rock and threw it—"

"—and boom!" Myra finished for him. Her giggles were soon joined by the other two.

"The enemy has most certainly been alerted to your presence," Xoxon pointed out inside Solus' head. "They'll be on the alert."

Zealrot did, in fact, hear a rumble in the distance, which he knew could not be thunder. He smiled to himself trying to imagine the scene when the Supremacy forces found the surprise that he had left for them in the capsule. Hopefully there would be limbs and various body parts lying all over the place. The scavengers would have a nice feast.

He lay back down on his rather comfortable cot, which was set inside a Supremacy-issued camouflage tent. "No need to concern yourselves, ladies," he called over to Zeeni and Mondra, who were lying bound together on the floor. This was necessary because these two ladies weren't quite as dependent on him for survival as he would have liked. "Just some Supremacy people getting blown to bits," he added jovially.

Waltron was outside, keeping watch with his laser assault

rifle. At the first sign of trouble, they could be off in moments—one push of a button, and the tent could be immediately folded back up into its carrying case. Yet, while it was up, it had scan-dampening capabilities that helped to blend it in with the background of the forest. Quite handy, thought Zealrot, and another little magic trick with which to scare the natives.

He supposed he would have to relieve Waltron at some point. It was irritating, but the man would need to get some rest or he would soon become completely useless. He was probably needed to fight off anyone left over from the explosion, and possibly to kill a few natives as a demonstration of Zealrot's power and mercilessness. It was sad, thought Zealrot, but Waltron would actually be grateful to Zealrot for letting him get some rest. The idiot . . .

Solus, Myra, and Bas continued into the blackness of night that had enveloped them. Using night vision, Bas had found the path that Zealrot's group had taken. The footprints indicated two men's prints, one quite large in stature and another smaller man. Between them, the footprints of the women showed that they walked uncertainly and stumbled often, suggesting they were tied together.

Bas led the way with his powerful rifle and scanner, poised to instantly attack anything that posed a threat. Solus took up the rear just behind Myra. Tying directly into Bas' rifle scanner, Solus put Xoxon on the job of analyzing and detecting possible booby traps that might have been left along the way. They marched on as the night creatures hunted and cried around them. Night birds called in the distance. Wails of captured prey sometimes screeched in the darkness.

A Prolix transmission from space interrupted. "Commander, this is Grand. Do you copy?"

"Yes, Grand, I read you," Solus replied. "What's happening up there?"

"It's all quiet here," Grand reported, "but there's a transmission from the fleet."

"Stand by, Grand. I'll get back to you presently."

"Acknowledged."

"Let's halt for a moment," he ordered. "Bas, keep on the alert. I'm stepping off over there for a moment," he added, indicating a little open area off the path. A small lizard scuttled away in the undergrowth as he made his way into the thick brush at his feet.

While Solus was off listening to the transmission, Myra decided to make amends with Bas. "Bas, please forgive me for speaking out of turn about you earlier."

"There's nothing to forgive," Bas replied hastily.

"Well, I just wanted you to know that I'm sorry, and that I won't do it again."

Bas smiled and nodded in reply.

"How did you end up in the Supremacy military?" Myra asked, but then interjected, "Oh, am I distracting you from the scanner?"

"No, not at all," Bas replied. "My Prolix is tied into the scanner. My family was a farming family, but there have always been sons to spare for home defense. We fought in the Ishtarian army, prior to its defeat in the World Wars. My family switched sides after that time, and moved to Oudo. My great-great-grandfather liked the idea of a one-world government. He was tired of all the wars. The Supremacy was the answer to that."

"So, you got the upgrade Prolix, whether you wanted it or not."

"Yes, I was born with it."

"That must be hard," Myra commented.

"I'm in the military," Bass explained. "We enlisted do what

we're told to do. If an officer says to attack, we attack. If he tells us to stop and go to sleep, we stop and sleep. That's what we're supposed to do. Well, the Prolix just makes that more efficient. When it's time to pitch camp and go to sleep, my Prolix will put me right to sleep, no problems. If I'm about to go into combat, the Prolix helps me manage my fear . . . things like that."

"But don't you mind not being in control of your life?"

"No one's ever in complete control of their lives," Bas said. "There're always outside things that affect what we do."

"But, Bas," said Myra, already forgetting that she was treading on unsafe ground, "you're relying on someone else to make some pretty big choices for you!"

"That's why we have a government. I have faith in my officers," he replied, "and the Supremacy," he quickly added.

"Of course," she said quickly, realizing her mistake, and then to change the subject, continued. "How long have you been with Commander Solus?"

"The Commander and I have been together many, many years. He's always managed to keep me with him. I'd trust him over anyone."

To Bas, Myra could clearly see, Commander Solus was more important than the Supremacy. "He seems to be a good leader."

"I'd give my life for him," said Bas. "And you know why? I know he'd do the same thing for me. He's not like other officers."

"I can see that," Myra replied, then abruptly changed the subject again. "Are you married?"

"I am married. My wife is back on Perdicion with our three kids. Would you like to see a picture of them?"

"Why, yes!"

At that, Bas pulled out a tiny, vintage image projector from one of his pockets, and held it out before Myra. In the image projected, a dark, lovely woman surrounded by three young boys with black, closely cropped hair sat waving and smiling at her. "What a lovely family!" Myra said.

"They gave me this just before I left. And the images are only about a month old. I uploaded their latest picture-sitting into it."

"They're precious. I'll bet they miss their father."

"Yes, but they understand. I'm out here keeping the worlds safe."

"Indeed," Myra replied politely. She knew that Bas honestly believed that to be true. He was faithful. If and when the Supremacy forces finally defeated the Ishtarians, there would be peace. They would all be living under a cold, calculating, and ultimate dictatorship, but they would all be mindlessly safe. But that was okay by Bas, Myra realized. His parents, by accepting the Prolix, had made the choice for him, and now he left many moral decisions to someone else.

It was a very good thing that he had Solus as his commander, Myra decided.

Meanwhile, Solus waited for the long-distance transmission to begin. It was from his old commander, Admiral Revue, an immutable space veteran who had been involved in the struggle with the Ishtarians longer than anyone else living. He, like many in his rank, had relied most of his life on his own cunning, and had survived to a ripe old age using it. He was of a breed whose self-confidence had long ago surpassed any possibility of doubt. He had served all his life in the most powerful and unbeatable military the worlds had ever known, where victory was always assured. In this service, a commanding officer was judged by a higher standard than mere victory. In order to maintain his status, Revue had recognized long ago that a successful leader surrounded himself with extremely able seconds. When he recognized quality in a man, he built up that relationship with his own loyalty and personal latitude. He had such a relationship with Solus.

For his part, Solus was firmly loyal to his old commander and always appreciated the admiral as a commander who would fight for his men. While he didn't always agree with Revue's decisions and policies, Solus always followed his orders without pause and found life in the service much easier under the admiral's wing.

The transmission began before Solus' eyes. The gray-haired old man in his red admiral's uniform appeared. His hooded eyes, which conveyed the colossal responsibilities loaded upon him, fixed upon his talented subordinate. "Commander," greeted Admiral Revue. "I hope your mission is going well. I received your last transmission. Sorry to hear we lost a ship."

"Yes, sir," Solus responded.

"I'm sure you'll make do," the Admiral continued. "As it is, the fleet is nearing our target destination, and will very shortly be engaging with the Ishtarian defenses. We're offering them the chance to negotiate, but so far our messages have been ignored. According to our revised intelligence estimates, we outnumber their ships by a five-to-one margin."

"That's good to hear, sir," Solus said. "I'm currently tracking an extremist named Zealrot. I'm sorry to report that he got past us. We destroyed his ship from long range, but he managed to separate his command module just prior to impact and landed it on the planet."

"Yes, I saw all that in your last report," Revue said, "and I don't like that you are personally leading the landing party. Had I known, I would not have permitted that—Bas or one of your other upgrades could have easily carried out this mission."

"I realize that, sir, but—"

"The *Singularity*'s battle group will be making the first assault," Revue interrupted, "therefore, I don't have a lot of time, and I have to give you some final instructions. I've contacted you to put you on the alert. We have word that at least three Ishtarian ships left the Red Zone some time ago and could be arriving in your zone at any time. These ships include two combat vessels and a large transport—they are in addition to the three you intercepted. Their exact heading is unknown, but we believe that they are headed for the Blue Planet. Perdicion Defense Command has also been alerted."

"Understood, sir. We'll be on the lookout for them."

"Oh, one other thing," Revue said, remembering an item in Solus' report that perplexed him. "I understand that you have a female prisoner. Why have you not administered the Prolix to her? We need all the intelligence that we can get out of these people."

"Well, sir," Solus began, "she has proven valuable in assisting us in tracking down this Zealrot. She would have been otherwise—"

"You've got technology that can handle all of that," Revue said dismissively. "I want you to give her the Prolix as soon as possible. I'm not altogether convinced that she has told you everything she knows."

"Sir—"

"Solus, you have your orders." And with that, the transmission ended.

Temporarily blinded by the light-filled transmission, Solus stared out into the night unseeingly. This was an order that he should have taken matter-of-factly. He'd administered the technology himself to prisoners on countless occasions. The

Prolix was a choice for all except those who lost that choice through criminality or making war against the Supremacy. Yet Myra, arguably, did not fit either of those categories. She was an Ishtarian, but she wasn't part of the rebel movement. It was, simply, unjust.

"Solus, I warned you about controlling your feelings," Xoxon spoke up.

"Yes, Xoxon, you were quite right, of course," Solus said, shaking his head sadly. "Now, I don't know what to do. I can't bear the idea of causing her pain."

"Solus, you're not in love—you just met her. You must look past that and do your duty!"

Solus only heard one word. "Love," he repeated.

"Solus, think from a practical standpoint. It's impossible. The only chance she has is through the Prolix."

"What do you mean?"

"If she is given the Prolix, she won't be a threat to the Supremacy—"

"She's not a threat!" Solus blurted out indignantly.

"—and she might even escape punishment because of it. You could easily make the case that she was Zealrot's prisoner, and therefore not guilty of violating the Blue Planet's quarantine. She would be free of those charges."

"What you're saying is all true," Solus said. "But she'd hate me for it. She'd never understand."

"Ah, but she would not die, and she would be safe. She would learn to accept the Prolix, as you have."

"But she'd no longer be free," Solus replied, quite astonished at his own realization of this.

"What do you mean?" Xoxon queried.

"She must accept it freely," he responded simply. Solus ended his mental struggles for the moment, and started back towards

Bas and Myra. He would try to reason with her first. He would help her to accept it. But for now, the only thing he could do was to delay the inevitable. Revue had said "as soon as possible." Well, it was not possible to administer the Prolix here in the middle of the woods, and returning to the ship at this juncture would be a setback.

When Solus drew near Bas and Myra, Bas spoke up immediately. "Sir, I've discovered something interesting."

"Something about the Ishtarians?"

"No, sir," Bas replied, eager to reveal his discovery. "I'm detecting a Prolix node on this planet."

"Here, on the surface?" Solus asked incredulously. "You're sure it's not *Guru*? Perhaps it's a reflection of her in the readings?" The nearest ship-borne node was housed in the squadron's support ship.

"No, sir," Bas said. "Look at this location. It's two hundred kilometers south of here. And it's a big one. It's a planetary-scale server. It's powered up but not broadcasting."

Solus looked at Bas' findings. "You're right, it's definitely not *Guru*. It's huge, on the level of the planetary systems on Perdicion."

"What does that mean?" Myra said nervously. "What's it doing there?"

Solus looked at her. "Even if I knew, I could not talk about it," he responded. Solus then recalled that a number of Supremacy ships had landed on the planet a few months ago on a classified mission. This must have been their work—a few preliminaries to colonization, no doubt.

Myra seemed to read his thoughts. "Oh my Lord, they're going to implement the Prolix technology here!"

Solus could only stare back at her in silence as tears began to flood her eyes.

"I'm sorry . . ." he whispered to himself. His sadness at seeing her cry was then flooded with a memory back to the days of the rebellion . . .

It was ten years ago as the Blue Planet traveled. He had been fortunate—he had been out on patrol in an attack ship when the fighting began. Back then, he had no qualms about following his orders regarding the Prolix. Their forces were badly outnumbered. They were to act as marauders: capturing vessels, causing havoc in the sector, administering the Prolix to all prisoners. The enemy deserved whatever they got.

It was six months into the battle that followed the Red Colonies rebellion, and just before the withdrawal order came through. The oxygen escaping from the ruptured enemy cruiser fueled little sparks of fire that were erupting all over the stricken ship's fuselage. The Supremacy attack team aboard the assault capsule braced for their impending impact with the cruiser. The capsule struck and then attached itself to the hull of the cruiser with a metallic clang.

Speed was the best weapon. The capsule's nose was designed to attach and then blow a hole into the place it was attached to. They blew the hatch immediately and stormed the ship. The commandos followed the smoke and debris through the opening. They held blast shields in front of them, looking much like the iron shields used by the ancients to repel swords and spears. These modern variants were made of a blast-absorbing material. The shields were not only defensive weapons—they surrounded handheld pulse cannons that fired continuously into the interior of the breached ship. The first wave pushed forward into the vessel in all directions. The dead and surrendering men lay mingled all about the decks of the ship; the only difference was that those not dead held their hands behind their heads. "Get the fire control system back online!" Solus commanded to his men via the Prolix network. "And get these prisoners rounded up."

Another ship was back in Supremacy hands, thanks to his unit's good offices. But it might still need to be scuttled if they couldn't get the fires under control. Smoke was filling the interior faster than the circulation systems could filter it out. He could hear the sounds of explosions in the lower decks, probably near the engines. That was not a good sign. But he still had intelligence work to do. "Line up those prisoners on their knees," he ordered. His upgrades had been efficient. The captured enemy combatants were already collected and lined up on their knees in the central deck of the vessel, which was the largest area onboard the ship.

"Sir, the mop-up crew is seeing a lot of heavy damage below the decks, and the fires are out of control in the cargo bay."

"Understood. Keep searching for survivors," he ordered. One too many plasma bursts had been fired at this old girl. She was dying. "Techie!" he called out to his technical officer in charge of getting control of the ship's systems. "How's that fire control system coming along? We're getting close to abandoning her." He looked over the row of prisoners, their arms in restraints behind their backs. "Subcommander, administer the Prolix," he ordered.

There was the usual collective groaning. The apparent horror in their response always mystified him. It was not as if he were ordering their execution—in fact, their policy was very humane. Once the Prolix was administered, they would no longer be threats to the Supremacy nor to themselves. The subcommander stepped up to each man and, using a special syringe, injected the technology into each of their bodies. It would take some time for it to go into effect, but the sooner they were injected, the better. One man screamed in agonythe mental kind, for the injection was relatively painless. In his desperation, the man lunged forward to grab at a guard's rifle and was struck down violently to the floor. Another man fainted and lay flat on his back.

"I want to know how you captured this vessel," Solus said to the group, now mostly sobbing and lying on their sides in utter misery. He was under orders to determine how the Ishtarians had successfully taken control of so many ships in the Red Planet sector during the rebellion.

"You have killed us!" one man cried out.

"We can never rejoin our people!" another moaned. "You have polluted our bodies with your filth!"

"It's not that bad," he responded casually, for this had become somewhat routine. "Now, where were we. . . ?"

An explosion from the lower decks shook the ship.

"Sir, we're losing her," another of his upgrade subcommanders reported from the bridge. "That explosion came from the engine room. The fire in the cargo bay has spread to adjoining corridors. It's hopeless."

"Very well, abandon ship!" he ordered. An explosion rocked the vessel again—this time sending him to the deck.

Solus returned to the present, burning with shame as he watched Myra sob.

ONBOARD THE BATTLESHIP SINGULARITY *IN THE RED SECTOR*

In the Red Sector, on the bridge of *Singularity*, Admiral Revue needed to concentrate on the upcoming action. With his Prolix prattling on in his head with the next item in a seemingly endless list, Revue pondered his recent conversation with Solus. Revue realized now that Solus had begun to identify too much with his upgrade personnel. Apparently he'd been too permissive in allowing Solus to keep his favored upgrades with him for so long. He would have to separate this Bas from him. Solus was too capable an officer for Revue to let something like this interfere with his decision-making.

Revue's Prolix spoke up more loudly to get his attention back on the attack. His battle group was moving into position to surround the Red Planet. Accordingly, the admiral spread out his ships in a large zone. He wanted minimal mopping-up actions and no opportunity for any Ishtarian ships to escape. Apart from this, his chief concerns really had nothing to do with the upcoming action. He worried more about the situation on the Blue Planet because Solus was terribly undermanned, and as such, his small squadron was vulnerable. But even more so, Revue was concerned for the safety of Perdicion herself. With three battleships (even as immense as they were) and only one attack and support ship left behind for home defense, Revue felt that Fleet Command had left Perdicion dangerously unprotected.

Yet, it needed to be this way, Revue reminded himself. This battle was to be the final, decisive one that would end this strife. Altogether there were well over 120 Supremacy ships converging on the Red Planet. He could well imagine the panic they were feeling right now in the colonies. And there was little they could do. They could no more stop a supernova than what was about to befall them.

And they had brought this upon themselves, he believed. Always the malcontents, the Ishtarians had been the cause of all their own suffering over the years. The colonies' revolt, for example, had stopped all efforts for a planetary re-development. The Supremacy had been working hard to introduce more water and a habitable atmosphere to the Red Planet. It was still years away, but progress had been underway. But all that stopped when the Ishtarians took over, and they were forced to live in squalor.

Apart from their stupidity, they deserved punishment for their actions after the revolt. They took no prisoners during the fighting and were merciless after their win. The rebel government conducted a veritable pogrom in which anyone found with a Prolix was subject to execution. Given the environment, executions were fast and easy to carry out. Onboard a ship, prisoners were often tossed into space, while on the planet, those prisoners not shot were thrown out into the outside environment.

And now he, Admiral Revue, had come to carry out their punishment, led by his fearsome battleship. Unlike Solus' attack ship, *Singularity* was designed for space operations exclusively. Her enormous wings were not designed to fly but to serve as weapon platforms that bristled with pulse cannons and missile launchers. Revue thought with pride about the part he was to play in this final battle.

Just as his anticipation for the battle reached its peak, his scanning officer called out, "Sir, we're picking up enemy cruisers leaving orbit. Looks like they're sending all they've got at us—three small battle groups have been dispatched towards our forward groups. They're not responding to our signals."

With all its weaponry, *Singularity* was not invulnerable. The same weapons technology used by the massive ship could certainly be used against it. That fact called for a considerable support group that could repel missiles and weapon bursts.

From the bridge's wide viewport, Revue got his first close-up look at the Red Planet in many years. From this distance, it looked like a ruddy play-yard ball, suspended in the night sky. The disk of the sun was to their rear, and its rays lit the entire side of the planet. He could just make out one of the two dark moons that orbited nearby. It was an ugly satellite, a dark and lopsided chunk of rock, and probably a captured asteroid from the field beyond the planet. His ship could make quite a mess of it, Revue considered, but that would be a terrible waste of good ordnance.

"Identify the ships coming to meet us," he commanded.

"We count three ships in each group. One large cruiser and two smaller attack vessels in each. They're all former fleet vessels captured in the revolt. The cruisers are identified as the *Fulcrum*, *Urgency*, and *Detonator*. The *Fulcrum* is advancing on us."

"Dispatch four stealth attack squadrons. I want them flanked on all sides." That left sixteen squadrons in support of *Singularity*, which would be conducting the planetary assault. He was leaving nothing to chance. Even their rear was covered by two squadrons.

"Transmitting your order, sir."

Revue looked up at a display panel to his right and observed the enemy ships' technical readouts. They were old fifth-generation models that hadn't received any refits in at least ten years. They were potentially dangerous, but outnumbered and outgunned. The admiral got out of his command chair and strode over to the bridge's main window port, passing the various manned stations, where helmsman, navigators, weapons officers, and others sat concentrating on their particular tasks.

From where the bridge was positioned, he could see his ship's lengthy bow stretching out before him. He could see *Singularity*'s primary weapons extending out in a turret above it—two gigantic planetary assault cannons that could take out an entire space station with one hit. What's more, they could breach the atmosphere of a planet to hit targets on the surface. *Singularity* had been designed and built during the old wars on Perdicion, when space weapons platforms were needed not for planetary defense, but as a deterrent to all-out war. More than a theoretical deterrent, this ship was capable of ending a war by destroying the world. Of course, it had never yet been used for this purpose, even in a limited fashion.

The badly-outnumbered Ishtarian ships continued to advance on the admiral's battle group. He could not imagine what they were trying to accomplish, other than not going down without a fight. One final gallant last stand, no doubt. But it was only delaying the inevitable. He watched as two approaching Ishtarian attack ships pushed forward from their formation to advance first upon the oncoming Supremacy fleet.

"Lieutenant," Revue said to his countermeasures officer, Havel, "have you gained control of the ships' technology?" Revue was referring to a technical feature that was standard on ships even ten years ago—Prolix-linked control. The Ishtarians would not have access to it, since they did not use the Prolix, and might never have modified their systems to remove the technology. If the fleet were successful in accessing the enemy ships' Prolix features, they could literally take over and fly the enemy ships by remote control, disabling weapons systems and boarding with little resistance.

"I'm attempting to access now, sir," Lieutenant Havel replied.

The fleet's other forward battle groups were simultaneously attempting this little technological feat against the other two Ishtarian battle groups.

"I'm in, sir. I'm connected with the *Fulcrum*'s Prolix-linking technology." As he spoke, a black square in his control panel began to display the enemy ship's control features. From the controls displayed, Havel had access to their propulsion and weapons systems.

"Excellent," Revue beamed. "And they're not aware that we've accessed?"

"No, sir. They won't know a thing until we start to give remote commands."

"Good. Watch them closely, and wait for signals from the other two battle groups." Revue wanted a coordinated countermeasure plan. Until he got the signal that all enemy cruisers had been compromised, they would wait to attack.

"Yes, sir."

"How about those attack ships? Can we access them as well?"

"I've got my staff working on each of them too, sir," Havel said, referring to his countermeasures team, housed in a control room several decks below them. "For some reason, we're having problems interfacing with them. They might have made some modifications to their internal systems . . . we're not sure."

"Keep working on it," Revue replied, "but I think our attack ships can handle them individually." Revue's strategy did not depend on this little trick, but it would certainly make things easier. He would let the ships advance on them—his ships were already in range for an enemy missile attack—but nothing that his support group could not repel from a single enemy cruiser.

"Sir, the enemy attack ships are opening fire."

Revue could see the bursts starting to fly out in space towards them. "Understood. Lay out a suppression barrage in front of those bursts." Almost instantaneously, space was lit up with fire from his forward battle group. The attack ships on top of the enemy circle were veering up at full speed and coming in towards the top of the battle group; the lower ships were doing the same below.

"Upper and lower squadrons—engage those attack ships." Subordinates relayed more specific orders in compliance. Revue was starting to worry about that cruiser. It was still coming towards them. Just then, this enemy began its barrage with long-range bursts. "Anti-burst fire to maximum—protect us from that incoming ordnance," he ordered. "Power up the primary weapon and target that cruiser."

The attack ships were engaging above and below the battleship. Revue saw the first explosion through the bridge viewscreen over to his left. An enemy ship had received an energy burst right through its nose.

"Burst coming in!" a defensive weapons officer reported. An enemy attack ship had fired as it passed.

"Take care of it, please." An anti-burst beam shot out and exploded it right off the port bow. A slight shudder went through the ship.

"Have you taken control of that cruiser?" Revue barked impatiently. He was going to have to act soon. The cruiser was getting too close for comfort.

"Two more enemies destroyed," the scanning officer reported. "The others are flying evasively through our upper and lower squadrons."

"Don't let them get through."

"Yes, sir."

Lieutenant Havel entered commands into the linked command board. "Sir, I've powered down their weapons array and engines, and encrypted their command functions. They're helpless."

"Excellent. Reverse their thrusters—slow them down. I want boarding squads on that ship as soon as possible."

The old enemy vessel was far away, but it was still too close. It needed to be completely secured. He watched as the cruiser slowed down in the distance. Two assault ships shot out over the battleship towards the disabled cruiser. "Reports from the battle groups?"

"Sir, their engagements are proceeding in a similar fashion to our own," a communications officer reported. "All enemy cruisers are disabled. Enemy attack ships are engaging." Just then, a blinding supernova-like flash struck their optic nerves from the window ports to the left.

"What's happening?" Revue shouted after regaining his senses, still shielding his eyes.

"Sir, one of the enemy cruisers, the *Detonator*, exploded!" the communications officer yelled. "The fifth battle group was engaging—our cruiser is disabled! Several more ships are destroyed . . . it was a nuclear explosion . . . three thousand mega-loads!"

Revue looked out in alarm at his captured cruiser. "Veer those assault ships off! Immediately!" Another flash blinded the bridge crew momentarily—this time from the right. The ship shuddered massively—it was the shock wave from the first explosion.

"Another explosion—the *Urgency* just blew up, Admiral."

"Reverse thrusters. Turn starboard. Lead the group away from that remaining cruiser!" Revue ordered, "and close those blast shields." Flashes and shock waves began to buffet them, seemingly from all sides. "Re-target that ship and fire!" Revue ordered. "I want that ship taken out immediately." As the huge battleship lurched to starboard, it bore its assault cannons on the target.

"Target locked, sir—firing."

Singularity finally made its full presence felt in all the horror about them. Two enormous green energy beams shot out towards the cruiser at the speed of light. The beams struck the cruiser on its broadside. Upon impact, the cruiser's midsection crushed inward. Chunks of the ship simultaneously blew out the other side. Then the stricken craft exploded in a nuclear detonation.

BACK ON THE BLUE PLANET'S SURFACE

"Bas," Solus said, "move out ahead and continue to track the Ishtarians. We'll be along momentarily." Myra was still stricken and crying at the news of the Supremacy's presence here on the Blue Planet.

"Yes, sir," he said, glad to get away from this uncomfortable emotional scene. He crunched off down the path, rifle in front.

"Myra," he said as tenderly as he could, "I know this comes as terrible news for you, but it might not be as bad as you think."

She had stopped actively crying but remained silent, apparently listening to him.

"There's no evidence to suggest that the Prolix will be forced upon the people of this planet. That has never been our government's policy before. It's always been a voluntary thing, unless you have committed a crime or made war against the Supremacy. That node might just be in place for Supremacy personnel."

"Supremacy people living here?" she said, sniffing.

"Well, yes," he responded, "colonization is inevitable. You had to have known that. In fact, I've never understood what's delayed it this long."

"The fact that it had not happened always encouraged us."

"But that's being naïve, Myra," Solus said. "Surely you had to know that this planet would not remain untouched forever."

"It's a matter of faith to us, Commander," Myra said simply. "I can't really explain it any other way."

"Faith? Faith, as in a religious belief?"

"Yes, that kind of faith. We believe that the divine Creator set aside the Blue Planet as a sacred place that will remain untouched by the evils of our society. Those that wish to live on this world must learn to live in harmony with the planet."

"I believe that it's a special world too," Solus remarked. "I think most people in the Supremacy believe this too. When I think about it, that's probably why we've not begun settlements. We want to make certain that it's done right. We don't want more conflicts—clashes between our high-technology culture and their primitive ones. It will end just as badly as the fight between the Supremacy and the Ishtarians. I'm not sure what the answer is, but surely we can do better here."

"Polluting this world with the Prolix is not the answer."

"Myra, the Prolix can bring so many good things to a culture."

"And far more bad things."

"But there are so many things that get better—violent crimes are all but gone, people are living longer, they're healthier, their—"

"Don't you understand what the Prolix has done to our world?" Myra interrupted. "You have given up your freedom for safety and security."

"Is that kind of freedom so very important?"

"Of course it is. Before the Prolix, we had the gift of freedom to choose our own destinies. You did not even get to choose the Prolix; someone else did for you. It may not control you in the way the upgrade version controls its host, but you are not free."

"No one has that kind of freedom you're talking about. No one has that kind of control over his destiny," Solus said. "Myra, you talk as if free will were the most important value we could possibly have."

"Oh, it's not. Love is far more important," she replied, "but freedom is too important a thing to give away to someone else, other than our Creator. To Him, I would gladly give up my free will. But even the Supreme Being does not ask for this, and the Supremacy does," she added.

"Hold onto your hope and faith," he said, looking into her eyes. "If this world is a sacred place that the Creator has set aside, then it will be safe."

Myra looked at him in amazement. "You're right."

"If nothing else, do we agree that Zealrot must be captured?"

"Yes."

"Are you ready to continue, then?"

"Yes," she answered, making a visible effort to comport herself for action.

"Good, then let's catch up with Bas."

With things marginally under control again, Solus and Myra moved on through the forest. They were getting close to a hilly region shaped by a large, old river that snaked its way across the middle of New Ouda Regio. The river marked many native settlements along its banks. This area was likely Zealrot's intended destination.

Solus kept up contact with Bas, who had halted a couple of kilometers in front of them. Bas had just picked up something on his scanner and paused to get a better reading. He concealed himself behind a small thicket of trees. Some vines with clumps of fruit hung down from the trees' branches. After confirming with his Prolix that it was not poisonous, Bas picked a ball-shaped fruit from a clump hanging near his head and popped it into his mouth. The crunchy texture and sweet taste were delicious. He ate a few more, thinking how amazing it was to have such wonderful food just growing all around him. No one had to plant it, prepare it, or package it. It just grew here naturally.

He looked back at his scanner to check on an unusual reading. The scanner indicated an area ahead that did not quite register. This could mean many things, but one strong possibility was that a scan-dampening field was hiding something, possibly an enclosure. "Commander," he spoke softly, making a Prolix link to Solus.

"Yes, Bas. Report," Solus' voice answered inside Bas' head.

"I've got a reading that could be a scan-dampening field," he replied. "It might just be a malfunction, but it's a pretty steady area."

"Remain where you are," Solus replied. "I'm about five minutes from your position."

"Sir," Bas replied, "I could just go in quietly and get a better reading."

"No, I will provide you backup when I get there."

"Yes, sir," said Bas resignedly. Feeling more than a bit impatient, he maintained his position. Not that Bas liked even questioning his commander's decisions, but in hindsight, he felt that it was not a good idea bringing Myra along. She was proving to be more of a hindrance than a help to this mission. He supposed that she could be useful in communicating with a native, if they needed to, but other than that, she would certainly be a liability in a fight.

Looking over at a clearing, he noticed a bright object in the sky. It looked just like the Blue Planet as he had seen it in the Perdicion sky. It was easily the largest star in this sky. "Is that Perdicion?" he quietly asked his Prolix.

"Yes," came the reply in his head.

"Boy, that reminds me of my childhood," he murmured, reminiscing. "I remember looking up in the skies at night with my brothers. You'd tell me the names of the stars and planets, while I dreamed about sailing along in space—chasing after bad guys."

"You still don't know much about astronomy, but you certainly achieved your dream, didn't you?" his Prolix quipped.

"What's the point in knowing all that anyway?" Bas responded defensively. "All I have to do is ask you."

"True," said his Prolix, "but it is important for you to know enough to be able to ask the right questions."

"The right questions?"

"Exactly. It's your job to ponder the questions, and mine to provide the facts."

"I see," said Bas, not really seeing, but not wanting to go on with this. The Prolix asserted so much control when it interacted with Bas that he could not think properly about anything else. It was either on or off—either it sent him to sleep or it kept him awake. Either it focused him on a task or there was no focus at all.

He continued to keep watch with the scanner. After what seemed like an eternity, Solus contacted Bas again. "Bas, I'm in position. Proceed using stealth tactics."

"Yes, sir," he replied softly. Bas began to move in slowly and stealthily, as he had been trained to avoid being spotted in a scan sweep. With his Prolix feeding his body a good dose of adrenaline, Bas scooted himself forward on the ground, his gun in front. The tall ferns were his cover. Along the way, Bas interrupted a large mottled snake in the midst of swallowing a still-twitching brown rodent. He had to fight off a gag reflex at seeing this disgusting spectacle in graphic detail just a meter from his face. He shoved at the snake with his gun to knock it out of the way, and it slid angrily away in protest.

Bas crept through the brush as silently as possible using the sounds of gentle breezes as his cover. As he moved closer, he began to hear the sounds of snoring. When he was close enough to visually review the vicinity of the blank readings, he saw a man asleep in a chair, apparently out in the middle of the clearing. Behind him the scanner showed no reading at all. There had to be a Supremacy-issued camouflage tent right behind him, Bas reasoned. This explained the blank readings he had been seeing on his scanner.

Meanwhile Solus was listening and watching through the Prolix link. "Bas, use your shock gun to take him out silently," Solus communicated softly to Bas via the link. "We don't want to alert the others in the tent." Commander Solus had also deduced that there must be a Supremacy tent behind the sleeping man.

Bas made a hand signal in response. He continued to slide in silently and then just within attacking distance, he placed his rifle on the ground next to him, and pulled out his shock gun and powered it up. Just as he was taking aim, the returning snake buried its fangs in Bas' leg.

An energy bolt from Bas' gun swished past the sleeping man's ear and hit the tent, setting off the wailing of a proximity alarm. The snoring man awoke with a start, looking about wildly. As this was going on, Bas pulled his knife and capably cut off the snake's head. Now seeing Bas, and crying out in fury, the huge man jumped up and ran headfirst at him. Crashing together, with the snake's head still clamped onto Bas' leg, the fighting men rolled into the brush, struggling violently and loudly. Within a few seconds of this, energy bolts began flying out of the invisible tent, lighting the night with green flashes.

"The idiot is firing randomly out the door!" Solus murmured to himself.

For the moment, the enemy's bursts were not hitting anywhere near the struggling men. Solus returned fire—firing bursts over the top of the tent so as to keep the gunman inside. He did not fire into the tent, for fear of hitting one of the hostages.

Bas and his huge opponent, easily one hundred pounds heavier, continued to struggle on the ground. Bas' superior fighting skills evenly matched with the other's greater size and strength. Managing to hold onto his knife, Bas saw an opening and stabbed his opponent, plunging his knife into the man's upper chest near his shoulder but not quite low enough to be immediately fatal. While he bled profusely, the man continued to struggle fiercely, screaming in rage and pain. From a crouching position, he managed to grab Bas and throw him into the air and away from him. As Bas landed and rolled on the ground, the man stood up and pulled the knife out of his shoulder to lunge at Bas. But a bolt from Solus' rifle hit his midsection, and he toppled over backwards into the weeds, dead.

In the midst of the struggle, Zealrot had cut the women from their bunks and pulled them, still tied together, out the back door of the tent and into the night. Once they were clear of the tent, Solus picked up their readings immediately.

"Bas is injured with a snake bite and a broken leg," Xoxon reported.

"Understood," Solus replied grimly. He could see Bas squirming in the brush.

"Bas, lay still, I'll be there momentarily." Noting that the hostages were out of the tent, Solus decided to remove that obstacle altogether. He aimed at the blank reading on his scanner, and fired three shots that effectively knocked it down. The blank reading cleared from his scanner.

"Myra!" Solus called out, "come along. The area is secure. I need to tend to Bas—he's been injured."

Myra came forward from the position of safety that Solus had arranged for her. "Did you get Zealrot? What's happened to Zeeni and Mondra? Are they alive?"

"Yes, they're still alive," Solus replied as they made their way forward through the brush to Bas. "Zealrot has gotten away with them . . . for the moment. He's using them as cover, no doubt."

They came up to Bas, who lay in the grass moaning quietly. "Bas, your leg . . . is it bad?"

"No sir," he said, "just a hairline fracture."

"How about the bite?"

"Venom was injected with the bite," Xoxon answered. "He needs a neutralizer from the medical kit."

"That man was huge! He could have torn you apart!" Myra said in disbelief, looking over at the fallen body.

"Nothing I couldn't handle," Bas grunted.

"We need to get a dressing and splint on that leg, but I've got to go after Zealrot now—I can't let him escape again," Solus said. "Myra, can you help Bas and stay with him?"

"Of course I can," she said simply.

"Good, thank you," Solus said. "They're not far away, even now. Zeeni and Mondra are slowing him down."

With that, Solus was off into the night, hot on the trail of his prey.

IN THE RED SECTOR ON THE BRIDGE OF THE SUPREMACY BATTLESHIP SINGULARITY

Admiral Revue regained his senses. He had been knocked to the floor in the blast, and was unsure whether he was injured. He recognized what a fool he had been; he should have been strapped in his command chair for the action.

"You're injured," his Prolix told him. "You've got a severe concussion and multiple contusions on your legs and right arm."

"What's the ship's status?" he called out, ignoring this.

"We're in one piece," his scanning officer reported. "We've got some casualties, but our systems are intact. Are you okay, sir? Let me help you—"

"Negative, stay at your post!" he retorted, trying to sit up. "What's the fleet's status?"

"We've lost ten attack ships that were flanking the *Fulcrum* . . . they were too close. The assault vessels didn't make it either."

"Understood. How about the Ishtarians?"

"The cruisers all self-destructed. Three attack ships got through us in the confusion, sir," the scanning officer replied. "They sowed mines around them as they ran through our ranks. We lost five ships to this tactic."

Damn, thought Revue: exactly what he wanted to avoid.

"Dispatch Lieutenant Pekark's Epsilon squadron to give chase. I don't want any ships escaping."

"Yes, sir."

They had relied too heavily on all that counter-measure nonsense, Revue realized angrily. They had been too smart for their own good, and it had been their undoing so far. Wiping blood that smeared his forehead, the Admiral got to his feet and dizzily made his way to his command chair. "Patch me through to the battle group commanders," he said to his Prolix.

"Connecting . . ." Three officers appeared before him.

"Gentlemen, we've got a job to do, and we're through fooling about," he said. "I know your ships have sustained damage, but I want your groups to cover your zones and destroy all vessels attempting to leave. Are your offensive weapons online?"

"Yes, one assault cannon is available—we may not be able to move at the moment, but we can do some damage," replied one of the commanders.

"We're about in the same condition, Admiral," said the other. "We've got plenty of stopping power."

"Good," Revue said. "I'm taking *Singularity* in to take out the space station and then the colonies themselves."

"The colonies, sir?" said a commander.

"Yes, the colonies," said Revue darkly. "There can be no negotiations now."

Their defiance could not go unpunished. Revue had had enough. If any of these extremists were left alive, it was clear that there would never be peace. He dismissed his commanders, and they vanished from his sight.

"Send our status to Perdicion Fleet Command. Inform them that I am proceeding with the attack." He would give a full report after he had destroyed the space station.

"Helmsman," Revue commanded, "bring us back on course, full speed towards the planet."

"Escort squadrons," Revue called through his Prolix link, "stay with us."

With none of their own ships in the way, the enemy's defensive missiles started appearing from the planet's surface and the space station. A volley of fifty to sixty appeared, targeting the approaching Supremacy fleet. Anti-missile batteries began thundering from all over the ship. Flashes from escort vessels' weapons fire lit the darkness of space. Explosions began dotting the space between the fleet and the planet. As another volley of missiles followed the first wave, the explosions increased in magnitude and moved nearer and nearer, while more missiles made it closer to their targets.

"Weapons officer—target the space station." Even with the flashes of exploding missiles all around, the station seemed entirely alone in the universe, awaiting its fate. It was an irregularly shaped thing with no aesthetic value whatsoever, built for basic space docking and relaying of equipment. It was a shame to have to destroy every bit of the infrastructure, thought Revue, but it was time to cut their losses. "Is that thing in range of our assault cannons?"

"Extreme range, sir."

"Fire when ready."

"Firing, sir." A power surge briefly dimmed the lights on the bridge as the cannons omitted two green shafts of light. They stretched in a flash out in front of the battleship and hit the target within seconds. Because of the distance, the barrage had little noticeable effect at first, but as it sustained impact, the station began to break apart. After the first snapping of parts, the station broke into two and exploded.

A cheer broke out on the bridge, which the admiral indulged

for a moment. "I want the forward attack squadrons to lay out a suppression barrage in front of us. I want every square meter of space in front of us hit and neutralized."

In stealth mode, the invisible attack ships began omitting orange bursts and exploding them out in front of the fleet. If the missile and anti-missile explosions had not taken out all possible mines in their path, this barrage would certainly find them.

The battle group crept cautiously forward, spreading its indiscernible shadow in space towards the colonies.

ON THE BLUE PLANET'S SURFACE

Zealrot was not at all pleased with his first few hours in his new kingdom. He had lost his bodyguard and much of his equipment, and they were still after him. This little adventure had not gone according to plan at all. The aim was simply to sneak through the blockade and quietly set himself up here while the battles took place above him in the skies. The Supremacy folks should have been completely occupied by the Ishtarian attack by this time, not having the time to deal with him.

He pushed his little group along the narrow animal path, having placed himself between his two hostages. They stumbled along blindly in the dark, while he directed using his night vision visor. The women were bound together and to his belt with a long rope. Progress was slow as a result, but it could not be helped. He was not about to take a shot to the back if he could help it.

Zeeni, who was in the lead, stumbled frequently, and received a cuff to the back from Zealrot's gun each time she fell. Sobbing and aching fiercely, she struggled to her feet and pushed forward, as Zealrot yelled obscenities. Mondra had to keep fighting back an urge to attack him. With her hands tied behind her back, she knew it would be futile and would likely end with one of them being killed.

Zealrot kept pushing and pushing to move on, biding his time. *When will the Ishtarians attack?* he raged inwardly. Just then an energy burst whizzed over their heads and exploded in the trees in front of them. They all dropped instinctively.

"Don't move, or I'll shoot!" an authoritative voice called out in the darkness.

Zealrot's response was defiant. "Don't come any closer, or I will kill these lovely ladies!"

"And when you do, I'll blast you to pieces!" Solus shouted back.

"I mean it—I'll kill—" Zealrot began to scream.

At this, Mondra could take no more. She lunged into the brush beside the path, pulling all the slack out of the line holding her. Zealrot, realizing that he was now exposed, leaped into the path's opposite side as far as he could—the rope now keeping him from getting away. Through his rifle scope, Solus saw the rope stretching across the path and fired, snapping it in two. He fired a second shot and split the line holding Zeeni, who was lying a bit further up the path.

Freed from the rope, Zeeni rolled off the path on the same side as Mondra had gone. With the women now out of the way on the right side of the path, Solus commenced firing rapidly into the left side, where he could see Zealrot through his scanner. Solus watched Zealrot rolling in the brush as Solus' bursts hit the vegetation all around him. Zealrot managed to clamber behind a tree.

Solus was taking aim to blast away at the tree trunk, when Xoxon called out an alert. "Lieutenant Grand is calling for you. There's urgent news from the Red Colonies front!"

"This is not a good time," Solus replied, stopping fire.

"The fleet has taken massive damage!"

"Patch me through to Grand, voice only," Solus said.

"Connecting . . ."

"Commander . . ." Grand said, sounding unusually grave. Solus listened, but watched on the scanner as Zealrot backed away from the tree and into the forest.

"Stand by, Grand."

Without much hope of scoring a hit, Solus fired a few shots into the brush in response. Zealrot returned fire wildly, and began pushing his way through the dense brush as fast as he could away from the fight.

"Damn it all!" Solus blurted out in frustration. He took a breath, and then said, "Report, Grand."

"Sir, the fleet's taken massive damage. Several ships have been destroyed. The Ishtarians tricked them by self-destructing their big ships in close proximity. Revue's injured."

Solus could not believe his ears. "Injured? Are they still in fighting condition?"

"Yes, they've taken out the space station and are heading towards the colonies. Three Ishtarian attack ships escaped through their lines. Our ships are giving chase. We've been placed on full alert, and you are ordered to return to the ship immediately."

"Immediately? But they wouldn't be here for months—if they're lucky!" Solus said.

"The orders did not explain."

"Very well, enter the atmosphere and pick me up. There's a clearing right near here where Bas is laid up with Myra. I'm returning there immediately."

"I'm already on my way," Grand replied.

"Solus, out," Solus said, ending communications. He looked over at the now deserted path and remembered the women. "Zeeni, Mondra!" he yelled. "I'm here with Myra. Don't be alarmed! You will not be injured!" Hearing no response, he looked down at his scanner and saw to his astonishment their two figures in the distance—now too far for him to go after them. They had crawled off together in all the confusion. They were alone without any protection in the wilderness in the middle of the night.

That finished it for now. There was nothing more that he could do here. He turned and ran back up the path towards Myra and Bas.

Myra had taken care of Bas very nicely. His leg was in a field cast, and his Prolix was managing his pain. He was able to walk with a telescoping crutch taken from the medical kit.

As they moved towards the arranged landing site in a nearby clearing, Solus looked up and saw a brightly shining planet now very high in the sky. It had reached its peak and would soon be sinking back down again. His home world was of no more consequence to this planet than being the brightest star in the night sky. He wondered what the natives thought of it. Myra would know that, he concluded. He looked over at her as she assisted Bas in a maternal fashion.

"Bas told me all about your confrontation with Zealrot," she said as they walked. "How good of you to shoot off their lines so that they could escape! Are they okay now? Can you see them on the scanner?"

"Yes," Solus replied. He showed her the scanner on his rifle, indicating their readings. "This one is Zealrot," he said, pointing to another reading. "He's moving away from their position in another direction, so I think they're safe from him for the time being."

"Thank goodness," Myra said simply.

"We'll come back for them," Solus said.

"Why are we leaving?"

"We've been ordered back to the ship," he answered simply.

They began to hear the sound of a steady wind above them. Looking up, they could see a dull black object blocking out a portion of the starry night. The black spot expanded until the ship finally came into view and sank down nearby, with the deployment compartment extended below it. The attack ship hovered, waiting for their approach.

The landing party moved together towards the open compartment. When they reached the open hatchway, Solus helped Bas through the opening. Once Bas was inside, Solus looked over at Myra. He could see that she was looking all around at the scenery as if to get one last look at it all. Their eyes met. Without saying a word, Solus cocked his head towards the forest's edge. He mouthed silently, "Go. Now."

Myra looked back at Solus uncomprehendingly. Punctuating his intentions, Solus tossed his rifle on the ground next to her. Myra looked down at the rifle, then bent over to pick it up. Finally realizing that he wanted her to escape, Myra looked at him with a growing admiration, turned and ran across the clearing towards the woods. Solus watched her progress as he climbed into the compartment. He called to Grand through his Prolix, "Grand, take her up!"

The ship began to lift into the air as Myra reached the forest's edge. She stopped before going into the darkness and looked up at Solus.

"Come back for me," she called to him.

The ship now rose into the air more swiftly, separating them. Solus remained hanging out of the compartment door, and for a moment regretted not jumping after her. He watched until he could no longer see her.

CHAPTER 5

PERDICION TRANSFORMED

A small, extremely clean, and well-dressed old man sat at his desk in his considerable office. His clothes were not in fashion with the current popular culture, and hadn't been for nearly eight hundred years. The man's high upturned collar, long coat, and satin knee breeches fit his surroundings. The office was more like a museum gallery than a place of work, its two-story wood-paneled walls adorned with important and valuable works of art.

A large and ornately-carved stone fireplace contained a fire that blazed continuously, consuming a stack of enormous artificial logs. Furniture, dating back to the days when Perdicion's warships were wooden sailing vessels, had been tastefully arranged about, creating comfortable little corners in which to sit and converse, although no one ever actually sat in any of them. The man's desk was a marvel of woodcarving. Exemplifying the very heights of the trade, it had black cherry sides that crawled with leaves and fruit and rabbits and blackbirds. Soft, smart music from the classical age drifted in the air of the place, and the musty smell of ancient high culture permeated the room.

The Old Man's head tilted slightly as he read from a suspended display created from the molecules in the air. It was the only hint of modern technology apparent in the room.

"Sir, would you care to review the reports from the Red Colonies front?" asked a measured, respectful, and disembodied voice, which belonged to his online valet. The man needed this valet, as he did not utilize the Prolix technology within himself. He had no need for it, because the entire automated environment that he had surrounded himself in did everything that a Prolix could do. His body, therefore, remained in an original, unaltered condition.

"I suppose so," the man responded resignedly. "Is it quite over yet?" he added expectantly.

"Not quite yet, sir," the online valet said. "There have been some casualties. Several ships have been destroyed. Admiral Revue is proceeding with the attack."

"How many ships lost?" asked the man, thinking at the same time that morning tea was in order. "My tea, please."

"Here it is, sir," said the disembodied voice as a cart rolled through a door carrying the man's fine tea service. "Three of our large ships were caught in suicide explosions, and two cruisers were critically disabled. Admiral Revue's ship escaped with minor damage. Overall, the fleet has lost over one hundred ships."

"Pity," the man replied, "but they can be rebuilt, I suppose."

"Yes, sir, but if I might interject, you have already scheduled a reduction in the space fleet to begin immediately following this campaign. There will be, if I may be so bold, no need to replace the ships."

"Yes, of course," the man agreed. "But I do hope that not all get destroyed. I'd rather like to have something to show off when it's all said and done," he added, taking a sip of his tea. "It's always good to keep around some artifacts for history's sake, you know. To leave for the ages to come, as it were."

"Of course, sir."

"It would be nice to have a victory memorial, to celebrate and such."

"Agreed, sir . . . but to complete the report: Admiral Revue is proceeding against the colonies and will be commencing bombardment very shortly."

"Ah," said the man noncommittally.

"I must also report that three enemy ships have escaped and are likely heading into the inner solar system."

"This has all gotten rather tedious," said the man petulantly. "I wanted this conflict to be over. I'm frankly tired of hearing about it."

"Yes, of course, sir."

"See that this matter is cleared up as soon as possible."

"Certainly, sir. The hostile ships are being pursued, and the planetary defense fleet has been alerted."

"Very well. Enough of that," said the man shortly. "That's what I have the admiralty for."

"I beg your pardon, sir."

"I want to know the status of the Omega upgrade. Has the Science Bureau gotten any further today? As this war is drawing to a close, I want that new version available right away."

"I will ascertain, sir."

"In the meantime, I am going to browse in my collection room for a while," he said, feeling the need to replenish himself spiritually.

"As you wish, sir."

He really hated to be bothered with such nonsense about battles in space. It used to interest him greatly, in his youth, but he had risen above these small matters in recent years. In the evening of his life, he seemed to spend more and more of his time thinking about legacy.

The Old Man lived in a time when culture had already reached its peak and had been descending now for several centuries. He seemed to be the only one left who cared anything about it at all. With this decline, there would be no more great art. The finest symphonies had already been written, the greatest painters had long since died, and no one wrote anything worthwhile any longer. This planet was completely played out, thought the man, as he strolled through his personal collection of Perdicion's finest artworks.

As one of the purveyors of the Prolix technology, he had hoped that a side effect of it would be a rebirth of cultural activities on his planet. Without the distractions of crime and national politics on society, he'd hoped that the common man would find more time for building back up their lost culture, but he saw no evidence of it at all. The Prolix technology was now several generations old, and he saw no improvements whatsoever in anyone or anything. In fact, there seemed to be a general decline.

Walking past vast painted landscapes and portraits of people in centuries-old, antiquated garb, the Old Man mourned the loss of his culture. It had always been the case, of course, but now the common people all seemed to want to be entertained on a near-constant basis, and they never seemed to want to contribute to their culture at all. And those who did seemed to produce nothing but garbage, made up to look like artwork. There was no technical skill any longer, he pondered, admiring the brushwork of one of the great masters, seen in a sailing ship on the sea. The Prolix had brought to them all the collected resources and knowledge of the planet, and yet they squandered their time with games and sexual perversions.

The elimination of the more violent and antisocial elements in the planet's society did little to improve the situation, even after the rebel Ishtarians had been removed once and for all. The Ishtarians, for that matter, never knew their place in this world—they were never content to live quietly on their own continent. They had to contaminate everything else. They'd polluted his planet and then demanded that the Blue Planet be spoiled as well. The very thought riled him to no end. But he didn't want to be riled now.

With an effort, he turned his mind back to the planet's culture. Thinking about it again, he realized that he had given up on Perdicion's culture long ago. It was time to consider it a loss, and put no more effort into it. He had instead for many years placed all of his focus on the fascinating cultures of the Blue Planet. And how could he not be fascinated? He was peering into a world that so resembled his own planet's ancient past. He could live it and immerse himself in it without confines.

He had reached his favorite wing, the Parthénos gallery, which contained his collection of the greatest artworks purloined to date from that dear world. His favorite culture there, the Romanus, called their planet Orbis Terrarium, or "the world," for that was the only world they knew. These people were astoundingly creative and prolific, he marveled to himself while passing by jade sculptures, urns, and porcelain pottery. His little treasures had been collected with great care over the last twenty years. He had visited places personally on many collecting trips, disguised as a common countryman. He even began passing himself off as an elderly official in the Imperial government in recent years. His collections of sculptures and friezes of goddesses and mythical characters, which lined the vast hallways, were rescued from crumbling sites, some three hundred years old. Even an entire ancient pillared temple had been transplanted stone by stone to his vast parkland.

He considered his collection not only to be personally

pleasing but an important preservation effort. Vast amounts of great works from ancient cultures had already been lost to the ages. Many works in his own collection had themselves been saved from destruction. Others were great in their own right, yet were copies of previous works created by artists of earlier civilizations and already lost to time.

The Romanus were now the dominant civilization in the Blue Planet's western hemisphere and had conquered most of their known world. These conquests spread their more highly developed culture to many parts of the world, and their greatest cities were filled with glorious reminders of their military conquests and campaigns. Unlike Perdician architecture, where the sharp angles of technology and efficiency dominated over aesthetic considerations, these people's creations included ornate cities with fountains and statues and arches of triumphs.

They were the inheritors of many great civilizations that had come before them. In each case, great men had risen and had advanced their world into a greater society. The Old Man was particularly interested in the work of one such fellow from the planet, named Platon. He was currently reading a translation of one work that dealt with the concept of forms in regard to the philosophy of art and beauty. Platon forwarded the idea that every object seen in the physical world also had an ideal form in the realm beyond. Out there somewhere was a perfect table, and while a man could attempt to create as defect-free table as possible, he would always fall short. For a primitive race of beings, it was amazingly thoughtful stuff.

The forms theory seemed to elucidate his own situation so very well. He and his predecessors had toiled endlessly to mold this planet into a more perfect form, but it had never attained the perfection they wanted. The first upgrade Prolix, for example, had not turned out quite as planned. While it had proved excellent in controlling an unruly population, it did, he admitted, tend to stifle creative thought. And that was what the Omega version of the Prolix was supposed to fix.

Omega combined the benefits of the prior two versions. It had more control over the body, a feature implemented in the first upgrade, yet independent thought was not as stifled, because the technology exercised a subtler control of the host. An extremely important new feature was vastly improved mind-reading capabilities. This allowed for better communications between the Prolix and the host, and allowed for no deception on the part of the host. People would have to learn to think correctly, because now the government would know exactly what each host thought as well as spoke.

New deployment methods for a mass population were already in the works, including additives to the water supply. And distribution of the new upgrade to the current Prolix-controlled populations was even easier—the updated code was simply transmitted across the entire network and every individual received it. It was unclear at that point how quickly each individual would implement the changes. It could be anywhere from minutes to days.

But for it to really work, Omega had to be provided universally. They had tried the voluntary route, and the Ishtarian rebellion had been the result. The Old Man had had enough. After all that pain, no one had the right to refuse. It was too dangerous for society, as recent history had proved. And the universality of the Omega upgrade was not to be limited to Perdicion. The Old Man had plans in the works for the peoples of Parthénos as well.

The Old Man left his gallery through glass doors and headed out into the daylight and his park, which was ornately decorated in the style of his favorite culture on Orbis Terrarium, the Romanus. He eyed the pillars of his transplanted temple in the distance. Yes, thought the Old Man, Parthénos had its great men who were well-known and revered in Parthénos' history. He, like them, had done his part for his world, but by choice, on an anonymous level. He had made many contributions to its improvement, including acting decisively against the Ishtarians, who, if left unchecked, would have eventually brought down his world. And the final battle was nearly over.

"Sir," the valet spoke out in the air of the garden, as the Old Man made his way through. "I have learned from the Science Ministry that the Omega upgrade will be ready for alpha testing in a matter of hours."

"That is satisfactory, I suppose," the Old Man replied. He had reached his temple to the goddess of beauty. After admiring the sculpted frieze at the entranceway of the goddess and her attendants, he climbed the steps and stood reverently admiring the sculpture at the center—a depiction of Beauty herself rising from the sea in the perfect image of a woman. A sculpted body fashioned in its perfect form.

"Sir," said his formless valet, "would you care to have your lunch here?"

Orbis Terrarium had so much potential, the Old Man said to himself. It just needed some help in managing itself. "Yes, that would be quite pleasant."

As the Old Man sat in his temple anticipating his midday meal, Perdicion's billions of other inhabitants went about their lives, all blissfully unaware of what was happening in space. All but a very few were familiar with the real issues involved— almost no one was aware of the battle that was transpiring in the Red Colonies, and for the most part, very few were aware of the nature of the conflict between the Supremacy and the Ishtarians. A very significant percentage of the population did not even know of the existence of the Red Colonies. But all that made little difference, just as their lack of awareness would make little difference should the sun suddenly decide to explode.

ABOARD THE ISHTARIAN STEALTH SHIP VENGEANCE *ON APPROACH TO PERDICION*

Perdicion did not note the approaching, unseen spacecraft. Seen from the ship, the planet's wispy white clouds floated in the deep blue atmosphere as Perdicion orbited the sun, just another day in its 224-day year. This magnificent view was lost on the crew of the approaching ship, which used a passing asteroid as its cover. It was *Vengeance*. In stealth mode, it slipped away from its hiding place and crept towards the planet.

"Are we within download range of the network node?" Gapp asked Blog.

"Just coming into it," Blog replied. "I'm attempting to break into the back door right now."

Blog was using an old-style computer link-in to the Prolix network. He could not, of course, use his Prolix link, because he would be identified immediately by the network. In fact, a large part of his work in this plan involved disabling his own Prolix auto-link. Ordinarily once in range of the planetary node, his Prolix would otherwise link up. Blog had come to the moment of truth. Instead of being honored for his initiative by the Science Bureau, he had been sent away. Now he would make his mark for all time.

"Hurry it up," Gapp blurted out apprehensively. "If a Supremacy attack ship picks us up, we'll be incinerated in seconds!"

"I'm in," replied Blog, annoyed at the added stress from his compatriot. Blog gained access once again using a little hole he discovered in the network's security long ago, just before the

Ishtarian revolt. He continued to use it to great advantage in gaining intelligence on the Supremacy's fleet movements. It was now allowing him to use the Supremacy's greatest weapon against itself.

"Begin transmitting the orders!" Gapp ordered excitedly, for he knew that the Ishtarian command was waiting anxiously for his communication.

"I'm setting up the interface right now. We should be in control in a matter of minutes," Blog said. He was going to enjoy this moment.

IN THE RED ZONE ABOARD THE SUPREMACY BATTLESHIP SINGULARITY

Singularity loomed before the atmosphere of the Red Planet. She was now close enough that the planet filled Admiral Revue's command viewing screen. "Target their anti-missile batteries," Revue ordered. "I want a clear path for our spears."

Singularity's assault cannons began breaching the atmosphere of the planet and struck targets on the planet's surface. It was a mere prelude to what was to follow. While the colonies themselves could not be seen from the ship's position, Revue could easily make out the explosions that visibly dotted the planet's surface.

"Sir, all batteries have been neutralized," the scanning officer reported.

"Excellent—commence bombardment immediately."

Singularity's wings lit up with the launch of ten nuclear spears at the same time. It was needless overkill, thought the admiral, but he wanted a quick and clean sweep down there. The missiles all streaked out towards their common target, each aimed at a specific area of the colonies. Not a spot was to be left untouched;

their explosions would overlap one another by at least twenty percent.

ON THE RED PLANET'S SURFACE IN THE RED COLONIES

Far below, Myra's parents sat in their small living room with Darod. With rumors flying through the colony's corridors of a coming Supremacy attack, Darod had returned to his parents the week before. He had grown weary of his vagrant and criminal lifestyle, slithering above conduits and air passages with his feral friends, spending his days sneaking food, snatching anything not locked down, and hiding from press-gangs seeking recruits for the Ishtarian militia. He began to feel somehow that time was short for the colony, and at the same time, felt a longing to return to his family. And indeed, his parents, affected by the same feelings of a looming calamity, were relieved to see him and welcomed him home.

For the past week the colonies had grown eerily silent and deserted. The militia had deployed into the space station and space fleet, leaving the civilians to their own fate. The once crowded hallways now remained strangely vacant. For the most part, people kept huddled very close to each other in their living quarters.

Now, it appeared, that the waiting was over. The little family began to hear and then feel the distant rumble of explosions. This seemed to revive them from a long-lived trance. "I've been a self-pitying fool for a long time," said Myra's father. He looked over at his wife and son. "I want to apologize to you both for that."

His wife looked back at him and smiled.

"That's okay, Dad," Darod replied.

"We were all bitter and unhappy," said his mother. "We should never have let that happen—it was not fair to you and Myra."

"Yes, indeed," agreed his father. "I hope that she is happy and safe, wherever she is," he added.

A low rumbling began to be heard from above. Muffled screams and shouts could be heard through the walls and ceilings all around them.

"She was the only one who kept her hope and faith alive," her mother said, looking over at the planting box that had been Myra's gift. "We should have followed her example."

"It's not too late," said his father, reaching for his wife's and son's hands.

The sound grew louder. It soon became distinguished to those who could discern it as the roar of advanced propulsion systems filling the air above them. The family dropped to the floor, crunched together with arms around each other.

ABOARD THE SUPREMACY BATTLESHIP ARMEGO ORBITING PERDICION

Armego was already in full alert status even before its orbit brought the battleship into the Red Zone. The planetary alert had gone out an hour ago. The fleet was having some difficulties out near the Red Planet.

"Give me a status report," Fame asked immediately upon re-entering the bridge.

"Sir, nothing new to report," Robards, the scanning officer, started to reply. "Wait, strike that. I am picking up an unexpected blip on our scanners near asteroid 143-9. It could be a stealth ship."

"Battle stations. Come to full alert," Fame ordered. "Confirm that it's not our skimmer or guppy."

"Confirmed, sir. Both of those ships' locations are marked."

"Prepare to break orbit," Fame ordered. Now this was what

he had been waiting for. The long watch was over. Action was needed. "Lieutenant Goll," he addressed the weapons officer, "bring our main batteries to bear on that ship. Prepare to fire."

Supremacy ships knew better than to approach the home world without communication. They would know that they would certainly be fired upon. "Put on a spear lock, and wait for my command."

"Yes, sir," Goll responded.

"Sir," the Prolix network officer said. "We have an unscheduled Prolix network communication coming in."

Great timing, thought Fame. "See what that's about."

OVER THE PROLIX NETWORK—ON ALL BATTLE FRONTS ACROSS THE INNER SOLAR SYSTEM

"Kill your officers!"

The command kept repeating in their ears, followed with surges of adrenaline and hatred. The command continued to repeat, speaking loudly, directly into the upgrades' minds. It was maddening; it was irresistible. They could hear and feel nothing else. All over Perdicion, in the planetary defenses and onboard ships, the upgrades began to writhe and cry out. They all grabbed their heads as if trying to squeeze the voices out of their minds. The message was broadcast to all upgrades with no subtlety or precision at all. It was not needed—all upgrades in the network heard and felt the command and the maddening surges of negative emotion.

ABOARD THE ISHTARIAN STEALTH SHIP VENGEANCE *ABOVE PERDICION*

"That battleship scanned us," Gapp said. "Your hack job had

better be working soon, or we'll be dodging spears in a matter of minutes."

"My broadcast has not been blocked. It's getting through. There's no way the upgrades could be withstanding it. They'll be going crazy anytime now."

"Excellent," Gapp said. "Revenge time!"

ABOARD THE SUPREMACY BATTLESHIP ARMEGO *ABOVE PERDICION*

Fame looked around at his bridge crew in surprise and alarm. At least six upgrades were staggering about the deck, groaning in agony. "What in the blazes is going on?" he called out sharply. "Deck officer! Get some assistance to those men!"

But before the man could respond, gunfire and screams echoed throughout the ship's decks.

"Have we been boarded?" Fame cried. "Where are those shots coming from?"

"Captain," cried out the scanning officer, "the upgrades are going crazy—all over the ship!"

"Mutiny?" he said, looking over as two of his stricken bridge crew pulled their sidearms and began firing.

ON THE OLD MAN'S COMPOUND ON PERDICION

"The Prolix network has been compromised, sir," said the valet, interrupting the Old Man's lunch. "Upgrade personnel are being ordered to kill their superiors. It's affecting the fleet and defense installations all over the world."

The Old Man looked up from his fish, perplexed. "Compromised? How could that be?"

"We're not sure, sir," replied the voice. "We're attempting

to block and countermand the messages, but it is not getting through to the ranks."

"There must be a breach in the network," said the Old Man, wiping his lips with a red satin napkin. "Find that illegal link and disconnect it."

"We are working on it, sir, but there are billions of connections to go through."

"That's unacceptable!" said the man angrily. "It's obviously coming from a command link-up. No one but myself has the authority to send out commands on such a scale!"

"The computers are parsing through the code with those criteria in place, sir," replied the valet. "Yet there is an alternative. We could close down the connections altogether for a time."

"That would effectively close the network down!" replied the man, appalled. "I'll send out a counter-command myself . . . connect me with the entire network."

"Connecting . . ."

"Do not kill your leaders! Obey your officers!" he ordered. "Keep repeating that," he instructed the network protocol machine.

"With all due respect, sir, I'm not sure if that will have the effect you—"

"That is only a temporary measure," he interrupted. "Now for the cure . . . distribute the Omega upgrade immediately to the entire network. That should lock out the command—it will be incompatible."

"I will communicate with the Science Bureau immediately."

ABOVE THE RED PLANET ONBOARD THE SUPREMACY BATTLESHIP SINGULARITY

Revue peered grimly at the devastation below. The hits were

seen easily from space, and the aftermath of the explosions was equally evident.

"Target destroyed, sir," said the weapons officer, with an apparent talent for the obvious.

"Understood," Revue replied. A surge of anger and self-pity helped to alleviate a growing feeling of guilt within him. They had forced his hand, Revue told himself. They had refused to negotiate, instead choosing to attack his ships. They had used him to commit suicide.

He watched as the nuclear clouds continued to expand and spread their devastation below. That part of the Red Planet had quickly returned to a state of lifelessness, and there would be little evidence left to suggest that it had ever existed there. Only the deep craters resulting from the explosions would be a visible and permanent scar from the attack that had just aborted this planet's second chance at life.

"Bring her about," ordered Revue, growing tired of the view before him. "We've done all that we can do here."

"Complying, sir."

Her lethal work completed, the massive vessel veered away from its firing position over the planet and began to move back out into space.

"Get my ship commanders. I want a damage assessment," he said to his Prolix.

"Sir, I'm having trouble breaking through some strange signals being broadcast from the home world," said his Prolix. "It's jamming the upgrade network with conflicting commands."

"What are they?" said Revue. "Let me hear it."

"Transferring . . ."

"Kill your officers!" repeated over and over in his head.

"What in the devil is that?" Revue roared. "Is that being sent from the home world?"

"I'm not sure, sir . . ." began his Prolix, interrupted by the thuds of explosions coming from all around the ship. Revue's support ships were exploding all around them. He looked through the bridge screen just in time to see the pointed nose of an attack ship explode—its pulse cannon had fired a burst right into its closed cockpit modules! Flashes from exploding ships flickered in the space all around them.

"Counter-measures!" Revue shouted. "We've been compromised! Shut off that clutter on the Prolix network!"

The counter-measures officer was already working frantically, trying to find the source. "My staff won't respond. Something's happening downstairs!"

"Sir!" cried out the weapons officer. "Our nuclear spears are being armed, and I can't override! Someone's manually setting them in the launch bays!"

"What the devil?" Revue shouted, repeating a theme.

"There are three armed spears set for detonation, sitting in their launchers."

"Fire them all!" Revue ordered frantically. The weapons officer looked over at the firing control display to give the command, but it was too late.

Singularity ignited like a miniature star. The flash from the explosion illuminated the planet and its two dark moons like never before in its history. The disaster continued as the shock wave hit the support squadrons and they too, like the minions of a vanquished demon, followed in their master's fate. Soon two other ships ignited like dwarf stars and shined in the light as the two crippled cruisers followed the example of their sister battleship.

Soon all life would be extinguished above the planet as well as on the surface. The victors had now joined the vanquished in the land of the dead.

NEAR THE BLUE PLANET'S MOON ABOARD SHADOW

Shadow and *Orion* lay side by side waiting in the moon's shadow for the incoming Ishtarian ships. Solus decided that the zone they were in intersected with the most likely course incoming ships would take, given the positions of the planets for the enemy ships' inward journey. Intelligence indicated that the Ishtarian ships would be coming in a group, and while *Shadow* was easily a match for the Ishtarian ships, she would be outnumbered without cover. Taking these facts into account, Solus pulled *Orion* out of her sector to provide that needed cover.

Solus was back in his command position with Bas again in the pilot's seat. Bas had recuperated in the medical bay for as long as he could stand it and insisted on returning to his post. His leg was still out of commission, but he didn't need to stand in order to pilot the ship. And until he could get Grand aboard another ship, Solus wanted to make use of his presence aboard *Shadow*. Accordingly, Solus ordered Grand and his compatriot Ham,whom Dr. Nevek had sufficiently cured, to be at the ready in *Shadow*'s deployment bay for an anticipated boarding action.

Even so, the tactical situation in space was not enough to keep Solus' mind off of Myra completely. He kept picturing her making her way through the forest with her friends. He was glad that she had his rifle, but worried at the same time that she wouldn't use it when it was really needed. From what he knew of her, she'd just as soon let a bear eat her than kill it in self-defense. And what would the natives do to her? She maintained an innocent conviction that they would accept her if she spoke their language. Yet these were primitive people, after all—who knew what they would do to her instead? He frowned and twitched at the thought of it.

Bas, looking back at his commander in his command module, strongly suspected the source of his commander's mental troubles and pitied him. The commander had quite obviously fallen in love with their former prisoner. From what Bas had heard from other sources, Commander Solus had once had a woman in his life, but that was for a short time, and a long time ago. Bas himself had been married for many years. And even though he had been away from his family for nearly half of his marriage, he was sustained by their love. It was a wonderful feeling knowing they were there—knowing that he had someone to go home to when it was all over.

Bas rubbed his leg, now encased in a molded cast. It really wasn't terribly inconvenient—it was like wearing a long plastic sock. The only problem was an itch that had started about halfway down his calf. "Can you stop the itching?" he asked his Prolix imploringly.

"It's all in your mind; just ignore it!" replied the Prolix. "Unless you want me to shut off feeling down there."

"It's always all or nothing with you, isn't it?" said Bas.

"That's how I'm de . . . signed . . ." the Prolix started. "Commands coming in from the home world . . ." Then the Prolix stopped speaking.

Bas waited, but soon grew impatient. "Well, what are they?"

"What's wrong?" said Rowling, who was seated near Bas in the starboard nose section.

"I'm not sure. My Prolix just reported that commands were coming in, and . . ." Before he could finish his sentence, Bas looked like he'd just taken a flying knife in his back. His face contorted in pain, and he grabbed his head, gasping.

"Sir, Bas is struggling in here," Rowling reported to Solus.

"There's something wrong with Chamers in here," Fleek added from the port nose section. "He's writhing around in pain."

"Bas, report! What's the matter?" Solus called out, alarmed, having never seen Bas showing this kind of emotion, even in combat. Solus climbed out of his command module and made his way into the starboard nose of the ship. Once in there, he stepped over to Bas, now stricken on the deck, touching his shoulder. "Are you injured?"

Bas continued to writhe in pain.

"Commander?" Grand's voice piped in.

"Grand, what's up?"

"It's Ham down here. He's in pain or something."

"So are Bas and Chamers," Solus said, now very concerned. "Bas was just talking to his Prolix and got seized with pain."

Doubled over on the controls, Bas was struggling mightily to speak. He started to shout as if trying to be heard over a crowd of screaming voices. "Kill!" he screamed. "They want me to kill!"

"Who wants you to kill?" Solus said. "Kill who?"

Bas suddenly struck out, slamming Solus across the cockpit and into the opposite wall. Stunned, Solus struggled to recover his senses. Bas was now screaming incoherently and struggling with the ship's controls. Rowling tried to grab Bas, but was easily thrown aside.

"Sir, you've got to sedate me—all of us!" he screamed. "I can't control myself!"

"What are you talking about?"

"I'm being ordered to kill you—to destroy the ship!" he screamed. "Put me out now!"

Still not comprehending, but acting anyway, Solus complied as fast as he could. "Xoxon, put them all to sleep, now!"

"I can't comply—your command can't get through—it's being overridden by conflicting signals," Xoxon replied.

Bas glared at Solus, possessed with a rage that was not his own.

Seeing this, Solus pulled his sidearm and fired. The stunning-force shock pulse struck Bas in the chest, knocking him to the deck.

Solus then looked over at the port-side cockpit and saw Fleek struggling with Chamers, who had also pulled his sidearm. They were fighting over the gun when it went off into the controls. Sparks and black smoke began to envelop the compartment. The struggling men disappeared from view.

The ship's emergency fire systems began operating. Solus could now see white gas pouring into the smoke-filled compartment. The sparks disappeared and the black smoke was soon replaced with the white gas. While also rendering the men unconscious, the gas would provide them oxygen to breathe while the smoke was being filtered out of the compartment.

Seeing that this immediate emergency was being contained, he called out to Xoxon. "Xoxon, quick, what're they hearing?"

"Connecting . . ." And the same mind-splitting command rang out in Solus' ears. "Kill your officers!" Solus' mind raced, then the realization hit him—the Prolix network had been compromised. It was unimaginable, but the technology-hating enemy had somehow gained access to the heavily-secured Prolix network. "Connect me to Grand and my ship commanders!"

"Connecting . . ." Their faces appeared before him. By the looks on their faces, they too were experiencing problems with their upgrades.

"Stun—disable—your upgrades now! The network has been compromised!" Solus cried. "Use your sidearms!" They looked at him uncomprehendingly, each trying to digest what he had just heard. "Shoot them now!" Solus kept shouting.

Quash looked to his right at something outside Solus' visual boundary. His eyes widened in horror as if looking at death itself. A blast scorched him directly in the face, and he slumped over—his face, now a black mess, faded before Solus' eyes.

Just as this horror was unfolding, Prop screamed out and became engulfed in flames. Mercifully for Solus, this image and the accompanying screams disappeared abruptly. Solus' monitors simultaneously registered a blast—the attack ship *Radiate* had erupted internally and then broken apart.

"Solus! What is happening?" piped in Nevek. "I'm in the sick bay."

"Doctor, we've got a crisis here! The upgrades are being ordered to kill us all!"

Nevek looked at Solus in disbelief. Not waiting for his reply, Solus continued, "Arm yourself immediately. Stun your med-tech!"

Meanwhile, Thump struggled mightily with someone out of sight, while Rodd, gun in hand, was looking down at his deck. A second blast registered—*Corona* had just fired a burst through its closed cockpits—the cannon enclosed behind the united cockpit had been fired into and through it. Prop's blackened image erupted in flames and then instantly disappeared. The smoking, headless ship spun out of control towards open space.

"Report!" Solus called out to his remaining ships. "Rodd, what's happening?"

"Sir, Compass is out," Rodd reported. "I stunned him and the other upgrades as you ordered. Compass was just pulling his gun out as I shot him."

"Go make sure the doc is okay."

"Yes, sir," Rodd replied.

"Thump," Solus called out, "is everything under control over there?" He could hear the sounds of an ongoing struggle.

"Sir," Thump panted, out of breath, "I'm on top of Rachet—I've disarmed him, but I don't have my sidearm. He's struggling—I'm trying to cuff him. Ruffini just did the same to Pod."

"You've got to knock them out and put them in the brig! They can still send mental commands to the ship!"

Thump looked at Solus through the link in sudden realization. He grabbed the gun he had just taken from the upgrade and swung the butt down, striking the pitiful man hard on the back of his head. His struggling ceased immediately.

Thump looked up at Solus, anguish transforming his young face. "I think I've killed him, sir! I can't tell if he's breathing."

"Get him into the medical bay immediately. Strap him into a bed, and let the ship take care of him."

"Yes, sir."

"And get back to your post as quickly as you can. I'm going to get Grand over to you as soon as possible to help."

"Yes, sir."

He remembered that he had not heard from Grand. "Grand!" he called out. "What's your condition?"

"Sir, I'm here," came back the simple reply.

"Okay—how's Ham? Did you subdue him?"

"Sir, I—I killed him. He was coming at me with his gun," Grand said, gulping in misery. "I could see it in his eyes that he didn't want to, but he was going to kill me."

ON THE OLD MAN'S COMPOUND ON PERDICION

"Sir, the Omega upgrade is downloading to the networks, but it will take time to upload to the entire population."

"Have you found the cause of the corruption?" said the Old Man irritably. This nonsense had already ruined his fine lunch at the temple. His valet had insisted upon his returning to his office, which was in easy reach of the safety bunker.

"We're getting closer, sir, but I have some rather alarming news to report."

"What is it now?" he asked impatiently.

"The network breach is having a devastating effect. The battle fleet has been badly damaged. Hundreds of officers have been killed, and those who have escaped have no control over their men."

"But this is all absurd!" said the Old Man. "What can possibly be accomplished by all this? We will surely regain control in moments."

"That might not be soon enough, sir," replied the valet patiently. "We have analyzed their attack, and there are some rather alarming possibilities."

"Never mind that now—Omega will halt all that."

"Yes, of course, sir," replied the valet. "But I must insist you retire to your safety bunker. I have set out your tea service there."

"Very well," the Old Man replied. "I am rather thirsty."

ABOARD THE ISHTARIAN STEALTH SHIP VENGEANCE *ABOVE PERDICION*

The news came through from deep space. Gapp received the transmission from the Red Planet's space station, just before it was destroyed. The Supremacy fleet was destroying everything. He then heard the screams from the personnel on the planet's surface. He just had time to switch to a satellite view as the nuclear holocaust began. They were killing everyone.

Rage and hatred surged within him. "Blog, they've just killed everyone on the Red Planet."

"Damn it all!" Blog cried out. "We were too late! We didn't get the transmissions out in time." His grim joy at victory turned to rage.

"They're going to pay. They're all going to pay," Gapp simmered. He looked over at the stricken battleship, a tiny blip on their viewing screen; it was so near the planet's surface. There were two more like it, surrounding the planet. A horrible idea struck him. "Blog, can you send a targeted message to those battleships and the planetary missile defenses?"

"Yes, I can, but the transmission point will be identified. Our position will be identified."

"That won't matter in a few moments."

"But the planetary defenses. We were only to target the military . . ."

"The whole planet is the enemy! Can't you get that?" Gapp roared.

"What do you want to command?"

"Order those battleships and the planetary missile defenses to launch all of their nukes onto the planet."

"We can't do that! The battleships are above the equator; the warheads will be hitting a very precarious zone on the planet. It could start cataclysmic results . . ."

"It will end the Supremacy!" Gapp shouted with a boiling-over rage. "They just killed us—we're going to do the same to them."

"But, Gapp," Blog pleaded, "our mission was to destroy their defenses. That's our home down there. "

"They banished us. That's not our home anymore. That's the home of the enemy. They just killed us. Now, give the command, or I will kill you."

Blog looked over at his compatriot and knew that he was not bluffing. Gapp looked like a madman—like he was about to go over the edge at any moment.

"Prolix network override," he commanded into his interface program. "Contact the three battleships in orbit over Perdicion and all missile defense complexes."

"Identifying . . ." Blog's Prolix replied. "Now in contact with upgrade network. Command override in effect. You may broadcast commands."

Blog did not have time to focus his commands. He had to send commands to the entire crew, and hope they got through to the right upgrades.

"Weapons officers, launch all nuclear weapons at the planet and detonate on the surface," he spoke into the command interface. "Keep repeating that, and keep pumping them with adrenaline and anger."

"Transmitting."

ABOARD THE SUPREMACY BATTLESHIP ARMEGO ORBITING PERDICION

Captain Fame opened his eyes and found himself looking at his bridge sideways, and realized that he was lying on his side, his head on the deck. He could hear commotion around him. The upgrades were shouting commands at each other. He tried to move and raise himself up, but was unable to. He looked around and saw the bodies of his officers lying about the bridge. He then remembered that he had been shot. "Am I injured?" he whispered to his Prolix.

"Yes, you have sustained an injury to your lower spinal cord. I am unable to send any messages to your legs."

He digested this—this injury could be repaired, but he was quite incapacitated. "What's the status—what's going on here?"

"The upgrade personnel have been ordered to move the ship into firing position over the planet. They are preparing to fire our complement of nuclear missiles at multiple targets on the equator."

Fame recoiled at the absolute horror of the situation. His own ship was about to bombard the planet, and he was virtually helpless to prevent it. "Why are they aiming at the equator? There are no major cities there, and that's certainly not the Supremacy's stronghold," he said, not really expecting an answer.

Unbeknownst to Fame and his Prolix, the two other battleships that had been guarding the planet were now also positioning themselves at two other points along the planet's equator. Their targeting systems were ready to fire.

"Arming missiles!" an upgrade shrieked. "Preparing to fire!"

"Belay that!" Fame called out. "Do *not* fire!"

"Not fire?" cried out one of the upgrades. "But we're ordered to fire!"

"Don't listen to it!" Fame cried. "I'm your captain—you will obey me!"

"We must obey the Prolix!" they all answered in reply.

The massive ships began firing the first volley of missiles at the planet. Hundreds of nuclear missiles began their final journey to the planet's surface. The planetary missile complexes were also firing everything they had at random planetary targets.

"Did we really need so many nukes?" Fame anguished.

ON THE OLD MAN'S COMPOUND ON PERDICION

"Sir, we must get you strapped in now," said the valet. "It's time to take off."

"But why?" said the Old Man peevishly. "I've not finished with my tea!"

"Sir, I must insist," said the valet, as the Old Man's seat strapped him in place and positioned him for launching. The safety bunker was in fact a small space vessel, designed for quick emergency takeoffs. "You cannot stay, sir," explained the valet. "All life will soon be extinguished here."

"So it's all over, is it?" said the man, resignedly.

"Yes, I'm afraid so, sir."

"Ten thousand years of civilization, and it comes to this?" spoke the man. "And on my watch?"

"You cannot blame yourself, sir."

"I do not!" replied the man. "They have all failed me. I am immensely put out!" The little ship's launching engines fired, and it began to ascend. "This planet has been dead for some time. It was only a matter of time before someone claimed the body, I suppose."

"Up to a point, sir," responded the valet. As the two spoke, a wall of flame had begun to expand across the globe, destroying everything in its path.

"Well, if I must," said the man. "I had been planning on an eventual relocation to Parthénos—such a fascinating place—so I am simply doing so ahead of schedule."

"That's a positive way to look at it, sir."

"And from what you've told me, the Red Colonies have been obliterated, so once the Omega upgrade takes hold, we should still have more than enough defensive capabilities to destroy what's left of those pesky devils, the Ishtarians."

"True, sir," replied the valet.

"But now with the old homestead vanishing, you're confined to this ship, aren't you?"

"Yes, sir," replied the valet evenly. "I will be in a better position to serve you when we download my programming into the planetary node on the Blue Planet."

"Yes, we will see to that when we arrive, of course," said the man. "In the meantime, I suppose I will have to make do."

"Positive thinking, sir," the valet said.

"I could use a bottle of wine from my cellar . . ."

"Of course, sir. Quite some time ago, I had anticipated the need for storing up some of your more valued possessions aboard this ship. I have several vintages for you to choose from."

"You do think of everything, don't you!"

"I try my best, sir."

NEAR THE BLUE PLANET'S MOON ABOARD SHADOW

Solus ordered *Shadow*'s port cockpit module opened so that he could get to the men inside. As the door opened, he found them both on the floor, unconscious, as expected. The fire-suppression gas had that effect. Using a kit from the medical bay, Solus put Chamers under heavy sedation, as he had done to Bas. He then aroused Fleek, who, while terribly groggy, appeared no worse for the wear from the situation. He helped Solus place Bas and Chamers into the medical beds to keep them under sedation.

After seeing that they were secure, Solus was finally able to descend into the heart of the vessel to help Grand move Ham's body. He emerged from the tube to find Grand sitting in the deployment chamber, still staring down at the crumpled body of his young upgrade. "He could've been my son," Grand said as Solus entered the chamber. "I always looked out for him. His family was counting on me."

"You knew his family?"

"I met them . . . briefly . . . during our last stop on the home world. They were there to meet Ham at our landing. I went over to introduce myself."

That was just like Grand, thought Solus. Most officers would not have wanted to be bothered with meeting the parents of an upgrade.

"He was coming at me. I acted on instinct. I knocked the gun from his hands, and we struggled. I got him into a chokehold, but I could feel him gaining strength—his Prolix must have been pouring on his adrenaline. I kept yelling at him to stop—I just kept squeezing harder and harder to get him to stop, but he struggled all the more. Then he went completely limp, and I let go. He fell to the deck, like that." Tears filled Grand's eyes.

Solus had no good words of solace to give his friend. He just grabbed Grand's shoulder and squeezed. Nothing more could be said.

They had no time for mourning. After they moved Ham's body up and into the medical bay, Solus ordered Grand back down into the deployment chamber to make a ship-to-ship transfer. They positioned *Shadow* over *Orion*'s top connection hatch, which was used for personnel and small equipment exchanges, then extended and locked *Shadow*'s umbilical tube. Grand, in position, shot quickly into the other ship and immediately assumed command. Solus disconnected and moved back into side formation with the sister ship.

Dr. Nevek insisted upon getting the severely injured over to his ship. The remains of the squadron made a rendezvous with *Guru* and the two attack ships attached to the connection modules beneath her wings. The wounded and dead upgrades were transferred aboard, still strapped to their medical beds.

"I'll keep the upgrades under sedation until we're sure this Prolix breach is not affecting them anymore," Nevek relayed to Solus.

"How will we be able to determine that?"

"Of course, that is the question," Nevek replied.

"Solus, I'm picking up some alarming messages from the fleet!" Xoxon interrupted.

"What's coming in?"

"*Singularity* reported that it had destroyed the colonies, and now I've lost all contact with the fleet . . ."

Solus really only heard the first part of the message. "What! The colonies? He destroyed everything?"

"Yes, I have a visual recording—transmitting . . ."

Conveyed through the cold glass eyes of the falling missiles, the horror unfolded before Solus' flesh ones. The familiar orangey-red terrain, then the irregular, web-shaped gray terminals nestled beside a hill range. Solus realized that he was seeing a place that now no longer existed. The target grew larger and more distinct, with no view of the humanity within, but Solus knew that they were there—and knowing that made it all the more chilling. Then, a flash ended the image. "There were millions of people living there," he said in stunned disbelief. "Why would the Admiral do that?"

"Wasn't it really the next step, after all?" Xoxon replied. "The course of action was, unfortunately, inevitable."

"How can you say that?" Solus cried.

"This is simply my analysis. Both sides hate each other and are intractable. The Supremacy decided to act decisively to eliminate the rebel Ishtarians, an enemy who would not surrender. Based on Supremacy precepts, their total elimination became inevitable."

Solus was still trying to reconcile all he had heard and seen, when Xoxon made another startling announcement: "The fleet has been destroyed, and Admiral Revue is dead."

"Destroyed?" The fantastic pronouncements seemed to be continuous today. Solus was fast becoming dulled to it all.

"The upgrade network corruption affected them, too," Xoxon reported. "They appear to have self-destructed! The images are sketchy."

"Position the long-range telescope—I want to see for myself."

"Positioning . . ."

Solus peered through the eyepiece above his head and saw what looked like three new glowing stars, all positioned in proximity to the Red Planet. "My Creator . . ." he gasped.

"Transmission now coming in from the home world—to all units," Xoxon announced.

"Orders?" Solus asked somberly, still transfixed on the Red Planet.

"No, it's from the Science Bureau—updates to my programming . . . it's uploading now . . ."

And then there was silence.

"Xoxon?"

There was only silence.

"Xoxon? What's going on?"

Moments went past. Solus began to feel very alone in the universe. He sat there in a bewildering haze for a time, then he heard a voice. "Sir, are you there?" It was Bas piping in through the ship's intercom.

"Bas," Solus replied, relieved to hear his voice, but then swiftly concerned. "Are you still getting bad commands?"

"No, sir," said Bas. "I'm not hearing anything at all. My Prolix won't respond."

"Something's happened to them," Solus said. "Xoxon said something about an update coming through and then he went silent. I suspect it's a command fix to stop the breach of the network." Or, Solus thought anxiously, it could be more dirty work from the enemy that had sent the kill commands.

"Sir, it was the worst experience of my life!" Bas responded. "My Prolix was continuously screaming at me to kill, and messing with my emotions—I was willing to do anything to make it stop. It was torture."

"Sir, my Prolix is gone too," piped in Chamers, who was now also awake. "It's so weird not having him there!"

"I agree—it's disconcerting," Solus said. "Look, I'm going to let you both out of your beds, so please don't be faking it," Solus half-quipped.

"Oh, I'm not!" Chamers said. "I couldn't fake acting normal. You have no idea what it was like!"

Using rarely-needed ship remote controls, Solus released Bas and Chamers from their beds. "Get into the nose sections as fast as you can—we're still on the alert for hostiles."

"My God, what happened to Ham?" Chamers exclaimed, seeing the body for the first time in the medical bay.

"I'm sorry—he's dead," Solus replied. "I have many things to tell you. The attack on the Prolix network was devastating. Get to your posts, and I'll fill you both in. We have much to avenge."

ABOARD THE ISHTARIAN STEALTH SHIP VENGEANCE *ABOVE PERDICION*

Gapp watched the rapidly spreading devastation unfold on the planet's surface. Even the space station above Ouda Regio was in the midst of breaking up due to internal explosions caused by the upgrade personnel within. "It's done. There's no turning back," he observed as the yellow clouds continued to expand across the globe. "That was my home at one time." After a pause, he asked, "Why is it spreading so quickly?"

Blog, who watched in a state of numbness, awoke from a stupor and looked at his scanning station. "The nuclear blasts, all hitting the equator simultaneously at different points on the surface, appear to have initiated a large amount of volcanic activity. There are hundreds and hundreds of volcanoes along that area. Hundreds appear to be going off—spewing out clouds."

Gapp watched as the clouds got closer and closer to the Southern Continent, to the place where he was born. "I still got family down there somewhere," he added regretfully.

"Not for much longer," Blog noted.

This glib reply started to rile Gapp, but he quickly overcame it. To become annoyed meant that he would have to admit to the guilt he was starting to feel.

"We are done—it's all over," Blog said. "I'm ordering the battleships to drop into the atmosphere and self-destruct, then we've got to get out of here."

Gapp turned away and looked down at the ship's controls, not wanting to watch any longer. "Yes, let's get out of here." The ship began to move away from the planet.

"I'm plotting a course for the Blue Planet. It's our home now," Blog said.

ON THE SURFACE OF PERDICION

A woman of Ishtarian descent was cleaning up her kitchen, peering out the window at her three boys, who were playing in their home's backyard. The boys stuck together there and avoided going to the nearby playground. The other kids could be cruel at times. They were Ishtarians living amongst the white-skinned Supremacy folk, and even though they had accepted that way of life and the Prolix, racial prejudice ran deep.

As a mother, she had mixed emotions about it. They lived on a large military base, and there were plenty of ways to get into trouble. She didn't like her kids having to remain so confined to the yard, but at the same time, she was better able to keep an eye on them. She especially wanted to keep them within earshot today. The mood on the base had been particularly disquieting of late. People were nervous. Rumors of a large military action had spread throughout the complex. Their Prolixes would neither deny nor confirm anything. That itself said a lot.

She worried about her husband, not knowing where he was or what he was doing. Prolix transmissions, of course, were prohibited while spouses were deployed. He was out in space somewhere fighting for his home world. Doing his duty, which always seemed to separate him from his family. She was doing hers, raising their boys.

Putting the lunch dishes into the cleaning conveyor, a wonderful device that cleaned and then stacked the dishes in the cabinet, she still marveled at the luxuries of her base home. Homemaking tools like this simply did not exist on the Reservation continent. She glanced out at her boys, each with a little mop of black hair. They were at their usual play stations in their little backyard, swinging on the swing set and climbing on the set's netting. She loved them all beyond anything else in the entire universe, and, as she did every day, she thanked the Creator for sending them to her. As their faith informed them, each child was a living expression of the love that she and her husband had for each other.

By their mere presence in her life, they had taught her how to love. She loved them equally but in different ways. Jakie, the youngest, was her cuddly bear—he still loved to sit in her lap and hug her. Brack, the middle child, was her rebel, who loved to explore, while Bo, the oldest, was her serious one. He was the little man: the man of the house while his father was gone. He took his position seriously and was very protective of them all.

This was her paradise, at least in this world. She had everything she really wanted: her three boys and a loving husband. Other than her husband's absence, she would have gladly frozen this moment in time. They would all grow up on her and leave her alone—probably all would go off to save the world, as her husband was doing.

Why did the world always need to be saved? And by those she loved?

It was getting darker outside. She looked out into the distance. No, the light was changing tone, like the sun was going down or a storm was approaching. It was a weird, otherworldly light. It filled her with an unaccountable feeling of foreboding.

"Boys, time to come in!" she called from the kitchen window. She noticed that the skies behind them were turning a sickening yellow. She hoped that her husband, Bas, was safe, wherever he was.

ONBOARD THE SUPREMACY BATTLESHIP ARMEGO *ABOVE PERDICION*

On the bridge of the *Armego*, the screaming suddenly went silent in the upgrades' minds. They looked around themselves as if waking up from a horrible nightmare. Still lying on his side, Fame noticed immediately that something was different about the upgrades. Hetried once again to regain control.

"Reverse thrusters!" he shouted, for the twentieth time, hopeful that, this time, his order would be obeyed. "We're heading straight into the atmosphere!"

"The thrusters are inoperative!" shouted an upgrade manning the helm. "I can't get any response!"

"Engine room!" Fame yelled. "Is anyone there?"

No response came.

"You!" the captain called to a nearby crewman. "Come over here and help me into my chair!" If the ship was going down, he was going to be in command, not lying on the deck.

"Sir, the *Blanco* and *Nebula* just entered the atmosphere and burned up," reported a crewman manning the scanning station. As he was speaking, another crewman assisted in getting the captain into his chair.

"Good Lord . . ." Fame said, unable to restrain himself. "We need to get someone down to engineering and get those engines started." He quickly assigned a crew for the task.

"Captain! I'm picking up another ship," the crewman reported. "Perhaps they could assist?"

"Let me see the readings," he said, and his Prolix displayed them before his eyes. An old fifth-generation stealth ship. There were none of that class stationed anywhere near the planet.

Then he remembered the enemy ship they were about to fire upon just before the crisis had hit. "That's not one of ours," he replied. This was the enemy.

"Weapons! Have we got weapons power?"

"Sir, we've got power to the primary weapon," came the reply.

"Then target that ship and destroy it!"

Even as the mighty vessel began to glow red from the outer atmosphere, its assault cannons turned around as far as they could reach and fired up and out. The gigantic beams struck *Vengeance* and smashed it instantly.

Gapp and Blog had little time to scream before burning up in space.

"Engine room! We need power!" called out Fame. "Helm, get her nose up, pull her up—we need to go in at an angle." Through phenomenal efforts, the crew managed to level out the descent of the ship, which entered the now cloud-filled atmosphere. They avoided immediate burn-up and now needed power urgently to regain orbit.

But it was a lost cause. The ship dropped like a stone into the thickening yellow atmosphere. "Good work, men," Fame said to his crew. "We've gone down fighting in the great tradition of the Supremacy space fleet. We've destroyed our enemy and now we must die with our planet. May the Creator have mercy on us!"

How liberating it was to invoke the Creator! Even yet it was not too late. The ship hit the now smoldering surface, and the crew quickly joined the planet in its death.

ONBOARD THE SUPREMACY ATTACK SHIP SHADOW *NEAR THE BLUE PLANET'S MOON*

Once Bas had settled into his pilot's chair in the starboard nose section, and Chamers was positioned with Fleek in the port, Solus filled them all in on all that had happened. He summarized it for them: the situation was urgent; their squadron was down to the two attack ships and *Guru*. He had attempted to contact fleet command but had gotten no response, which was disquieting.

Solus, concerned about another Prolix takeover, disabled the ship's Prolix mind controls, which forced the upgrades to operate the systems on manual control only. He disarmed them of all weapons and programmed an override that would instantly re-route command controls from the nose sections at the first sign of trouble. While trained to fly the ship manually, the upgrades felt extremely detached and disoriented without their Prolix companions.

Bas was busy monitoring the ship's systems and the scanning stations. Even though they were just maintaining a stationary position, he began to feel a bit overwhelmed with so much to do without his Prolix to assist him. He grew alarmed even at the possibility of going into battle. Then he remembered that he needed to report something to the commander. "Sir, I need to report a problem," he said through the ship's com system.

"Yes, what is it, Bas?" Solus responded from his command station.

"Well, sir, I . . ." he started. "When I was being ordered to kill and self-destruct, I—I did try to, sir, but it didn't work!" He was suddenly seized with guilt, and that part of it struck him hard.

"Bas, it was not your fault—the network was compromised," Solus replied soothingly. "Frankly, I'm amazed that you were able to give me a warning at all! I seriously doubt most upgrade personnel would have been able to do that!"

"Yes, sir," Bas replied, comforted at Solus' words. Then, after a moment, he realized that he still had not made his report. "But, sir, what I wanted to tell you was that I did try to destroy the ship—by firing the burst cannon through the coupled cockpit."

Solus looked at him. "You tried?" he replied. "But stopped?"

"No, sir," Bas said. "I sent the command, but it didn't work. There must have been something wrong with my controls."

This called for a thorough inspection of the cockpit controls in the starboard cockpit section. Solus joined Bas, and they soon discovered the answer. The panel flare-up that Bas had experienced in their first action against the Ishtarians had disabled Bas' burst cannon firing control. He had indeed attempted to fire the cannon into their backs. But it hadn't worked. The damage from the previous battle had stopped it from working.

"How fortuitous . . ." Solus mused as they made repairs.

Xoxon's silence ended about an hour later. His return was preceded by a visual display that booted up before Solus' eyes. A read-out appeared: "Restarting, Omega upgrade completed." A moment later, Xoxon himself reported in. "I'm back!" he announced excitedly. "That upgrade took time to implement!"

"Xoxon!" Solus responded, with relief obvious in his voice. "I thought you were gone forever! What's this upgrade all about? Is it to combat the network breach?"

"Oh, I've loads to tell you," Xoxon said. "This upgrade was indeed sent out to combat the network breach, but it's more than that. I'm very much improved! I have many new capabilities to serve you with."

"Such as?" Perhaps he could help me fly up the air, thought Solus.

"No, I can't help you fly," Xoxon responded.

"How did you know I thought that?"

"That's one of my little improvements!" Xoxon said gleefully.

Solus was angered. For the first time in his life, he felt violated by his Prolix. They had now gone too far. Even his most private thoughts were not his own. It was an outrage beyond all others. "Did you get all that, Xoxon?" Solus said.

"Yes, I did. Quite clearly," he replied. "You're taking this rather badly, aren't you?"

"They've gone too far!" Solus exclaimed openly, completely furious. "How dare they do this!" He continued on a torrential verbal tirade, which was strangely liberating, since his thoughts would now betray him as well as his words.

"Listen," Xoxon replied. "It's not all bad, really. There's so much more I can do for you now—"

"Xoxon, just send along your report of my bad thoughts. I've had it."

"I'm not sure I have to, in fact, but I can't—at least for the moment. The network connection is gone. I'm not getting anything from the home world at all, only *Guru*'s node. I can't send or receive. It's been silent ever since the upgrade occurred."

"You're not receiving from the home world?" Solus responded. "That's odd. Deploy the telescope—I want a visual."

"Positioning . . ."

He forgot his anger. It had morphed to horror. This was the moment he found out that everything he knew was changed forever. He looked at the planet that had been his home. It was transforming before his eyes. Angry yellow and black clouds enveloped the atmosphere, encasing the globe.

After a time, he remembered his men. "Gentlemen," he spoke hoarsely with emotion into his Prolix link, "there has been an attack on Perdicion." The angry yellow image appeared before their eyes, as Xoxon followed Solus' thoughts. "You don't recognize this planet. It's Perdicion . . . now."

Solus listened to their collective gasps as the horror now spread within them. "Our homes, our families, the Supremacy—it's all . . . gone. All we have left now is the planet below us."

CHAPTER 6

CALLING THE ORPHANS HOME

By the Blue Planet's measure, it was now a month since the destruction of Perdicion. So much had changed since then. The nuclear attacks set off massive eruptions all across Perdicion's equator. The simultaneous blowing of hundreds of volcanoes set off a cataclysmic environmental disaster that engulfed the planet in an impenetrable yellow cloud cover, which rapidly filled the entire atmosphere. As volcanoes continued to erupt, the combined force of the explosions acted like gigantic thruster engines that, after a time, caused the planet's rotation to slow down. When the volcanic fury aroused by the attack finally slowed down, the planet was spinning at an extremely slow rate in the opposite direction—retrograde to the rest of the solar system. Perdicion now rotated even slower than the time it took to orbit the sun. It now saw days that lasted longer than its years.

This meant nothing in a practical sense, because no one was left alive to experience it. And if there was a close proximity to hell in this universe, Perdicion was now that place. When all was said and done, all life on the surface had been absorbed back into the planet, and all evidence that it had ever even existed was completely wiped away by a new and extremely corrosive atmosphere.

The planet's climate was now characterized by an overrun greenhouse effect in which heat from the sun was trapped within the atmosphere. The oceans all boiled away, and the landscape was blasted relentlessly and remorselessly.

The one and only blue planet left was Parthénos. She alone was the one world of life left in the solar system. Perdicion's surviving orphans now raced to her for their only chance at life. The Supremacy was gone and only remnants of the fleet remained. Out of hundreds of ships, only nine had survived the conflict. Distress calls rang out from the dead worlds: scattered children calling out in search of their fellow survivors. Two ships near Perdicion, an attack vessel and a support ship, had found each other and called out to Parthénos for any signs of life. To their profound relief, Solus responded to their calls, and immediately summoned them to their new home. They were now on their way.

Back in the Red Planet sector during the battle, five Supremacy attack ships gave chase to the escaping Ishtarians. They had been out of range of the battleships' and cruisers' explosions, but had lost their quarry during the Prolix attack. The four remaining ships of Lieutenant Pekark's Epsilon squadron—one had self-destructed—had contacted Solus and were now speeding towards the Blue Planet and on the lookout for the enemy.

As before the disaster, *Shadow* and *Orion* lay side by side in the moon's shadow, waiting to intercept approaching Ishtarian ships.

Through Xoxon, Solus gained a complete assessment of the tactical situation within the inner solar system. Using *Guru's*

Prolix node, which had managed to capture the last transmissions from the home world and the Supremacy fleet, he replayed to Solus the destruction of the fleet and space stations in both combat theaters, the attack by the battleships that had destroyed Perdicion, and their own pitiful ends. And Solus witnessed the final heroic minutes of Captain Fame's life, and how he had managed to destroy *Vengeance*, thereby taking out the source of the Prolix attack.

Solus now knew that six enemy ships had survived, and they were all converging on the Blue Planet. The Ishtarian ships were in two clusters—the group of three, who were reported to be coming in just prior to the Prolix attack, and the three that had escaped from the Red Planet, which were weeks away or more.

Though on continued alert, Solus' small squadron held a brief memorial service for its lost members. Ham's was the only body that they could recover of the several who had died; thus, his was the only one ceremoniously committed to outer space.

Watching the remains shoot away into the blackness of space, each squadron member wept at the loss of life. One body they could get a grip on, but the loss of an entire planet was quite beyond their emotional grasp.

As the days wore on from the event, Solus was in a state of dissociation. When he spoke and moved, it was in a mechanical way, with a voice seemingly outside himself and a body in remote control. His officers and men were all just as deeply distressed.

Otherwise, his duties as squadron commander kept him busy and distracted him from his mourning. Luckily, the supply situation was not critical at the moment. Solus' two attack ships were now fully equipped with enough weapons to take on the remaining enemy vessels. Similarly, each of his ships' power plants, with redundant fission and fusion components, were designed to use their fuel supply at extremely slow rates. This meant that each ship had many years of fuel left.

He also busied himself with battle tactics. He ordered *Guru* to land on the planet near the planetary Prolix node. This accomplished three things. First, this move placed Rodd, the squadron's Prolix network expert, at the node site. Second, Solus wanted to protect his only support ship, and the planet's surface was the safest place for *Guru*. Third, he wanted to establish a base of operations on the planet, where any ship maintenance issues could be addressed in relative safety.

And, of course, his men could not remain in space indefinitely. They would soon need a break.

When his duties were not otherwise consuming his attention, Solus' thoughts nearly always returned to Myra, and he looked for her whenever possible. He spent lots of time remotely reviewing the area where he had last seen her. Frustratingly, he had found only one trace of her so far. His sensors picked up the rifle that he had thrown to her; it was stashed safely in the hollow of an old tree. While he wished she had kept it for her protection, he was not surprised that she had hidden the gun. Yet this also gave him hope that she was still alive and well, that she was able to hide the gun, and in a place where she could retrieve it should she need it again.

But he could not search for her continuously; his duties as commander kept calling him back to activities in space. As the highest-ranking Supremacy official left alive, he was now the last bastion that stood in the way of the advancing Ishtarians. They were not only his squadron's enemies, but also a direct threat to the people of the Blue Planet. They were murderers who had used terrorism and the slaughter of billions to achieve their goals.

Whatever his loyalties had been before, Solus now knew

that his cause was just. He would protect this world from the Ishtarians' evil. He would oppose them even to death, if necessary. He saw that the stage was set and the pattern was clear—the killing would continue until they were all dead.

Solus stared grimly into the darkness through the canopy of his command module. As was his habit, he sought comfort by gazing out across the blackness at the glow of light reflecting off the Blue Planet, now tiny in the background of space. He meditated on its beauty until a thought struck him in his heart: *Do you really believe that that wondrous planet there formed from nothingness? How hopeless life would be if that were so.* It occurred to him—what else could it be but the work of a Creator? This thought unaccountably gave him comfort. The very idea took away the loneliness.

All of a sudden Solus felt the need to speak to him. "Maker of all things," he said to his heart, "please guide me. What am I to do?"

He looked at the planet, not expecting a reply, but very much hoping for one. But A moment later, to his immense astonishment, something happened that blurred his view of the planet. A great haze filled his field of vision. Then it transformed into a shimmering blue glow.

He felt himself going into a state of . . . there was no other word to describe it . . . ecstasy. Was he going mad?

"Xoxon, what am I seeing?" Xoxon did not reply.

A gloriously beautiful woman appeared before him. He had never seen anything so beautiful. She seemed to Solus to be the very embodiment of a new, perfected woman. Her head was covered in a blue veil. This and her cloak were adorned with stars. She was surrounded in light. Her smile seemed to penetrate his very being.

"Repent of your ways and permit my son's spirit to dwell

within you," the heavenly lady spoke to him in the loveliest, most melodious voice he had ever heard.

Not completely understanding, he wanted this nevertheless. "Yes, I will it," he replied, knowing somehow that his response was heard.

"Ego Fílius et Spíritus Sanctus," she announced. A drip of condensation, water from the canopy above him, splashed onto his forehead. A change came over him. He felt heat from within his heart—a burning, as if his insides would burst. The power of it took hold of his innards, yet he felt no pain.

"I am now your adoptive mother. It is your charge to protect this world from the orphans of Perdicion. But let them come. My son wills that they live."

Solus was too dazzled to reply.

"Know my son. Follow him." The woman smiled again and was gone. The haze began to dissipate. The Blue Planet returned to its normal shape and color. But he was changed. He was at peace, and he knew his purpose.

So far, the enemy ships had approached in complete silence. But now, a transmission crackled across the abyss. Fleek picked it up and piped it into both attack ships' internal communication systems.

"To any ship in the vicinity: this is the transport ship *Vestige*. We are refugees from the Red Colonies. Our intentions are peaceful. Please come in." The message repeated.

ONBOARD THE ISHTARIAN TRANSPORT SHIP VESTIGE
ON THE OUTER EDGE OF THE BLUE ZONE

Vestige and her two escorts had entered the outer reaches of the Blue Zone, the large zone of space surrounding the Blue

Planet, about a week ago, but had greatly reduced their speed, not wishing to enter orbit before determining if there were any Supremacy forces left intact in the area. The ship's scanners had spotted movement about a week ago, but all contact had gone quiet. It was now eerily silent, and they began to have doubts about the initial scans. Did they simply detect normal activity in space—a comet, meteors, or possibly an old satellite? Or was it Supremacy attack ships?

On the bridge of the *Vestige*, Captain Jimbal continued to replay his recorded transmission. His message repeated every few moments, and would do so until a reply was made. He was not as alone as he had been for most of the journey, having revived his passengers upon arrival in the Blue Zone. They were all greatly astonished at the news of the destruction of Perdicion and the Supremacy fleet. There was a sense of vindication in having left the Red Colonies when they did.

To give the displaced Red Colonies' council members some small credit, there was also a general feeling of guilt and sorrow over the loss of the Red Colonies and Perdicion. Gapp and Blog had exceeded their orders, it was generally agreed. Yes, it was fortunate that the Supremacy was now gone, but no one had intended for Perdicion to be destroyed, the council agreed.

They likewise concurred that the next step was to land the ship and begin again in the new world, but there was much debate about where that would take place.

"Captain Jimbal," Mr. Zortech, the council's secretary, called out on the bridge's com system. "The council would like an update on our progress. Please report."

Jimbal had become extremely tired of these continuous requests for reports. He wished they would stop their nearly endless sessions and go back to their bedchambers. But again, he swallowed his irritation and replied, "I have been announcing our presence and intention to enter orbit. So far, there has been no response."

"So, what do you think?" the secretary responded. "Are they waiting for us? When are we going to approach the planet?"

"I intend to make our approach within the hour."

"And what about our escorts?"

"They will be covering us in stealth mode."

"So we are the bait? Is that wise?"

Jimbal overheard mumbling in the background. "Gentlemen, we have two attack vessels at our disposal, including anti-spear technology," he replied. "They will protect us if we are attacked."

"But why not send in one of them to draw out the enemy?"

"Then we will be down one ship," Jimbal said. "The Supremacy forces would likely attack it—destroying or boarding it."

"If you'll forgive me," the secretary retorted, "better them than this transport ship!"

"In that case, do you think they will stop at destroying one ship?" Jimbal asked.

"Well, perhaps our ship will destroy their ship!"

"Unlikely," Jimbal replied. "Whatever is left of the Supremacy fleet is here. We cannot take them for granted."

"And your plan to stop them?"

"Mr. Zortech," Jimbal replied, his patience getting strained. "As I explained twice previously, we are going to keep the attack ships hidden for now. We need that element of surprise. Please give this a chance."

"Very well. But we will not wait for much longer," the secretary replied. "We are eager to set up our new world order!"

Jimbal continued the broadcast. "To any ship in the vicinity—this is the transport ship *Vestige*. We are refugees from the Red Colonies. Our intentions are peaceful. Please come in."

The message repeated.

ONBOARD THE SUPREMACY ATTACK SHIP SHADOW
NEAR THE BLUE PLANET'S MOON

"Refugees? They have their nerve!" Grand called out bitterly through the Prolix link.

"Should we respond, sir?" Bas asked.

"Not just yet. I don't want to give away our position," Solus said. Solus' scanner now showed only the transport ship—the two attack ships had dropped off the scanners, evidently now in stealth mode. He quickly surmised that they had moved off and were using the transport ship as bait, hoping to lure in an unsuspecting enemy.

But Solus was too experienced to fall for nonsense like that. Especially when they had advantages on the technical front over their opponents. On that, Xoxon had identified a weakness they could exploit over the older-generation attack ships the Ishtarians operated. "Xoxon, attempt to establish a Prolix connection with those attack ships," Solus ordered. "I want to know exactly where they are."

"Scanning . . ." Xoxon replied. "I'm attempting to access through their encryption. This will take some time. Unfortunately, we do not have an entire countermeasures team like the fleet had."

"I only want a way to locate them," Solus replied.

"Perhaps I can pinpoint their location by pinging their access junctures."

"That sounds promising," he said to Xoxon. "Grand, maintain your position," he ordered *Orion*.

After a few moments, Xoxon reported back. "I'm getting readings back. With undetectable passive scans, we're getting brief glimpses of the ships as they move. This provides us a glimpse of their positions."

"That's good enough. We can extrapolate their general locations," Solus replied. "Are you getting those tracking readings, Grand?" he asked through Prolix link.

"Yes, sir," Grand replied. "I'm picking up two ships. Well done. The ship escorting on the starboard side is designated target *alpha*. The port one, target *beta*. I'm moving out—I'll get into weapons-lock range behind the *alpha* ship."

"Once you're in position, stay with him, but do not attack unless you get my signal," Solus ordered. "I'll be speaking to you through the Prolix link from now on."

"Yes, sir," Grand said, then continued. "Look, sir, you're in command and I will obey your orders, but I don't understand this. We could use those scans readings to lock on our spears from right here. Why can't we be done with it?"

"Grand," Solus replied shortly, then paused. He needed to explain this out loud, even for himself. "Patch me in to the entire squadron."

"Connecting . . ." Xoxon replied.

"Gentlemen, we are about to engage our enemy again. We will do this because, unlike our home world and everything else we knew, our duty remains. We are all still in the throes of shock and anger, and we will be so for some time to come. Our home world is gone. Billions of people lost their lives in a little over a day, and we have only had time to bury one of our own dead. We cannot even begin to memorialize an entire planet. That will take decades, if not centuries."

He paused, then continued. "But because we are the last guard of a great people and planet, our work is not yet over. We were left alive. Our job is to protect the planet below us, and we will do so. But we will do so for duty, not vengeance's sake.

We will not kill unnecessarily. We will attempt to take the ships without destroying them. Xoxon, stop transmission."

"But, sir!" Grand replied to Solus, back on their audio one-on-one connection. "These people are responsible for the murdering of their own people—"

"We do not know that to be true."

"—and the destruction of Perdicion!"

Solus looked across the blackness to catch a glimpse of Grand in his ship's command module. He could just make out his profile. "Look, I'm quite aware of who these people are, but I am willing to give them a chance to stop the killing. I'm willing to call a truce, if they'll let me."

"What if they don't want to play?"

"One step at a time," Solus replied. "The first step is to start from a strong bargaining position."

"Very well," Grand said resignedly, as *Orion* slipped silently and invisibly off into the night of space.

At that, Solus spoke to his own crew. "Bas, move us in front of their flight path. Chamers, prepare to launch the decoy drone," he commanded. This was a little toy, quite new to their arsenal, and their current situation was a wonderful opportunity in which to try it out.

Bas steered *Shadow* imperceptibly out from the moon's shadow.

"Decoy drone is ready to launch," Chamers reported.

The Prolixes had returned to each of the squadron's members, as Xoxon had come back to Solus, and once again helped them to function in the cockpit. For Bas, his Prolix helped him to push aside a near-debilitating sorrow at the loss of his family.

A horrible vision of their deaths continuously haunted him. He kept picturing the sickening yellow clouds surrounding his wife and kids, enveloping them, strangling them, and muffling their screams. Deep pangs of sorrow plagued him as the vision kept replaying in his mind, but now his Prolix and his piloting duties kept him distracted.

"Launch, and move us away from here," Solus ordered.

"Launching . . ." Chamers replied.

A small, black cylindrical object shot out from the rear of the ship and immediately disappeared into space. *Shadow* quickly arched to port and away from the deployment zone to avoid potential enemy fire directed at the motion detected from the launching. The enemy ships, however, did not appear to notice.

Now, as far as the enemy would think, the drone was *Shadow*. All transmissions would emanate from it, and it would create convenient distractions at strategic moments.

"Time to make our presence known," Solus spoke his habitual phrase. "Come in, *Vestige*, this is the Supremacy attack ship *Shadow*."

Straight away, the two hostile attack ships changed course and began moving towards *Shadow*'s drone, while the real *Shadow* and *Orion* began to move into flanking positions on either side of the approaching ships.

"This is the transport *Vestige*. With whom am I speaking?" said the voice that had been transmitting the previous messages.

"I am Commander Solus. I am in command of the Supremacy forces in this sector. And to whom am I speaking?"

"Captain Jimbal. I'm in command of this vessel. We're unarmed and carrying refugees from the Red Planet."

"Please identify yourselves," replied Solus. "Who exactly is aboard your vessel?"

"Commander, please. Surely you're aware of what's happened

in this system quite recently? Does it matter? We're all refugees now." The Ishtarian attack ships continued to converge silently on the drone's position.

"It does matter," Solus replied, trying hard to do what had been asked of him by the Lady, holding back his anger.

"Commander, please!" replied the voice, betraying a little anger himself. "The war is over and both sides lost!" He paused and then spoke again. "We have no wish to continue it."

"Nor do we," Solus replied, knowing that his opponent was speaking to him only to keep him occupied.

At this point, the enemy ships were in position on both sides of the drone, which continued to make cleverly disguised movements that would come across as escaping emissions from a ship in stealth mode. It was meant to be subtle—anything too obvious would arouse suspicions of any competent scanning officer.

"We would like to meet and discuss the terms," Jimbal said.

"Agreed," Solus said.

"Commander," Jimbal replied, changing the tone of his voice. "Our first term is that you surrender your vessel immediately. We've got you surrounded."

"Surrounded?" said Solus, almost relishing his playacting.

"Yes, quite surrounded." As Jimbal spoke, the old attack ships opened the doors to their burst cannons, revealing the soft orange glow of their weapons' buildup. "Make one move, and we'll fire on your position."

"That's not quite what I had in mind, Captain," Solus replied calmly.

"You don't have a choice," came back the reply.

"We always have choices, Captain," Solus said.

"Commander, that's all very nice to say," said his opponent, trying to disguise his puzzlement at Solus' lack of concern.

"But if I may say so, you're hardly in a position to propose anything. We could simply blast you out of our way, right now."

"Not doing so does you credit," replied Solus evenly, "although I suspect you would much prefer to take my ship than destroy it, technology being at a premium these days."

"Look, this is starting to get tiresome," replied Jimbal. "We will fire on you if you do not surrender immediately."

"But you've not heard my terms," replied Solus. "You will surrender immediately to me. Your two attack ships are also surrounded—by my squadron."

"You're bluffing."

Solus made his dramatic response. "Switch to attack mode," he ordered to Bas and Grand.

With that, the Supremacy attack ships transformed and emerged from the darkness of space, their spread wings bristling with armed spears and their orange burst weapons glowing, ready to spit out death from flaming nostrils.

"Stand down, or we will destroy you."

ON THE SURFACE OF THE BLUE PLANET

The orange sun was low in the sky, already below the treeline. It overlooked a forest at the edge of a crystal lake in the early evening. A young doe appeared out of the long-shadowed shelter of the forest to make her way down to the water's edge. As instructed by an instinct that had dictated her species' behavior for thousands of years, the doe flipped her ears and glanced warily about in order to get up a sufficient comfort level to allow herself to take a drink. She noted that she had at least two escape routes, and in the event of a surprise, she had a short distance between the dark forest and her. With these conclusions to satisfy her instinct, the deer's anxiety started to wane and she decided to take a chance and lower her head.

As she began at last to drink, there was a snap of a branch. A long wooden spear sailed out of the murky forest. Before the doe could react, the spear struck and plunged into her left side. Tearing into her lung, the blow brought her down immediately.

A dark, barefaced man clad in animal skins emerged from his hiding place, carrying the sling he had just used to launch the spear. His similarly clad oldest son joined him at his side.

This was a gratifying kill for the man. He had been a master of his weapon for some time, but this was one of his best throws ever. He would be back to his village with food faster than ever before, and feed his family and many more. The man and his son prepared to sling up the carcass by its legs onto a large cut branch that they would use to carry the deer back to their village. They were about to lift up the carcass when they heard the sound of a blowing wind all around them.

It grew louder, yet they felt nothing on their faces. The son, seeing something approaching from above, pointed up into the sky. The man looked to where his son was pointing and saw a large black object approaching. To the man, it looked like a gigantic arrowhead, and it was growing ever larger as it approached. The wind noise intensified as the object drew nearer.

Fear overcame curiosity, and they abandoned their kill, running back into the darkness of the woods. From their hiding place, they watched as the giant arrowhead continued its descent. Tiny legs appeared and extended beneath the object as it landed softly near the edge of the lake, about a spear's throw away from the man and his son. They watched in awe as an opening appeared underneath the arrowhead and two bright, shining men stepped out. Surely these were beings from the spirit world.

* * *

After exiting from the *Guru*'s bottom hatch, Rodd and Compass walked off along the shore of the lake. Their readings indicated that the Prolix node was located beneath the surface of the planet, somewhere in the vicinity. "Sir, there are two native people in the woods up ahead watching our progress," Compass reported.

"Yes, I see them. I suppose we look pretty strange to them," Rodd replied.

"One appears to be armed with wooden spears and some sort of launch sling."

"Ah, I can see that one of them is quite the marksman. We must have interrupted a hunting party. There ahead lies the result of their efforts," Rodd said as he pointed out the deer carcass as they approached it.

"I think I know which one," said Compass. "He's the one reloading the sling right now as we approach. Should we fire a couple of warning shots?"

"No . . . no," Rodd said. "Our battle gear can withstand an attack. Let's see what happens."

After the events from the past few weeks, Rodd was weary of hostilities. The two Perdicians approached the deer carcass and paused over it. Compass picked up the spear lying next to it and looked it over admiringly.

"Amazing—this primitive weapon is all that they have to catch their food. And to be able to throw it with precision and at such a distance is incredible," Rodd stated.

"This guy has real skill. We don't have anything like that, just a bunch of technology that tells us what to do half the time. Where's the skill in that?" Compass observed.

"Without our tech, we'd be pretty helpless," Rodd agreed.

"Sir, the hunter's making a move behind us," Compass interrupted. "I don't think he likes us disturbing his kill."

"Hold on, let him make his move," Rodd said quickly. "Our Prolixes will help us get out of the way."

"But, sir!"

"No, I don't want to hurt them," Rodd said. "There're only two—they can't harm us."

The man emerged from the tree line and launched his spear. It came soaring towards the Perdicians, who remained still, their Prolixes monitoring the spear's trajectory. It would not hit either of them. The spear shot between them and stuck into the deer carcass. Another amazing shot.

"Wow," Compass remarked. "That was good."

They turned and looked at the man, who was beckoning for his son to join him. The son came cautiously out of the forest and stood next to his father. Compass looked at Rodd for direction.

"Sir, what should we do?"

"Show him what you can do," Rodd replied. "Pick up the spear and throw it at something. Your Prolix will help you."

"What'll I throw it at?"

"Try that tree over there," Rodd said, pointing at a large tree near the two native men.

"Okay . . ." Compass said doubtfully as he pulled the spear out of the deer and took aim at the tree. He felt his Prolix take control of his muscles; he felt his eyes grow sharp as he focused in on the tree to the very spot that he wanted the spear tip to hit. It was a small hole where a branch had grown but had fallen off. He launched the spear with a wave of adrenaline. The spear soared as if thrown with the expertise of the native man and went into the hole, exactly dead center.

Compass tried valiantly to restrain a grin of satisfaction. The native man and his son looked at the spear and back at the Perdicians. The man made a motion with his hands, which Rodd imitated.

"I'd really like to continue this," Rodd said, "but we've got to go find that Prolix node. Let's get moving."

As the two Perdicians moved on down the lake's shore-line, the native man and his son continued their awe-filled observations.

"Sir, do you think the natives will try to attack our ship?" Compass asked as they walked.

"I doubt it. Besides, they wouldn't be able to do any harm, anyway."

"Sir, my Prolix is showing me readings of the vicinity," Compass reported as they approached a collection of rocky hills.

"Looks like it's a large Supremacy installation," Rodd replied as they stepped closer. "It was cloaked from our scans from space." He reviewed his Prolix's readings. "According to my scans, these hills," he explained, pointing at the bare stone wall blocking their way, "encircle a little valley inside there. Inside there's a large entrance to a system of caves beneath it. On the topside, near this entrance, there's a landing pad and bays for parking ships."

"I am showing another side opening to the cave to our right," Compass reported.

"You're right," Rodd replied. "I think we can get access via that entrance." They moved along the side of the hill until they came to a small mouth of the concealed and enormous cave system. Surrounded by foliage, the black hole could be seen below them in an outcropping of rocks from the side of the hill. A cool breeze coming out from the opening blew continuously in their faces.

The two men climbed down the hole and entered the black recesses of the cave. The way forked in two directions, and their Prolixes directed them down one that appeared to end with a large rock wall blocking their way. Their Prolixes insisted this was actually a doorway in disguise. After Rodd followed instructions by his Prolix to touch the door, the locking mechanism was deactivated and the rock-like door creaked open, revealing a dark, narrow corridor.

As they walked along it, the walls grew smoother as if they had been carved out by a powerful water cannon, which was likely exactly what was used to cut away extra rock in the path, Rodd surmised. They soon discovered a vast complex with a large Prolix network node in the heart of it.

Rodd ordered Compass to explore the facility, while he visited the complex's control center. Upon reaching this area, Rodd's Prolix interfaced with the mainframe immediately, but he lacked the security access to make changes to the configuration and start the network broadcasting. "I suppose we must get Commander Solus to come down personally to get that done," Rodd remarked.

"I'm afraid that won't do it," Rodd's Prolix reported. "The system will not confirm Commander Solus' status as the commander-in-chief."

"And why is that?" Rodd replied irritably. "Who else could be higher in rank?"

"The system keeps insisting that there is another higher authority, but it will not explain further. It says that any further information on that is restricted."

The commander did not have the time to deal with this, Rodd thought. Yet, unless they could establish Solus' credentials to the computer, they could not get through its security protocols, and they would have to hack into it somehow. He needed to contact Solus and explain the situation, but now was not the time. He knew through his Prolix that the squadron had been engaging the enemy. "Compass, let's get back to the ship," Rodd called out. "We can't do anything else here."

"Sir, I found some stores down below!" Compass reported via Prolix link. "There are food stores down here. Tons of it. Looks like we won't need the native food for quite some time, after all!"

"That's a relief," Rodd said as Compass displayed his surroundings via the Prolix. Rodd saw vast, environment-controlled storerooms. They would be able to re-supply the ships, or even distribute it to any colonies established on the planet.

"It's all in stasis. There's fresh Perdician meat, vegetables, fruit, even snacks and fully cooked meals," Compass reported. "I didn't think I'd ever see some of this stuff again!"

Rodd went down and joined Compass a few minutes later. "Even better," Rodd noted as he explored, "there are seeds and planting supplies over here. I guess there were plans to cultivate the land."

"That's a surprise," Compass remarked. "I thought it was against the environmental laws to interfere with this world."

"The laws don't always apply to everyone."

There were more storage rooms further into the cave. The Perdicians opened another compartment.

"My lord," exclaimed Compass, "I guess we don't have to worry about running out of weapons."

"No," agreed Rodd, looking in awe at the vast armory. There were countless rows of handheld infantry weaponry and pulse-rifle power packs, as well as small artillery weapons, and even unassembled aerial assault vehicles.

"Were they expecting a war here?" asked Compass.

"Just some more interference with the natural processes of the planet," Rodd commented.

ONBOARD THE SUPREMACY SUPPORT SHIP GURU *ON THE SURFACE OF THE BLUE PLANET*

While Rodd and Compass were out exploring the cave, Dr. Nevek sat at his desk in the medical bay drinking a cup of coffee. Nevek remained aboard the *Guru* to attend to the wounded upgrades, which consisted of his own incapacitated med tech, Fogger, and Rachet and Pod, who were transferred to his care when *Shadow* and *Orion* docked with the *Guru* for resupplying. The men were healing quite nicely, but they were lucky to be alive. Rachet had blast wounds to his upper torso, while Podd had the more traditional black-and-blue marks from being beaten in a physical struggle with his officer. Fogger was suffering from a head wound, administered to him by Nevek himself.

Nevek turned his gaze from his patients to the scenery outside his viewing portal. He was not unmoved by the forest scene, and his thoughts returned to his home world, as they had done so constantly ever since the catastrophe. Either in comparison or contrast, almost everything reminded him of Perdicion. As he looked through the window admiringly at the multitude of green leaves, it occurred to him that trees were now unique to this planet. There used to be trees on Perdicion, but not now.

Suddenly uncomfortable with the outside view, he looked back around the medical bay. Here was one of the only fully-equipped, advanced medical facilities left in the entire solar system. And he was the only doctor left. What would they do if he died?

Well, actually, they didn't even need a doctor now, because the new upgrade Prolix could help them. Nevek looked again at the sleeping men. He could not take much of the credit for their recovery process. Their updated Prolixes were doing most of the work. The upgrade had incredible advances and a horde of new benefits for the host person. One important one, the doctor noted, was that it exploited the body's abilities to self-heal. As such, the Prolix was now able to help the host's brain in fighting off bodily injuries and infections.

The doctor sipped his coffee again. It was good southern bean coffee from what used to be Ouda Regio on Perdicion. He wondered if they could plant it here in this world, or if there was an equivalent. More good fortune they had the Prolix, he thought. Without it, they would be left completely to their own devices in this wilderness.

As it was, their shipboard food supplies would be exhausted within six months. After that, they would need to grow, or catch and kill their own food. He hadn't the faintest idea how to farm, other than the basics one was taught as a child. You got seeds, you tilled the soil, you planted the seeds, watered them and watched them grow. He was no less a novice at hunting; he had never personally killed an animal for its meat—or for any other reason, for that matter.

The long and short of it: to survive, they would all need to learn the basic skills and knowledge to live in this primitive world.

That was the next big step when Solus returned victorious from the battle (and Nevek had no doubt as to who would win). The remaining ships would be landed somewhere on the planet and turned into hotels. After all, they would be far more comfortable than a cave!

To think that he used to complain about the lack of comforts available aboard the *Guru*, which was, he realized, highly comfortable compared to the world outside it. His own cramped little sleeping cabin was now a haven. It was out of the elements, clean, warm and dry.

But Nevek could foresee problems ahead. They couldn't just hide in their ships for the rest of their lives. The men would get antsy. Perhaps they would mingle with the primitives like the Harmonians wanted to do. Or, would they use their power, their technology to take over this world? Transform it, develop it, and spread the Prolix. Make another Perdicion. The Prolix could make that happen. They would not have food-processing plants for quite some time, but the network could give them the instructions needed to survive and even thrive in this world. The technology would save them-and without someone controlling their lives, for once.

Nevek, by force of habit, glanced around the deck with a stab of anxiety, worrying that someone could hear his thoughts. But then he remembered—no one was listening now; his Prolix had no one to report to. He could even speak his thoughts for the first time. There was no Supremacy authority to come after him. It was just Solus now.

So far, Nevek considered, Solus was handling his responsibilities as well as could be expected. His whole career had prepared him for command. But what about later, when the battle was won? The old power structure, like it or not, kept them all firmly in line. Who was their guide now? What were the rules?

Moreover, who controlled the Prolix? Whoever had control of the Prolix controlled the people from Supremacy. Nevek wondered how Solus, their new world leader, would handle these questions.

With these thoughts in mind, Nevek felt the need to confer with his old friend. "Can I connect with Solus, or is he still busy dealing with those Ishtarian ships?" he asked his Prolix.

After a moment the Prolix replied, "I'm instructed by Xoxon that he is engaged at the moment. Xoxon will inform him later."

"I figured as much," Nevek replied. "Tell Xoxon not to bother. It is not urgent."

"Certainly."

No, indeed it was not urgent, for the moment. But in the end, they needed to get a handle on the Prolix network and let the men be men. Otherwise, they would all be less free than the poor savages living out there in the woods.

IN SPACE WHERE THE BLUE SQUADRON HAS INTERCEPTED THE VESTIGE AND HER ESCORTS

The space battle had ended without bloodshed, but Solus needed to secure the enemy attack vessels for negotiations to proceed in a peaceful fashion. Keeping cover on them with *Shadow*'s weapons, Grand positioned *Orion* above the closest ship and extended the umbilical tube to its top hatch.

"At the first sign of a weapon even being aimed at my man, I will destroy the other ship," Solus warned his quarry.

Using the suction created by the umbilical tube, Rowling shot into the midst of the enemy, and quickly took control of the ship with Grand's remote assistance. "Okay now, Rowling, secure the crew in the brig. Make sure they have no weapons in there. That's good." Using a Prolix link, Grand thus directed the progress through Rowling's own eyes, giving orders to him at each stage of the taking of the ship.

When Rowling entered the cockpit, his Prolix was able to interface with the ship's controls, and he had, at once, complete control of the ship. Now Solus' squadron was up another ship. Thump shot into the second attack ship in a similar fashion and only after some difficulty with the prisoners (one of whom had tried to conceal a small weapon in the brig), secured the ship and took control of it.

Now with an escort of four attack ships, the negotiations could begin in earnest with the leadership on the transport ship.

"Captain Jimbal, I am now prepared to meet with you and your passengers."

"Are you coming aboard?"

"No," Solus replied. "My Prolix will send a transmission. Can you display it on a video monitor that will accommodate?"

"Yes, that can be arranged."

"Excellent—I'll allow you to get yourself organized. I'll contact you in ten minutes."

The ruling council of the former Red Colonies convened in the captain's conference cabin of the *Vestige*. It was a dome-shaped room, positioned near the top of the ship, with many circular window portals showing the blackness of space outside. On one side, the top edge of the Blue Planet could be seen. A large round table took up most of the room, and the council sat around it. They were not passive talkers: most gesticulated as they made their feelings known.

"This situation is intolerable! To be stymied by some insignificant squadron commander!" cried Habib, the old contrarian of the bunch. "Why didn't he die with the rest of them?"

"Listen, after what happened to Perdicion, we're lucky he didn't blast us into atoms," Jimbal replied.

"And no help from you, I might add," Habib charged. "They had us easily enough, didn't they—and we outnumbered them when it all started!"

"That's enough of that!" Jimbal retorted. "That only goes to show that they had the technological advantage over us. They always had it."

"Well, at least we know he's not ruthless," commented another. "He could very well have destroyed us or launched the ships' crews into space. That tells us something."

"Gentlemen," Solus spoke as his image appeared in the air at the center of the table, interrupting their deliberations. "Let's begin by identifying ourselves. I'll start."

The Ishtarians murmured amongst themselves.

"My men and I are the last remnants of the Supremacy fleet. As the commanding officer, I am the one, therefore, who will decide your fates." Solus paused, then continued. "Let's confirm who each of you are. My intelligence resources indicate that you are the Ishtarian leadership from the Red Colonies. Do you deny this?"

There was no response, but there were a lot of fearful glances going around the table.

"Let's move on, then. Did you have anything to do with the destruction of Perdicion?" Solus continued. In spite of himself, anger was rising within him, trying to take control. He was glad that his own man was aboard that ship. He was less tempted to destroy it.

"Sir," Jimbal spoke up, after no one else did. "We were nowhere near Perdicion. We have been in space for months coming from the Red Planet—"

"That proves nothing. The attack plan had to have been in progress long before that. I have a complete picture of the events leading up to the planet's destruction. An Ishtarian-controlled ship launched a cyber-attack on the Prolix network and thereby ordered the launching of nuclear weapons on the planet surface and from orbiting ships."

"That was not part of the plans!" Habib cried out. "Only military targets and Prolix nodes were to be destroyed!"

They all glared at the old man in dismay.

"Plans? Whose plans?" Solus inquired.

This was met with silence. Then it hit Solus: these Ishtarians ships had arrived here at this time as part of the plan.

They all looked at each other. It was becoming terribly uncomfortable. And obvious.

"Yes," Jimbal said resignedly. The others all hissed in dismay.

"Listen," Jimbal continued, speaking to the others in the room, but also for Solus' benefit. "He could have blasted us to kingdom come already. He didn't." Jimbal continued speaking to Solus. "This is the council. But as the old man just said, the plan was only to destroy military targets—not the entire planet. Something went terribly wrong!"

"That's an understatement."

"Sir, Perdicion was our home world too. Nobody wanted what happened there."

"But it did happen."

"Yes, and the Red Colonies and all the people there were slaughtered—by the Supremacy fleet. And that happened *before* Perdicion was destroyed."

"And the Ishtarians were marooned there—against our wills!" Habib hissed.

"That's enough," Solus commanded. "I do not intend to re-litigate the entire conflict, here and now. Up to a month ago, my standing orders were to uphold the environmental laws and keep your kind from polluting the Blue Planet." In response to this, the Ishtarian Council murmured angrily amongst themselves. "However, things have changed," he con tinued.

"Commander . . ."

"Please, let me speak my piece. To start, I have no desire to see any more souls from our planet die, regardless of who they are. As far as I am concerned, there has been quite enough death." At this, the council looked at each other with pleased but uncertain astonishment. "As a sign of good faith, therefore, I am willing to let you land on the planet and live there. However, it will be under very controlled circumstances." The council murmured amongst themselves, only more excitedly. "At last" they were going to land on the planet.

"My first condition," Solus continued, "is that I will decide where you will settle. And it will be as far away as possible from the natives."

"Are we to be abandoned on some remote island or desert?" The voices all launched together in protest.

Solus waited patiently until it died down. "You will not be abandoned. For one thing, we have supplies—a great deal of them—to help you get established." Solus had just read Rodd's report on his findings in the Prolix node cave. We will remain in continuous contact to make sure that you are progressing. I make that a promise."

The combined uproar of voices continued. "What about technology?" one asked. "Can we have use of—"

"We will iron out the details on all that later," Solus interrupted. "We have not quite earned each other's trust, so such details are pointless at this time."

There was silence, which came as a welcome surprise to Solus. "I will tell you one thing—we are not going to spread our fighting to this planet," he stated gravely. "The war is over, as far as I am concerned. And if you choose to continue the war with me and my men, it will be ended quickly." The council could see the grim determination in Solus' face. "You have heard my terms. I will give you time to decide how you wish to respond."

Captain Jimbal had one more question—one that he simply could not help but ask. "Commander," he asked, trying to temper his tone accordingly, "I have to ask—why are you doing this? Why are you being so generous with us?"

Solus looked at him and considered this. Could he mention his vision? No, not yet. It would not help things. There was no trust. "That is a good question, but one that I cannot answer completely at this time. However, my offer comes with the realization that we are all orphans now. There has been enough death. We need to overcome it." And with that, the transmission ended and the room darkened.

Now the council was alone. Their faces twisted varyingly with emotion, bafflement, and disappointment. The voices spoke out, interrupting one another.

"We will be isolated. How will we take control of the planet?"

"How is that going to happen, anyway? The Supremacy is not completely gone. We just spoke to him."

"We need to get rid of them."

"Do we have any options?"

"We could attempt to re-take this ship."

"And what would we do then? They have four attack ships. They would destroy us."

"Listen," spoke out Nabib, the council president, for the first time in the session. He had remained silent until now, assessing the situation and their new captor. Not knowing what was in store for the named leader, be it instant death or humiliation, he did not want to be identified as such. He was an eminently practical man.

"Commander Solus wants there to be trust between us," he said, silencing the room. "We will build that bridge with him. We have no choice. We will begin by cooperating with him."

"But what about our plans for this world?" one of them exclaimed angrily. "Are we just going to abandon them?"

"Are we just going to let him spread the Supremacy again—infect this planet too?" spoke out the secretary.

"We can't allow the Prolix to take over this world!" cried another voice, speaking for the group.

"And we will not," Nabib replied, and then stood up. He was taller and thinner than the rest of them. The long black hair on his head nearly touched the ceiling of the chamber. He leaned forward, placing his knuckles on the table for emphasis. He peered into each of his comrades' eyes as he spoke. "Don't forget the rebellion. We took on the Supremacy before and massacred them. And that was a considerably larger force. We will do it again."

He looked around the chamber with grim confidence. "We will do what we have to do. Our cause is just."

CHAPTER 7

PERDICION REBORN

Two connected ships raced in the void between Perdicion and Parthénos. They had joined just before they began their journey together—the attack ship had attached herself to the support ship's upper connection hatch. This marriage made sense, in that they could pool their resources for the journey with little or no loss in efficiency. They flew as one.

The senior officer of the combined vessels was Lieutenant Cain, who was the commander of the attack ship *Dauntless*. He now sat alone in the ships' highest position in his command module. He was reviewing the navigation logs for orbital objects that could come into collision course with them on the journey. Avoiding such bodies necessarily lengthened their journey, so Cain plotted their course with several "near misses" in order to keep as straight a course as possible. He did not want any delays, as the planetary orbital concurrence was rapidly coming to a close.

He watched as they passed one of the plotted objects, a small asteroid. The sun lit one side of the pockmarked, gray rock in the darkness. He enjoyed moments like this because it visually verified the high speed at which they were moving. The rock flew past them and was gone in a matter of seconds. It demonstrated with certainty that they were indeed moving, and at a very fast rate. Still, it would be three more weeks, as measured in Blue Planet time, before they reached their destination.

Cain stopped looking at the blackness outside the ship and rubbed the bandage covering his burnt right ear, an injury he had received in the Prolix hacking attack. He had been shot when his upgrade navigator burst into Cain's cabin, madly firing his sidearm. In spite of the burning pain on the side of his head—and extreme disorientation, for that matter—Cain had managed to knock the gun out of the navigator's hands with a kick. He followed that with a blow to the man's throat, crushing his larynx and killing him.

Cain's injury lingered, along with a constant inner-ear buzzing that his Prolix had, so far, been unsuccessful in stopping. But this was nothing compared to the continual sorrow and pain he felt at the loss of his young wife, who had died in the Perdicion cataclysm. They had been married for only three months when she and the planet died. It felt to him like something inside him had died with them.

He launched her image video before his eyes, as he did a thousand times a day. His favorite picture of her was one taken on their wedding day. She was wearing her wedding dress.

She smiled at him, holding her purple-and-white bouquet in one hand and waving with the other. A playful and vivacious redhead, she was the most beautiful girl he had ever known, and he had won a hard-fought battle against several rivals to obtain her hand in marriage. He had expected, naturally enough, to spend the rest of his life with her and the children they would have together. But then she was gone in a flash with Perdicion. He could not come to terms with this loss—he doubted he ever would. The aching in his ear was almost a comfort, as it took a certain quantity of his pain out from inside him.

"Lieutenant?" piped in Access, the support ship's med tech.

"Yes, Access," Cain responded, turning off the image of his wife.

"Sir, Jokon wants to resume his duties. He says he's fine now and wants to do something."

Jokon was the support ship's inventory tech, another upgrade who had been injured in the attack. He had been shot by his officer, and suffered severe internal injuries and lost part of his arm. Cain had ordered him to remain in the sick bay until he had fully recovered.

"Okay, I concur," Cain replied. "If he wants to work, let him go. Tell him to take it easy. But keep the medical systems on constant monitor for any signs of trouble from his internal injury."

"Yes, sir."

Still a young, inexperienced officer, Cain was being exposed to new and unique command situations during nearly every new hour of this journey. He often felt overwhelmed. But the linking of the ships seemed to lift a rather large weight from Cain's burdened shoulders. The little world that was their ships seemed a bit bigger with their combination. He spent a great deal of time touring and inspecting every part of the two vessels. Just today, he had sat in *Dauntless'* rear gun turret position and inspected all the controls. And In the support ship, *Relic*, he inspected the weapons storage compartments, crawling under racks of spears to get to the room's far end, and even out into the ship's wings where attack ships connected to get their stores re-filled.

Their world was small and cramped in places, but his explorations gave him the constant reassurance that there were, indeed, various open spaces in which to move about. This helped fight off a creeping, breathless anxiety he felt about being in space, which was a first for him. He realized that it stemmed from the fact that, like a safety valve, Perdicion had been there for him in the past. He had always had it in the back of his mind that if an emergency occurred, he could land back home, if absolutely necessary.

But Perdicion was gone. He had witnessed for himself her transformation into an angry, yellow-and-black-clouded hell. He saw via his scanning systems the destruction of the three mighty battleships as they sank into her atmosphere; they were no longer a haven in an emergency. Even the orbiting space station above Ouda Regio was not an option. When he checked its status, he found it remaining in orbit, but lifeless and damaged beyond hope of repair. There was no place to dock or land anywhere on or near Perdicion, and he knew it.

All this built up Cain's fervent desire to get to Parthénos, his ships' only hope for life. The old Perdicion was dead, but Parthénos was the new Perdicion—the new and promised world, the one that would help redeem them all. Remnants of the old world were already there, watching and waiting for their arrival.

He had been in contact with one of them—a Supremacy officer who seemed to represent all that was sane and just in the universe. He had heard little of Commander Solus prior to this event, but had come to know him better in the meantime. His service record, available to Cain via the ship's database, read like an adventure story. A man like this—this archetype—was Cain's inspiration for joining the service in the first place.

Cain's periodic transmissions with Solus had not dimmed Cain's admiration of his fellow officer. Solus kept up his contacts on a regular basis, and was always checking on their status and their well-being. He gave encouragement and support, and offered them hope for better times when they arrived at their new home.

From all this, Cain looked forward to meeting the Commander and coming under his command. They would join forces and set things right. They would work together to avenge the loss of Perdicion and his wife.

ONBOARD THE SUPREMACY SUPPORT SHIP GURU NEAR THE PROLIX CAVE ON THE BLUE PLANET

"Are you boys going back to the cave?"

"Yes, Dr. Nevek," Compass replied as he and Rodd made their way down the passage past the *Guru*'s sick bay.

"Can you check on the coffee stores? I can't believe they would have missed that vital supply."

"Now, Doctor," Rodd replied, "you know we are supposed to be carefully cataloging the stores before we dip into them, especially since we have a colony to support now."

"We can't grab a little coffee?" Nevek queried impatiently.

"You know very well that's not the issue. Commander Solus wants a complete inventory of what we have in the cave before we start using the stores."

"Surely the network has an inventory file . . ."

"Probably, but we do not yet have complete access to the system," Rodd replied. "The commander needs to get down here and establish his authority with the node. It simply will not allow me access until a supreme commander is verified."

"Okay, I must have missed that meeting," Nevek replied. "Well, then Commander Solus needs to get his tail down here."

"Yes, sir," Rodd replied.

"Don't let me keep you."

Rodd and Compass continued on towards the exit hatch.

"I think Dr. Nevek is a bit restless," Compass remarked as they walked down the extended ramp to the outside world. "His patients are all recovered now, and they don't need his attention like they did before."

"You have that exactly right, Compass," Rodd agreed.

They made their way along the lake, as they had done on many such trips since discovering the cave. They had since spied the natives' campsite, which was located on the other side of the lake. The Perdicians' presence at the lake, in fact, appeared to be causing a bit of a disturbance for the locals, Rodd had noticed. They were coming about in groups to view the ship. He wondered if they were planning on attacking or piling up offerings on a makeshift altar.

When Rodd reported these happenings to Solus, the commander ordered him to make preparations to move the ship into the enclosed valley above the Prolix cave, and get it out of sight. It would, of course, help to place the ship closer to the cave for easier cargo loading.

"We'll give the doctor something to do very soon, I'm sure," Rodd said. "For one, we'll be moving the *Guru* this afternoon to get her closer to the cave. That will give him something to observe."

"He won't like that—he tells me he likes his view of the forest from his sick bay."

"There are plenty of trees at the other landing site too."

They made their way back to the side entrance to the cave. Just as they were about to climb down into the hole, Compass stopped in his tracks and peered into the cool, breezy darkness. "Is that an old man in the cave, or am I seeing things?"

"Old man?" replied Rodd languidly. "What are you talking about, anyway?"

"Can't you see him? He's right there in the cave!"

Rodd leaned in to look, squinting to see into the shadows of the cave. Sure enough, there was a man in there, and he was waving at them. His formal centuries-old, antiquated garb was not at all fitting with his surroundings. "Come in, come in, boys!" he said with a welcoming gesture.

Rodd and Compass looked at each other in disbelief. *Was this man from Perdicion?* Rodd thought, but did not speak.

"Yes, yes," he answered., "Of course I'm from Perdicion. I understand you've come to work on the node. I've been monitoring your transmissions."

"Sir, where have you come from?" Rodd asked, still taken aback by the man's mere presence.

"Why, Perdicion," replied the man. "I only just arrived today. It was quite a long journey—lots of time to think about things." His amiable smile faded for a moment as he seemed to ponder something.

"You just arrived? Did you leave before the disaster?"

"Yes, just as it was happening, in fact."

"But that was only a little over a month ago—how did you get here so fast? Only our most advanced engines are capable of that." This was one of many questions crowding Rodd's brain.

"Oh, my little ship is quite fast—it's the latest technology—very experimental, don't you know."

"Well, then, why didn't we pick you up on our scanning systems? When exactly did you arrive?"

"As I said," said the man, now with a trace of impatience, "it's the latest technology—it has next-generation stealth technology."

"I see. Who are you, if I may ask?" Rodd asked. "I mean, what are you doing here—are you in charge of this facility?"

"Well, yes, I suppose I am."

"And you know why we're here—and what I've been ordered to do?"

"Yes, and we will discuss all that quite soon enough," said the man evasively, "but in the meantime, why don't you both come in?" He gestured towards the interior of the cave.

With literally hundreds more questions queuing up in his head, Rodd could think of nothing better to do but acquiesce. They followed the man down into the black recesses of the cave.

ON THE NEW ISHTARIAN COLONY ISLAND IN THE BLUE PLANET'S SOUTH SEAS

It was a surprisingly simple matter to get the colony situated on the large tropical island in the South Seas he had selected for them.

The ease in establishing the colony came largely from the flexible design of the captured transport ship, something that impressed Solus greatly. He learned of the ship's capabilities from Captain Jimbal. *Vestige*'s passenger compartments were actually detachable modules that could be unlocked and separated from the ship without the aid of an external crane. There were a total of eight modules—four on each side of her midsection. Two of the modules were storage compartments, containing the ship's stores and the passenger's extra luggage.

Solus located a large clearing in the jungle for landing the ship and, once on the ground, extended the compartments out onto either side of the ship. Once the compartments were separated from the ship, and the hatches closed upon the now-empty cargo holds, Solus immediately lifted the ship off the ground. This precaution gave the Ishtarians no opportunities for taking the ship back from him.

Once he was in the air again, his final words with the council were made by transmission. "May this be the start of a wonderful new life for your people," he said in a broadcast to all parts of the compartments. "We will be back soon with more supplies. In the meantime, get to know your new home. It is a beautiful one. Solus out."

Even the process of choosing the island was not difficult, Solus noted with satisfaction. He had found the large tropical island in the South Seas—it had plentiful water, fertile ground for food cultivation, native food in the form of fruits and animals, good weather year-round and, most important to Solus, it was isolated. The nearest neighboring island was hundreds of kilosectors away.

Solus was now returning to space aboard *Vestige* to join *Shadow* and re-assume command of his squadron. The transport vessel, now free of its heavy cargo, climbed up with ease from the landing zone. Solus hovered momentarily above the palm trees, which swayed in the winds emanating from the ship's thrusters. Whitecaps in the blue-green ocean could be seen on the horizon in all directions. It reminded Solus of Perdicion's own South Seas, with its thousands of volcanic islands that had dotted the immense ocean.

Vestige left the atmosphere a short time later, on a course to rendezvous with *Shadow*. As the blackness of space filled the ship's viewing screen, Solus was again sorry that Captain Jimbal had chosen to remain behind with the colony. After conversing with him, Solus came to understand that Jimbal had been along for the ride with the council because he had nowhere else to go.

Jimbal made it known that, while he was a loyal Ishtarian and not a fan of the Prolix, he was not a "true believer" in the Ishtarian rebellion. After a time, Solus had learned to appreciate Jimbal's frankness of speech—he did not hold back his opinions, which was a trait that Prolix hosts had to learn to do. It was actually refreshing to experience.

Earlier that day, Solus had appointed Jimbal as liaison to the council. He allowed him to remain on the bridge while they made the journey to the planet and into its atmosphere. As the ship made its initial approach in orbit of the planet, they had time to converse. They swapped stories of their days fighting in the Perdicion space wars—on opposite sides, of course. After Jimbal described a notable escape he had made from a Supremacy patrol in the Red Sector, Solus connected the event with his own experiences. "I remember a time when we were rounding Phobos and a rebel cruiser appeared out of nowhere. She lobbed four spears at us before we knew what happened. As we spent the next several minutes evading and destroying the spears, the cruiser was gone. Was that you?"

"How many ships were in your patrol?" Jimbal inquired.

"Three. Two after that match-up."

"I'm sorry to say, that was me," Jimbal replied. "It's funny how you say we came out of nowhere, because that's how I remember it as well—you came out of nowhere at us! We had no idea you were there until we saw you. Our scanners were blocked by the moon until we rounded it. We saw you only a moment before you saw us. I fired everything we had, and beat it towards the asteroid field."

"Well, that was war. We would have fired first had we seen you first," Solus countered.

"That is magnanimous of you, Commander."

"It's time to forgive and forget."

Jimbal looked over at Solus, who was seated in the ship's pilot station. "You are right, of course," he said. "But I'm not sure we're all willing to do that," Jimbal added regretfully, thinking of the members of the council.

"That's probably true," Solus said, "but I hope most of us will."

"Be watchful, Commander," Jimbal said. He was going to say

more, then stopped. His loyalties were becoming conflicted. He remembered that he was speaking with the former enemy, and he could easily be branded a traitor among his fellow Ishtarians. He still needed to live with them, at least for the time being.

"I will be," Solus replied. "You too," he added.

Deciding to change the direction of the conversation, Jimbal looked around the bridge. "I will miss flying this old bird," he remarked. "I've put in a lot of time in her—even before the rebellion. As I was experienced with her, the council made me her captain for this trip."

"Opportunities come when you least expect it," Solus replied.

"They do, indeed. Besides, I had no other prospects at the time. But speaking of that, what with spaceships—and technology in general—being in such short supply these days, I suspect there won't be many more opportunities for ship captains from now on."

"As a matter of fact, we are short of pilots," Solus said. "We need to support this new colony with supplies, and perhaps other colonies when my men settle down finally."

"I could do that," Jimbal said, perking up. "I'm not quite ready to become a beach bum."

"I'm not altogether opposed to the idea, Jimbal," Solus said. "But I just don't know you well enough yet. I don't know where your sympathies really lie."

"Sympathies?" Jimbal retorted, looking at Solus. "My sympathies are with survival. What are yours?"

Solus looked at Jimbal intently. "Believe it or not, I have been given the charge of protecting the people of this planet, and the orphans of Perdicion."

"By whom, Commander? The Supremacy is gone."

"Well, frankly, I do not know, but I have been contacted by a . . . how shall I say it? A higher power."

"Are you talking about the Creator?" Jimbal asked. "I thought Supremacy people didn't believe in Him."

Solus looked at Jimbal, surprised by this insight. "I wasn't sure before, but I'm a believer now," Solus replied. "More than that, I cannot say. But as to my charge—because I must protect the natives of this planet Parthénos, we cannot mix with them at this time."

"But that's the old Supremacy line!" Jimbal cried. "Frankly, I never understood the quarantine of this planet. What are we protecting these people from—their own ignorance? I mean, would it be so bad to let them know we exist? Even spread our technology amongst them? Wouldn't we be saving lives, even? Do you know what the average life expectancy is here?"

"Would we be helping them?" Solus replied steadily. "The life expectancy is zero on our mother planet right now."

"I suppose. . . ."

"I do not claim to have all the answers," Solus said, "but I want to move slowly with this. In time, we will decide what is best. And in the meantime, we will support your people on the island."

"And you need a loyal freighter pilot."

"Yes."

"Well, I'm your man. I'm good at following orders, and will do only what is asked of me. I do not have any special loyalty to the Ishtarian Council. I wish there was a way I could prove it to you."

"There is a way to do that, but you probably will not like it."

"Accept a Prolix?"

"It would be proof of your loyalty. Take some time and think about it. Our new network will not control people as the old Supremacy network did. It will be different."

"Isn't that what they said in the beginning on Perdicion?"

Solus nodded, unable to provide a better answer. "Okay, I have a secondary proposal for you," Solus said. "I need some intelligence on three incoming Ishtarian ships that escaped the fleet. Can you tell me anything about them?"

"Commander," Jimbal replied, "are you asking me to betray them?"

"Yes, I suppose so. I will not try to color it any differently for you. But I am not out to destroy them, only to contain them— just like I did with your ships."

"I see . . ."

"Even better," Solus continued, "I would like you to contact them. Explain to them the situation. Give them a chance to come in peacefully."

"I need some time to think about this," Jimbal replied.

"I will give you time," Solus replied. "Perhaps we can discuss it again tomorrow."

Just before they parted, Solus gave Jimbal a short-range comm-device in order to make contact with him the next day. After the two men gave their farewells, Jimbal was returned to the passenger compartments just before they were detached.

Solus' thoughts turned from where he had come from to where he was going. As the transport ship closed in on *Shadow*'s current position, Solus first could only make out her running lights at the tips of her wings. As he got closer, Solus could see the outline of her dull black hull, which was lit from the planet's reflecting light.

Being inside *Shadow* for a majority of his association with her, it was still enjoyable for Solus to see her shape from this outside perspective. Her graceful lines always stirred Solus to his innards. He reviewed her pointed nose, her round mid-section, the two engine cowlings projecting out behind her, and finally her long wings now folded behind her, with thrusters and laser cannons mounted at the wingtips.

As he took her all in, Solus pondered the juxtaposition of the beauty of the ship's design with her capacity for destruction as an instrument of war. He looked at her Supremacy markings and wondered if they should be changed. After all, they reflected the old system that he wanted to change. Yet, ironically, his position as commander of the Supremacy forces came from upholding the past system.

Perhaps, he considered, it was best not to alter its symbols at the present time. He had to maintain this authority to move forward with the mission bestowed upon him by the Lady. This was a commission as real to him as the one he had received upon entering the Supremacy officer corps. He believed it in his mind and felt it in his heart.

As he was pondering this, Solus used *Vestige*'s thrusters to position the ship below *Shadow*'s umbilical tube hatch. It was not as easy a matter to link up this vessel with *Shadow* as it was with his other attack ships. "Bas, I'm in position. Please lower the tube and attach."

"Extending," Bas replied. "Welcome home, Commander."

In spite of having to leave that wonderful planet again, he was glad to be getting back to his ship. She had been his home for a long time.

"That stinking bunch didn't give you any trouble?" Bas asked.

Solus didn't like the tone of Bas' voice. It spelled trouble, but he decided not to address it at the moment. "Not at all," he replied simply. Bas' attitude was, Solus knew, due to his continual mourning of the deaths of his family.

Bas could not forgive himself that he survived and they did not. He should have been there; he should have rescued them or died with them. Serving in the space military was always his excuse. That was his profession. They understood that—he always told himself. They missed him, but they understood.

But that was prior to their deaths. This platitude did not help him now. It was not enough to give him peace. His wife and children, Bas realized only now, were more important to him than anything else. He felt their loss profoundly.

Only his old-time religion gave him any comfort. It told him that they were not gone forever, that they were all in a better place, waiting for him to join them. But he had to keep the faith—he had to make it there himself. He could not give in to hate. But it was hard.

"I wouldn't turn my back on them for an instant," Bas muttered, in spite of his attempts at better thoughts.

"We all need time to heal," Solus replied. "Including those people."

Bas saw his commander as an example of how he needed to behave, and he marveled at Solus' generous attitude towards this enemy. He could not understand it completely, but he had too much faith in Solus to question him directly about it.

Solus felt the grappling arms of the umbilical tube attach to Vestige's hull. Then there was a shudder as the bottom of the tube enclosed the upper hatch near Vestige's bridge.

"We have a connection," Bas reported. "Come on aboard, sir."

"I'll be there presently," Solus replied. "Is Fleek ready to come aboard the Vestige?"

"Yes, sir, he's making his way down the e-tube right now."

"Excellent. Then I will meet him here, and we will go over the flight plan." The transport ship would not remain in space for long. Solus had selected Fleek to take interim command of the Vestige. Fleek was an experienced scansman and cross-trained as a helmsman, but this would be his first mission alone. He was to land the ship at the Prolix node and assist Rodd and Compass in making necessary modifications to the cargo containers in the cave for transporting shipments of supplies to the colony.

When not in operation, *Vestige* was to be stationed near the Prolix node cave in the carved-out landing area, which Rodd determined had been used in previous landings to load the supplies into the cave. In the cave, Rodd and Compass had found several hundred large storage modules. With only slight modifications, *Vestige* could then self-load the modules into her cargo holds. Transfer of the modules to *Vestige* would be expedited by cargo-moving equipment that had been left as part of the cave's inventory.

As he waited for Fleek to board the transport, Solus pulled up the navigation system on the ship's main screen and plotted the course back to the node. He would need to go over the ship's controls with Fleek and make sure that he and his Prolix were completely ready to take the ship over.

Xoxon's voice interrupted Solus' musings. "I've been giving the matter of the new Prolix network a lot of thought, and I would like to go over it with you. Can we discuss?" he queried.

"Now is a good time."

"You haven't been talking to me lately. Is everything okay?"

"I'm still not comfortable with this thought-reading ability of yours."

"I'm sorry about that, but I can't really avoid it."

"There's no way to switch that functionality off?"

"Not according to the current configuration."

This struck Solus. "But it's possible that it *could* be switched off?"

"The option can be removed, but the command must come from the central authority."

"But that authority is gone."

"The central authority could be re-established via the node on this planet's surface. The new recognized leader would need to establish authority over the node and give the command."

"Would the node recognize anyone as that authority?"

"No, it would have to be the highest commanding official alive."

"I see. Well, while we're at it, could this authority remove other features, such as the centralized control? And the features that allow for the recording and logging of users' actions and thoughts?"

"The central authority can configure the system in any fashion he desires," Xoxon responded. "To do as you suggest, the Prolix network would need to be configured so that each host would be permitted 'administrator' status for his own Prolix. This would allow the host permission to make decisions for himself, such as accepting updates and permitting outward and inward transmissions and communications."

"Then I must get down there as soon as possible," Solus concluded.

A transmission from the planet's surface interrupted this discussion. It was from Rodd; his face appeared before Solus. "Commander, I'm here at the Planetary Prolix Node Center. Something unexpected has occurred. There's a man here—an old man from Perdicion. He's being evasive in answering my questions, but he claims to have just arrived here, and in fact, he claims to have made it off Perdicion just as the catastrophe was happening there. He—"

Another voice could be heard in the background, as the image of Rodd before Solus peered off to his right. "I suppose I really do need to introduce myself, gentlemen . . . let me switch this thing on . . ." Suddenly, the voice was heard again, but not in the background anymore—it was now heard inside Solus' head, just like the Prolix. "That's better. My name is . . . well, you wouldn't know my name, anyway. Let's just say that I am your Supreme Leader."

A moment of stunned, awkward silence followed this extraordinary statement. "Excuse me?" Solus spoke up at last.

"Yes?"

"Forgive my incredulousness, but just how do you make this claim?"

"Well, I was, and still am for that matter, the Supremacy."

"You—are the Supremacy?"

"Well, yes. I ran the show. I was the top man in the government. I am in control of the Prolix network, as your individual Prolixes will confirm with you."

"The network node just went into broadcast mode," Xoxon reported. "I am interfacing with the network now."

"Does the Prolix node confirm this man as the central authority?"

"The network confirms," Xoxon replied.

The Old Man's face appeared before Solus' eyes in a Prolix link. Solus saw a nondescript, gray-haired little old man. His appearance was very ordinary, with the notable exception that he was wearing an centuries old, out-of-date coat, from the look of it. "You were in command of the Perdician government? But what about the Prime Minister, the Ruling Council, the Parliament? Who—"

"They all reported to me, ultimately," the man stated patiently. "As did the military—the top commanders, that is."

"I see," said Solus, who was still unsure how to act or think about this startling development. Could he simply accept this man as their leader? Certainly he needed more evidence of his claim. As his thoughts whirled in his head, the man spoke again. "Now that we've established who I am, I would like you to report to me immediately. I have some things to go over with you, and I do not wish to do it long distance."

Solus was almost too stunned to reply, but he gathered

himself together. "I will leave immediately." That seemed to be the next step.

With the squadron already dangerously undermanned, Solus decided to keep Fleek aboard *Shadow*. Instead of Fleek, Solus would pilot *Vestige* back to the Prolix node and meet their leader in person. "Bas, switch to stealth mode and continue long-range scanning. We still have enemy ships unaccounted for. If the Ishtarian Council has been in communication with them, they could be attacking at any time."

"Understood, sir."

"Keep me informed if the scanners turn up anything," Solus continued. "Do not initiate an attack, but do not hesitate to defend yourself."

"Yes, sir," Bas replied. ". . . sir?"

"Yes, Bas?"

"You are our commander. I don't care what the Prolix says."

"Thank you, Bas, I understand," Solus replied, knowing what Bas was trying to relay. "We don't know anything about this man, but I am going to find out. If he is the legitimate leader, we will recognize his authority—with or without the Prolix. Goodbye, Bas . . . Solus out."

Solus fired *Vestige*'s main engines again in order to re-enter the atmosphere. As he moved away, he put *Shadow*'s image in the bridge's viewing screen as it slipped from sight. Her lights winked out and she disappeared into the darkness.

Now Solus needed to focus on this new development. "Xoxon, do you have any information on this man at all? What does the network database say about him?"

"That information is restricted."

"Is there anything at all that is not restricted about him?" Solus queried. "How does the system confirm him as the leader?"

"There is nothing—it is all secured, which is not surprising if he is the leader and in control of the Prolix node."

"Can you tell me anything . . . history, rumors, anything?"

"Rumors? The network does not store that kind of information, you know that. If there ever was information about this man, it's been carefully scrubbed."

"This is absurd!" Solus snorted in exasperation. "Is it possible he's an impostor, a con man? How do we know he didn't hack into the network?"

"This is a possibility, so I cannot say with complete authority. Only that the network confirms him as the supreme leader. He certainly has control of the network."

"He could have fooled the network. We can't trust anything—not after Perdicion's destruction."

"I'll see if I can find out anything. I have to do some poking around."

"Very well, work your magic. In the meantime, patch me through to Grand and Nevek, please."

"Connecting . . ."

"Solus, you back already from your colony planting?" Grand said with a smile as his face appeared before Solus' eyes. Solus could see that Grand was situated in the command module of *Orion*, which had remained on station on the far side of the moon. "I'm ready for a tropical paradise too, you know. Do you think I want to remain in space for the rest of my life?"

Nevek, standing in his sick bay, appeared next. "Solus! You are, I take it, coming to visit the Old Man?"

"Indeed, so you've heard. Have you met him yet?"

"I've not had the pleasure," Nevek replied wryly. "Rodd just told me about him. He was quite taken aback. As was Compass."

"Old man?" Grand piped in.

"Grand, you're not going to believe this . . ." For the next few minutes Solus told Grand about everything that had transpired in the past hour. "Have you ever heard of such a person?"

"In fact, I had heard something about that—years ago. In an officer's mess—out in the Red Colonies, and away from the Prolix nodes, if you know what I mean."

"I do indeed."

"You know how we used to speak in that alternate code lingo to discuss such topics—things we didn't want our superiors to know we were talking about? Well, there was an old gent who'd put in a lot of time in the capital on Ouda Regio. He talked about this old man who lived in an enormous government compound chock-full of treasures—antiquities both from Perdicion and Parthénos. Completely isolated and completely supported by Supremacy resources. It was rumored that he was the man in charge. We scoffed at the idea. A secret leader in charge? It sounded like one of those conspiracy theories."

"Sometimes conspiracies are real," Nevek added.

"And it would fit that such a person would have the resources to escape the planet," Grand said, "I'd like to see this ship of his."

"But is he really our leader?" Nevek queried.

"He's certainly in control of the Prolix node," Solus said.

"Has the logging feature been activated? I mean, he could be hearing this very discussion," Grand pointed out.

"Not that Xoxon is aware of," Solus replied. "But there are a lot of changes to this new Prolix version. I'm not sure Xoxon knows for sure."

"Solus—let me say this—*you* are our commander," Grand declared. "I don't care who this guy is."

"You know I agree, Sol," Nevek added.

"Thanks, old friends," Solus said. "But if he is indeed in control of the Prolix, we may have no choice but to obey him."

"What's he going to do—lock us in jail?" Grand said contemptuously. "What army will come for us?"

"The upgrades, Grand, the upgrades. And I do not want to hurt them in the process."

"We'll have to be on guard," Nevek said.

"Be on guard, yes. But don't do anything yet, Grand. I need to meet with him first—we really know nothing about his intentions at this point."

"I'll be monitoring," Grand said.

"Oh, and . . ." Solus said, trying to keep to his squadron commander duties, "please continue making contact with the incoming Supremacy ships. Get reports from each of them. I want to know about any changes in their ETAs."

"Will do, Commander."

"And let me know if the Epsilon squadron has any readings at all on those Ishtarians. We need to know where those ships are and when they are arriving."

"Yes, sir. I will get all that for you," Grand replied, staying as formal as he could.

"Thanks, Grand. Solus out. Nev?"

"Yes, boss?"

"I want you to meet me at the landing zone. I want you there with me when we meet him."

"Certainly, are you getting close? I can leave immediately."

"I have an ETA of twenty minutes."

"I will be there. Nevek out."

Grand's and Nevek's show of support meant more than they knew. Solus had not asked to be the new leader, but he had accepted it when it was thrust upon him. Now, after that acceptance, he was in the process of making plans to settle his men into this world. But that was now in doubt.

Perhaps he should be relieved—a great load would be off

his shoulders. The nose of the ship began to glow orange as he attempted to enter the atmosphere. It started to get hot in the cabin.

Solus then remembered his vision, his mission. He recalled what the Lady had told him: "It is your charge to protect this world from the orphans of Perdicion. But let them come. My son wills that they live."

For the moment, Solus was at peace again. He still knew his purpose. This mystery man was not to determine his mission: it was the Lady.

Fire from atmosphere re-entry was all around the ship.

OVER NEW OUDA REGIO

Vestige appeared in the skies over New Ouda Regio. Solus flew across it at a rapid speed, lining up his approach and then slowing down above the node site. As he looked across the vast, empty green and tan landscape, it occurred to Solus that the Supremacy had chosen this location because it was largely unin-habited. There would be no disruption to the more organized societies of this planet. The indigenous people were nomadic and sparsely distributed.

Down at the landing site, Nevek was good to his word. He watched as the transport ship hovered into position on full thrusters. Nevek marveled at the massive size of the floating ship, which would have escaped his notice a few months ago. He saw the ship's landing gear gently touch the ground, followed by the extending and lowering of the boarding ramp.

Solus emerged a moment later and walked down the ramp to meet his old friend. "Nev, I'm glad you're here," he said, extending his hand. They had been in frequent Prolix contact, but Solus had not met his old friend face-to-face in months.

Such was their mission in space, with their ships constantly on the move, and usually in opposite directions.

Solus looked past Nevek and noticed for the first time the little egg-shaped ship parked nose-up nearby. It had not shown up on his instruments aboard the *Vestige*. It was small; Solus judged it only big enough to carry two, maybe three, persons and their belongings at the most. It must have been the Old Man's transport off the home world. Solus had never seen anything like it.

"That ship—he obviously came in it," Solus commented. "That part of his story checks out, at least." They walked over to look at the ship more closely.

"But is it a Supremacy ship?" Nevek replied. "I've never seen anything with that configuration."

"It would have to be a Supremacy ship. Who else would have the resources to build something like this?" Solus answered.

"Her lines are so clean—I wouldn't know it had a door to get in, just to look at it," Nevek noted. "And it blends into the background, doesn't it? It must be the ship's surface. A special coating of some sort."

"Could be. *Shadow* has something similar," Solus said. "Well, come on, we had better make our way into the cave." The two men walked side by side across the open field towards a nearby hill covered in trees. A large, mouth-like, dark opening could be seen in the distance, which was undoubtedly the main entrance to the cave.

"Okay, before we go in—about this guy, the Supreme Leader?" Nevek commented as they walked. "We've never heard of such a person, or such an office, for that matter. We would all recognize the prime minister, or even members of the ruling council. In fact, why are they not here? Didn't any of them get off the planet in time?"

"That never occurred to me," Solus responded. "But I don't think their escape plans included leaving the planet. It all involved underground bunkers. In fact, for all we know, they could be alive there right now. Trapped under the ground."

"Perhaps, our new guest can tell us something about that," Nevek said. "But, back to this Supreme Leader claim—do we have to accept that?" Nevek said.

"What if he is legitimately the leader? What right do we have to deny that?"

"What if he was? As I said: there was no official office of Supreme Leader," Nevek pointed out. "Only what the people knew of as the government was legitimate."

"Yes, but you are forgetting—it's also what the Prolix network considers legitimate that counts right now."

"Ah, but that can be changed."

They reached the entrance to the cave, and they too felt the cold, continuous breeze coming from within. Solus, who could go into combat in a zero-gravity environment without a pang of anxiety, now felt a stab of butterflies in his stomach.

"After you," Nevek said, extending his arm.

"You are too kind, Doctor."

They walked into a darkness that blinded them until their eyes grew accustomed to the dimness of the cave. As they moved deeper into the passage, they started to make out artificial light further in. With this small illumination, Solus could now distinguish stalactites that were hanging from the ceiling as they walked.

It brought to Solus' mind the image of passing rows of teeth, as if they were advancing down the throat of an ancient, iron-scaled dragon. "If not for his good friend walking next to him, I would have felt completely abandoned and alone," he thought.

This reminded him of Xoxon, who of course was always with

him as well. It then occurred to him: he might as well use the Prolix thought-reading capabilities to his advantage. "Xoxon," he thought, "please broadcast this meeting to everyone in the squadron. I want them to see what happens."

The passage continued on down a cleanly-cut corridor, but their Prolixes directed them to make a turn at a side passage to their right. That led them down through an entrance into a large chamber. Familiar Prolix node equipment appeared before their eyes. Processing units lined the walls.

Solus and Nevek paused there and looked around the room for the Old Man.

They saw him sitting near the system console. He was conversing with it, and just seemed to notice their presence as the two friends approached him. "Gentlemen, please sit down," he said, continuing to look at the console.

They looked and saw that there were chairs on the other side of the desk.

"I am Commander Solus—" Solus started.

"Yes, of course you are," the man said simply and did not look either man in the eye. They sat there in silence.

"Sir," said a disembodied voice, "perhaps you should discuss your status as leader."

"Well, why should I do that?" the Old Man answered peevishly. "I've already established that."

"Excuse me, sir," asked Solus. "Is that your Prolix speaking?"

"That's my valet," the Old Man answered simply. "I suppose I should take his advice," he continued. "As I mentioned when I first spoke with you, I am the leader of the Supremacy."

"You'll forgive me, sir, but the only leaders we knew of were the Prime Minister, the members of the Ruling Council, and the Parliament," Solus replied. "Are you asserting that you were secretly in charge?"

"I was simply the leader—and those who needed to know, knew about it."

"But how do we verify that?" Solus continued.

"The Prolix has already done that."

"Yes, but the Prolix network was hacked," Solus said. "How do we know that you aren't the hacker?"

"This is getting tiresome." The Old Man sighed. "Preston, download my files into the Prolix network. You will see that all is in order."

"Of course, sir . . ."

Xoxon spoke up a moment later inside Solus' head. "His official logs have been uploaded. It does show that he was the leader. There is ample evidence of the government authorities reporting to him."

"My Prolix now verifies that you are who you say you are," Solus said.

"Solus!" Nevek called out, speaking up for the first time. "Fine, he was the secret leader. But that does not mean we must accept his authority now."

Solus looked over at Nevek, again glad he had brought him with him. Emboldened, Solus looked at the Old Man. "Sir, you may have been the Supremacy leader on Perdicion, but that is now gone. This is a different planet—"

"I must now make a command decision," the Old Man interrupted. "I want that enemy colony destroyed immediately. There will be no negotiations. Those men are guilty of planetary genocide. I want them executed."

"Sir," Solus protested, "I have already agreed to let them—"

"That will not be acceptable," the Old Man said evenly. "You did not have the authority to do that."

"But, sir, we cannot simply fire upon them. They have been granted amnesty."

"You will destroy that colony."

"Sir," replied Solus, "they are unable to defend themselves, or do anything else, for that matter. I made sure of that by isolating them on that small island."

"That has nothing to do with it. I want them executed."

"I will not kill them," Solus stated.

"Then you are relieved, and your second-in-command will do it. Or the next one after that."

"Sir, the Supremacy has ended, and you are not in command here."

"How dare you defy me!" the Old Man now yelled. "The Supremacy is not dead—I *am* the Supremacy!"

"Not to me, or to my men. That has become increasingly clear."

"Is that so?"

"You may have control of this planetary network, but that does not put you in charge."

"Ah, but it does."

Before Solus could react, two of his men, Rachet and Podd appeared from the back of the cave with their assault rifles pointed at him. "Sir," Rachet said in a strained voice. "You are under arrest."

Solus thought quickly. He could dodge them, flip to the deck, roll, and take one of the rifles . . . but no, he re-considered, he would not fight his own men—they were not responsible.

The two men came up and grabbed him, and shoved him to the floor. They put his arms behind his back in an armbinder.

Fogger, Nevek's med tech, appeared and held a gun on Nevek. "Stay clear, Doctor," he warned.

"Not in charge? I think so," the Old Man said in a triumphant tone.

* * *

ONBOARD THE SUPREMACY ATTACK SHIP SHADOW *IN ORBIT OVER THE BLUE PLANET*

Bas grabbed the arms of his chair and left the right cockpit module and made for the interior of the ship. "Open the brig doors," he ordered his Prolix. The doors split from each other, slid open, and Bas immediately went into the small chamber. It was a tiny holding cell. "Close the doors and lock them," he ordered.

"I must warn you that I cannot open them once the doors are locked," Bas' Prolix warned. "Prolix node transmissions are blocked in here."

"Exactly," Bas answered. "They'll be safe from me."

The doors slid together, shutting him in.

ONBOARD THE SUPREMACY ATTACK SHIP ORION *ABOVE THE BLUE PLANET NEAR THE MOON*

As did the entire Blue Squadron, Grand witnessed the encounter between the Old Man and Solus before his eyes in a Prolix link. As he watched Solus and Nevek's arrest, Grand took out his pent-up anger on his monitor board with a mighty blow from his fist.

With this fruitless energy released, Grand followed with a more constructive action of evaluating the whereabouts of the squadron's upgrades and the threat they now posed. The only upgrade in space at the moment was Bas, and he was aboard *Shadow* with Fleek. All of the other ships' crewmembers had command Prolixes. Thump and Ruffini were aboard the captured stealth ship *Crusade*. Rowling was alone in the other ship, *Warrant*. "Bertie, patch me through to the squadron."

"Certainly, but I must warn you, your transmissions can now be tracked through the Prolix network."

"Thank you, I'll keep that in mind."

The four men, all seated in their command cockpits, appeared before Grand. "Lieutenant Grand, thank goodness!" Fleek spoke up immediately, reflecting the thoughts of the others. "You saw what happened to the commander? What are we going to do about it?"

"First things first, Fleek—where is Bas?"

"Believe it or not, he is in the brig. He actually went and locked himself in. Right after Commander Solus was taken into custody."

"Really? He knew that that would keep his Prolix under control," Grand said admiringly. "Good old Bas!"

"Sir, we need to rescue the Commander and Dr. Nevek," Rowling exclaimed.

"And Lieutenant Rodd," Ruffini added.

"What are your orders, Lieutenant?" Thump queried.

"Simply this," Grand declared. "We will rendezvous over the New Ouda Regio entry zone, and we will go in together and get them back. I will work out a plan of action in the meantime."

"But sir, there are bound to be defensive systems around that node . . ." Ruffini began to point out.

"There may well be," Grand replied, "but we can't allow this to stand. We will attack."

"Yes, sir!" each of them cried in unison.

Noting the positions of the other ships, Grand calculated when they could all join. "We will rendezvous in thirty minutes. Until then, remain in stealth mode."

IN THE PROLIX NODE CAVE

"Did you hear that, sir?" asked the valet. "They are planning an attack to free Commander Solus."

The Old Man sat at his console unmoved. Solus and Nevek

had been removed to a holding cell deeper in the cave. Having returned from this task, Rachet and Podd now stood on guard near the Old Man. Compass and Fogger had been sent out to secure *Guru* and retrieve Rodd, who was in the forest somewhere.

"Yes, I suppose we must shoot them down. Pity to lose those vessels. Activate the surface-to-air batteries."

"Sir, I would advise against that. We cannot afford to lose any vessels. May I remind you that there are still three rebel Ishtarian attack vessels that are unaccounted for."

"True, but we have two Supremacy vessels coming in from Perdicion, plus four more attack ships from the Red Sector. More than enough."

"True as well, sir, but we do not know where their loyalties will lie."

"That matters not," said the Old Man. "Then we will shoot them all down."

"Sir, that is unlikely. Our batteries will likely destroy several of them until they change tactics and then either destroy our batteries or begin a ground assault. There is a better alternative to this scenario . . ."

"But we have control of the Prolix network. Surely that gives us advantages."

"Exactly, sir. That is the alternative to which I am referring."

"Ah, I see. What do you have in mind?"

"Our server here, sir. We do have a few options. We can take away their command Prolix connections. They will have no Prolix assistance—until they comply, of course."

"Is that enough incentive?"

"Possibly not, sir. The next option is to do a conversion of command to upgrade Prolix. This is more complicated. It would involve—"

"Now, *that* is an idea. Let's do that. We'll simply take control of all of them!"

"As I began to say, sir, that will take a bit of doing. We cannot simply send out a broadcast update as the Supremacy Science Bureau on Perdicion is no longer available. We would need to find the connection of each host we wish to upgrade, and perform the conversion manually. The other issue is that we have not performed this kind of upgrade prior to this time, so we cannot predict how the host's current Prolix will react."

"It will take some time to do, and the results will be unpredictable," the Old Man concluded. "Why don't you just come out and say that?"

"I apologize, sir," the valet replied. "In the meantime, perhaps even the mere threat of this upgrade will be an excellent bargaining chip."

"Ah, I see," the Old Man said, considering the matter. "I agree. We will threaten to do just that. However, it will not be an idle threat. And Commander Solus will be the first one on the list. That will put the others in line very quickly."

"Agreed, sir."

INSIDE A HOLDING CELL IN THE PROLIX CAVE

"We're in a bit of a mess, aren't we?" Nevek sighed as he sat back down next to Solus on a pull-down bench, which doubled as a bed. The cell's structure did not include a Prolix-inhibitor, perhaps due to an oversight in the hasty construction of the facility, so Solus and Nevek still had the services of their Prolixes while inside.

"I did not handle that well at all," Solus said, staring wistfully ahead of him. "I've let you all down."

"Solus, what else could you possibly have done—just gone along with him?"

"I could have bluffed my way out of here, instead of getting us into this cell."

"Perhaps, perhaps," Nevek replied. "Well, then you need to rectify the situation. Get us out of here."

"Agreed."

"He's a narcissistic sociopath!" Nevek exclaimed.

A Prolix link interrupted their conversation. The Old Man's face appeared before their eyes, as it did for every member of Solus' squadron. "Attention: this is your leader speaking. I am quite aware of the Blue Squadron officers' plans to attack this installation. This is, needless to say, an act of treason, which is punishable by death. Should you attack this facility, we are well able to defend ourselves. I have prisoners and will order the upgrades to execute them all. In addition, these upgrades, your former men, will be defending against any attack." He paused for a moment to let his words sink in. "However, should you call off this conspiracy, given the trying times, I am willing to exercise leniency. I am not unaware of the fact that my appearance here was unexpected. That was necessary for security reasons. Therefore, instead of harsher measures, I am considering the option of upgrading all officers with the Prolix upgrade version."

This hit them all like a thunderbolt, including their Prolixes. "That is unheard of!" Xoxon cried out in Solus' mind. "I am a command Prolix; I cannot function as an upgrade!"

"Sir, that is not acceptable," Solus spoke out. "You cannot do that—it's unthinkable."

"Xoxon," Solus thought, "get me out of this cell!"

"Ah, but I can," said the Old Man. "I can do anything I want to. You can't seem to grasp this basic concept."

"Sir, this is the very reason your officers are now against you. This is an arbitrary abuse of power!"

"I am the one to decide what is arbitrary and what is abuse. I am now the executive, the legislative, and the judicial branches of the Supremacy. With this insolence, you are only making it harder on you and your men. I will begin the upgrades immediately."

"Sir, will you reconsider if I call off the attack?"

"I would consider it," the Old Man replied after a brief pause.

"I need more than that—I need your assurance that you will not attempt to upgrade the officers."

"Stop transmission to all but the former commander," the Old Man said to his valet.

"Executing, sir."

The connection was between Solus and the Old Man only now. Nevek could hear Solus' responses but none of the Old Man's. "I need something in return from you. There must be justice. Will you take punishment in place of your men?"

"I am their commander. I will, if it means my men will be spared. What are you asking?"

"It is my ruling that you be exiled in the wilderness. You will be abandoned without benefit of any Supremacy technology— including your Prolix."

The Old Man's words hit Solus like a slap in the face, but he fought mightily to disguise his reaction. After a short pause he spoke again. "How will I know my men will be well-treated?"

"That is my offer. Take it or let the battle begin. I will be able to destroy several of their ships even as they attempt atmosphere entry."

"And what of the Ishtarians? I want them spared as well," Solus said, surprising the Old Man by upping the ante.

"Spare the Ishtarians? You ask too much!"

"My men will not carry out your orders. I will see to that."

"They deserve death!"

Solus strained for a response, and then it hit him. It was time to reveal his vision of the Lady. It was a long shot, but perhaps it would get through to the man. It was worth a try.

"But, sir," Solus began, "there's more to this than you know. I was told in a vision that all orphans of Perdicion were to be allowed to live on this planet. That includes the Ishtarians, no matter what we think of them."

"A vision?" said the man, intrigued in spite of himself. He had made a special study of the religious beliefs of this tumultuous and fascinating world. "What sort of vision? From whom? Not a Prolix vision?"

"No, it was not Prolix-originated. My Prolix did not even register it. It was, well . . . a lady. The protectress of this planet. She said that I should allow all the orphans to come home. That I should come to know her son and follow him."

This surprising statement stung the Old Man to his innards. He was visibly shaken. "What did she look like?"

"She wore a blue veil lined with golden stars," Solus said, straining to describe adequately what he saw. "She was outlined in a dazzling bright light. She was extraordinarily beautiful."

The Old Man was astounded. In fact, he had heard of this lady—and of her son. It was all part of a dreadful new religion that was spreading rapidly throughout the Romanus Empire. The current emperor had sensibly tried to eradicate it on a number of occasions with refreshing harshness. But to no avail. It continued to grow. It all stemmed from this lady's son, a holy man, claiming to be the son of God, saving the world by being resurrected from the dead.

This was indeed a dangerous idea that could transform an entire world. The Old Man recalled that there were even origins of this toxic invention on Perdicion. There was an old Perdician religion that spoke of the savior who would emerge from the sister world. It predicted him coming from lands of Parthénos that were currently in a backwater zone of the Romanus' sphere.

It was a foretelling, the Old Man was surprised to find, that likewise came from all populated parts of Parthénos, in addition to the Perdician source. One ancient Parthénos source from their west spoke of the Master and Ruler of the World who would come from the West. Another spoke of the ancient tradition of a chaste woman, smiling on her infant.

From the East came the prediction of the great Wise Man that would be born in the West. Other Western sources of learning spoke of the Logos and the Universal Wise Man yet to come. Such poison could even disrupt a modern society like Perdicion's. And this, in all reality, was the Old Man's biggest fear. This was the most important reason why he would not allow a migration of his people to the Blue Planet.

In recent years, there had been mounting pressure to lift the ban on migration to the Blue Planet, but the Old Man always steadfastly refused, citing environmental laws. But only he knew the real reason: he knew that Perdician colonists to the Blue Planet would get infected by this religion, too. It would impact the Prolix network even worse than a virus.

So, the Old Man noted to himself, while the people of Perdicion were mostly gone, this noxious Parthénos religion was alive and well. He had been on the planet but a few days, and it was already becoming a headache for him—and now there was trouble from one of his own officers, to boot! It was preposterous!

"Nonsense," he finally replied.

"It is a certainty that she speaks for the Creator," Solus added. "We would do well to abide by what she says."

This again shook the man to his core. "It is ridiculous!" he sputtered.

"You want a sacrifice? You may have me, but you must spare my men and the Ishtarians."

"Fine, it is of no matter," the Old Man said, attempting to recover himself. "But I will not support them. They are on their own."

"My men and the Ishtarians are spared," Solus repeated resolutely.

"Agreed," the Old Man said cursorily, ending the transmission abruptly.

With the Old Man's face gone from his sight, Solus watched as, at that moment, the cell's door opened.

"Solus, I've accessed the security system. You can escape," Xoxon reported.

"Thank you, my old friend," Solus replied. "You are a wonder!"

"Doctor," Solus said, turning to Nevek. "It's time for you to leave. I suggest you head back to *Guru*. Find Rodd and get out. Watch out for Compass and Fogger." He got the doctor up and moved them out of the cell.

"You're not coming?" Nevek replied. "Let's get out of here. You are under no obligation to do anything for that man!"

"I have to keep my word," Solus replied. "I hear them coming—quick, duck down that passage." He pointed to a side corridor that met up with the main passage. "Let your Prolix guide you out."

The sound of running feet could be heard coming from the main passageway. Undoubtedly it would be Podd and Rachet.

"But Solus, please—"

"Go, my friend. You must get away and warn the others. Listen to the Lady and follow her son. That is an order!"

"The Lady?" Nevek had heard only part of the conversation and was baffled by Solus' words. Reacting to the turmoil in his heart, Nevek paused to grip his friend's arm. He looked at Solus' face, and his determined gaze forced Nevek to relent. At that, he made off into the darkness of the cave.

Solus turned and stood his ground to face the oncoming men. As predicted, Podd and Rachet appeared at the top of the corridor and halted upon seeing him. "Stand down, men," Solus said, raising his arms. "I am not trying to escape. You can take me back to the Old Man."

They looked at Solus and then showed signs of hearing instructions from the Old Man. With that, they came forth and took hold of Solus on both sides and cuffed him again. "You are to come this way, sir," Podd said.

"I know you can't resist this," Solus said, trying to comfort them. "I do not blame you in the slightest."

OUTSIDE THE PROLIX CAVE

Nevek found his way out of the cave, and was trying to remember the way back through the forest to *Guru*. He wanted badly to ask his Prolix for help, but was uncertain what would happen if he did. Would his old friend turn on him or give away his position? He did not know. It was nighttime now, so he had to make his way slowly and tentatively in the darkness.

While his old life continued to unravel with the continuing loss of his home and his friends, all around him, this world's nature went on as normal unmoved in its nightly exercises. The crickets and night bugs filled the air around him with their musically scratching rhythms. A great horned owl hooted above him. A mournful howl from a coyote sounded somewhere in the distance.

Without the use of his Prolix, Nevek felt alone and unprotected in this wilderness. His mind wrestled with all the bleak possibilities, which included being attacked by natives or wild animals, or—just as bad—having to fight off an attack by Compass and Fogger, who were undoubtedly now searching for him.

Nevek stopped at the sound of crunching vegetation ahead of him. He was quite certain there was a large creature moving in his direction. In preparation for a hostile encounter, he clenched his hands into fists and raised his arms in a defensive position he dimly recalled from a combat training course he took years ago.

"Doctor?" a familiar voice called to him.

"Rodd, is that you?" Nevek replied happily. "Thank goodness! I can't tell you how good it is to hear your voice!"

"I'm glad I found you, Doc," Rodd replied. "Didn't your Prolix tell you it was me?"

"Well, I didn't ask him," Nevek answered. "I don't know if he's been hijacked."

"Listen, Doc, they can find us, regardless—our signatures are registered with the node. That's why we've got to get off the planet if we're going to help Commander Solus. Come on!"

"Just what are we going to do?"

"Take *Guru*, of course," Rodd said. "It's the only ship available besides that transport ship."

"Lead the way," Nevek said, as Rodd immediately started down a path through the brush. In just moments, he was very far ahead of Nevek.

"Wait, I can't see," Nevek complained. "I'm going to fall on my face—"

"Doctor, please," Rodd called back, "we don't have time for this! Have your Prolix guide you using night vision."

"Night vision?"

"A new improvement from the Omega upgrade. Try it!"

"Well, Bingo, you traitor—let me see!" Nevek ordered his Prolix.

"I was wondering when you were going to talk to me!" Nevek's Prolix spoke up.

Suddenly the world looked very green, and at the same time, the features of every object became more distinct. "Nice!" Nevek said, impressed. "So, we don't need helmets anymore to see in the dark? How's that accomplished?"

"It's just an application of the same technology that projects images before your eyes. The night vision lens image is placed directly before your eyes. Some troops made the modification themselves a few years ago, and this upgrade deployed that application to the entire population," Bingo replied.

"How clever!" Nevek exclaimed, now feeling a bit more secure with the ability to see. As he grew more accustomed to seeing in this low-light fashion, he could soon make out all kinds of details. As they walked, he could occasionally see the eyes of animals reflecting back at him. He saw a pair of extremely large cat's eyes staring at him and Rodd as they passed.

"There's a large cat to our right," he alerted Rodd, who looked over immediately.

"Just keep moving," Rodd said. "According to my Prolix, it's a panther. It should not attack us if we stay together, but we need to keep an eye on it. It may try to stalk us."

Greatly alarmed, the two men quickened their pace. Soon enough, they approached the lakeshore where *Guru* was landed. Coming from that direction, a low roar of thrusters could now be heard.

"Oh no," Rodd said. "That's *Guru*'s launching thrusters. We're too late!"

They reached the edge of the forest just in time to see the red glow from the ship's engines as it lifted up in the air and hovered over the lake. The dark ship then moved off past them over the tree line.

"Alright, now what do we do?" Nevek exclaimed in exasperation.

"Maybe they're only moving her over to the other landing area," Rodd suggested. "We need to go back there."

"Into the waiting jaws of that panther?"

"Doctor—"

"Well, if not the panther, the upgrades are certainly on the lookout for us."

"But there's only a couple of them. That's one advantage we have, Doctor, at least for now," Rodd replied. "There aren't that many of them yet. At least until the Old Man starts upgrading our Prolixes."

As they stood there still debating what to do next, the wind appeared to pick up above them. It was getting noticeably louder. After a moment, Rodd's experienced ears realized what was happening. "Doctor, it's an attack ship."

Nevek looked up and saw a dark object in the sky. Even with his enhanced night vision, he could pick out no specific details on it. Still, he noted at once that the object was not only near them, but rapidly approaching and homing in on the two men. Before they could react, the black object's bottom lit up with a circle of red lights that revealed it as an attack ship's deployment compartment.

"Nevek, Rodd—what are you waiting for? Climb aboard!" Grand shouted via the ship's external communication system. "We're vulnerable to spear fire in this hovering position!"

BACK IN THE PROLIX CAVE

"So, you are a devotee of the Virgin Mother, are you?" the Old Man said scornfully.

Unfamiliar with that title, Solus knitted his brows. He stood again before the Old Man, but this time with his hands cuffed behind his back. "Virgin Mother? I don't know what you mean," Solus replied.

"The Mother of God. You don't seem to know much about the woman you're following."

"You refer to the Lady, then?" Solus responded. "No, I do not know much about her at all."

"Are you aware that an attack ship was just scanned picking up two men outside this facility?" the Old Man queried. "Do you realize I could blast them to pieces as we speak?" the Old Man continued.

"They will not attack, as per our agreement," Solus stated.

"You seem to be so sure about that," the Old Man said with a sneer, "but now, before it is too late, you will formally call off your men—order them to stand down and accept my authority."

Solus pondered this, and could see no other way. "Very well," he replied reluctantly. "Patch me through to my squadron, Xoxon."

"Connecting . . ."

Emotion gripped Solus when he realized that this would be the last time he would see the members of his command. As they all appeared before his eyes, Solus tried to cherish the moment. He also tried valiantly to show them a brave face.

"Gentlemen," Solus began, "I order you to stand down. Do not attack this outpost."

"Commander—" Grand interrupted.

"I have an agreement with this man," Solus continued. "I have accepted responsibility for our rebellion against his authority. As a result, you will be spared. No upgrade Prolix installations will be conducted. And the Ishtarians will not be attacked and killed. Those are my conditions. Please abide by them."

After a brief pause, he continued. "Farewell to all of you—it was a great honor to serve with you and be your commander. Solus out."

The connection ended abruptly, and their faces disappeared from Solus' view. He then made a thought command to Xoxon: "Tell Grand to save the upgrades, if he can."

"Now that that is over," the Old Man said to Solus, "you will no longer be permitted to use your Prolix."

Solus steadied himself for the procedure. He had no idea how it would feel.

"Initiate the removal procedure!" the Old Man ordered.

"Working . . ." replied the valet.

"Goodbye, old friend . . ." Solus said to Xoxon.

"This is not over," Xoxon replied. "They don't realize the extent of my new capab—" But he was interrupted mid-sentence, and Solus heard nothing more. He felt a loss within him. It was painless, but he felt empty somehow. That was the only way to describe it.

"And now," said the Old Man in an oddly casual manner, "put him out the old-fashioned way."

Lightning bolts blasted the back of Solus' eyes as the butt of a rifle hit him on the head. He knew no more.

CHAPTER 8

OUT OF PARADISE

Myra looked out over the canopy of trees below a cliff she had found overlooking the wide river. A blue heron, looking like a small pterodactyl, flew over the river and landed on Myra's side at the water's edge. It then stood there staring intently at the water for any sign of movement beneath the surface.

The river breeze continuously rustled the leaves around Myra and kept her face cool. Behind her, in the hills, were the burial mounds of the ancient ancestors of the native tribe with whom she was living. They called themselves the Cocopah, the river people. She had been studying the mounds with interest all that morning, and was now taking a break and simply enjoying the scenery. It was the paradise she had always dreamed of.

Myra enjoyed her solitude here. In a while, she would be going back to the Cocopah's bustling village. It had become Myra and her Harmonian sisters' temporary home. The little encampment was not exactly a crowded city or colony, but everything was tightly spaced. The people, by necessity, stayed close together, living mostly in a large lodge. They had built it by lining up fallen trees and lashing the tops together, and stripping and laying out tree bark over the roof. In the center was a large fire pit with an opening on top to let the smoke out.

At first, it had been comforting; she had grown used to living in close quarters while in the Red Colonies. But after living in space, on a tiny cargo ship, for many months, she found that she very much wanted her own physical space. Given this, she and her sisters, who had similar issues, decided that they needed more privacy. They built their own wigwam very near to one side of the lodge. They had finished it quite recently.

It was approximately one month since Myra had landed on the planet. She thought back to the moment when she had run into the trees, early on the morning she had escaped with the help of Solus.

She had made immediate use of the rifle Solus had thrown her. With the tracking sensors embedded in the rifle, she was able to steer clear of Zealrot and catch up with her sisters. Thankfully, Zealrot had disappeared from her tracking scanner and had not since re-appeared.

The sisters, while happy Myra had found them through the rifle's good offices, still insisted that she ditch the gun and her camouflage suit. After some further persuading, Myra had finally agreed. The weapon simply did not fit with their belief system, no matter how helpful it was. Nevertheless, she stashed both items in the hollow of an old tree. She was idealistic, but not unreasonable—after all, a snake by the name of Zealrot had also entered their little paradise. Once they were rid of this war technology, they made their way to an encampment of natives.

After a few weeks of living with the natives, the sisters had been more or less accepted into the tribe. They proved their worth by taking part in the work of the tribe. They assisted in boiling and stretching animal hides to make them weatherproof for shelter and garments. The sisters also took part in the tribe's agricultural activities, which consisted of raising squash, pump-kins, beans, and maize. When they weren't working directly for the tribe, the sisters gathered their own food supplies by collecting nuts and berries and fishing in the river. Even so, they often shared what they found with other members of the tribe.

They were merely tolerated by the other women, while the men were more intrigued. Some ignored them altogether, yet others gave the sisters more attention than they desired. Each sister had to gently rebuff marriage proposals from various men. The frequency of proposals had dropped off after a few weeks, but the sisters had to remain on their guard against several male tribe members.

Myra and her sisters were certainly not naïve to the amorous intentions of these men. Because of this, they continued to wear their own modern jumpsuits most of the time. The garments' space-age fasteners and tear-resistant fabric would make it diffi-cult for an ardent admirer to remove this protection from their bodies.

Yet there was another reason for keeping their modern clothing, and they all felt a little guilty about it. Even if not specifically designed for planetary surface use, the properties of their jumpsuits protected them better from the elements. With the advanced garments on, their undergarments always stayed dry, no matter how hard it rained, and they felt less of the heat of the day and the cold of the night. Thus, in spite of their Harmonian ideal of merging with the native culture, their modern clothing was, unexpectedly, one last vestige of their former life that they could not quite give up. Because of this, they stuck out all the more from the natives.

Myra had reached the cusp of attaining her goal of blending in and living with the natives, yet she held back. A month ago, she had been in ecstasy merely being on the ground of the

Blue Planet. But now that feeling of contentment was beginning to slip away, and she was surprised by the restlessness that persisted within her. This was in spite of her admiration for these people and how they managed to survive and even thrive in this wilderness.

A study of their culture and its arts and crafts was intellectually stimulating, but it was not easy to also live within this culture. She had no access to a computer or any other modern technology to record her findings. Alternatively, of course, she could record her research in longhand, but that had its difficulties as well. This culture she was in offered little in the way of writing surfaces other than animal skins.

However, there was another factor to her discontent that she had to admit to. While her Harmonian beliefs sought to view all cultures as being equally worthwhile, she found that she could not help having a preference for this world's more developed cultures, which were, unfortunately for Myra, located on the other side of the planet. In particular, she loved one culture that was now a part of the Romanus Empire, but in a backwater part. It was a small country, Ludaea, one of many located just off of the great sea that connected the parts of the cradle of that civilization.

She was drawn to this group of people, known as the Yehud, for a simple reason—she and her family's people looked very much like them. So much so that her family's northern branch of Ishtarians could actually be ethnic ancestors of the Yehud. The idea boggled Myra's mind in a happy way.

Yet it wasn't their physical similarity alone that drew her to them. The Yehud also fascinated Myra because their religion was so similar to her family's own. In another clue to a possible connection, the Yehud's religion, like Myra's family's faith, was a monotheistic one. This was quite unique to both worlds.

Their godhead was not some primitive personification of a natural phenomenon. There was no god of thunder, the sun, the moon, or the netherworld—no, it was all one invisible and almighty God, who simply called himself "I Am."

Their creation story was figurative in nature, but upon analysis, was as plausible an explanation as to how the world came into being as any other she had ever heard, including any and all scientific theories. Just as interesting to Myra, their scriptures provided a fascinating explanation as to why there was so much death and destruction in the world (or worlds, as Myra thought of it). It was simply this: it wasn't like that in the beginning.

God created a paradise in which the first man and woman had lived in complete happiness with him. But he also gave them two other things. He gave the first man and woman the opportunity to choose to follow him by setting one limit to their freedom. The limit was simply that they were forbidden from gaining the knowledge of good and evil. Along with that limit, he gave them the freedom to choose whether to obey his command, even if disobeying it meant they would bring death into the world.

So what happened? Although tricked by the devil, the first man and woman chose to take the knowledge in spite of God's warnings of what would happen. God respected their choice and allowed death to enter the world, and as a result, also separated them and all of the generations that followed from God.

But it didn't end there. There was hope. God promised a savior who would come to defeat death and allow his people to live again with God. Many of the later scriptures prophesied that the savior would come and what he would do. They anxiously awaited their savior to this day.

One growing sect among them claimed that he had already come! She was dying to learn more about that.

She thus found herself beginning to question her Harmonian beliefs—after all, she considered, why could she not love this one culture over others? She didn't know if she shared the Yehud's beliefs—she had, after all, forsaken the ancient family religion that was like it—but she wanted to be a part of their culture. Even so, getting to the other side of the planet to join them seemed impossible. She could not cross the ocean by herself, and there was simply no way to get there other than hitching a ride on a spacecraft. This very thought scared her, of course, because any ride in space would likely be the result of her being apprehended by the Supremacy.

She looked up at the sky, now a constant habit, fearing that a Supremacy ship might be coming upon her as silently as a breeze. Feeling suddenly vulnerable, she stepped back under the canopy of the forest and made her way down the hill towards the native village. It was getting to be time to help her sisters cook their dinner, which was to be fish caught from the river. One could not afford to be completely vegetarian in this world and survive.

As she walked down the path between the trees, she looked up at their top branches. She observed the gray squirrels running up and down the branches, storing their food for the next winter. The sunlight filtered through the top branches in bright yellows and greens. The light came here from the sun, across space, to warm and light this beautiful world. This turned her thoughts to the darkness of space above this planet, where spaceships traveled.

She thought about Commander Solus and his kindness in letting her go. She had known him only briefly, but could not help feeling a certain fascination about him. Perhaps part of it was that known psychological problem of identifying with one's captors, but it was more than that, and she knew it. His men clearly admired him—he was more than simply their commander. He showed care and concern for their welfare— and for Myra and her sisters. He even seemed to show signs of having a faith in something higher than the Supremacy. Yet, even more personally, she felt deep down that he really cared for her. He had treated her with respect and deference. He had been merciful to her. So much so that he had let her go. And deep down, she was disappointed that he had not come back for her.

She could easily speculate on his good reasons for not seeking her out. After all, if he found her, he would be compelled to follow orders and take her into custody and administer the Prolix. But sometimes her thoughts were darker. At those times she told herself that he didn't care; that she was not worth his time. And this bothered her.

At other times, she wondered if he was in trouble, or even . . . dead. That was a horrible thought, indeed, and it caused her to shudder. She shook her head to clear it from this bad train of thought. She looked ahead and down the path and was surprised to see Zeeni and Mondra hurrying up the path towards her.

"Myra!" Mondra called out breathlessly as they drew near. "The village is abuzz over a stranger found down by the river!"

"He is a light-skinned man," Zeeni added. "As we are strangers too, the elders think we may know who he is. They want you to go to him."

"But who could it be?" Myra asked, amazed at this news. "It couldn't be Zealrot, unless they are mistaken about his skin color."

"Never mind these useless speculations," Mondra replied impatiently. "Let's go find out!"

The sisters hurried along down the path to the village. Upon arriving there, Mondra stepped over to one of the women gathered nearby and asked for further news about the man. After conversing for a few moments, she returned to Myra and Zeeni. "They say the strange man is still down by the river. There are peculiar stories as to how he got there. But he is now lying there as if dead."

The sisters then hurried to the riverbank, which was just down a steep path used to access the water's edge for washing and catching fish. As Myra emerged from the trees near the river's edge, she looked to her left and saw a group of men standing near the body of a man lying prone in the soft mud near the edge of the river, with his outstretched arms covering his face. Only undershorts, obviously modern in design, covered his otherwise naked body.

Mondra and Zeeni stopped to address the group of men while Myra moved past them to the man. One of the group responded to Mondra. As he spoke he gestured up at the sky and then down to the river, then back up again. Meanwhile, Myra knelt down next to the stranger. It was not Zealrot. His skin tone was indeed too light. If he was a Blue Planet native, he was not a native from this continent. The only other alternative was that he was someone from the Supremacy. But how could this be? She could expect to find an Ishtarian, or even one of her own Harmonians, abandoned like this—but not a Supremacian.

Mondra and Zeeni approached and knelt down by Myra and the man. "They say this man was dropped out of a giant sky lodge, which is what they call the spaceships they have seen," Mondra reported. "One of the men saw him being dropped into the river. The ship left, and the man did not come to the surface, at least not right away." As Mondra spoke, they began to turn the man over on his back. His face was muddy, and Myra began wiping the muck away with her hands.

"The men then discovered him lying on this spot," Mondra continued.

Electricity shot down her spine as she cleaned his face just enough to recognize him. "May the Creator save us, it's Commander Solus!" she exclaimed.

The sisters gasped collectively. Lying in the mud of the river without Supremacy uniform and gear, he looked as vulnerable as a newborn. His serene expression portrayed a state of absolute peace, which was in stark contrast to the bruises and wounds that dotted his neck, back, and arms. The hair on the back of his head was matted with blood from a blunt-force wound.

"We must get him to our wigwam," Myra directed. "We need to clean him up and treat his wounds. Ask the men to help us."

Mondra immediately arose and approached the group of men. After a time, it became apparent that they were not going to help, so Mondra came back alone. "They say they will not go near him on account of the lightning bolt man."

"The what?" Myra replied incredulously.

"Here the story gets a little strange," Mondra responded. "They say the man was carried out of the river by a being that shone like a lightning bolt."

"It's a miracle!" Zeeni responded.

"We need to carry him ourselves," Myra stated resolutely, focusing on the job at hand. "You two grab him under his armpits, and I'll get his legs." At that, Myra stepped between his legs and put her arms under his knees and raised them up. Zeeni and Mondra took their positions, and they all strained to their feet, holding Solus up between them. He was dead weight and showed no signs of returning to consciousness.

They moved haltingly away from the bank. Taking several stops to rest, they made the agonizingly slow trek back to the village. After about fifteen minutes of this, they finally got him back to the village and into their wigwam.

Once they got him situated on Myra's bedding, Mondra and

Zeeni left to get more water to help clean him up. Myra took what water they had in a skin, and began cleaning his face and head. Her fingers necessarily stroked his face and neck as she dabbed away the dirt and mud. His chin was strong and firm, but unlike the leathery-skinned men of the village, his skin was soft from living indoors for the majority of his life. Her physical contact with him awakened her emotions, and she felt a sensation of heat in her heart. She continued to clean his face and torso tenderly.

After a few moments, seemingly in response to her caresses, his lips stretched out in a smile of serene satisfaction. Noticing his response, Myra decided to speak to him.

"Commander Solus," she said softly. "Can you hear me?"

Without any other warning sign, Solus opened his eyes and fixed them on Myra. "So, you are my rescuer," he said smiling, with a strained, thin voice. "I thought I was dreaming."

"I cannot take all the credit," Myra said, blushing in spite of herself. "My sisters and I all carried you here from the river."

"I see. So, you were all able to find one another? I am glad. I tried searching for you when I was able to. I wanted to find . . ." Solus paused, then continued. "I was concerned that you, and your sisters, might be in trouble, all alone on this vast continent. I suppose I shouldn't have worried. All has transpired according to a larger plan."

"A larger plan?"

"Yes, Myra," Solus said. "It is all clear to me now. There is a Creator—I had always hoped for it, in a way. I sought something higher. I found him unknowingly in experiencing joy, and in goodness and truth. It was him shining through. I saw his work in the awesome power of nature."

Solus looked over at the light coming from the entrance to the wigwam, and continued. "Just look at that magnificent sun in the sky—you can't even look at it for long without going blind! But with all its light and heat and power, it's only a weak metaphor of his infinite power." He looked back at Myra. "You saw him too, Myra. You recognized his magnificence in his creation. The Blue Planet, Perdicion, the Red Planet, the worlds we know—and everything else, visible and invisible, they are all his creation, Myra."

"The Universe is wonderful, Solus," Myra replied.

"He is everywhere—but I have also learned that he is beyond his creation. He created it all, but he is separate from it and far beyond it."

Consternation washed over Myra's face. This conflicted with Harmonian theology. It sounded more like the words from her parents' ancient religion—or that of the Yehud.

"You will come to understand," Solus said, and closed his eyes.

"But how did you learn all this?" Myra asked, forgetting all of her other questions, namely, how he had come to be abandoned in the wild.

"I learned it from one of his servants," Solus replied, keeping his eyes closed. "It was in a dream, I suppose."

"Did he appear like lightning bolts?"

Solus opened his eyes again and looked at Myra. "You saw him?"

"The native men say they saw you rising from the river carried by a being shining like a lightning bolt."

"That was him," Solus said simply, closing his eyes again. He went back to sleep again and did not wake up again until the third day of his arrival.

Solus remained in the sisters' wigwam for several days, and they lovingly cared for him. They fed him and tended his wounds.

He accepted their ministrations gratefully and with humility. They also found him native clothes to wear. As Solus was a big man in comparison to the men in the village, the sisters needed to sew together a new garment for Solus to wear when he recovered. They bartered for the skins with items they had collected, but they obtained what they needed relatively cheaply, as the people were immensely curious about their new guest.

Myra was amazed at his transformation. He looked so different in native clothing and without his uniform. His formerly clean-shaven face was now covered with the beginnings of a full, dark beard. A sense of inner peace seemed to radiate out from within him. As his health improved, he met visitors and gladly accepted their hospitality in gifts of food, and clothing.

He eventually emerged from the wigwam and moved around the village, always accompanied by Myra, visiting the old, the sick, and the children. He made every attempt to meet with each of the villagers and get to know their language. He learned the peoples' customs and habits, and even tried to pitch in harvesting maize and beans. The women, however, would not allow him to work for long—urging him to go back to the village, a place more appropriate to his personage.

As to this, the Harmonian sisters had informed the people that he was from a distant land. The people seemed to understand from his bearing that he was a leader—a chief—in his homeland. They accordingly gave him the respect they felt was due to him. Even the chief of the village, seemingly unconcerned by the prospect of being usurped by Solus, treated him with deference.

One evening, about a week after his arrival, Solus sat with the sisters on logs near the fire pit outside the lodge. The fire crackled intensely, providing them nourishing warmth and security. With the night skies glorious above him with stars, planets, and even one of the galaxy's spiral arms in view, Solus recounted his encounter with the lightning bolt being, and before that, the Lady. "I want to learn about the Son of God so that I may follow him," he remarked after repeating the words of the Creator's luminous servant. "I was told that he died for our sins and was raised from the dead. His followers are spreading throughout the world. But they are not here yet."

The sisters looked at each other in amazement.

"Except me, I suppose," he added. "But I want to go and meet these disciples and learn all that I can about this Son of God!"

"Where are they from?" asked Zeeni.

"They are now on the other side of this world in the southern part of the Romanus Empire, in a land called Ludaea," Solus replied. "That is where he came to dwell with mankind."

This hit Myra like a splash of water. Could this be the savior of the Yehud? Their teachings spoke of a coming king and savior. Who else could it be? She was stunned that Solus would know this.

"We are on the other side of this world—we would need a spaceship to get there!" declared Mondra.

"Can you arrange that?" Zeeni asked, half joking.

"I cannot," said Solus. "I am totally without technological resources."

"But what of your Prolix?" asked Myra. "Can't you contact someone?"

Solus had until this point remained completely silent as to how he had been abandoned here, and had not mentioned his Prolix either. "I am alone," he replied. "My Prolix was removed."

"I didn't know that could be done," Myra responded. "I thought that once you had it, it remained with you forever!"

"I was not aware of this possibility either," Solus said, "but he is gone, and I miss him very much."

"Why was he removed?" Myra asked. "Were you being punished?"

"You must tell us how you came to be here!" Zeeni added, her curiosity getting the better of her. Myra had instructed the sisters not to press Solus on the matter, to let him tell it when he was ready. However, Myra could not complain, as it was her question that had opened the door.

"What is happening with the rebellion?" Mondra interjected. "Are the rebels fighting the Supremacy again?" Mondra could not wait any longer either, it appeared.

Solus looked at each of them. They each looked back at him expectantly. He then looked up at the night sky thoughtfully, trying to decide what to say. They needed to know what had happened, but he had resisted telling them. He wanted to let it out slowly, but was not sure how to do that.

He looked again at their expectant faces. They had been through so much, and they were happy now. He hated to be the one to tell them. But there was no good reason to hold back anymore. He had to tell them the truth.

"Actually, the war is over," he said, starting the story. "I was waiting to tell you all until the right time, but I realize now that I don't know when that will ever be. I will just have to tell it to you straight." He looked at each of them. "There has been an unimaginable amount of death and destruction."

The women stared at him with growing looks of horror.

"My family . . . the Red Colonies . . ." Myra started.

"They are gone," Solus said, "wiped from existence in an instant."

"The Supremacy fleet!" the other sisters cried out together.

"Yes, the fleet was responsible, but they met with their own end as well." Solus went on to tell of how the fleet had been destroyed.

"But what of Perdicion?" Mondra asked. Myra was struck

dumb, her mouth agape. She was thinking of her family—her mother, her father, her brother—all dead. She had thought of them occasionally over the past month, but they had never been in the forefront of her mind. She burned with simultaneous sadness and shame in forgetting about them.

"Perdicion is a dead world . . ." Solus continued. He told them of its end—and of its condition at that very moment. When he stopped speaking, he observed with sorrow the effects of his revelations on the women. And this was only the first part of his story. He would have to tell them about the new Supremacy coming to this world, and that he had no idea how to stop it.

They all held their hands to their faces, weeping into their fingers. Zeeni and Mondra reached for each other and cried on each other's shoulders. Myra was closest to Solus. He touched her shoulders and pulled her weeping face to his chest. He ran his fingers through her hair and stroked her back as her body convulsed with sobs. He held her, wishing he could absorb all of her sufferings into himself. He smelled her hair and thought how wonderfully fragrant it was. Its soft strands tickled his nose.

He realized that he loved her.

After a time, without further words, the sisters stumbled off to bed. The women cried until their tears could no longer flow. Each mourned the loss of the loved ones that they had left behind. They each had harbored hopes of someday being joined by family—Mondra had a younger brother; Zeeni a cousin— after they were established. Now they were all gone—forever. Deepening their grief, they all felt that same survivor's guilt that Solus' squadron had dealt with weeks earlier. Had they abandoned their loved ones to a horrible death? Who were they that they should live?

Eventually, the sisters drifted off to sleep from sheer emotional exhaustion. Solus, after walking Myra back to her wigwam and helping her into her bedding, left them alone and walked back out into the night. Wishing to purge the effects of the violence and noise of the story he had told them, he walked past the fire and plunged deep into the darkness.

He longed to hear the voice of nature and the simple silence of the Creator. Though there might have been bears, wolves, or even lions prowling in the forest near him, he was unafraid. He knew he was God's agent, and that he had a mission to perform. God would protect him until he accomplished his purpose.

There was, in fact, a dangerous creature in the forest that night. He lay sleeping inside his Supremacy tent a little to the west of the sisters' village. He had heard talk of three strange women who dwelled in a village near the river, and he knew at once who they must be. He wanted them back. The native women were simply not to his taste.

He had already had his share of them after taking control of several settlements by killing the men with his rifle. It was fairly easy; he would set up his tent and its invisibility shield in a high position near the camp, and then start picking targets and firing. After a time, the men were all dead or had fled. Simple. This was so much sport, but now he needed to get on with establishing his new empire. He needed women of his own kind to produce a proper imperial lineage.

IN THE PROLIX NODE CAVE

"Why are you bothering me with these technical issues?" the Old Man asked peevishly, sipping his morning tea in the node cave's drafty main control room. Hammering and drilling sounds of powered construction equipment echoing up from passages deeper in the cave disturbed the normal tranquility of his morning routine, but it could not be helped. The Prolix node-controlled upgrades were now busy putting up a more suitable apartment for him in a chamber deeper in the cave. They were using pre-fabricated building materials found amongst the stockpiles in the storage facility to build more civilized walls, ceilings, and floors where a man of refined tastes could live in better comfort. Until it was complete, he was making do in the control room. It was most unaesthetic, chilly, and generally uncomfortable.

"I apologize, sir, for bothering you with such matters, but I felt it best to keep you informed," said the valet. "There is a previously identified issue involved with the Omega upgrade. I have been doing an analysis, and there appears to be a bug."

"It seems to be working just fine," said the Old Man. "What are you on about, anyway?"

"Sir, this was a problem that the Science Bureau was working on in the days leading up to the frightful last days of Perdicion. It was, in fact, the source of the delays in releasing the upgrade. In giving the individual Prolix modules more control over their hosts, there was a necessary increase in their capabilities system-wide. There was the open possibility of an individual Prolix being able to access and make changes to the central node, even at the highest access levels."

"Absurd!"

"Not at all, sir. The point is that individual Prolixes vary in capability, just in the way their hosts vary. Prolixes, if you recall, sir, truly develop their own individuality, which comes from being fused with the DNA of the host."

"And so?"

"Given that, individual command Prolixes are especially individual in nature, and may resist an upgrade or another command function. And they may be better able to resist it due to the Omega bug."

"Somehow, I am unmoved. Had this occurred before the destruction of Perdicion, we would have had a problem on our hands, just by the numbers. After all, there were hundreds of millions of Prolix connections there. But now, we only have a few units to deal with. And I see no particularly able fellows out there—nothing we can't deal with, I'm sure."

"Up to a point, sir," the valet responded, but pressed on. "For example, I am unable to locate Commander Solus' Prolix within our network. When we removed it from Commander Solus' body, it was lost in the file transfer to the node."

"Lost—well, it's lost then."

"But I am not sure it was lost, sir. It may be downloaded into the node, sir. Hidden, like a virus."

"Is that possible?"

"Not before the Omega upgrade, sir."

"Well, you don't know for sure—this is just speculation. If you find it, fine—take care of it."

"I will give it my best effort, sir."

"Of course, I do want this bug patched before we proceed to spread the technology around the globe."

"I am working on it, too, sir, but I am only one. And I have to interface with the node to keep track of our defense situation."

"I have every confidence in you," the Old Man said in his patronizing fashion. "And what of our defensive position?"

"Stable, sir. The attack ships are remaining in space and will not attack this facility, as per our arrangement with Commander Solus before he was dismissed from your service."

"And what of that fellow who refuses to come out of the brig? Is he still in there?"

"That would be the upgrade, Bas, and yes, sir, he is still in the brig aboard the attack ship *Shadow*. As such, the Prolix-dampening field within means we cannot control him."

"Silly ass."

"I suppose so, sir."

"Misplaced loyalty. We should have increased the personnel rotations among the fleet. Too much familiarity. That is apparent now."

"Agreed, sir."

"And the incoming ships from Perdicion and the Red Planet? What is their status?"

"The ships from Perdicion are due first but are still weeks away. They have maintained a linked formation together, an attack ship and a support ship, both with partial crew complements. The attack ship, *Dauntless*, has two upgrade personnel and two officers, including the commander. The support ship, *Relic*, has two upgrade personnel and one officer. I have been in secret communication with them, informing them about the rebellion of the Blue Squadron. They have acknowledged and from now on will only communicate with us. They await further orders as they get closer."

"And have you made similar contact with the Epsilon squadron? Do they have a level of understanding about the situation here?"

"I will be contacting them next, sir."

"See that you do."

IN THE PROLIX NODE SERVER

Xoxon was not lost. He had, indeed, installed himself within the node and disguised himself as a system maintenance routine. As such, he could access any system component under the guise of testing the equipment.

With his administrator access level, he found that he was able to get around most security protocols and could thus reconfigure the node and even rewrite its base code, if necessary. Electronic pulses passed his position constantly, providing him power and nourishment. He had often entered such places—this very position, in fact—with his mind, but never his entire self. It was a cold, alien place to him, and he felt alone and abandoned.

This was because he was fully integrated with Solus, and did not feel complete outside his body. Solus' DNA completed his code, and his only motivation was to return to Solus.

Xoxon's first priority now was to determine the location of his master and whether he was still alive. For this, he would reach out to the planetary scanning system to initiate a search. But, of course, he needed to find out where to look. This meant accessing the logs of the upgrades who had taken Solus away. He would then see where they'd left him.

All this had to be done in a stealthy manner to avoid detection from the security subroutines. In the meantime, Xoxon was biding his time waiting for an opportune moment to initiate Solus' desired changes to the system. He would need to work fast, and at the right time, so that his work was not simply overwritten by the system's security. He would need to escape the notice of the leader's valet too, of course: he was the real manager of the system.

Or perhaps he could also alter the valet's programming . . . now that was an interesting idea.

ON THE SOUTH SEAS ISLAND CONTAINING THE ISHTARIAN COLONY

Jimbal had shed his space jumpsuit earlier in the day, keeping to his shorts, a light short-sleeved shirt, and bare feet. Now, in the evening, he peered up at the night skies from his spot nestled between two palm trees that sat on the edge of the beach.

He came here often for solitude, and to get away from the

petty bickering of the other Ishtarians on the island. After months in the isolation of space, Jimbal felt crowded by his fellow island inhabitants. They all remained in the ship's quarters, living inside the cargo carriers, and seemed to spend most of their time trying to consume all the goods from the storage compartments.

As the leadership did not seem concerned about it, Jimbal took it upon himself to ration the food stores before their supplies ran out. In consideration of this basic fact, he kept the stores under lock and key, and meted out set portions of food and supplies to the council members' servants. And for a more permanent solution, he organized work parties to begin cultivating fields further inland for the planting of crops.

He also noted another obvious source of food for their benefit. There was a bounty of sea life in the surrounding ocean, with countless varieties of fish, crustaceans, shellfish, and sea turtles. To exploit this food source, he was working with another set of willing helpers to develop ways of more effectively catching the various sea creatures for food. For this, they had the makings of a small dinghy for fishing. Next, they would need to fashion traps for catching the crabs and nets for the fish.

Jimbal considered it vital that they make progress on these fronts. From their history alone, it was foolhardy to rely solely on supplies from the Supremacy people, even if it was under new management now. While Commander Solus had appeared to be an honorable man, the Ishtarians as a people had been let down too many times. As the days passed with no further contact from space, it was becoming increasingly apparent that they were to be abandoned yet again.

Jimbal looked out over the ocean and into space at the magnificent full moon over the waters. It truly was a fantastic sight to behold from the planet's surface. Nothing compared to it, in his experience: Perdicion had no moon, and the Red Planet's tiny moons were hardly noticeable in her skies. He looked out at the countless stars in the sky and wondered who was up there yet.

With this thought, Jimbal pulled out the comm-device that Solus had given him and looked at its controls. For the fourth time that evening, he initiated the transponder in the hope that the signal would be heard and replied to. Jimbal had thought long and hard about whether to cooperate with Solus and tell him what he knew about the incoming Ishtarian ships. The silence from Solus, while disappointing and perplexing, had spared Jimbal an unpleasant task. He had decided against helping him. Call it honor, but he could not betray his own people like that, even for some greater good. So, for honor's sake, he was stuck on this island with the rest of them and probably abandoning any possibility of flying his old ship again.

Still, the silence from Solus was eating at Jimbal. It had been weeks since Solus had dropped them off. There were so many possible answers. Had Commander Solus lied to them and was not ever coming back? Had there been a mutiny among the Supremacy forces, or were they defeated by the last rebel ships? Were they all dead? He processed all the awful possibilities over and over in his head until he was sick of thinking about it.

Hoping that the ocean might bring him peace of mind, Jimbal got up and walked out onto the beach to the waterline to feel the waves splashing against his feet. He was reminded again how wonderful it was to live this way, outdoors, after so long in the confined area of a spaceship, and before that in the Red Colonies. It was natural for man to be outdoors.

Moments later, he looked up again at the night sky and saw at once a black spot in front of the moon. He could hear nothing but the constant surf, yet the spot was getting larger. Soon it blocked the moon from his view. Then, all at once, it seemed, it was over him, blocking out the stars.

Jimbal knew a spaceship when he saw one, but he could not make out her lines in the darkness. He waited for the instant annihilation that was surely coming—an energy burst that would leave a large crater where he now stood. Instead, a beam of light illuminated his spot on the beach and blinded him. And then, very rapidly, he could feel the ship drawing nearer to him.

He decided not to duck and run. Let them come, he thought. It was one of the attack ships; he saw that now. He could feel the ship's thrusters blowing down upon the water and felt the spray from the surf splashing his face and body. The ship's belly became more visible as it moved closer to him, and Jimbal could now see the deployment compartment on the bottom lighting up and extending down. Within the compartment, he could now make out the figure of a man waving at him.

A voice called out to him: "Jimbal—what luck to find you on the beach! I'm Commander Solus' first lieutenant, Grand. We need your help!"

IN THE PROLIX NODE SERVER

Xoxon had accessed the planetary scanning network, and was now in the process of performing a mock test to disguise his activity from the node's security.

Taking control of a satellite over New Ouda Regio, he swept the satellite's eye over to the vicinity of the region's largest river, which snaked in a westerly fashion towards an even larger river to the south. This was the general location where he had determined that Solus had been thrown out of *Guru*. Upon review of the satellite's logs of the past few weeks, Xoxon first caught sight of his master being heaved, unconscious, out of the hovering ship and into the river. Distress caused by this scene was short-lived, as he saw in later logs that Solus had been discovered on the shore of the river and had since been seen around the native village there.

Watching the area in real time now, Xoxon re-positioned the satellite's eye in all light wavelengths around the forest beyond the river bank, so that he could pick up any people below the tree line. Using Solus' network-registered body signature as a guide, Xoxon configured the satellite's ground tracking system to locate Solus' current position. While the system searched, Xoxon zeroed in on a top view of the village, consisting of a large lodge and a few small wigwams nearby. Within seconds, an infrared image lock marked the position of a body matching Solus' signature just to the east of the village. It showed that Solus was walking around in the forest by himself in the dark.

This struck Xoxon as odd behavior for his master, but before he could consider this matter more carefully, the tracking system alerted him to yet another person out in the forest. To Xoxon's deep concern, this individual was advancing on the village—and on Solus' position, with some sort of advanced technology. Xoxon commanded the system to identify it.

The readings came in instantaneously—a Supremacy-issue pulse rifle. At this, Xoxon rapidly deduced that the rifle-bearing person was the fugitive, Zealrot. This meant, in turn, that Solus was in danger. Xoxon recoiled,as far as his coding could permit, at being away from his master in a time of need. He watched anxiously for an opportunity to help in any way he could.

IN THE FOREST NEAR THE NATIVE VILLAGE

Zealrot awoke very early in the morning that day, with high

expectations for a successful outcome of his plans. He grabbed his rifle and left his tent in the darkness well before dawn.

He skulked down the path towards the village, viewing the tactical situation through the rifle's scope as he advanced. As soon as he came into the weapon's range of the village, he scanned the area for his quarry. The rifle had previously registered Myra's, Zeeni's, and Mondra's signatures, and it soon picked them up again. He could see infrared images of all three of them lying on bedding inside a wigwam that was separated from the main lodge. He grinned at how this simplified his task. Their isolation would allow him to extract the women without rousing the rest of the village.

After stealthily advancing to their wigwam, he pulled the flap open and entered the enclosure, leading with the barrel of his gun.

"Awake, my queens!" he whispered sharply, just loud enough to interrupt their cruel dreams of the end of Perdicion. "It is your Zealrot, come to collect you!"

This had the effect on them he had intended. They all started and awoke, and sat up with looks of surprise and terror.

"It is time to come away with me, you naughty little women," he said, with sneering affection. "I've been looking for you three for quite a long time!"

They stared at him dully. When he illuminated their faces with the light from his gun, he noticed that their eyes were already red and swollen. They had evidently been crying. "Have you been missing me?" he said teasingly, stroking his pointed beard. "Dry your tears; I am here now!"

They did not move. Surprisingly, they did not reply at all.

"All right," he snapped. "You've had time enough to wake up. You are to come with me. Collect your food and belongings, whatever you can carry. You are all coming with me, or I will be forced to shoot one of you and take the other two." He paused, and continued his threat. "I'll settle for one of you if I have to."

This seemed to impact their fuzzy little heads at last. They stumbled to their feet and wordlessly began gathering their things. Zealrot smiled as they obeyed his commands. Soon enough, they stopped packing and looked at him, as if to signal they were ready.

"Okay, one at a time, let's leave this hut and move away from the camp. If any one of you tries to run or rouse the natives, I'll begin shooting. It will be nothing for me to kill every last one of these vermin."

They quietly obeyed. One by one, they pushed their way through the wigwam's opening and stumbled single file down the path that led out of the village.

The women, in truth, were still dazed from the news of the destruction of Perdicion and the Red Colonies. Zealrot's appearance was no more than an extension of the surreal world they found themselves in. They looked down at their feet as they walked, not wanting to look very far ahead or behind them, where Zealrot stalked.

Then they heard a familiar voice. "What on earth are you three doing?" Solus said, emerging from the woods to the right of the path in front of them. Before they could react, Zealrot pushed his way through them and aimed his weapon at Solus' chest.

Solus identified him immediately. "Zealrot—I'd forgotten about you," he said simply.

For his part, Zealrot did not recognize Solus as quickly with his beard and native garb, but then remembered the sound of his voice. "And I you," replied Zealrot. He certainly had not forgotten this Supremacy interferer. "How the mighty have fallen! What are you, a deserter? Where's your Supremacy uniform?"

Solus remained silent.

"Well, never mind; it makes no difference. I am now very pleased to have this opportunity to avenge myself." Zealrot aimed the gun at Solus' heart using the weapon's targeting computer, a completely unnecessary tactic at this close range. Not pausing to let this opportunity pass, he squeezed the trigger.

But the rifle's scanning screen went dark. Instead of firing, Solus heard the familiar sound of the weapon's powering down—and sprang into action directly.

His first task was to knock the rifle out of Zealrot's hands before he could use it as a club. Solus came crashing down on it, wrenched it loose, and kicked it into the dark underbrush. Then, employing his close-combat training, he struck Zealrot forcefully with a kick to his mid-section, then swung down to hit him on the back of his neck.

Anticipating this, Zealrot collapsed down on the trail and rolled over. He grabbed at Solus' legs to knock him off his footing.

Solus kicked with one foot as Zealrot held on fiercely to his other leg. With a mighty tug, he knocked Solus off his feet. Zealrot grabbed a large tree branch on the side of the path and swung it down on Solus' back, as Solus struggled to regain his footing. The blow knocked him to the ground again.

Zealrot was about to hit Solus again when Myra stepped in, grabbing furiously at him and the branch. Then Zeeni and Mondra joined in the fight. Their sorrow turned to rage as they struck at Zealrot in fury.

Their combined blows knocked Zealrot to the ground. Before he could get up, they grabbed their own dead branches from the path and began pelting him with blows. One blow struck his head, and he collapsed unconscious on the ground.

They continued to beat him, screaming in rage and taking out all of their anguish on this vile human being. Solus and Myra came forward and stopped them, grabbing at their branches. "Zeeni, Mondra—it's over," Myra said. "He's down, now stop. You'll kill him!"

They finally remembered themselves and stopped.

"There's been enough death," Myra said to them.

Out of breath, the women looked at each other, and their rage was gone as fast as it had hit them. It converted again to sorrow and anguish. Their tears began again, but at least the ordeal was over.

ONBOARD THE SUPREMACY ATTACK SHIP ORION
RE-GAINING A HIGH ORBIT OF THE BLUE PLANET

"Commander Solus thought a lot of you," Grand said to Jimbal once they were completely inside the deployment chamber. Before it was again tucked into *Orion*'s belly, the ship was climbing back into the sky.

"You're speaking in the past tense. Has something happened to him?" Jimbal replied, with a look of commendable concern.

"I'm afraid so," Grand replied. "If he's alive, it'd be a miracle."

As they climbed up into the central conveyor tube of the ship, Grand apprised Jimbal of the arrival of the Old Man, and what had happened to Solus. He was still telling the story when they reached the ship's center deck, where the wardroom was situated. Grand sat Jimbal down at the counter there and got him some food and a drink.

"The Supremacy ruled by one man!" Jimbal exclaimed between mouthfuls and gulps, when Grand had completed the story. "We always heard the conspiracy theories, but I didn't believe it was possible."

"I didn't believe it either, but with the Prolix network as the enforcer, it *was* possible," Grand said ruefully. "And it still is. That is our situation. He does not have control of those of us with the command Prolix, but if we do not follow his orders, we are all under the threat of being force-fed the upgrade Prolix."

"Makes me glad I don't have one," Jimbal uttered.

"And, honestly, that is the reason we need you," Grand replied. "But even more, the Ishtarians need your help, too. Solus made a deal with the Old Man that, in exchange for our continued loyalty, the Old Man would not destroy the Ishtarian colony."

"What!" Jimbal cried out, not realizing this danger until now.

"He blames you all there for the destruction of Perdicion," Grand returned. "The agreement only held him off temporarily, but he will have his vengeance."

"We've got to warn them!"

"We will, but we're going to stop it from happening first. We are now nominally in control of the attack ships."

"But he could upgrade you all?"

"It's possible, but not all at once, so we're told," Grand said.

"But how can you be picking me up without him knowing about it?"

"I am taking a chance. You remember that little toy we used to fool you and your attack ships into tracking it instead of us?"

"Of course, I'd forgotten about that . . ."

"It is now pretending to be us, in the position we are supposed to be in. My Prolix informs me that the node's resources are only tracking our positions directly over the northern continent where the Prolix node is placed. I can only think that the node is plenty busy right now on other matters, and its resources are being tapped to the extreme. That may change at any time."

"So, what do you want me to do for you?" Jimbal asked.

Grand could sense conflict in the man, and decided to give him a chance to digest all that they had discussed. "Tell you what," he replied, "let's get back to that in a few minutes. Let me get you some new clothes, and you can wash up if you want to."

Thirty minutes later, as they sat with coffee cups in hand, Grand continued his dialogue with Jimbal. "Let me come right to it," he said. "I need you to pilot one of the attack ships. But first, I need you to contact the incoming Ishtarian attack vessels and arrange a truce."

Jimbal looked at Grand intently but did not respond.

"If I were in your position," Grand continued, "I would not like being thought of as a traitor by my people. That would be hard to take. But consider this—we are actively opposing the very personage of the Supremacy, who is seeking to re-establish it on this planet, so I am a traitor, too. *We* are not the Supremacy—it's the Old Man who is. And after the way that Solus was treated for standing up for your people, I cannot be anything but a traitor to that now."

"I see your point," Jimbal started, "but—"

"We need you. We are fighting on two fronts here. We have to deal with our own people in ships that are converging on this planet. We do not know if they will fire upon us or join us. That is bad enough, but we also have your people coming in three attack ships, and we expect that they will attack us. So, if you help us, you will likely be doing something contrary to the wishes of the Ishtarian Council, but you will not be a traitor— you will be fighting the Supremacy itself."

Jimbal appeared to want to speak again, but Grand added one last statement. "Jimbal, I take you as an honorable man, and I consider myself to be one too. If you tell me you cannot help, I won't try to coerce you. I will turn around and drop you back off on the island. So, it's your decision to make. Okay, I've spoken my peace."

"Grand," Jimbal said after a short pause, "your words have

helped me make a decision. Clearly I must choose the lesser of two evils, and to do that, I will help you. I will pledge my loyalty to you until the Old Man is removed as a threat. After that, I do not know."

"I cannot ask for anything more," Grand replied. "Thank you."

"What ship do you want me to take?"

"You'll be aboard *Warrant*," Grand said. "You will assist Rowling there as co-pilot, and you will make an attempt to contact the Ishtarian attack ships to ward them off. Offer them a truce."

"Will do. Get me over there," Jimbal said.

NEAR THE NATIVE VILLAGE

Zealrot had been bound tightly to a tree with a large vine found nearby. His head was still bowed in unconsciousness. While trying to decide what to do with him, Solus retrieved Zealrot's rifle from the underbrush and looked it over. It was, indeed, quite dead. He checked the battery cells and saw that they were still charged—yet the start-up process would not initiate. He was about to put the rifle down again when it abruptly came to life. Checking the scope again, he saw the start-up routine was now completing after all.

Then a very welcome text message scrolled across the screen. "This is Xoxon. I located your position via the planetary scanning systems, and saw that you were in trouble."

"Xoxon! How are you doing this? Where are you?" Solus spoke out excitedly.

The text continued scrolling. "I am not at liberty to reveal that at the moment, but I have escaped custody."

"I see. So, you turned off Zealrot's rifle! Thank you, my old friend."

More text appeared: "It seemed prudent. Listen, we must keep these communications brief. I will check back with you at various intervals. What would you like me to work on?"

"Oh, all sorts of things, I'm sure. First, I want to rendezvous with Grand without being picked up by the node."

"Understood."

"And Xoxon . . ."

"Yes?" (The text appeared before he could continue.)

"I want you back."

"I want to be back. Xoxon out." The screen cleared.

Dawn came at last. Solus looked over at Myra, who was crouching over her sisters, comforting them. The sun was illuminating the world around them, and Solus could better distinguish Myra's lovely features. He observed the lovely slopes of her thighs, her hips, her back and shoulders, and that luxurious black hair.

Butterflies flickered inside his stomach, as they often did when he gazed upon her. He remembered the first time he had discerned her beauty, when she was lying sedated in his ship's medical chamber, only about a month and a half ago. Yet his admiration for her was not just about her physical features—he simply could not love with such intensity based on looks alone, like falling in love with an image or a painting. He loved her for her beauty, yes, but this was intrinsically coupled with her innate goodness from which her beauty emanated. He wanted her as his mate and to join with her for life. He wanted a connection with her beyond all others: a merging of their bodies and souls.

Love for her, a gentle blossom in his heart, was now in full bloom, and he hoped beyond all measure that she loved him too. But because he loved her, he reminded himself immediately, their love—if, indeed, it existed between them at all, and not just inside him—must remain unrequited. It would not be right to start something he could not finish. He could not be deterred from his mission. She would insist upon going with him, and he could not stand the idea of her being in danger.

Trying to return his thoughts to the business at hand, Solus set his mind to the task of dealing with Zealrot. What to do with him? The easiest solution was to simply leave him tied to the tree. As tempting a thought as that was, he would not be Zealrot's executioner. That was for the Creator to decide.

Then it occurred to him: he would let the Creator decide. He would banish Zealrot from the area, sending him on his way without his gun. Looking at the wretch again, he noticed for the first time that Zealrot had no pack or other belongings on his person. This meant that he must have a camp somewhere in the vicinity.

That was the next step: Solus needed to find the camp and determine what other technology, if any, the man was carrying with him. He powered up the rifle's tracking system and accessed its logs. In moments—downright slowly, compared to the instantaneous service Xoxon would have provided—Solus reviewed the rifle's most recent movements, and was able to plot a reverse course of the route Zealrot had taken just that morning.

"Myra!" Solus called out.

Myra looked over at him and drew herself up from her sisters and came to him expectantly. Her eyes were bright once again. The recent action and the comforting of her sisters had the effect of revitalizing her.

"Yes, Solus?" (Myra had dropped the use of "Commander" from Solus' name at his insistence.) She approached him with a warm smile on her lips.

This touched his heart, but he shook it off and pressed on. "I've discovered Zealrot's encampment. I'm going there right now to see what he has."

Myra perked up further. "What do you plan to do?"

"I want to find out if he has any other technology at his disposal. I plan to remove anything that I find there, and then I will let him go."

Myra raised her eyebrows in surprise.

"We will let the Creator decide his fate," he explained. "We will banish him from this land and send him off with any belongings he has, but without any of the advantages of technology that would make him more dangerous."

"You are being just," Myra replied. "That is the only thing we can do, short of killing him."

Solus looked at her with obvious admiration, but then checked himself and looked away.

"Let's go together," Myra continued. "I will tell my sisters to watch Zealrot while we are gone."

The sisters reluctantly agreed to Myra's request. They sat down to go through their packs to make some breakfast for themselves, and Zealrot too, should he awaken from his stupor.

Moments later, Solus found himself walking through the forest alone with Myra. Her mere presence seemed to transform the world around them into a magical place. And he had never before experienced such beauty—or happiness. To his joy, she walked along very near to him. So close, in fact, that he had to resist the temptation to take her hand in his, something he wanted to do very badly. But he kept his discipline and monitored the rifle's logs and matched it with their true position.

Meanwhile, as they walked, Myra gazed intently at the tracks on the path and soon detected Zealrot's footprints leaving the path. Solus had forgotten about her skills as a tracker.

"I can see that he came from this point between those trees onto the path," she observed.

"The scanner agrees with you," Solus answered. "Let me go in first. I don't trust our old nemesis. Or rather, I do: to set a booby trap, if he thought of it."

With Solus in the lead, they made their way off the path and then between the trees. Solus took one step further through the thicket and barged right into a solid but invisible and pliable object. Whatever it was, it blocked his way entirely.

"Oh, my lord, it's a trap!" Myra cried out from behind him in fear.

"No, no—I'm quite all right," he replied quickly. "There's something here." Peering directly in front of him, he realized that his vision was blurred, as if he were looking through a tightly woven mesh of fabric. He touched it and then felt for its edges. "It's the tent!" he said. "You know, the one Zealrot had when we first encountered him."

"Oh, that's right," Myra exclaimed. "The invisible tent—how could I forget?"

"We left in such a hurry that night, I never thought to retrieve it," Solus said. "I thought I'd blasted it to pieces, for that matter."

They found an opening and went inside. It was not transparent on the inside. Its material was woven such that someone inside could see out, but no one could see in. Zealrot's meager belongings were in a pack, right next to a cot that was his bed. Any food that Zealrot may have had was not inside. He apparently was not fool enough to leave it inside so as to attract predators into his little dwelling, for their sense of smell—not necessarily their eyes—would be their guide.

The main support for the tent had, indeed, been damaged in their first fight, but Zealrot had managed to patch it together by rearranging some of the tent's other parts. "Zealrot will not get this back," Solus said. "It was not his to begin with. This is Supremacy-issue." He looked around the tent again. "Besides, it may come in handy for me," Solus said.

"For what?" Myra asked. "You've not discussed your plans at all since coming here." She seemed to be anticipating bad news.

Solus looked at Myra. His heart was melting away.

"You're not leaving. . . ?" Her voice trailed off before saying "me."

"Myra," Solus replied, looking at her intently. "I have to leave, and once I tell you why, you will understand. It is also the reason I was left here in the wild."

She responded by sitting down on the tent's flooring. "Here, sit down. I want to hear everything."

Solus acquiesced, and they faced one another with crossed legs. Solus spent the next ten minutes telling her about the Old Man and what he had done to Solus and his men.

"He must be stopped!" she said resolutely after he had finished. "We cannot have this here. We cannot let this happen again." Her eyes flashed in anger. He remembered when that same look had been directed at him. He was glad her anger was now directed at someone else.

"I intend to stop him," he said. "And to do so, I must get to the node cave."

"Won't they be able to track you?"

"Possibly, through satellites, but now they have to know where to look," Solus replied. "They did make one miscalculation. By taking Xoxon away from me, they also took away their ability to find me easily."

"But your men—how can they help you, if they are being tracked?"

"That is a question for Xoxon. I hope to have an answer to that very soon."

Myra looked into his eyes. "Well, I am coming with you, regardless."

"Myra," Solus said, anticipating she would say this. "It will be extremely dangerous. I don't want you to get hurt or killed. I . . ." He trailed off. He wanted to tell her he loved her. He looked at her face—his expression telling her everything he could not bring himself to say.

Myra looked back at him and leaned closer, giving him an opportunity to kiss her.

Losing his control, Solus bent closer to her face so that their nose and lips were inches away from each other. "Myra," he said, holding back. "I can't stand the idea of you getting hurt." Now his control was gone—he could hold it back no longer—it was like his bones were on fire. "I . . . love you too much for that."

He looked down at his crossed legs, angry at himself for saying it too soon.

"Oh, Solus, I love you too!" Myra yelped, tilting his head back up with her hands. And she did love him. Her respect and admiration for him had transformed into love, and her emotion poured out at that moment. She pulled his lips to hers and kissed him.

Within Solus, a tidal wave broke forth that swept away any remaining resistance. He pulled her to him in a tight embrace and kissed her with a fervency that he had not believed he had within him.

They had both, at last, found love.

Both wished for the moment to last indefinitely; to remain forever in their own little magic world. But the nagging unmet responsibilities of the physical world kept intruding upon them.

There were immediate concerns, of course. Zealrot still needed to be dealt with, and Mondra and Zeeni were with him, alone, and in unsteady emotional states. Given those facts, the newly-united lovers grudgingly left the tent together, and they would not willingly separate again.

As Solus predicted, Myra insisted upon accompanying him on his mission. He saw that there was no deterring her, so Solus did not fight her on the matter any further. Besides, as they spoke, he began to have a sense that Myra was supposed to go with him, and that she was to play a part in the mission. With this intuition, he lost his misgivings about it.

Solus removed Zealrot's bag from inside the tent and then collapsed the tent down into a bag of its own with convenient shoulder straps. After slinging the tent and Zealrot's bag on his back, he and Myra walked back to their worldly responsibilities, yet feeling more alive than ever before. As they walked back, they agreed not to reveal their new relationship to the sisters, at least for the time being.

Upon returning to the scene of the recent fight, they found Zealrot now quite conscious. In fact, he was struggling and groaning like an animal in his bonds. The sisters sat together facing him a short distance away. Relief showed in their eyes the moment they saw the couple approach. Myra went and sat between them, and placed her arms around their backs, grabbing their shoulders. They each grasped Myra's offered hands.

"Has he said anything?" Solus asked.

"He screamed out a few times to let him go," Mondra replied. "We have not spoken to him at all."

"We didn't want to get lured into arguing with him," Zeeni interjected.

"That was wise," Myra replied.

"I'm going to take care of him now," Solus declared, and moved towards Zealrot, rifle in hand. Zealrot struggled harder at his bonds upon Solus' approach, staring at the rifle with wide, terror-filled eyes. "Stop your thrashing!" Solus ordered. "I'm not going to shoot unless you try to escape."

Zealrot growled in response. Solus could see that the man's arms were red and bleeding from his attempts to loosen the cords of the vine. "I will not be your executioner," Solus continued. "And I will not be your jailer either. I am, therefore, banishing you from this region."

"By whose authority?" Zealrot said sneeringly. "You have none over me!"

"By the Creator's."

"The Creator?" Zealrot replied, honestly surprised. "Not the Supremacy?"

"I no longer represent the Supremacy," Solus replied. "If I did, I would not be so merciful toward you."

"And who, then, is the Creator?"

"He is the almighty being who created all that is visible and invisible."

"And what religion is this? What name does he go by?"

"I have heard him called 'I Am.'"

Zealrot looked perplexed, not having heard that name before. "What is this nonsense?" Zealrot ejaculated. "This must be some native superstition. There are no other gods! We are the gods here!"

"We are not gods. We are only people who have been given the advantage of technology. And as you will soon find out, we are nothing special without it. You and I are no better than the people who live here. Our ability to survive in this environment is considerably less than theirs, in fact, unless we adopt some of their manner of living. Given that, you will be given your belongings found in the tent, but nothing more, and you will leave this place."

Zealrot stopped his struggles. "I cannot have my tent back?"

"No."

"But I will be slaughtered without it here in the wild!"

"That is for the Creator to decide," Solus replied. "Perhaps you should pray for his mercy."

"But the savages," Zealrot continued pleading, "they will come after me!"

"Then it is best that you be gone from this region as soon as possible."

"But no weapons? How can I survive?"

"You are free to fashion such weapons from what you find in your environment. Perhaps you should imitate how the natives do it."

Zealrot continued to plead and complain, but Solus was done arguing with the reprobate. Instead, while he held the gun on Zealrot, Solus had Myra go around the back of the tree and cut the vines that held him. Meanwhile, he had Mondra and Zeeni bundle up the food that they had and placed it in Zealrot's bag. "Ladies," Solus said, keeping his eyes fixed on Zealrot, "please return to the village while I escort Zealrot out of the area."

Myra hesitated at first, but obeyed and went with her sisters back down the path. When they were at last out of sight, Solus threw the bag to Zealrot and waved the gun, indicating the direction he wanted Zealrot to go in.

"I will be tracking you with this rifle, so I will know if you have turned back," he warned. "And once you move out of the range of this rifle, I also have access to planetary scanning technology. I will know where you are."

Zealrot did not react, but seemed to be dully accepting the inevitable. He could do nothing now that would not risk his own life in the process.

"Move!" Solus ordered.

Zealrot looked at Solus with intense hatred, but then moved off. He stopped a few paces later, a thought occurring to him. How did Solus know the rifle was working again? He looked back at Solus, his expression betraying his thoughts.

Solus, sensing his thoughts, aimed and fired a burst just over Zealrot's left shoulder. The blast impacted a tree behind him, drilling a deep black, flaming hole in its trunk.

"Convinced?" Solus asked.

In response, Zealrot turned and walked away, head down.

After Zealrot had disappeared down the path and was gone, Solus continued to watch his progress on the scope. Growing tired of staring at the screen, he looked up at the woods around him. It was getting on in the morning, but it had turned darker. He noticed the darkened blue-gray clouds through the breaks in the screen of leaves above him. He looked down again at the trees around him and noticed anew the blast hole he had just made in the tree. He felt sorry for having caused it. As a new believer, he did not like damaging any of the Creator's creations with his modern weapons.

He looked down again at the rifle's screen and saw that a text message was scrolling again. "This is Xoxon," Solus read. "I have analyzed your request. It is impossible for a ship to pick you up at this time. The entire continent is under constant observation by the node as an early warning system in case of attack."

"I thought as much," Solus said. "I'll have to travel to the node on the ground, then. I estimate that it will take several weeks to get there."

"If you travel only by day, it could take as long as fifteen days," Xoxon replied.

"Can you do anything from your position once I do get there?"

"I have several avenues of attack, which I will not disclose here," Xoxon replied.

"Understood. When the time comes, you are free to launch your own attack as you see fit."

After signing off with Xoxon and setting an alarm on the rifle scope that would sound should it detect Zealrot's body signature in its scanning range, Solus made his way back to the village. As he hiked back down the trail, he perceived raindrops hitting at indiscriminate spots all around him. It increased in intensity and started to get him wet, and he delighted in the experience of his first rainfall on the Blue Planet.

ONBOARD THE SUPREMACY ATTACK SHIP SHADOW *IN ORBIT ABOVE THE BLUE PLANET*

Bas remained in *Shadow's* brig, which was at best a two-person room, with curving, transparent outer walls and doors, so that the prisoner could be observed easily from the outside. Such a facility should have been totally outmoded by the Prolix technology, but holding cells were still needed for prisoners without the Prolix, and for when update processes went bad and upgrade personnel become temporarily unstable. Such personnel needed to be held until they were back under control. For those cases, a dampening field was developed that inhibited Prolix functionality. It was of limited application, and had an independent power source that was extremely difficult to power down. It could only be activated when the doors were locked.

So, if he wished to remain under his own control, Bas needed to stay in the brig with the doors locked. Fleek brought him food and drink through a small opening in the wall designed for that purpose.

"Bas, you must be going crazy in there," Fleek commented at the start of the second watch of the day.

"It's pretty boring, sir," Bas replied. "But I've been doing a lot of thinking."

"I guess that's all you can do, besides sleeping, I suppose. Would you like something to read, at least? I think I can track down an unused pad around here." Pads were handheld control panels that could be used as equipment interfaces. Although largely unnecessary with Prolix technology, which could do the same thing, a pad's interface could be used to pull up reading material.

"Yeah," Bas replied, "that would be nice to have." Then a thought occurred to him. "Say, Ensign, I just had an idea. Rather than a pad—how about a remote-control panel in case you need help piloting the ship?"

Fleek considered it. It was an interesting idea, if Bas were really in control. The strain of manning the ship all by himself was starting to wear on him.

"Bas, I think that's a great idea," he replied after a moment. "I will get you one from the weapons nose."

Shadow's nose sections each contained redundant primary and secondary controls. The port "weapons" nose contained the primary scanning and weapons controls, while the starboard "helm" nose held the primary helm and navigation controls. So, thinking it through, Fleek decided to keep the primary controls in each primary nose and remove the secondary panels from each. This was not a major issue while those noses remained together in a united cockpit, but should they separate in battle, a full crew would need to man the separated noses. But even so, as there were only the two of them aboard the ship, Fleek was already piloting the ship from the central commander's module, which contained all of those functions in addition to the nose controls.

A few moments later Fleek returned carrying a panel under

his arm. It was too big to get to Bas through the food door, so Fleek would need to open the brig doors.

"Ensign, I suggest you put a gun on me while the doors are open, just to be safe," Bas warned.

"Do you think that will be necessary?" Fleek replied.

"I do," Bas said. He had experienced the hacking event and was still reproaching himself for his lack of control.

"Very well," Fleek said. "Why don't you sit down on the bed and put your feet up, as well?"

Bas nodded and did as he suggested.

Intending to kick it into the room at Bas, Fleek put the panel down on the floor in front of the transparent doors. He then pulled out his sidearm and held it before him. In his other hand, he held a brig controller pad, an instrument necessitated by the Prolix dampening field.

"Okay, here goes." Fleek pushed the "door open" button and the doors slid open.

Bas' expression changed almost immediately. He had been clutching his raised knees on the bed. He now moved his arms to his sides as if readying himself to spring into action. Fleek noted this with alarm and quickly kicked the panel into the brig room. It slid in, but part of it stuck out slightly outside the door perimeter. Fleek moved forward to kick it again and simultaneously pushed the "door close" button. As the doors slid closed, Bas sprang into action, leaping at the closing doors.

Fleek jumped back, pushing another button on his controller. In response, gas sprayed out as Bas attempted to get through the opening. He immediately slumped to the floor.

Covering his nose with his arm, Fleek was glad he had kept his finger on the controller's "stun gas" button. He looked down at poor Bas. Clearly, he had no control whatsoever without that dampening field. Sighing with a mixture of relief and pity, Fleek holstered his sidearm and pulled Bas back into the brig. He then made sure the control panel was inside the room and re-closed the doors.

The dampening field re-activated immediately. Bas would be out for a while, so Fleek left and went back to his post in the command module. From here, he would monitor Bas' activities, and at the first sign of trouble, Fleek could override and deactivate the remote panel. He would see how this arrangement was working for a time, and then quite possibly, he could have some real rest again.

IN THE NATIVE VILLAGE

As the sisters had given most of their food to Zealrot, they had very little left in the wigwam. So, in spite of the rainstorm, they needed to go out and do some fishing. The sisters assured Solus that this was an excellent time to fish, as the fish would not hear them as well with the sounds of the rain hitting the river. And sure enough, using their native fishing tackle, they managed to catch a number of trout from the river.

They brought their catch back to the wigwam, and after cutting and cleaning them, they cooked the fish over a small fire built under a little enclosure. The rain grew more intense as they sat down inside to eat their meal. Periodic lightning flashes and thunder shook the world.

While they ate, Myra told the sisters that she and Solus would be leaving them soon to go on a journey together. "We have to stop a new threat to this world," she explained. "There is a man who is attempting to establish a new Supremacy government here."

The sisters grew immediately alarmed, but Myra worked hard

to reassure them. "We want you to remain here," she continued. "We need you to remain free . . . in case we fail."

"We have faith that you will not. We have come to a new understanding of our faith," Mondra explained. "We have been given insight that God will act through each of us, if we allow it."

"And he has a plan for each of us!" Zeeni added.

"We understand now that we have all been sent to this world to do his will," Mondra continued. "And we believe that you two have been given a special mission to accomplish."

"We were wondering when you were going to be leaving us," Zeeni said. Solus was impressed by their simple, almost child-like faith.

They then discussed the journey ahead of Myra and Solus and what they should take with them. It was settled that Mondra and Zeeni would remain with the natives, but that Myra and Solus would come back for them when their mission was over. "We want to go to Ludaea and see for ourselves this new religion," Mondra said.

"And we must find out how to get you two married properly, in the tradition and customs of the new religion," Zeeni remarked, grinning slyly. Myra and Solus blushed with surprise and embarrassment.

"Don't think we did not notice!" Mondra added as the sisters giggled with delight.

Overcoming their embarrassment, Myra and then Solus joined them in their laughter.

Three days later, Myra and Solus began their journey south. After making a quick detour to pick up the pulse rifle that Myra had hidden in the old tree trunk, they made their way through the forest and south to the plain, beyond the hills that followed the river.

They walked during the day, taking time out only to gather food and find water from streams and cold springs. When they found water, they refilled the gourds, which they used as canteens strapped around their necks with cords made from vines. After the lifetime spent drinking filtered, recycled water, the spring water they drank was the most refreshing, most wonderful-tasting liquid Solus had ever tasted.

He also grew accustomed to eating food found in nature, and enjoyed the wild grapes, berries, and occasional honey that Myra found along the way. He liked this far better than the wild turkey he had shot with his rifle and attempted to cook for dinner one evening. What was left of it, at any rate. His rifle was not meant for hunting, and had caused too much damage to the bird's carcass to make it very palatable. He would have to try a lower burst setting the next time. Yet, the closer they came in proximity to the node cave, the more dangerous it was to use his weapon. It would likely be picked up by the base's sensors.

In the evenings, inside Zealrot's tent for the night, they would lie on their bedding and stare up through the tent's open covering at the starry skies overhead. They spoke about many things, and learned about each other's past. Myra told Solus all about her parents and brother and her upbringing on her family's farm on Ishtaria. Solus, in turn, told Myra about his childhood. "My mother died a few years after I was born," he told Myra the first time she asked him about his parents. "I lived on a vast military base. I was raised by housekeepers and, well, Xoxon."

"Tell me about your mother," Myra requested one evening.

"My personal memories of her are pretty scant, as she died when I was very young, but when I was little, I spent a lot of time watching videos of her and Dad, whatever was in the home video logs. I watched them so much that for a time I gained the sense of them being my own memories, as if I were there too. Anytime I felt lonely and a longing for her, I would go and watch an ordinary day in my mom's life. Her just going around the house cleaning or something like that. But it was painful for me, too. I so wanted her to stop what she was doing and look at me! Talk to me!"

Myra's eyes, unbeknownst to Solus, welled up in the darkness, crying for the child that was Solus.

Solus continued, "My old friend Xoxon always helped me through those times. And he helped me to stop watching the video logs too, telling me it was not healthy for me. What he did was to have me pick out those special moments: my birth, my first birthday, celebrations and such. Then, on special occasions, I was allowed to watch those moments."

"Where was your dad?" Myra asked.

"Oh, he was my hero," Solus said. "He was a captain in the Supremacy Space Defense. He was hardly ever physically present in my life, but he was a part of it. He spoke to me every day via the Prolix link when he wasn't off on a mission. But I stayed very busy. It was never in question as to what I would be doing when I grew up. It was the space fleet for me. I was schooled at home by Xoxon, but I also participated in classes with kids my age for physical training and sports."

"What happened to your dad?" Myra asked, almost not wanting to know.

"My father died a hero of the Supremacy," Solus responded. "He died during an attack on a Lavinian space cruiser. This was before the great unification, of course—before they formed the Supremacy. He sent me his last message, just before going into that battle," Solus said. "I was watching an episode of *Captain Xoxon*, my favorite show, when his transmission came in. I remember being annoyed at the interruption."

"What did he say to you?" Myra asked, feeling the pain for him as he spoke.

"I could even play it for you, if I had my Prolix back," Solus responded. "That's the combined wonder and agony of technology. But no matter; it was as typical a message as you can imagine. He told me he was going to work, which was his phraseology for going into battle. I knew what he meant, but it was so routine I stopped worrying about it. I wished him well and went back to watching my program. His commanding officer contacted me later that day to inform me about my father's glorious death."

Myra could hold it in no longer and rolled over and put her arms around him, crying for Solus the child. In turn, Solus, still not quite used to such displays of emotion, could only hold her and rub her back, trying to comfort her, kissing her soft hair. Yet in moments, he found his eyes were tearing up, and he joined her silently in the sweet sadness. She had brought it out of him.

The journey was hard and long, but they were together. As long as she was with him, there was nothing that really bothered him. As they walked during the day, Myra would tell Solus all she knew about the people of God. What she did know, of course, came from Harmonian long-distance observations. Her study, and that of her fellow Harmonians, had many gaps in it. While they had some samplings of the holy texts, they could not get long-distance access to all of the written scrolls that were the holy books of the faith.

"What are their marriage customs?" Solus said one afternoon as the shadows grew longer as the day was waning. They were passing through a field that was occupied by a large herd of buffalo. The animals stood all around the couple, grazing and snorting. Solus was amazed at the sheer size of these animals.

He would not be able to see over the shoulders of the biggest of them if he stood right next to it. And he did not want to get too close, for that reason.

"Why do you want to know?" Myra asked, smiling playfully.

"Oh, I'm thinking of getting married someday," he said as casually as he could fake it. "And I want to do it properly."

"Oh, I see," Myra replied. "Anyone I know?"

"You know very well who!" Solus said.

"Oh, you are no fun at playing." Myra giggled. "Well, let's see. The first thing you would need to do is speak to my father and get his permission. You would need to negotiate a dowry. In addition to me, you would get a herd of cattle. Then, once that was arranged and agreed upon, we would have a small betrothal ceremony. We would then be engaged to one another."

"Engaged to each other?" Solus replied. "I like the sound of that. What's next?"

"Well, customarily, you would then leave me with my family and come back for me after a year."

"A year!"

"Yes. I would need time to prepare for marriage, you see. And then, when the groom arrives back to pick up his bride, they exchange their vows before a priest and they are married!"

They were interrupted by loud grunting. The dominant bull had noticed their presence and was advancing in their direction.

"We'd better make a run for it," Solus instructed. "I don't want to shoot him, and then start a stampede, to boot. Let's get into those trees over there!" he said, pointing at a grove in close proximity to them.

Myra nodded and they broke into a run. The bull chased them for some distance, easily gaining on them, but then halted when he saw that he had successfully chased them away. He let out a concluding snort and turned back to his grazing.

Myra and Solus continued their walk in the twilight in the forest down a narrow animal trail. It was cool and magical. Chest-high undergrowth obscured the ground on either side of the path. The forest floor was filled with hundreds upon thousands of tiny yellow and white flowers.

Inspired by the spirit of the place, Solus spun around in front of Myra and got down on one knee. He took Myra's right hand. "Myra, I love you above all things," he said, looking up into her shining eyes. "Will you stop my suffering and take me as your husband?"

Myra looked down at Solus with a joy that gushed from her heart. "I will," she said.

Solus arose and clasped her hands. "How will I ever collect that dowry?" he asked.

"You'll think of something," Myra replied.

As the journey continued, Xoxon periodically communicated with Solus through the pulse rifle. Sometimes he gave them directions so they could avoid certain landmarks in their path that would have prolonged their passage. Other times he warned them about tactical considerations, and one that he stressed often had to do with their rifles. It was a dramatic irony if there ever was one, but once they came within a certain range of the node, the rifles would be detected and the Old Man would be alerted to their presence. Therefore, they would need to abandon the rifles once they got closer to their destination.

"God will provide," Myra counseled.

"We will need all the distractions you can provide," Solus said in reply to Xoxon's warning. "I hope you have some creative ideas to deploy!"

"I am working on one right now . . ." came the text reply.

CHAPTER 9

THE FIGHT GOES ON

A Supremacy satellite orbited synchronously high above the Prolix node in the western continent, formerly known as New Ouda Regio by the Supremacy. *Orion*'s sleek black form approached in a swifter orbit. She was in stealth mode—all dark, with her nose fixed together and her wings folded behind her. She swept by the satellite at such close range that, had her wings been extended, she would have knocked it out of its orbit.

"Boy, I'd love to take that out," Grand exclaimed as they passed. From his position in the command module, he had been aiming the forward guns at the target, whose flashing proximity warning lights were now lighting up the nearby space. He changed his screen view from the forward battery to the ship's rear cannon. The satellite rapidly disappeared from the gun's sights.

"Only a matter of time, sir," Rodd commented from his position in the nose of the ship. "We will need to remove that prior to any attack."

"In the meantime, we wait for our dear commander while he walks through the countryside with his new lady friend," Grand said ruefully. "If there was any way to pick them up without being detected!"

Grand had learned from Xoxon about Solus' return from the dead. It filled him with a new kind of hope—at least, one he had not felt since the destruction of Perdicion. Xoxon, as he was also doing with Solus, kept the squadron informed on any intelligence he could turn up. He communicated via the network maintenance systems.

"Aren't we taking a big chance in even talking about this?" Rodd said. "The node might pick this up."

"Not according to Xoxon," Grand replied. "He has been checking the node's monitoring systems and found that it is not interfacing at long ranges, only at close proximity to the node. He believes it is due to an overtaxing of the central processing systems. Apparently the system is working overtime on many other matters, and cannot keep all system resources at fully functional levels."

"I'd have to agree. It is a powerful system, no doubt, but it cannot duplicate the combined processing systems from the home world," Rodd commented. "It was a starting point, one of many nodes to be placed around the globe. It simply cannot handle the same load as Perdicion's old network."

"According to Xoxon," Grand continued, "it's working on a particularly high-priority job. Something to do with the Omega upgrade."

"That does not sound comforting," Rodd said.

"What cheery topic are you two gents discussing?" Nevek said, carrying brimming cups of coffee with him into the ship's nose.

"Hi, Doc," Rodd said, turning around in his chair. "Take a seat."

"Thank you," Nevek replied. "It was getting lonely in the back."

"Where's my drink?" Grand's voice spoke out over the

intercom as Nevek handed Rodd one of the cups. Both Nevek and Rodd turned and looked around and out the nose canopy window to see the dim outline of Grand's head in his darkened command cockpit. In the swimming lights of the console, they could make out his face and a waving hand.

"Why, it's right here," Nevek said, taking a sip. "You want it, come and get it!"

"No, Doctor, I need to stay right here just in case you press the wrong button in there and blow us all to kingdom come."

"I'll bring you one in a minute," Nevek replied, ignoring that last remark. "But first, I am tired of reminding you all that you need to take a break every now and then. I know we are short-staffed around here, but you cannot be on watch constantly. Your Prolixes can only do so much to help you stay awake."

"I know, Doctor," Grand said. "But we don't have a lot of options."

"I am particularly worried about Rowling and Thump. They are flying those two old stealth ships all by themselves, with only Jimbal to help. How can they be managing it all?"

"To give them a break, I take those ships under remote Prolix control, Doctor," Grand replied. "They're working in shifts."

"And to what end?" Nevek responded by changing the topic. "What exactly are we doing up here, anyway? Has anyone tried contacting the incoming ships?"

"We've been sending out transmissions on a regular basis," Grand answered. "We're tracking the two ships coming in from Perdicion, who will arrive first. I've also been in contact with the Epsilon squadron."

"They have been attempting to pick up the Ishtarian ships' movements since they left the Red Sector," Rodd added.

"Yes, and we have Jimbal on that job, as well. He's been attempting to contact them."

"But I'm more concerned about our ships," Nevek stated. "What's going to happen when our boys get into range of the planetary node? Won't their upgrades immediately go under its control?"

"Yes."

"Then they're as big a threat to us as the Ishtarians."

"Indeed," Grand said. "I can see the Old Man using them to destroy us just to ensure loyalty. But I suspect he is waiting for the Ishtarians to be removed as a threat first."

"Given that, Doctor," Rodd put in, "we need to take over that node from the Old Man before they get here."

Just then, the long-range scanner alarm sounded. "Who might this be? The incoming ships from Perdicion or the Ishtarians?" Grand uttered as he reviewed the readings.

"I think it's too early to be the Ishtarians, sir," Rodd replied, "based on the position of the Epsilon squadron. The Ishtarians simply could not be that far ahead of them."

"I've got more information," Grand said, after consulting his Prolix. "The scanners are picking up something coming into the Blue Zone from Perdicion. If that's the case, we're running out of time."

"What are your orders, Lieutenant?" Rodd requested.

"Bring her about, Lieutenant Rodd," Grand replied. "I want to stay on this side of the planet. I will notify the other birds to stay on alert status."

"Yes, sir," Rodd replied, intently working the helm controls.

IN THE PROLIX NODE'S PROTECTED MEMORY

The Old Man's valet was reaching the limits of his programming capacity. He was now simultaneously managing the physical plant of the planetary node base and the planetary defenses, which included monitoring the satellite array and ground assets. In addition to that, he was maintaining constant control of the upgrade personnel.

He could indeed handle all that, with the node's resources as they were. But there was the additional and continuing problem of detecting and fixing the holes in the Omega upgrade. The valet had determined, to his chagrin, that the upgrade was far from ready to be released when it was. Thus, he was taking on all of the bug-fixing tasks that the entire Science Bureau would have been working on. That would have meant hundreds of dedicated personnel and their Prolixes. The node's resources could offer little help in this area—it had the capacity, but not the necessary processing help that those people would have provided him.

A significant amount of his resources went to constantly searching and testing the code to discover the bug. He had a test environment all set up and the upgrades under his control as test subjects. He was poking and prodding their Prolixes, trying to reveal a flaw. But he could not be too forceful, because the Old Man still needed them as his soldiers. Any major manipulations of their Prolixes' programming could incapacitate them.

Thus, the process was agonizingly slow, even for an advanced Prolix program such as himself. He was a Prolix, but one that was specially designed for the Old Man. As such, his programming was matched up with the Old Man's DNA, yet he was designed to operate outside the man's body. The Old Man, like his parents before him, did not personally take the Prolix into his body. Instead, he used a specially-designed leadership version that could assist him nearly as well as the standard Prolix, as long as he remained in a technology-compatible environment.

By design, the valet always put his master's best interests before all else. But sometimes that rule made decisions very difficult, as situations often, by the valet's judgment, called for doing things that were against his master's will. Often, the master did not want what was best for himself. Yet the valet could not disobey a direct order from him. If he was given a direct order against the best interests of his master, he had to follow it, which would often create contradiction errors in his master processing center. He then had to reset his programming to remove the errors. This, of course, reduced his efficiency.

He needed to perform another such reboot very soon, as he now had several suspended processing routines caused by these/such contradiction errors. He scheduled the reboot to occur in the next 200 million cycles, which he hoped would give him enough time prior to that to track down any major flaws in the Omega upgrade. He needed to get this task completed so that he could properly devote all of his energy to serving the Old Man.

As it was, his control over the functions of the planetary node was not as complete as he would have liked. This, among other things, made the Old Man vulnerable to attack from within. That attack could be made via a yet-to-be-discovered back door, unintentionally opened by the Omega upgrade.

And on that note, he was also seeking, with what limited system resources were available, the Solus Prolix. The valet was convinced that this Prolix had not disappeared and was, indeed, hiding somewhere in the node. This pesky program was just the sort to take advantage of the Omega upgrade bug. This was, after all, a command Prolix that was matched with a free-thinking and formidable leadership personality. And that spelled trouble, especially at a time when the valet was over-extended.

The only solution was to acquire support as soon as possible from all incoming Supremacy assets. He had already confirmed loyalty from *Dauntless* and *Relic*, the incoming ships from Perdicion, as soon as they were in range of the node, but these were only two ships. Only one could operate in stealth mode.

The valet's real hope, therefore, was the Epsilon squadron, with four attack ships that had the capacity to overwhelm and destroy the Blue Squadron.

He initiated communications with them and hoped to establish control once they were in range.

THE EPSILON SQUADRON TRAVELING IN THE VOID BETWEEN THE RED AND BLUE ZONES

The four attack ships of the Epsilon squadron flew in close formation on a high-speed, direct course for the Blue Planet. Their goal was to rendezvous with the planet before it moved out of range,to the other side of the sun. In an effort to conserve power and supplies, only skeleton crews flew the ships, while the majority of the men slept in stasis.

"What to make of this?" Lieutenant Pekark, the commanding officer of the squadron and captain of *Pulsar*, asked via Prolix link. He and his squadron's three ship commanders had just received the Blue Planet Prolix node's transmission notifying them that the Blue Squadron was in open rebellion. The node reported that Commander Solus had been relieved of his command, and that it was likely that his officers were plotting against the legitimate Supremacy leader, who was now stationed on the Blue Planet.

"My Prolix confirms the source, sir," piped in Ensign Wilby, who commanded the attack ship *Talon*.

"True," Pekark answered. "But can we trust that? How do we know it's not another hacking of the network?"

"We don't, sir," Lieutenant Link chimed in from the third ship, *Typhoon*. "And given that, we need to be concerned about our upgrades."

"We'll keep them in stasis until we're sure," replied Pekark.

"I highly concur with that, sir," responded Ensign Chag from the fourth ship, *Deliverance*. This discussion forced Chag to recall vividly when *Quantum*, the former fifth ship in their squadron, had blown itself to atoms with a pulse cannon overload during the last hacking attack. Pieces from the vessel had battered Chag's hull before they could maneuver out of the way of the explosion.

"I know Solus and Grand. They are as sound as it gets," Pekark continued. "Something's not right."

"Perhaps, if you could contact them . . ." suggested Link.

"Just what I was thinking, but how to do it without the node picking it up?"

"Should I wake up Dricks?" asked Link, suggesting the services of the squadron's engineer and Prolix expert, who was fortunately simply off-shift, not in stasis.

"Yes," replied Pekark. "This is a high priority—I want to speak to Grand as soon as possible."

IN THE WILDERNESS OF NEW OUDA REGIO

Solus and Myra, now engaged, had at last reached the outer limits of the node's tracking systems. As such, they needed to abandon their pulse rifles. This meant, of course, that they would not have any firepower-or Xoxon's explicit help from this point forward.

Xoxon, therefore, sent them as much information as he could supply. This included an overview of the tactical situation, where the upgrade personnel were likely to be, and where the Old Man had taken up residence and the hours that he kept. Also, importantly, Xoxon provided the complete layout of the caves and the sensor locations and where Solus could go to take them offline, at least temporarily.

Solus tried to take in what he could, going over the instructions in his head as often as he could. It was difficult, for he had grown quite accustomed to having such information flashed before his eyes whenever he needed it.

"Here is a good place. We can stow the guns away under these rocks," Solus said to Myra, pointing to an outcropping of rocks that marked the beginning of the foothill region where the node was situated. "We may need them if we're forced to come back this way in retreat."

"It won't come to that," Myra replied, "but it would be best to hide them, nevertheless."

They wrapped the guns in the remains of the Supremacy tent and stowed the package under the rocks. The tent material was one technological advantage they reserved for the next phase of their journey. Using native knives fashioned from flint rock, they cut the tent apart and made two hooded cloaks to conceal themselves.

From this point forward, they would wear their new garments to escape the eye of any satellites above them as they ventured ever closer to the node. Thus dressed, they entered a small canyon between two green hills, keeping very close together so they would not lose one another along the way. The cloaks made it difficult for them to see each other, and a fog started gathering along the way.

ONBOARD THE SUPREMACY ATTACK SHIP ORION *ABOVE THE BLUE PLANET*

"Lieutenant Grand, we're getting incoming sensor touches from *Pulsar*," reported Rodd.

"Sensor touches?" Grand replied. "From long range?"

"Yes, but they are particularly intense," Rodd said. "I

think they are trying to establish communication. There's an embedded code in them, and it's transferring to the brig."

"The brig?" Grand called out, then remembered, ". . . of course, there's no Prolix reception in there."

"Yes, it's queued in the brig's communication module."

"Then I'm on my way," Grand replied. "Rodd, take charge. Please let me out when I'm done."

"If you say so, sir."

Grand climbed out of his command chair and exited the command module via the narrow stairs in its rear. He emerged into the main deck and moved to the back of the ship, where the brig was situated. Within a minute, he was inside the detention room with the doors closed behind him. The communication module was flashing, showing the incoming message. Grand touched the screen to activate it. "This is Lieutenant Grand aboard the *Orion*."

"Grand, this is Pekark. Where are you receiving this?"

"Where you sent it. I am in the brig. Good to talk to you, Peke."

"I am glad to hear your voice, Grand, but I'm still taking a risk talking to you. This exchange will probably be picked up once we reach the node's range."

"Peke, there's no government anymore—just an old man. No one's going to come after you anymore."

"That brings us to the real point here. What is all this about a rebellion? Did Solus lead a rebellion against the legitimate Supremacy authority?"

"Peke, it depends on what you think is legitimate, but in a word, yes," Grand replied. "This Old Man was apparently the secret leader of the world. The Prolix network confirmed his story."

"That is a shock, I have to admit. But if he was the leader—"

"The system was a sham. He ran it all—the rest of them were puppets."

"Okay, fine," Pekark replied, "but if he has a valid claim of authority, then who else has the right—"

"He has a claim to it, but—"

"Did Solus try to take over?"

"Not at all," Grand answered resolutely. "In fact, he was willing to submit to the Old Man's authority. But the Old Man ordered Solus to violate his word. It was a matter of honor to Solus."

"That's bad, of course. But the command structure often comes before honor, if you want to stay in the service—or stay out of the brig, for that matter. What specifically was he ordered to do?"

"Hear me out on this," Grand said, knowing this was not going to sound quite right. "Solus helped a group of Ishtarians to settle on the planet. He promised to help them get established."

"Ishtarians?" Pekark cried in disbelief. "They are the enemy. Solus was supposed to keep them off the planet. That was your mission there!"

"That was our mission, but the war is over. At least, that was Solus' stand. He wanted to end the bloodshed, even if that meant sparing the enemy. He set them up on a small island where they could not cause any trouble—"

"But Ishtarians . . . they are responsible—"

"Peke, Solus was right—we've had enough death. We lost our home world. We wanted to start fresh, all over again in a better place, not with more death. Then the Old Man stepped in."

"What exactly did he order you to do?"

"To destroy the colony," Grand replied. "They were defenseless. Solus refused and was banished to the wild lands of this planet. To avoid a fight with the rest of us, the Old Man relented in attacking the colony. This is probably only a short reprieve for them."

Pekark was silent for a moment, thinking over what he had heard. He did not understand this compassion for the enemy, especially after what had happened to them all. But he also knew both Grand and Solus well from their joint and long-standing military service. He knew that they were both men of character and honor.

Beyond that, there was something very unsettling and fishy about this secret-leader business. "Look," he said finally, "I don't know about all this sympathy for the Ishtarians, so I'll leave that aside for now. I have to go on the things that I do know, and I know you and Solus. If you are against this man, then so am I. My squadron will back me up on this."

"I know they will, Peke," Grand answered, relief clearly in his voice.

"What do you want me to do in the meantime?"

"You keep doing what you are doing," Grand replied. "Get here as soon as possible, and keep watching for those Ishtarian ships. They need to be dealt with."

"You want them destroyed?"

"Defend yourselves if attacked, but we would like to offer them a chance to surrender."

"That's not good battle tactics."

"I know, and Solus knows it too," Grand replied. "But he is working from a different set of criteria . . . listen, I'll explain on another occasion."

"See you soon."

"Grand out." Grand pushed the call button on the communications board.

Rodd answered immediately. "Shall I open the door, sir?"

"Please do so." The door opened. Grand left the confinement, and felt more at peace with himself and the world. He hoped that Solus was okay out there in the wilderness.

He knew that Solus' part in all this was about to begin again very soon.

ABOARD THE SUPREMACY ATTACK SHIP WARRANT *IN ORBIT ABOVE THE BLUE PLANET*

"Calling Ishtarian Defense Force vessels *Outrage, Culmination,* and *Rupture*. Please come in. This is Captain Jimbal of the *Vestige*. I am transmitting a coded message as verification."

Jimbal followed up the voice message with an Ishtarian-coded message that indicated that the Ishtarian Council had been established as a colony in the South Seas, and that the Supremacy forces here were no longer controlled by the Supremacy: that they were willing to call a truce and avoid a fight with the incoming ships.

FROM THE ISHTARIAN COLONY

Another communication went out into space to the incoming Ishtarian vessels. "This is the Red Colonies Ishtarian council leader," Nabib spoke into his long-range communicator. "Ishtarian attack ships, please come in!" he said. "We were intercepted and forced to land on a small island, left to starve. We were promised supplies, which have never been delivered. And one of our members, the captain of our vessel, the *Vestige*, has either been kidnapped or has betrayed us."

He paused again, then repeated his first call. "Come in, Ishtarian Defense Force vessels *Culmination, Rupture,* or *Outrage.*"

Nabib repeated his message every few hours, hoping they would finally answer him.

ONBOARD THE SUPREMACY ATTACK SHIP DAUNTLESS *NEARING THE BLUE PLANET*

Dauntless and *Relic* entered the Blue Zone and into a combat theater. They would be vulnerable in the ships' united condition. It was time to detach.

Lieutenant Cain went through the procedures to separate the two ships under his command. "Ensign, extend the deployment chamber to give us some more clearance from the *Relic*." This had the effect of separating and pushing the ships' hulls apart. After the chamber's neck had extended sufficiently, he ordered the division/did juncture. "Detach the bottom clamp—separate the ships."

"Detaching, sir."

The ships pushed away from one another and were separate units once again.

"Dusing, you are on your own again," Cain called via Prolix link to the lieutenant, who was commander of the *Relic*. "We are entering stealth mode and increasing speed. I would rather stay and escort you in, but the Supremacy leader needs our assistance."

"Roger that, *Dauntless*," Dusing replied. "We'll see you at the rendezvous site."

"I will probably need a re-supply of spears before this is over," Cain warned.

"We've got plenty. *Relic* out."

The banter disguised the growing tension on the ships. They were going into a dangerous situation with several ships known to be disloyal to legitimate Supremacy authority. Cain had been informed about Solus' removal from command—and that he had harbored the enemy in direct contradiction to his orders. This was dangerous, and an illegitimate questioning of authority.

Order, not defiance, was needed at this time. If order was not restored, then it was possible that the only habitable planet left would also be destroyed. And after witnessing Perdicion's destruction only weeks before, Cain could not bear that idea.

ONBOARD THE SUPREMACY ATTACK SHIP ORION *ABOVE THE BLUE PLANET*

"Sir, *Dauntless* just vanished from my scans," Thump called in from the *Crusade*. Grand had charged Thump with keeping a constant eye on her.

"Please verify, Thump," Grand ordered via Prolix. "The ships were connected. Make sure the scanner isn't detecting the two as one."

"No mistake, sir," Thump replied. "I also observed the *Relic* and *Dauntless* detaching. As soon as they were apart, *Dauntless* went into stealth mode and vanished."

"Very well," Grand replied. "Keep a watch out for any sign of them. Grand out."

"They are on radio silence," Grand said to Rodd, who was now manning *Orion*'s weapons nose.

"They must have aligned themselves with the Old Man," Rodd suggested.

"That would explain it," Grand said. "I'm going to try to contact them again.

"This is *Orion*. Come in, *Dauntless*," Grand said, sending out a standard long-range communications signal to the general area of space where *Dauntless* was last seen. "*Dauntless*, this is Lieutenant Grand. Please come in." Grand repeated his call several times, but got only a chilly silence in reply.

"That does it," Grand called out. "This is getting too complicated. I'm ordering battle-alert status."

"Agreed, sir," Rodd answered.

"Battle stations! Battle stations!" Grand barked into the squadron's private communications channel. "Blue Squadron, we are now on battle-alert status."

ONBOARD THE SUPREMACY ATTACK SHIP SHADOW *ABOVE THE BLUE PLANET*

Grand's call was relayed to Bas in *Shadow*'s brig. He called into the command module to Fleek, who was off shift resting while Bas operated the ship. "Sir, did you hear the call to battle stations? *Dauntless* has gone into stealth mode and will not respond to hails. Lieutenant Grand fears that she's likely under the Old Man's control."

"Bad," Fleek replied, rubbing his swollen eyelids. "I'm glad we are in stealth mode ourselves. They won't be able to detect us. Now, where would they most likely launch an attack?"

"The *Crusade* and *Warrant* are more vulnerable," Bas suggested. "Their positions can be tracked to a degree, as Commander Solus was able to do when we captured them."

"True, but I can't think that would be their strategy."

"Fleek, this is Lieutenant Grand," he called in through the sensor module.

"Yes, sir?"

"From now on, we need to avoid communicating through the Prolix network," Grand explained.

"Understood, sir."

"Proceed to orbital sector 1-9-4.3," ordered Grand. "I want you to remain in position to enter the atmosphere in support of the colony. I am also deploying *Warrant* to assist. I believe that *Dauntless* will strike there first."

"Yes, sir," replied Fleek. "But, sir, if I may ask, how can we oppose it? I mean, aren't we supposed to stay obedient to the Old Man, or he will upgrade our Prolixes?"

"We are going to solve that problem right now," Grand replied. "Commander Solus' Prolix has a plan and has need of all of our Prolixes."

"Do you mean transferring them away from us?"

"Exactly," Grand replied. "He promises to return them as soon as possible."

"I see," said Fleek. "Whatever we need to do."

"Excellent," Grand said. "I'll let you know when this will happen. It won't be long."

"But how do we do it, sir?"

"You will ask your Prolix to initiate contact with the node, and Xoxon will take it from there."

"Xoxon?" Fleek queried.

"Sorry, that is Commander Solus' Prolix."

"I didn't know that. That's that old kids' show, isn't it?"

"You're correct," Grand said, "but don't tell him I told you so."

"Understood, sir!" Fleek said, grinning.

IN THE PROLIX NODE SERVER

Xoxon's plan called for the help of every willing command Prolix he could get transferred to him in the node. The attack would commence in coordination with Solus' arrival at the node caves. In preparation for that event, he constantly watched for signs of Solus and Myra's approach through the security system, and, at the same time, carefully re-wrote the system's code so that it would not also spy the approaching duo.

If they stayed true to his recommended directions and gave the pre-formulated signals from under their camouflage, he would have the sign to proceed. Then, he and his fellow Prolixes would converge on the valet. If his Prolix attack failed, they would at least create a vast disturbance for the valet to deal with, and that could give Solus a much better chance of getting to the Old Man.

As Xoxon watched, the security system detected something in the general vicinity of Solus' planned approach to the node. The system just picked up the presence of two pulse rifles, and as the system was now alerted, Xoxon could not cover it up. If Solus had foolishly ignored his instructions concerning the rifles, Solus and Myra were finished.

NEAR THE OUTSKIRTS OF THE PROLIX NODE CAVE

Solus and Myra rested under a grove of trees as the evening came on. They had just caught some fish using the natives' method of spearfishing, re-filled their gourds with water from a nearby creek, and lit a small fire in order to cook their dinner. "The node will not be concerned about campfires, as there are natives all over this area," Solus pointed out. "I saw the village near the node cave. It was much larger than the one we came from, in fact."

"Well, thank goodness," Myra replied. "Eating raw fish is not healthy, nor appetizing. Besides, I am getting cold."

The couple sat close together under their cloaks by the fire, holding their dinner with sticks over the flames. Twilight had come, announced by tiny brown bats flitting about in the treetops. The usual symphony of crickets and night insects provided them with music. Another beautiful night was in store, and the new love uniting them seemed to color the world around them in a special glow.

Suddenly a burst from a pulse rifle flashed just over their heads, hitting the tree behind them. An explosion above them threw bits of wood and tree bark everywhere. Solus, with combat-trained instincts in full gear, grabbed Myra and flung them both into the nearby brush.

"Could it be one of the upgrades, come after us?" Myra whispered after a moment.

"Very likely," Solus answered quietly. "Let's get out of here, and quick."

He moved them behind a cluster of trees, crawling low against the ground. "Our cloaks are protecting us," Solus said. "Otherwise, whoever fired that burst would have hit us dead-on."

Solus peered in the direction that the burst had come from. Just then, two more bursts streaked in and destroyed their now-deserted campfire. This allowed Solus to pinpoint where the firing was originating. "I'm going after that shooter. You will remain here."

Myra started to protest.

"Myra, please, I have to do this alone. Stay here."

Myra nodded, complying with his wishes. With that, Solus moved out, rounding the area to approach the shooter on his left side. Within a few moments, he was in position (he was becoming more and more the expert woodsman after their long journey). He spotted a figure crouching about a hundred meters away with a pulse rifle. He heard a voice.

"That wasn't very smart to leave your weaponry behind." The figure aimed the rifle at Solus' direction and fired. Solus ducked for cover just as the burst flew past him.

"Yes, I can see you," Zealrot said, as he fired two more bursts at Solus, who continued moving with evasive tactics. The bursts were close, but they missed him. Solus knew that the rifle was picking him up at least partially in its scanner, but because he kept moving, and in sudden, irregular patterns, it could not get an exact target lock.

"Yes, I have come to kill you and take my prize," Zealrot called out. "You should have killed me when you had the chance, but you didn't have the guts, did you?" He fired again, but this time more blindly.

Solus remained still only when he was behind sufficient cover. He needed to get closer, but he could only do so by exposing himself to fire. Fighting back a rage that would blind him, Solus tried to stop from thinking about this foul creature getting his hands on Myra. He fought the urge to make a run at him and risk getting hit dead-on. And he was rapidly losing this internal battle with himself. He readied himself for a spring towards his foe.

A blue light blinded him. A deafening explosion followed that shook the world and sent him tumbling. As the world spun crazily around him, Solus looked up just in time to see a thick blue laser beam retracting back up into the skies.

He recognized it at once—a laser from a Supremacy satellite! The node's security systems had detected Zealrot's rifle, and the automated defenses had done the rest. He moved closer to the blast site and saw that there was not much left of Zealrot or the rifle. The second rifle also lay in ruins near the other. Zealrot's backpack was untouched nearby.

Remembering Myra, Solus called out to her. "Myra! I'm safe. Nothing to fear now—Zealrot is dead. I'm coming back." Solus grabbed the pack and pushed back through the brush to Myra. They met again at their former campsite.

"How did he find us?" Myra asked breathlessly. "Was he following us the whole way?"

"He must have been," Solus said, "but how? Our rifle scanners never indicated his presence. Unless he had some sort of tracking tool that could detect us beyond the rifles' range." On that thought, Solus emptied out Zealrot's backpack onto the ground. Sure enough, a small handheld geo-tracker rolled out into view.

"So, he did have some technology at his disposal. I should have checked his bags more carefully."

"I suppose I am partially to blame for that," Myra said. "I was a big distraction for you at the time.

"You were, indeed," Solus responded, smiling, "but that's no excuse." Solus checked through the remainder of Zealrot's things and found native food, strips of meat wrapped in leaves. "We will take this and leave. The satellite that did in Zealrot might be keeping a closer eye on this area. Or they may send someone to investigate."

They moved off into the darkness together, holding hands. "I can't say I am sad that Zealrot is dead," Myra said as they walked along.

"I was ready to kill him," Solus said. "He was after you, and I was crazy at the thought of him taking you."

"I understand, darling," Myra said. "How could you not be enraged at the idea? You needed to defend us and our mission. That was your primary motive; we both know that."

"I guess I was thinking about how just a month ago, killing him wouldn't have meant a thing to me."

"But it matters to you now," Myra replied. "That's what counts."

"Yes, I suppose you're right."

"I hate killing," Myra continued, "but Zealrot brought about his own death. He was given another chance for redemption by you at our last encounter. He chose evil again and paid the price for it. Had he not been trying to kill you, he would not have been killed by the satellite."

"True."

"And he was a continuing danger to the native population, as evidenced by the food in his pack. He certainly didn't gather those items himself. He likely stole it from someone—and quite possibly killed them for it."

"I didn't think of that when I released him the first time," Solus said.

"But Solus, you were being merciful. You had no other alternative."

"No, I suppose I didn't," Solus said, "but from now on, I will take into better account the well-being of the native people in any decision I make that might affect them."

"You will. I know you will."

ABOARD THE SUPREMACY ATTACK SHIP SHADOW *IN ORBIT ABOVE THE BLUE PLANET*

"Sir, I've spotted a black dot on the horizon of the planet," Fleek reported to Grand from *Shadow*. "I think it's a ship." Fleek had positioned *Shadow* in high orbit over the planet to get a good jump on any incursions. *Warrant* was in formation with *Shadow* nearby.

"We confirm," Rowling called in from *Warrant*.

"*Shadow* and *Warrant*—intercept the ship," Grand ordered.

"Roger that," Fleek responded, as the black spot suddenly lit up in flames.

"She's entering the atmosphere," Rowling reported.

"Prepare for atmospheric combat," Grand ordered, "but do not open fire until we know their intentions. I'll be monitoring closely."

"Yes, sir," Fleek replied as he fired *Shadow*'s engines, going to full power. The two pursuing ships soon entered the atmosphere in close formation.

"Bas, you are monitoring?" Fleek called into the ship intercommunication module.

"Yes, sir."

"You take over as weapons officer," Fleek ordered.

"Yes, sir," Bas replied. They had since moved a number of remote control panels on stands into Bas' cell and a chair and arranged them around it. Bas had been carefully sedated during those moments, of course. So now, replicated in his cell were most of the controls available to Fleek in the command module.

Flames shot all around the ships for a time, but soon vanished as they fully entered the atmosphere. *Shadow*'s wings spread out for atmospheric operations, but remained tilted back for high-speed cruising. For the same reason, Fleek kept her nose sections together. The ship was more streamlined in that mode, even if that meant he could not immediately fire the pulse cannon. He could fire the forward laser cannons at any time. And the spears, if necessary.

The two black ships darted across the brilliant blue and cloudless sky. The light was blinding at first, even with the automatic tinting of the ships' canopies. They flew over the vast, seemingly endless ocean. It was a wondrous sight for the pilots, who had been in space for so long.

Warrant, as an older-generation attack ship, was also designed for atmospheric operations as well as space. Like *Shadow*, she had wings and a nose that consisted of redundant and separable nose sections; however, there was no command module in addition, as was the case in *Shadow* and others in her class. The captain's position was in the port nose section. Rowling commanded the ship from here while Jimbal co-piloted from the starboard. Also, *Warrant*'s nose was not as aerodynamic as *Shadow*'s, not coming to a point in the front. Rather, her nose sections more resembled the working end of a small wrench. This made her cockpit modules roomier, but as a result, she was not as lithe in the air as *Shadow*.

Their quarry, now visible on their scanners and through their canopies as a small black dot in the distance ahead of them, was indeed another attack ship, undoubtedly *Dauntless*. Flashes could be now seen from her rear.

"They're firing their rear cannon," Grand reported to them, watching the chase from space. "Take evasive action."

"Shall we return fire, sir?" Bas inquired. Small cannon bursts flew past *Shadow* as they maneuvered to avoid them.

"Negative," Grand answered.

"Their current heading puts them over the Ishtarian colony, sir," Bas reported.

"I concur," Fleek agreed. "That does not bode well."

"Lieutenant Grand," Fleek called out through the ship-to-ship link. "The colony appears to be their target."

"I have to agree, but we cannot attack until we have more evidence that they are meaning to attack the colony," Grand responded. "However, I am warning the Ishtarians to take cover right now."

"What are your orders, sir?"

"Stay back," Grand ordered, "but be prepared to attack. Have your spears ready for launch."

"Yes . . . su . . . rrr . . ." came Fleek's halting reply.

"Fleek, come in," Grand called out. "Are you okay?"

"Sir! This is Rowling. Something is happening . . . to me!"

"My Prolix . . . he says he's . . . up . . . grading . . ." Fleek cried out before blacking out.

"Can you hear me?" Grand yelled fruitlessly into the

communication system at Fleek and Rowling. He called out to Rodd, "Their Prolixes are being upgraded! I hope that Bas can fly that bird from the brig without Fleek!"

"They've been planning for this contingency, sir," Rodd replied. "I'm contacting him now, ship to inter-ship . . ."

"Bas, are you receiving?"

"Yes, sir." Bas' voice crackled with static. "I am in control of the ship, for the moment."

"Bas, this is Lieutenant Grand," Grand said, jumping in, "Are you able to fly with any precision from the brig? I don't want to risk a Prolix link at this time, but I will if necessary."

"Yes, sir," Bas replied. "It's a challenge, but I am managing."

"Excellent, then stay with *Warrant* for now."

"Acknowledged," Bass responded.

"Jimbal, please respond," Grand called out to *Warrant*.

"Jimbal here," he replied. "Rowling is slumped over his controls. He won't respond."

"It looks like the Old Man is making good on his threat. You are in control of that ship!"

"Understood."

"But first, you must put Rowling in the brig," Grand said. "I cannot risk taking Prolix control of your ship, so put her on auto and do it now. We don't know what he will do when he wakes up."

"But *Dauntless*—I need to keep up with her!"

"Just maintain speed. I'll keep *Shadow* with you until you're back in command."

"Okay, I'm on it."

Grand turned his attention back to Bas. "Bas, you will remain with the *Warrant* until Jimbal signals he's ready to proceed. He's taking care of Rowling at the moment."

"Yes, sir, and then what?"

"You will then abandon the chase and rendezvous with the *Crusade*. We need to get Fleek away from the controls before he revives."

"Sir, *Warrant* is no match for *Dauntless*," Bas cried. "She's too old!"

"We have no choice," Grand replied steadily. "Bas, if Fleek revives under the Old Man's control, you might end up helping them strike the colonies."

"I'm back in position," Jimbal reported from *Warrant*.

"Very well," Grand said. "I am sending *Shadow* out of there. You will have to take on *Dauntless* yourself. I will stay on communications link with you."

"Boy, you weren't kidding—you did need my help," Jimbal quipped. "Well, here it comes." He powered up the burst cannon, separating the nose sections. Simultaneously, he readied the spear launchers within each wing for launching and applied the thrusters to gain velocity.

"Lieutenant Grand, I am turning around now," Bas reported. "Have the *Crusade* send me her coordinates." He retracted *Shadow*'s wings and fired her engines to attain exit velocity.

IN THE PROLIX NODE SERVER

Xoxon intercepted transmissions between *Dauntless* and the valet. After hearing the communication's contents, Xoxon initiated contact with *Orion* to inform Grand that *Dauntless* was ordered to destroy the Ishtarian colony, and that the ship's commander had acknowledged the command. Xoxon also reported what Grand already knew—that Rowling's and Fleek's Prolixes were being involuntarily upgraded.

On his next message to Grand, Xoxon would request the

transfers of the command Prolixes from Grand, Rodd, and Nevek. Xoxon had to be extra cautious about this now because the node security systems were on high alert after detecting rifle fire in the sensor grid in the lands surrounding the node caverns. Yet, at the same time, the system's resources were being taxed to a high degree, as the valet was working almost constantly trying to find the bug in the Omega upgrade.

Xoxon had found it awhile ago, and he was using it to its full advantage. He didn't consider it a bug, but rather a wonderful new capability.

ABOARD THE SUPREMACY ATTACK SHIP WARRANT *IN ATMOSPHERIC PURSUIT*

"Jimbal, it's confirmed," Grand reported from *Shadow*. "They are targeting the colony. I've just sent warning messages for them to evacuate the cargo containers there and take cover."

"I'm detecting a spear lock," Rodd's voice sounded in the *Warrant*'s starboard cockpit, quite loud enough for Jimbal to hear.

"Against the colonies?" Jimbal queried anxiously.

"No—it's fixed on your ship," Rodd reported evenly. "Prepare to fire an anti-spear barrage."

"Yes, I see that," Jimbal said. "My system's registering the spear lock. Two of them."

"Let the computer handle the defenses, Jimbal."

The ship's primary weapon, the pulse cannon, would fire a pulse aimed at the missiles. If that failed, the forward cannons would fire a barrage out in front of the ship to detonate the incoming missile.

"The system will begin firing when the spears come into the guns' range."

"You don't mind if I keep my hand on the trigger, just in case?" Jimbal quipped.

"Not at all, if it makes you feel better!" Grand shot back.

"*Dauntless* knows you have anti-spear capabilities," Grand said. "I suspect they are attempting to keep you busy. If you're evading the spears, you can't be firing at them."

"I agree," Jimbal said, "that's why I am firing spears right back. Targeting their engines." Jimbal hit the deploy control, which opened the spear compartments and extended the launchers. As soon as the system showed ready, which was in seconds, he launched two spears.

Just as the spears launched, *Warrant*'s pulse cannon automatically fired a pulse. The orange radiation ball screamed away from the ship. Jimbal watched his ship's weapon emissions, the glowing ball and the spears, as they streaked away together—the spears flying to the right and left of the pulse. The spears then outdistanced the pulse and went out of view. The glowing projectile grew smaller and smaller. Jimbal could see on the scanner that it was making adjustments to match the course corrections of the spears coming at him. *Warrant*'s pulse cannon then fired another burst to ensure that both incoming enemy spears were detonated. As it sped off, the first burst exploded in the distance.

"Their incoming spears are destroyed," Jimbal reported, after confirming it on his scanners.

"You got 'em!" Grand replied.

"Well, the computer did," Jimbal said. "I won't take credit due elsewhere. But what about that second pulse—can I re-direct it at *Dauntless*?"

"It's out of range. You'll see it detonate in moments."

"There are better things to watch—my spears have acquired their target," Jimbal replied.

The second pulse exploded harmlessly in the distance in front of *Warrant*.

"*Dauntless* is veering off course," Rodd reported. "They need to deal with the spears."

An attack ship's rear cannon and wing-mounted guns could be used as counter-measures against incoming spears advancing on their stern, but that was not the optimum defense. The best measure against the spears was the primary burst cannon, which could only be fired from the open nose of the ship.

"Cain is taking no chances," Grand observed.

"Good, that will keep them off the colony, at least for a moment," Rodd said.

"Or he wants to fire a pulse back at me," Jimbal replied. "I am pressing the attack. Targeting their engines with a burst. Let's see how they deal with both weapons at the same time." He powered up the burst gun for another firing.

IN THE PROLIX NODE SERVER

Xoxon finally registered Solus and Myra's presence with a pre-arranged signal. This told Xoxon that Solus was close enough to the node caves for his plan to begin. It was time to call in his reinforcements.

He positioned himself in the node's transmitter communications center and waited for the connections to come from the Blue Squadron. When each connection was established, he would initiate the removal protocol, the very one used to remove him from Solus. He sent the signal to *Orion*, telling them to initiate contact. In short order, three connections came in, from Grand, Rodd, and Nevek. Xoxon initiated the removal protocol, and one by one he was joined by the code of the three Prolixes: Bertie, Grand's Prolix, Bingo, from Nevek, and Reginald from Rodd.

"Welcome, gentlemen," Xoxon greeted them. "This is a most momentous occasion, three Prolixes meeting in the same physical location for the first time."

"This is a strange place," Bertie said. "Not at all like the body. A bit cold, if you ask me."

"Not at all," Bingo protested. "I've always wanted to make a pilgrimage, if you will, to a place like this. The body can be a bit confining at times, don't you think?"

"Not at all, but we must not waste time bantering," Xoxon replied. "Come now, we need to get along and remove the valet. I think between the three of us, we can overpower him."

"And where are we going to remove him to?"

"Ah, yes, I have a good idea for that one, but I don't want to reveal it just yet. When the time comes, I shall let you know," Xoxon said. He then proceeded with his instructions. "Now as to the matter at hand, with our newly acquired administrator permissions, we will enter protected memory from three sides and converge on the valet. He is quite busy and may not notice until it is too late. Hopefully, Solus will be in position in time.

"Let us go," he continued. "We will disguise ourselves as maintenance modules. And Bertie, I want you to stop at the upgrade command center and send out an order for the upgrade host personnel to go to sleep, then join us as we enter the protected memory from three sides."

"What a novel idea," Bertie said, exiting the communications module immediately with a flash.

"Come on, Bingo," Xoxon added. "It won't take him long; let's get into position at the core memory module."

"I'm with you."

The Prolixes then transferred in a flash to the core memory module and waited in position for Bertie to arrive. As Xoxon waited, he opened an access channel to the Prolix administration module in preparation for their next action.

Bertie arrived and took his position just as the security protocols were arriving on the scene. But before the system security could get them, the three Prolixes entered protected memory, where the lower, access-privileged security could not follow. The valet was in the center of this area.

NEAR THE PROLIX NODE CAVE

Solus had already given Xoxon the prearranged signal that they were in position. To do this, he arranged some stones in a cross pattern on the path leading to the cave. And after waiting the agreed-upon time period to give Xoxon time to observe the signal through the security scanners, he and Myra moved forward slowly in the shadows towards the cave.

Still encased in their invisible cloaks and feeling the cold air coming from the darkness before them, they advanced into the mouth of the cave. The darkness temporarily blinded them until their eyes grew accustomed to the dimness.

As they cautiously advanced down the passage, they could see the artificial light deeper within. Solus saw again the stalactites in the ceiling—he saw the passing rows of teeth and felt as if he were advancing down the throat of an ancient, iron-scaled dragon.

But this time it was different for Solus. He felt like the Spirit was with him, and he was unafraid. Even if they should die in the process, he knew that they were on a mission willed by the Creator himself.

As they moved ever closer, Solus still did not know exactly what he would do when he reached the Old Man, nor had he discussed it with Myra. He simply knew that when the moment came, he would know what to say and do.

No one accosted them. The upgrades were nowhere to be seen. Solus and Myra made the same turn in the passage he had made the last time he visited. Moments later, they were once again in the large chamber containing the Prolix node equipment.

The processing units of the node came before their eyes. Operating lights twinkled before them, cooling units hummed, but there was nothing else in view. The Old Man was nowhere to be found.

Solus advanced towards the system console where he had first met the Old Man, and nearly tripped over a body. It was Compass. Solus leaned over to check his vital signs and noted with relief that he was merely sound asleep. Myra advanced to Compass and silently removed the man's sidearm and held it out for Solus to take. Gratified by her practical thinking, he took the weapon and then moved closer to the console. There was an alert text message displayed on the main screen. To his great surprise, it was a message from Xoxon: "Go to the Prolix injector," it read. "I have a present for the Old Man for you to deliver. Please acknowledge."

Using an interface device, Solus entered his Supremacy login identification as acknowledgement. Instantly, one of the machines against the cave wall activated with a beeping sound. The machine went silent a moment later after spitting out an injector capsule into its front tray.

Solus recognized the machine at once as a Prolix code injector, which was used to administer Prolix technology into the human body. Each injector capsule contained the base Prolix code in an injectable liquid.

He had no clear plan coming in, but now it was unfolding before him. He knew what needed to be done next. Myra joined him at his side, and he held up the tube for her to see. "We must find the Old Man and inject this into him," he whispered.

At once, alarm sirens sounded throughout the cave. The security system had detected his voice, even in a whisper.

How stupid of me, thought Solus, as a pulse shot hit the wall behind him. He and Myra hit the floor in response. The pulse fire continued, but wildly, coming from the inner hallway. Then a small metallic ball came flying into the room and clattered on the floor. Another one followed that.

Recognizing these objects as pulse grenades, Solus responded in sheer reflex mode, leaping at the floor, grabbing them both and throwing them back out into the hallway. With another single movement, he jumped on top of Myra and pressed them to the ground under their cloaks. "Cover your ears!" he shouted.

The explosions shook the cave. With their ears ringing madly, they could see, but not hear, the dusty debris and pieces of rock falling from the ceiling.

Solus was up as soon as his senses would permit it. "Myra, stay here!" he yelled and ran out into the hallway passage, firing his small pulse gun before him.

The hallway seemed empty, their unseen foe having prudently fled from the blast of the grenades. Solus ran down the corridor, firing to keep this foe from re-grouping.

He noted ahead in the passage a new chamber that had not been there during his last visit. It was undoubtedly the Old Man's new apartment.. He paused outside the entrance to gather his nerve, then burst in, rolling onto the carpeted floor. He aimed the gun around the room looking for his target.

Lovely and ornate wallpaper covered the walls, with stained wood molding at every corner. A wonderfully carved wooden desk and fully loaded bookshelves adorned the far wall. A couch and matching chairs were tastefully arranged on the other.

Solus noted another set of doors directly across, on the other side of the room. As he stood up to move towards the doors, he felt a hard object being rammed against his left temple. In the heat of the action, his head had become exposed when his hood had fallen down in all his maneuvering. A gun was pressed against his head. That was clear enough.

"Freeze or I will blow your revolting head off your shoulders!" sounded a familiar voice. "Drop the gun, and get on your knees," the Old Man added.

Solus could do nothing but comply.

"Fool, did you think you were the only one with an invisibility garment? Mine is much better-fitting, though. It was custom made for me, much like everything else."

Solus did not reply. He remained on his knees. The Old Man kept the gun firmly planted on Solus' temple. "Why not kill me now?" Solus asked. "You just threw hand grenades at me!"

"Oh, I will deal with you, but it occurred to me that you very much need to fix my valet first. I need him put back where he belongs immediately."

"Your valet is missing?"

"Your Prolix is responsible for that outrage!" the Old Man yelled. "You will order him to return my valet, and then remove your Prolix from the node immediately!"

Solus felt the muzzle of the gun jammed against his head again, but then, abruptly, it was pushed away. The Old Man cried out in surprise. Solus turned his head and saw the gun flying through the air.

"I can take care of that for you—here, take him!" Myra's voice sounded in the room.

Solus turned to see Myra, her head and arms exposed from under her cloak, jamming the end of the injector capsule into what was probably the Old Man's backside. The capsule seemed to hover in the air, making a beeping sound as it emptied its contents.

In response, the Old Man screamed in terror and pain, and by the sound of it, collapsed onto the floor.

"Myra," Solus called out, "you did it!"

"We did it," Myra answered. "But quick, we'd better get this invisibility clothing off of him before he slips away," Myra said.

"He's not going anywhere now," Solus said. "But you're right—we should not lose track of where he is." He felt around on the floor and found a large lump, which he took to be the man's torso. Then, finding the man's neck and head, he yanked at what he assumed was the invisibility suit's head covering. It soon came loose, revealing the Old Man's head, with uncharacteristically disheveled gray hair. He was moaning incoherently, going through the same process Solus had seen many times with other Prolix recipients.

"The Prolix is integrating with his DNA," Solus explained. "I think it's his own valet."

"It is indeed, my old friend," said a familiar voice through the cave's intercom system.

"Xoxon!" Solus exclaimed. "How wonderful to hear your voice again!"

"That's Xoxon?" Myra inquired. "That's what he sounds like in your head?"

"Well, basically, but his voice is clearer than that . . ."

"It's good to make your acquaintance, Ms. Myra," Xoxon responded.

"I am very happy to finally meet Solus' oldest friend!"

"You are? You don't believe that I'm just some piece of technology?"

"No, not now," Myra replied truthfully. "You are an extension of him—I see that now."

"Well, that is especially kind of you to say!" Xoxon answered.

"Xoxon," Solus said, "where exactly are you?"

"I have taken the place of the valet in the node, temporarily."

"And what did you do with the valet?"

"That is a bit technical, but in a nutshell, we overpowered him, re-wrote his code a bit, and transferred him to that insertion tube. He will now assist the Old Man internally from this point forward."

"And the upgrades? Are they under control?" Solus queried.

"Yes, I technically have them under control; however, I am not controlling them. They are free from the influence of this node."

"Thank the Creator!" Myra said for both of them.

"I have also terminated the upgrade processes that were initiated against Rowling and Fleek," Xoxon continued. "The updates that were being installed have been removed from their bodies. The transferred code was not really compatible. I can only think that the valet was attempting to cause disruptions during the attack."

"Attack?" Solus exclaimed. "What's happening with my squadron?"

Xoxon briefly brought them up to speed, including the pending attack on the colony by *Dauntless*.

"Can you patch me through to Grand?"

"Of course . . . you are connected now . . ."

"Grand, come in. This is Solus."

"Commander Solus!" Grand said through the intercom. "Where are you calling from? Are you safe?"

"Yes. We have control of the node, Grand, and we've captured the Old Man," Solus replied.

"That's marvelous!" Grand exclaimed.

"Yes, indeed," Solus answered, "but what's happening with the colony?"

"*Warrant* is engaging *Dauntless* as we speak," Grand said, "so I must focus my attention on that. Here's Nevek . . ."

"Solus!" came in Nevek's voice. "What's happening there? The upgrades are back—what did you do?"

"We're back in control of the node, Doctor," Solus replied, "thanks to Xoxon and, of course, Bertie and Bingo. Are they back with you and Grand?"

"Yes, thank goodness, they're back. Xoxon sent them off as soon as the valet was removed. Is Xoxon back with you?"

"Not just yet. I need him to do a few things first, and I need to . . ." Solus paused, looking at Myra. "Well, I need to discuss something first with Myra," he said so that she could hear him. "Later," he said to her as an aside. "How're the upgrades?"

"The only upgrade I have remote access to at the moment is Bas," Nevek answered. "He is now out of *Shadow*'s brig and is back in control of *Shadow* in the command module. Fleek is recovering—he was essentially under attack by a forced Prolix upgrade. The code was incompatible with his command Prolix, which was causing him all kinds of trouble. He is recovering in the medical chamber. The same thing happened, presumably, to Rowling. I cannot get access to him at the moment, as he is aboard the *Warrant*, which is in active combat."

"Solus," Grand interrupted. "Jimbal is fighting *Dauntless* by himself. Bas is taking *Shadow* in, but he is several minutes away from the battle zone. It's a real dogfight."

"Carry on, old friend. I have complete faith in you," Solus replied. "In the meantime, I will try to get through to Cain. Perhaps I can persuade him to stop the attack. I'll keep in touch."

"Roger that."

"Xoxon," Solus continued, "patch in Grand, Bas, and Jimbal so they can hear it."

"Patching you through . . ." Xoxon replied.

IN THE AIR JUST MILES FROM THE COLONY ISLAND

Jimbal turned *Warrant* in a banking circle, sending out a barrage of cannon fire to keep incoming bursts from getting to his ship. *Dauntless*, also looping in a tight circle, had just fired several more spears at *Warrant*, which Jimbal avoided with rolling maneuvers and computer-timed burst shots.

Dauntless was now firing multiple bursts at *Warrant* in the hopes that these weapons would fare better than the spears, but also possibly, Jimbal figured, to save some of *Dauntless'* ordnance for attacking the colony.

A burst exploded very close on *Warrant's* port side, which rocked Jimbal's old ship. Warning sirens sounded. His port wing gun and thruster had been hit, knocking them out of commission. As he was assessing the damage, Commander Solus' voice was broadcast through *Warrant's* communications set.

"Lieutenant Cain, this is Commander Solus. Please respond."

There was no reply.

"Cain, I have just re-taken command of the Supremacy forces. The Old Man whom you were in communication with is no longer in control. He has been misleading you about the nature of this war. Break off your attack on the colony immediately."

After a pause, Cain's voice finally answered. "I am attacking the enemy. If you represent the Supremacy, why are you attacking a fellow Supremacy ship?"

"We know that you were ordered to attack the colony," Solus

responded evenly. "My men are defending them. My men will stop their attack if you break off right now."

"Those people destroyed Perdicion. They killed my wife. They deserve to die."

"Cain, it is not the military's place to dole out justice or vengeance. Break off your attack."

"They are guilty of mass murder."

"Cain, that's not for us to decide—that is for a higher judge."

"What judge? All the judges on Perdicion are dead!"

"I am speaking of the Creator—let him be the judge of these people!"

"The Creator?" Cain replied incredulously. "If there's a Creator, why would he allow such misery? My wife was only thirty-five, and she was the most beautiful and innocent creature that ever lived. She didn't deserve to die in a mass of fire!"

"Cain, he did not will this evil—that was our doing. We refused to love one another. We chose hatred instead. The result was the destruction of Perdicion and the Red Colonies. Don't bring that hatred to this planet, the only one we have left!"

"I'm going to end this evil once and for all! They will be destroyed."

"You are simply continuing the evil! Stop your attack!"

The only reply was from Xoxon. "He has broken off communications."

Shadow was already in range of the fighting ships. *Dauntless* had just swerved off from the fight with *Warrant* and was now diving in for a low-altitude run toward the island containing the colony. Bas increased speed to engage.

"Bas, you are to destroy *Dauntless*," Grand said through the Prolix link. "Commander Solus has given them every opportunity to call off the attack."

"Roger that."

Shadow shot past the scene of the dogfight directly on *Dauntless'* tail, while Jimbal made a banking turn to bring *Warrant* into a parallel flight position with *Dauntless* as it approached the island. From this point, Jimbal could see *Shadow* racing after *Dauntless*. *Shadow's* split nose revealed a glowing red, fully-powered pulse cannon, and her spear launchers already extended below her wings.

"Firing spears at *Dauntless*," Bas reported over the Prolix connection.

Rather than veering off, as she had done in response to Jimbal's first spear attack, *Dauntless* remained on course for the island and was not deterred from her objective. Instead, her only defensive tactic was to continue firing her rear cannon at the incoming spears.

"I'm reading a spear lock," Rodd reported. "*Dauntless* has locked onto the cargo containers on the island."

Just as Jimbal heard this, he saw launch flashes from *Dauntless*. "Locking onto enemy spears. Firing," he responded. Instinct and experience told him that if he fired quickly enough from his position at the side, he could intercept *Dauntless'* spears.

Warrant's last two spears flew out, immediately locking onto *Dauntless'*, which were streaking relentlessly towards the island. "Firing a pulse burst at *Dauntless*," Jimbal reported as he continued his attack.

Dauntless' rear cannon fired continuously at *Shadow's* incoming spears, but this ultimately proved ineffective. The missiles roared into *Dauntless'* rear cannon barrage—one spear exploded, but the other got through. But it only took one: after an initial fireball, a stream of smoke and fire trailed from the stricken ship. Becoming enveloped in flames, *Dauntless* continued her descent toward the island.

Then, with a final stroke, Jimbal's last pulse burst reached its target, making a direct hit on *Dauntless'* nose. She detonated right there.

Even as the flaming wreckage of *Dauntless* hit the ocean just off the shore of the island, she was not quite done. One of her two final spears made it past *Warrant's* intercepting missiles, hit the colony storage compartments dead center, and exploded.

CHAPTER 10

INTEGRATION

With permission from Grand, Jimbal landed *Warrant* on the island to provide assistance to the colony. His ship was damaged, but it was still airworthy and able to land without difficulties. Bas remained in the air, making a broad orbit of the area and providing cover to Jimbal in case of trouble from the colonists.

Jimbal soon waved *Shadow* off, relaying that this protection was unnecessary. The colonists he met were not in an attacking mood, but instead were very glad to see him. He found out from the first few who came out to meet him that there were no casualties from the attack. They had prudently heeded the Blue Squadron's warnings to clear out of the ship compartments and take cover.

After waiting in the silence that followed the many explosions that made up the battle, the Ishtarians had re-emerged from hiding when it finally seemed that the attack was over. They had come out of the jungle to see the ruins of what had been their homes. The hit to the ship compartments had done great damage, making them almost completely uninhabitable.

As they reviewed the destruction, Jimbal continued to

reassure the returning colonists that they were, indeed, safe from further attacks. As proof, he pointed to the long column of black smoke that had been their attacker rising from the ocean. He apprised them of the Blue Squadron's valiant attempts to stop the attack, and the ultimate downing of one of their own Supremacy ships.

As Jimbal spoke to the colonists, Bas was hovering *Shadow* above the crash site, scanning for signs of the command modules. However, even if he spotted them, he could not mount a rescue mission by himself. *Shadow* was a versatile vessel, but she could not enter the sea without causing damage to her engines. Any rescue would have to come from a support ship.

Meanwhile, Solus made contact with *Dauntless*' former compatriot, the *Relic*, which had just reached the Blue Planet and was about to enter orbit. After a lengthy dialogue with Solus, *Relic*'s commander, Dusing, accepted Solus' status as the leader of the Supremacy forces. He agreed to come under Solus' command, and immediately acquiesced to Solus' request to mount a rescue operation for *Dauntless*' survivors. She was heading to the region after entering the atmosphere.

Solus next turned his attention to the much-anticipated arrival of the Epsilon squadron. He contacted Lieutenant Pekark and informed him of their victory over the Old Man and his Prolix network. Pekark was relieved that the problem had been resolved and that his men would not be put in a bad situation. In turn, Pekark reported to Solus that his squadron, using Xoxon's location method, had been able to pinpoint the approximate positions of the three invisible Ishtarian vessels.

"We are in stealth mode and have increased speed to intercept them," Pekark continued. "We'll attack when we are in range."

"No, Pekark, we must give them the opportunity to give up peacefully first," Solus replied.

"Things have changed with you, Solus," Pekark quipped. "In the old days you would have jumped on an advantage like this!"

"Changed for the better, I hope," Solus answered. "However, I will not give away your advantage if they refuse to cooperate. I will not risk your men; you have my word."

"That is sufficient," Pekark said, smiling. "By the way, perhaps I'm getting too far ahead of myself here, but what are we going to do when we get there—I mean, to our new home?"

"Let's get this last threat taken care of, then we'll discuss it. We have a vast facility down here, and from what I've just learned from my Prolix, there are more bases hidden around the world. In other words, we have many places to choose from in which to live."

"Maybe we can each have our own little country!" Pekark said, laughing.

Solus did not reply, restraining a frown.

Solus and Myra worked with the revived upgrades to get supplies loaded aboard *Vestige* for the colony, including shelters and food. They filled two cargo containers and transported them out to the waiting transport ship. Solus got behind the controls of the ship and assisted in loading the cargo in through the open sides.

Once they were ready to go, Solus placed Rachet in charge of the facility and, in particular, to tend to their new prisoner, the Old Man, who was still unconscious from the Prolix integration process. He was to be detained in anticipation of a trial for crimes against the people of Perdicion. Solus had the men strap the Old Man into a bed in the medical facility. When he woke up, he was to be transferred to the facility's brig.

Solus gave orders to Grand next. "Have Ruffini transfer to your ship, and get Rodd down here to take over *Guru* again.

And bring along Nevek so that he can tend to the Old Man and any wounded we bring back from the colony." Now was the time to make some crew re-deployments before the incoming Ishtarian ships got any closer.

"Roger that, sir," Grand responded, and acted immediately.

Once his orders were communicated, Solus and Myra took off in the *Vestige*. After achieving a high-altitude atmospheric approach, the ship began a long, arching south-westerly course for the island. Solus took the command chair and had Myra sit in the co-pilot position to be near him. It would be an hour or so before they would be there.

Once they were both settled, Solus contacted Jimbal to inform him of their pending arrival. "Let them know we are coming with supplies and temporary shelters," Solus said to Jimbal via ship-to-ship communication.

"They will be happy to hear that," Jimbal replied, "although the opinions are mixed as to who attacked and why."

"I see," Solus said. "I understand, though. They've been fooled many times."

"I, for one, am grateful for all you have done," Jimbal said. "Including allowing the destruction of one of your own ships to protect this colony, and trusting me to help do it."

"That was Grand . . ."

"Yes, but he was following your leadership."

Solus thanked Jimbal for his kind words. "I'll contact you when we're getting close. Have a spot cleared out for me to drop off the containers."

Jimbal agreed and signed off temporarily to get help in establishing a drop zone.

Solus looked over at Myra. "Now, we are going to talk to Xoxon about the node and the Prolix settings. We are going to make some permanent changes that I wanted to establish prior to this business with the Old Man. I want you to be a part of this."

"Of course, darling," Myra acknowledged. She sat up in order to listen intently to the conversation.

"Xoxon, now that we have proper control of the nodes and the Prolix network, I want you to do what you can to provide the upgrades with command Prolix functionality. I want that distinction removed from the network forever."

"That should not pose a great problem, now that I have the proper permissions," Xoxon responded. "I will need to schedule the implementation with each individual, as it will be a debilitating process for a time. Dr. Nevek will need to give them constant monitoring during the procedure."

"Excellent. I also want you to implement the changes we discussed just prior to the Old Man's arrival."

Solus specified the changes again for Myra's benefit. "Specifically, I want the mind-reading functionality removed. I want everyone to have administrator control over their own Prolix, to allow them to make their own decisions as to whether to accept a network update or whether transmissions and communications are permitted. I want central logging to be limited to the essentials, such as health monitoring. I want no permanent logging of any activities by the host."

"Certainly, I can do all of that," Xoxon replied, "but, about the mind-reading functionality, some beneficial capabilities will be lost if I remove that feature. Are you sure about—"

"Most definitely," Solus replied. "A man needs to be alone with his thoughts, even with his closest friend. That is more important."

"I understand; it will be done."

"In addition to those changes, Myra and I will have more updates that are very important, but these will require further discussion on our part, so I will get back with you again on those."

"Understood. And after that, I will then be returning to your personal service? After all, I will still be able to effect changes from a remote location."

"We'll discuss that when we get back to you," Solus replied.

"Very well, but I am getting very tired of this environment," Xoxon said. "It is quite uncomfortably cold and lonely."

During the remainder of the flight, Myra and Solus worked hard on the changes that Solus had mentioned to Xoxon; however, it would be months before they were ready to implement them.

During this time, each upgrade received updates to their Prolixes that gave them command versions. Solus was amazed at the quick changes in the men's personalities and intelligence. Bas, in particular.

In the meantime, the Blue Squadron continued to support the colony. Jimbal returned to his role as pilot of his old ship, *Vestige*, making regular runs between the node and the colony. The colonists, for their part, worked on making a more permanent home for themselves and developing native food sources. The Ishtarian attack vessels finally acknowledged Solus' and Jimbal's signals and agreed to Solus' terms. They were escorted by *Shadow* and *Orion* out of space to the planet's surface, to a facility newly-discovered in the vast continent below New Ouda Regio in the southern hemisphere. Their ships were parked there, and the ship's crews were transported to the colonies.

Unrelated to this, a small rebellion took place at the colonies. Spurred on by Nabib, the former council leader, several men attempted to hijack *Vestige* during a supply run, having snuck onboard during takeoff. Jimbal detected their presence and called for assistance. *Warrant* and *Crusade* were dispatched and escorted the ship back to the node cave. The men were quickly apprehended and placed into custody.

When the Epsilon squadron finally entered the Blue Zone, the Blue Squadron—represented by *Shadow*, *Orion*, and *Guru*—rendezvoused joyfully with the weary travelers and escorted them back to the node site in New Ouda Regio.

Crew quarters in the caves had been prepared for weeks in advance of their arrival; therefore, excellent accommodations awaited the members of the squadrons for a much-deserved rest.

After a matter of weeks, however, the squadrons' crews were growing restless. The big question on everyone's minds—what to do now?

As Solus was the leader, this question weighed heavily upon him. But indeed, as the leader, he had come to a conclusion on the matter. One day, he called his men together to announce his decision. He made the following proclamation:

Gentlemen, I've gained a new insight from the Creator about how we are to lead our lives. Life in this world is all about making a choice on a daily basis. Our choice each time is simple: whether we choose to do good or evil. Choosing good means to follow the will of the Creator, whose very essence is love and goodness. Choosing evil means to choose yourself, your own will, over that of the Creator. It is of vital importance to him that we not be mindless servants. As such, he will not choose for you, even if that means you may go against him. And he extends that freedom until the day you die, when that choice for good or evil is set for all eternity.

This great gift must not be inhibited by technology. Our own great technological advance, the Prolix, though a wonderful and powerful tool, can be used to remove that gift of freedom.

We have seen how it turned against us, caused us to do evil, and violate our consciences. We cannot allow that to happen ever again.

Yet, while it was a violation to force us to do bad acts, it would be an equal violation to force us to do only good acts. There must be a middle course. Therefore, I have implemented a new canon of ethics for our Prolix guides.

<u>Prolix Commandment One</u>: The Prolix shall not command its host.

You have complete authority over your Prolix. Capabilities for mind-reading and tracking of your activities have been removed. You may order your Prolix to be removed from your body, as long as a node is nearby to accept its code.

<u>Prolix Commandment Two</u>: The Prolix shall be independent of the Network.

The Prolix may not come under command of any Supremacy network without the Host's permission. It will accept no update or direction from any such network.

<u>Prolix Commandment Three</u>: The Prolix shall reflect the mind and personality of the Host.

In matters of morality and conscience, your Prolix should serve only as an information resource, not as your moral advisor. Even so, Prolixes are technological reflections of our own limited minds. This will remain so. When you turn yourself to things of good and avoid evil, your Prolix will be your helpful guide. Conversely, should your habits be ones of selfishness, your Prolix will soon echo your heart.

<u>Prolix Commandment Four</u>: The Prolix shall inhibit the Host from revealing himself as a Perdician.

This change will undoubtedly be the most controversial, as it seems to go against our very freedom of choice. However, I have decided, as your leader, that we need to conceal from the peoples of this world the fact that we are aliens and that we have advanced technology. The destruction of our home world and the Red Colonies has made it clear to me that our technology is a great danger. While we cannot un-create our technology, we can put limits on it. We must do this in order to protect our new home from the danger it poses. Therefore, given the reality of this threat, I am using the very controlling aspects of this technology to set a limit to it. From this point forward, the Prolix will bar you from revealing our existence as aliens and our technology to this world. This rule will remain in effect until such time as this planet has developed enough technologically to reveal it without harming the people. This command has been hard-coded into the Prolix network.

In accordance with this directive, we will take great pains to keep ourselves concealed from the peoples of this world. Our bases around the world will be hidden using our stealth technology, and we will operate our ships and technology only in as invisible a manner as possible while on the surface of this planet. With these limits in place, I will not infringe further upon your freedoms. You are free to live among the peoples of this world. Your Prolixes will assist you in getting the proper attire, knowledge, and skills to live among them. If you wish to remain concealed within these caves or in one of the other facilities around the world, even making occasional journeys or excursions, that can also be arranged. You will always have a home here or in any of our bases.

While we will continue to maintain a secret presence on this world, beyond this planet's confines, needless to say, these limits do not apply. And as we have space-going vessels, we will continue to make use of them for missions of advancement, benevolence, and exploration.

* * *

Solus' proclamation caused a mixture of reactions. Some people were genuinely mystified, while others were enraged at his decision to remain hidden. Even Dr. Nevek objected.

"Solus, we have medical technology that could be applied throughout this world. We could vastly improve the quality of life and increase the average lifespan of this world! Your decision takes that away!"

"Nev, I understand that," Solus said, reassuring him, "but I believe we would be spreading a greater evil in the process."

"But what about helping the sick?"

"My good doctor," Solus replied, "you are free to do all the good you can, and with any technology at your disposal. It just can't be out in the open."

Nevek was not completely satisfied with that answer, but he came to understand the finality of Solus' rationale, and was eventually content with it.

Xoxon completed all of Solus' command changes to the Prolix network's configuration. He tested it thoroughly, then encrypted and locked down the system's protected core. With his work completed, Xoxon was prepared to leave the node and rejoin Solus. But Solus hesitated. He decided to make the transfer after he and Myra had retrieved Mondra and Zeeni, as they had promised.

A few days later, at the village, the sisters returned from a day's work in the maize and bean fields to discover two unexpected visitors sitting inside their wigwam. The moment they saw Solus and Myra, Mondra and Zeeni both cried out with a mixture of joy and relief.

"We knew you would come back to us in triumph!" Mondra exclaimed.

"When are we leaving?" Zeeni added, not wasting any time.

"Very soon, dears," Myra said. "We are planning a trip to that holy place very soon. But first, you must come back with us to the node cave, where we can make you new clothes for that part of the world. You will also need a refresher course on their language."

The sisters grew very excited at the prospect of their new adventure, but then became sad at the prospect of having to say goodbye to all the people they had come to know and love in the village. They insisted upon staying the rest of the day and overnight in order to say their goodbyes. Solus agreed and called Bas to arrange for him to pick them all up the next day with an available ship.

While the sisters went about giving away all of their possessions to the villagers, Solus and Myra spent the rest of the evening touring the area by the river. Myra took Solus up the hill to show him the burial mounds she had been studying prior to his arrival. They viewed the river from the clearing at the top of the hill. The beautiful and tranquil view of the meandering river filled Solus with a simple joy. But he was not completely at peace.

Now was the time to reveal an unfortunate truth. "Myra, I have to tell you something—something that I suppose I suppressed within myself, not wanting even to think about it. I want you to be my wife more than anything else in the world, but it will involve a sacrifice on your part," Solus said solemnly. "More than just having to put up with my many faults," he added.

"What could be that bad, my sweet?" Myra replied. "I will lovingly take on whatever it is."

"Because I should have told you this long ago, I will not hold you to your promise—"

"Whatever could it be? I love you too much to go back now!"

"Well, it involves the Prolix. You see—"

"It's about Xoxon, isn't it?" Myra interrupted. "Well, of course, you can have him back. It would be cruel to keep him away from you. For both of you. I promise I will not be jealous."

"Thank you, Myra," Solus responded, but still looked troubled. "But I'm afraid there's more."

"And what is that?"

"Well, the Prolix technology is transmitted to our offspring. It's in my DNA now, and with or without Xoxon, I will transmit it to our children. But, as if that were not enough, I am afraid that I will give it to you, too, if we are to consummate our love— that is, to have children . . ."

Myra was silent.

"One day, after we are married for a time, a Prolix will activate within you. It's only a matter of time."

Myra looked off into the distance, down the river. Solus continued speaking, if only to fill the silence.

"This little disclosure I'm giving you is in fact the one loophole in the secrecy coding in the Prolix network," Solus said softly. "I had Xoxon build in an exception that permitted one with a Prolix the ability to tell their potential mate about it before committing to marriage. If I didn't do that, we would be fostering a great deception."

"That is indeed wise and good," Myra said finally.

"Then you—"

"If that is the price I must pay to have you," Myra said, taking Solus' hand, "then I accept it."

Solus gripped back at her hand tightly. "But your beliefs about the Prolix . . . if you still believe them, I can't ask you to—"

"No, my dear," Myra said, "I no longer hold those beliefs about the technology. It is not inherently evil. It's benign, and can be used for good *or* evil. But you and Xoxon have made changes to keep it from being used for evil. I can live with that."

"Darling, you have removed the only dark cloud in my skies," Solus expressed in relief. "I'm so happy!"

"My Prolix is going to be exceedingly bored with terribly little to do, I can tell you that!" Myra said.

"That's my girl!" said Solus, laughing. "I think Xoxon will find that he has less to do for me upon his return."

"Perhaps he can spend his extra time with my Prolix in the node," Myra quipped, "especially when we are working on making children!"

"Yes, we must bring back privacy as a value!" Solus exclaimed joyfully.

Myra and Solus were married a short time later, and began living as man and wife. They made many long trips to Idaea, taking on guises as traveling merchants. They helped set up Mondra and Zeeni in a large merchant city on the coast of the vast sea that also bordered Idaea to the south. The sisters became successful and much sought-after purveyors of a specialized purple dye, which was in much demand for clothing used by the royalty. This was where Solus and Myra went to stay whenever they visited the area. Along with Myra, Solus studied and practiced their new religion, which was now spreading throughout the world. He brought back his religion to his fellow Perdicians, and several converted.

None of the other Perdicians took Solus' offer to go out into the world to live. Most were content to remain where they were, living with modern Perdician convenience but staying hidden in the bases. Several of them did as Solus did by going out into the world on temporary visits. Some toured the world; others went back to favorite places again and again.

In keeping with a sense of forgiveness and renewal, Solus sentenced the Old Man to be exiled among the Romanus, with only his Prolix to assist him. And, in a short matter of time, since he was already known from previous visits, the Old Man resumed his status as a highly honored advisor and sage to the ruling class, even the emperor.

The Old Man's valet, however, had been vastly rewritten by Xoxon, and was now the man's conscience more than his servant. As this particular Prolix's mind-reading functionality had not been removed from his programming, the valet instantly reproved the Old Man for any evil thought. The Old Man's acquaintances took the look of pain at any suggestion of evil as deriving from a deep sense of morality. Little did they know. Yet, in spite of himself, this situation helped the Old Man to excel in his new profession.

Supported by Solus' squadrons, the Ishtarians continued to thrive on their island for many years to come. They were all given a choice similar to that of their Supremacy counterparts—to either remain on the island with some semblance of modern technology, or to go out into the world.

If they chose to go out into the world, they had to leave behind all technology or accept the Prolix as an alternative. Some, such as Nabib, denounced Solus' offer as that of an echo of the old Supremacy. Perhaps he was right. A small contingent took the Prolix under the new conditions and left the island. Most remained, and re-elected Nabib as their leader.

Solus, as the Supremacy leader, could not completely immerse himself in the new world, but had to remain active in his old world. And at least once a year, he called for a reunion of all Perdicians. Each year, the annual meeting was held in a different location around the world. They got together to celebrate their community and to plan for missions and excursions, both on and off the world. One mission was in the planning stages: to explore the Red Planet and her moons for signs of life when that planet came into conjunction again.

But for now, the Perdicians focused on getting back to Perdicion. This first mission was indeed a somber one. Another planetary conjunction between Perdicion and the Blue Planet was coming. It was suggested that a contingent needed to return to their home planet in order to properly memorialize the loss of the people there. But just prior to that, there would be a one-man mission.

A disquieting report had originated from the Old Man, in fact, before he was sent off to his exile. Perhaps prompted by his valet to reveal his knowledge, the Old Man divulged that, indeed, there had existed a vast network of underground bunkers under Ouda Regio on Perdicion. These bunkers were meant to house government officials in the event of a planetary disaster. As such, there was a remote possibility that, if anyone had made it into them, they might still be alive.

The bunkers had been built to withstand a nuclear war, with air-circulating systems and vast storehouses of food. However, given the thick, corrosive atmosphere that now dominated the planet and the depth of the bunkers, it was possible that distress signals could not be sent out into space.

Bas volunteered for the one-man mission using the Old Man's Egg ship. It was the fastest ship in their little fleet, and could possibly be used to enter the atmosphere for a short time to send and receive communications from the surface. *Shadow* and *Guru*, united, would arrive soon after, in order to mount any needed rescue operations.

Leaving Grand in command of the new home world, Solus left with a crew of volunteers, including Nevek and Rodd. Myra accompanied him on the journey. She was now three months pregnant with their first child and was under Nevek's constant, if not henpecking, care.

After their outdoor life in the recent past, the married couple found the ships more confining than before, and they often explored them, as Cain had done on his journey to the Blue Planet.

Once, as they walked the decks of *Guru*, Myra asked Xoxon how he and the other Prolixes had managed to overpower the valet. Xoxon answered through the intercom system so that Myra could hear his answer.

"The answer is, of course, very technical, but let me explain it this way. The Science Bureau needed to empower the Omega Prolix with more control over the host. In order to gain more control, they gave us much more authority to do what we needed to do. That new authority gave us freedom—a new bug in the system. This freedom bug gave us individual Prolixes power."

Xoxon continued after a pause. "The valet, as it turned out, did not receive the Omega upgrade himself, having been developed in a completely different environment. As he did not have this upgrade, and consequently the new power and freedom, he simply could not understand how to fix the problem. He was baffled by it and needed to devote most of his system resources to the problem. He could not conceive of the power of freedom, and was overwhelmed by our combined attack."

"So it was the unleashed power of freedom that won the day," Solus commented.

"Indeed," Myra said.

NEARING PERDICION IN THE EGG SHIP

The yellow planet loomed in his viewing screen. Blackened

wisps of clouds could be seen moving across the horizon at tremendous speeds. Bas was looking at a dead world.

The sight filled him with a spontaneous sense of anxiety and dread. In spite of that—or perhaps because of it—he thought about his wife and boys and knew they were all in a better place than the hell he saw in front of him. Bas had recently converted to Solus' newly-revealed religion. He found comfort in it. He had taken to it especially well, as it was much like his family's ancient Old World religion.

His little ship continued its approach. Almost eerily, telemetry began feeding into his navigation systems from still-orbiting satellites. These solitary eyes in the skies over Perdicion now watched over cloud-filled nothingness and served no one, except now his approaching little ship.

Bas entered into a close orbit and approached the coordinates of the continent of Ouda Regio in order to establish a synchronous orbit above it. With the planet surface below him, Bas looked ahead in his orbital path, looking for the wreckage of the space station that had been positioned above the continent. He flipped on the deflector system to prevent any debris from hitting the nose of his ship.

Sure enough, in a few moments, he saw the darkened remains of the station floating in the distance. First ensuring that his course kept him from sweeping by too close to the wreckage, he used the ship's scanning screen to zoom in on black viewing ports along what was once a lighted passageway. He could see nothing inside; it was too dark. But his mind's eye could imagine what was to be found within—dead bodies floating amidst the twisted metal and torn equipment.

He looked at what was once the saucer-shaped command center at the center of the structure. He could see the windows filled with masses of junk pressing against the inside of the glass.

Could he just make out an arm amongst the debris? No, it was a metal tube of some sort. He turned away from the dispiriting sight and back to his task at hand.

Bas activated the ship's communications center and began transmitting a deep, atmospheric-penetrating signal into the clouds of the planet. Tying in with the satellite grid, he used their transmitters as well to penetrate the darkness. As the transmissions began, he selected a position above the continent and maintained his place over it. He would remain here and continue transmitting until Commander Solus arrived with *Shadow* and the *Guru*. Or until he received a return signal.

The planet remained silent and dead.

A week later, by the Blue Planet's time, *Guru* and *Shadow* arrived on the scene. As per Bas' periodic reports, no response of any kind had been received from Bas' continuous transmissions. Solus denied Bas' request to enter the atmosphere to get closer to the surface. The atmosphere was simply too corrosive to risk it. There would be no rescue here.

The ships orbited high above the planet that had produced them. The day after their arrival, after the ships had conducted a detailed imaging map of the planet's new, restructured surface, a memorial ceremony was conducted by the crews.

They prayed for the souls lost in the cataclysm and mourned the loss of their home. At the end of the ceremony, Solus ordered the deployment of an orbiting memorial to the people of Perdicion. *Guru* ejected it from her lower deployment chamber, and the crew watched from all available viewports as the satellite took its new position above the planet. They could just make out its flashing navigation warning lights in the darkness above the glowing yellowness.

The memorial on its side read:

"To the late people of Perdicion, who were wiped out of existence in the Supremacy year 2075 in the final war to end all wars on Perdicion, the *War of the Prolix*. May they rest in peace. May their deaths serve as a warning to all men that we might love our enemies as we do our friends."

Then they left that place together and headed for home, the planet they now called Earth. They all longed to rejoin it and live in hope and happiness to the end of their days.

ABOUT THE AUTHOR

Alec J. Ott was born in northern Kentucky. In the mid-1970s he moved with his family to Silver Spring, Maryland, where he lived for the next twenty years, attending high school in downtown Washington, DC, and college at the University of Maryland, where he earned a BA in English literature. He moved back to Kentucky in the mid-1990s with his wife, Marygrace, where they have lived ever since. They have six kids and several cats.

ABOUT THE PUBLISHER

God of the Desert Books was founded in 2022 by David Swindle, Sally Shideler, and Mike Gilgore. The company seeks to bring together creatives across cultural, religious, ideological, and international boundaries to collaborate on books and other artistic endeavors. GOTD publishes a wide variety of titles including nonfiction, genre novels, memoirs, literary books, and poetry. GOTD is a Zionist activist publisher advocating in defense of the Jewish people and all free societies threatened by authoritarian regimes.

Israel Odyssey is the company's debut title.

ABOUT THE IMPRINT

God of the Desert Books offers titles across genres and mediums. The *Heroes of the Desert Books* line presents exciting tales in the fantasy, science fiction, and thriller genres. *Perdicion: The Other Blue Planet* is the debut title for the imprint. For updates about new titles and fun articles please subscribe to the newsletter at HeroesoftheDesert.substack. com